BAD MONEY

'A rattling good city thriller'   *Evening Standard*

'Patten knows her world intimately and with an authority and knowledge which few previous financial novelists have enjoyed. Her detail is meticulous and authentic, but never gets in the way of the story which moves along at a hectic pace'   *Independent*

'They'll be twittering in the wine bars around Threadneedle Street as to who was the inspiration for the power-crazed CEO of a biotechnology company and his partner in crime, a grasping, coked-up investment banker who makes Gordon Gecko look like a tender-hearted philanthropist'   *Scotsman*

'Louise Patten is certainly qualified to write this novel . . . there are less entertaining ways to spend a few hours'
                    City AM

'Patten knows her gilts from her derivatives'   *Mail on Sunday*

'Exciting and highly topical thriller'   *Good Book Guide*

Louise Patten has worked in business since 1977, first in the banking world and then with strategy consultants Bain & Company. While still in her thirties, Louise broke through the corporate glass ceiling to become a main board director of her first FTSE 100 company. She has served on a number of multi-national boards, not only as a director, but also as one of a handful of female chairmen of major UK businesses. Married with one daughter, Louise lives in London and Somerset.

BAD MONEY

Louise Patten

Quercus

First published in Great Britain in 2009 by Quercus
This paperback edition first published in 2010 by

Quercus
21 Bloomsbury Square
London
WC1A 2NS

A CIP catalogue record for this book is available
from the British Library

ISBN 978 1 84916 220 3

10 9 8 7 6 5 4 3 2 1

Printed and bound in Great Britain by Clays Ltd, St Ives plc

For John
sine quo non

'Just shut up! I'm chucking you out of the window if you make another sound.' As Mary Kersey turned through a pair of wide stone gates, the mobile on the seat beside her rang again.

She swung her Land Rover over on to the verge and stamped on the brake pedal, scoring muddy tyre marks through the neat turf edging the long, twisting drive to her daughter's school. A blackbird, chattering in alarm, took off from almost under the wheels. Mary switched off the engine and glanced at her watch. Ten minutes until she was due to see the headmistress. Just time to sort out whatever drama had erupted back in the office.

'Welcome to your mobile messaging service. Please enter your PIN number followed by the hash key. You have twen-ty-se-ven new messages. To listen to your messages, press one.'

'Damn! I really haven't got time for this.' She ended the call and dialled her office number.

'Hi, Mary, what's up?'

'Bella, help! My mobile's got a ton of messages on it and I absolutely haven't got time to go through them. D'you know what's going on?'

'I'm so sorry you've been disturbed. You just won't turn that mobile off, will you? But if you really want to know, I've got the list of your calls here. I must say, the phone's been ringing itself off the hook. Hang on a second.'

There was a long pause. Mary caught herself chewing her

knuckles in agitation as she waited for Bella to come back to her.

'Still there?'

'Still here, but in a bit of a screaming hurry.'

'I'll talk fast then.' Bella laughed cheerfully. 'Let's see, the London Business School want you to speak at their Top Women conference in September – no, that can wait. Here's another, I don't know if this one's urgent or not. Your block of flats rang about that water leak you've had in your ceiling. Your own insurance has to pay, apparently. Oh, and here's some good news. You know that card company with an unpronounceable name that you were pitching to in Sweden last week? They called to say Lock Chase has won the business. They want to talk to you about arrangements but I'm sure that can wait till tomorrow.'

'Listen, Bella, I've only got time to deal with anything if it's seriously urgent.' Mary often wished that her PA was a bit quicker on the uptake, but she'd never dream of telling her so. She depended on Bella to keep her office life in order. And besides, Bella would always watch her back for her.

Mary had seen this only a few days ago when she'd dashed into the Ladies for a quick pee and had been unable to miss overhearing two of the Lock Chase assistants who had sauntered in shortly afterwards for a gossip in front of the mirror.

From her embarrassing perch, Mary recognized one of the voices as belonging to an assistant whom she'd caught helping herself to the contents of the office stationery cupboard and who clearly resented being told off for it. 'Bossy cow' had been one of the less offensive things she heard about herself. 'None of her business, was it? Nag, nag, nag. Taking a pencil that doesn't belong to me isn't exactly the Great Train Robbery, is it?'

There was the audible click of a lipstick top being removed

before her companion replied, 'That Mary Kersey and her bloody ethics. Gave me a right bollocking when she heard I'd taken an extra forty minutes on my lunch break the other day while my boss was out. She said it was like stealing from the company.'

Then came the sound of a door opening and 'Oh, hi Bella' came clearly through her cubicle door. 'We were just talking about your Mary and her flipping morals.'

'And what's wrong with having morals?' Mary felt a flash of gratitude for her assistant's immediate response. 'She's always ready to help anyone out, as you both know perfectly well.'

'Keep your hair on. I didn't say she was bad, I meant she was a goody-goody.'

'That's rubbish. She's a lovely person and lots of fun!' Hearing this, Mary wanted to rush out and give Bella a hug. 'And anyway, she only sticks by the same way of working as the whole company does. If you don't like being in a place with morals, you shouldn't stay at Lock Chase.'

'Oh, don't be such a prig, you know why I stay.' There was a giggle. 'I'm hanging around in case Urban needs a new assistant.'

There was a general murmur of understanding. 'Mmmm. Heaven, isn't he?'

Desperate to get back to her office, Mary had then been forced to listen to a eulogy about Urban Palewski's hawkish good looks, his marriageability and his earning power as Managing Partner of Lock Chase's London office. It was a good five minutes before she heard the final snap of a powder compact and then at last the door sighed shut. Good old Bella. Rushing out a couple of minutes later, Mary vowed never be annoyed again by Bella's tendency to focus on detail rather than speed.

That vow was sorely tested as she sat in her car, willing Bella to run through her messages a bit faster.

'Matt from Accounts rang to say your December expenses still aren't in. I've got them here. You just need to sign them.'

'Anything *really* urgent?' Mary controlled her impatience with some difficulty.

'There's one call you'll definitely need to make today. The new head of Cirrus Bank wants to talk to you. I've sent a diary note about it.' There was a pause. 'Mary, you have checked your calendar, haven't you?'

Scrabbling guiltily in her briefcase, Mary pulled out her personal organizer. Sure enough, there was the message about Cirrus. 'You're a duck, Bella, thanks.'

From a corner of her organizer, the digital time blinked at her. Only five minutes till her appointment, and it would take at least four of them to get down the drive. No point in trying to ring the client now. She'd need to keep the meeting with Grace's headmistress short and get on the phone straight afterwards. There was *never* enough time.

Starting the engine in a hurry, Mary took her foot off the clutch too fast for the old car, which bounded off down the drive in a series of staccato leaps. Round the next bend, she passed the school groundsman raking up fallen leaves and hoped he wouldn't guess who it was who had gouged tracks through one of his perfect verges. Guiltily, she slowed down to the school's mandatory fifteen miles per hour. Her day wouldn't be improved if she flattened a bunch of schoolgirls loitering on the drive.

Mary wound down the window to let the cold, fresh air into the car and forced herself to calm down. It was a perfect winter's day. She noticed for the first time how blue the sky was, that milky sapphire only seen near the sea. Even at Trister, scarcely ten miles inland, they never got skies like this, while in London the sky never seemed to be any colour at all. How lovely it was here, and so peaceful. How *could* her daughter not be happy?

She and Guy had agonized over the right school for their only child. One of the big London day schools was an option. They could have kept on the nanny and Grace could simply have gone on staying with Mary in the London flat during the week, coming down to Trister at the weekends. But Grace was eleven, still a child. Girls grew up too fast in cities.

Grace herself had been enthusiastic about St Blaise's, but that was before she had started boarding, before she'd been hit by a terrible homesickness. This was her second term and it wasn't getting any better. The last week of the Christmas holidays had been almost insupportable, as were her letters. At first they'd been tear-blotched litanies of misery. More recently, Grace just wrote, 'Mummy, Mummy, Mummy,' which was even worse.

Mary was at her wits' end. The only answer seemed to be for Grace to go to St Blaise's as a day-girl, but her long hours working in London made a daily commute from Suffolk quite impossible. Guy, deep in Cambridge academic life, wouldn't be much of a help either.

Mary had finally accepted that she was going to have to do something when she received a letter from Grace's headmistress:

Dear Mrs Kersey

I am sorry to have to trouble you again about Grace. She is working hard and is a good little Catholic, of whom we are all very fond. I fear, however, that she continues to be far from happy. When you and I last discussed the matter, we agreed that it would take her a little time to settle in, but that she should ultimately be a happy boarder.

I am no longer convinced that this is going to be the case and suggest that we meet to discuss Grace's future. I do appreciate that you are a busy woman but I am sure that your daughter's happiness and security will weigh strongly with you. Perhaps you could arrange to see me here during the course of next week?

Yours in Christ,
M. Ligouri

Mary pulled up in front of the stolid grey Victoriana of St Blaise's Convent School. She flipped her mobile on to Silent and was just reaching to turn off her personal organizer when she saw its red light flashing with a new message.

Reminder: Partner meeting moved to 7.00 pm tonight. Imperative whole Partner group attends. Urban.

Damn, she'd forgotten to change the date. That was the trouble with this electronic diary system. Lock Chase insisted on it, as it made global time management simple, but Mary loathed it and was always forgetting to click on the updates. Paper diaries were so much easier.

She had planned to stop off at Trister for a couple of hours once she'd seen Grace's headmistress. Now she would have to drive straight to Ipswich station and go back to London for the Partner meeting. Climbing from the car, Mary tugged down the woollen jacket of her fawn suit, rather too tight across the stomach, and hurried across to the school's main entrance. The big double doors swung open before she had a chance to ring the bell.

'Ah, Mrs Kersey, now isn't it wonderful to see you! An honour, indeed. Do come in. And won't you be careful of the step? Sister

Ligouri is waiting to see you right this very minute. I'll be bringing the tea in straight away. I've Earl Grey for you, Mrs Kersey. And biscuits. If you'll just be so very good as to follow me.'

The school secretary always met Mary with this mixture of unctuousness and awe. Word had got out that she was a direct descendant of the Earls of Ivybridge on her mother's side. Not only were they one of England's leading Catholic families, but there was a real saint in their ancestry, one of the Blessed Martyrs, hanged, drawn and quartered. A particularly nasty evisceration, or so Mary had always been told.

Sister Ligouri came straight to the point. 'Grace is very happy here as a pupil, Mrs Kersey, but extremely *un*happy as a boarder. If we allow this to continue, her academic work and her health will suffer.' She paused to let the words sink in. 'I suggest that Grace comes as a day-girl from next term and we'll see how she settles down.'

Mary found herself gabbling, 'Oh! But that would be so difficult. My husband's in Cambridge all week and I'm in London. I work ridiculously long hours.' She stopped, ashamed to be caught making excuses. 'But of course you're right, Sister. We'll just have to thrash out a way to make it work.' She smiled at the headmistress. 'I've got to rush back to London now, but I'll talk to my husband as soon as I can. May I let you know by the end of next week?'

Outside Sister Ligouri's office Mary found Grace sitting in the panelled window seat usually occupied by miscreants waiting for a ticking-off. Her body was almost hidden by the shapeless green jersey and long kilt which the school thought a suitably warm and sexless uniform for pubescent girls.

'Gracie, how nice! I thought you'd be in lessons.'

Her daughter flew across the narrow corridor. 'I'm so sorry to be a trouble. What did Gory say?' Grace's grey eyes stared up anxiously, and as she hugged her, Mary was shocked by how thin her daughter had got.

'Sister Ligouri and I had a nice chat and we've agreed we'll see how things are at the end of this term. You think you can manage till then?'

'Oh yes, I'm sure I can.' Grace forced a smile but Mary could see her eyes filling with tears.

'Gracie, darling one. *Please* try not to cry.' Catching sight of a clock, she felt her throat tighten. She'd never make the Partner meeting at this rate. 'I don't want to but I simply must go now. Don't forget next weekend's an *exeat*, so Daddy or I'll be here on Friday to take you to Trister.'

Grace clutched at her hand. 'Oh Mummy, please don't go yet. Just come and see the dorm. My cubie's got more pony posters than anyone else's.'

'Oh, I'd love to. I'd much, much rather stay here with you, but I've got such a lot of work to get through.'

Grace was gripping Mary's hand amazingly hard for someone so frail-looking. 'OK, Mummy,' she gulped. 'I'm sorry, I know you're really busy. But couldn't you stay for a few minutes more?' Mary felt near to tears herself as Grace looked imploringly up at her. 'Please?'

'Honestly darling, I think the longer I stay the worse it will be for both of us.' Mary waved at two smiling girls coming down the corridor towards them. 'Look, here are Cordelia and Alicia to look after you.'

Cordelia put her arms around Grace.

'Poor Gracie, don't be sad.'

'Everyone gets homesick, Mrs Kersey,' said Alicia earnestly. 'I was so homesick I was really and actually sick. I had to go to the San. But I'm better now.'

'It's jam puffs for tea, Gracie, Mrs Jones just told us.'

'Don't worry, Mrs Kersey, we'll look after her.'

After a few minutes of this, Mary was relieved to see Grace looking a bit more cheerful. 'I'll just go and see Mummy off then. Meet you in the Ref.'

With her arm round Grace and trying to chat about ordinary things, Mary went out to her car. Although she felt wretchedly guilty at abandoning her child, common sense told her that it was the right thing to do. Giving her a firm but final hug, Mary climbed into the Land Rover and after a last wave, drove off straight away, in the hope that Grace would settle down quicker if she didn't hang around.

The school was soon hidden as the drive twisted between dark banks of rhododendron. Mary was thinking abstractedly how ominous they looked when a movement in her rear-view mirror caught her eye. Grace was running at full tilt after the car. As she neared a bend in the drive, another glance showed the child tripping on her long kilt and falling to her knees.

Beside her, her mobile phone sang unheeded. At the first possible turning space she swung the car round and drove back to stop beside Grace. She scrambled out and knelt down beside her sobbing daughter, not caring at all if she stained the light fawn wool of her suit. Her arms reached out for Grace, who clung to her, eyes and nose streaming, collar-bones sticking out.

'It's all right, Gracie.'

'No, Mummy, it isn't.' The voice rose to a wail. 'I'm sorry, but I miss you so much I can't bear it.'

Mary was suddenly and completely certain about what she should do.

'Grace, look at me! *I'm* the one who's sorry. I love you more than the whole world and I've made you miserable. I'll never do it again, I promise. You're coming home to Trister with me now and you'll never be a boarder again. I love you, Gracie, more than anything. Stop crying now. It's all right. I'm taking you home.'

Mary half carried her daughter to the car, feeling Grace's breath coming in jerky shudders as she started to calm down.

'I'll just pop back into school to let them know what's happening.'

'But what about my things, Mummy, and my homework? Won't they be cross with me?' Grace's voice started to rise again.

'I'll make sure they don't care if you miss a bit of homework. And there's everything else you need at home, though you might have to share my toothbrush for the night if you don't mind my spit? Stop worrying. It'll be all right, Grace.' Mary stroked her child's hair and repeated under her breath, 'It *will* all be all right.'

Ivan Straw ground out a cigarette on his glass reproduction of the Virgin and Child and paced up and down the grey carpet of his office. Thank Christ he was on his own. He could move about when he wanted to, with no one to raise an eyebrow when one of his hyperactive moods came on. Wolkenbank had finally got the message that he preferred to work solo. Human Resources hadn't tried to saddle him with another bag-carrier since he'd managed to get rid of that woman.

He'd been quite pleased with Cherry at first. She was quite sexy if you went for that spiky dyke look in a woman. And she had rarity value, since virtually no girls got into the aggressively deal-driven Mergers and Acquisitions department. Normally they were put in the softer areas like Corporate Banking, where their job was primarily oiling up to clients. Or they went into Syndicated Loans and sucked up to other bankers, but it came down to the same thing. Girls were good at toadying but they were useless at closing deals. Mergers and Acquisitions was too tough for them.

In M & A you were hustling all the time, looking for clients who might want to buy a company, pushing to get their business, shafting any other banks that tried to elbow their way in. Then you watched everyone getting legless when the deal completed before setting straight out to find the next one.

Cherry hadn't been able to get her cropped head round the

fact that M & A was just about doing deals. She had some idiot idea that Wolkenbank should be adding value to its clients and she'd simply lost it over that mega estate agency merger. He'd put ten million into last year's bonus pool with that deal, though she'd nearly managed to fuck it up.

'But Ivan,' she'd whined at him, 'I studied this sector during my MBA. Estate agency's just a series of local businesses. There simply aren't any merger synergies and I don't believe the numbers. If our client goes ahead with this deal it'll destroy massive amounts of value and I really think we should tell them.'

'I don't care if both companies go bust five minutes after the deal's closed,' he had hissed at her. 'My bonus gets paid if the deal gets done, so the deal gets done. Period.'

He'd had another bust-up with her when one of the bulge bracket Yanks had tried to nick a client from him. He'd told her to see his client's Chief Financial Officer. 'Just have a bit of a weep,' he'd said. 'Say that if Wolkenbank don't get the deal it'll be very career-limiting for you. Flirt with the bugger. Just get me back on track and you won't regret it.' Cherry had refused. He couldn't believe it. And she'd sat and sniffed disapprovingly when he'd had to make the call himself.

He'd managed to get rid of her pretty sharpish after that. She said she was leaving the City for ever, it was too amoral. Off to some do-gooding career. He pitied the poor sods she was doing good to.

Ivan perched on a corner of his desk and gazed thoughtfully out of the window at the murky rain dripping down on the City of London. Shame he'd never managed to get a leg over Cherry. His mind wandered to a brief fantasy about what he'd have done once he had tugged down those black tights of hers, but it didn't stay there for long. His thoughts reverted to how he could get his earnings up high enough this year.

The phone rang and he reached behind his back to pick it up.

'Your wife for you, Ivan.'

'Thanks, doll. Put her through.'

'Oh, hi babes,' Francesca purred. 'It's the builders. They need to know what kind of lights you want in your shooting range.'

He felt a rush of pleasure. Not only did he have a gorgeous wife and a six-million-quid house in Kensington, but soon he'd have his own shooting gallery in the basement. He was pretty good with a gun now, but with regular practice he'd be fantastic. And he'd be ready for any little shit who came thieving. He'd fire first and ask questions later.

'And we *have* to buy the mews at the end of the garden,' Francesca's honeyed voice sighed into his ear. 'Daddy says house prices are never going to stop rising and it'd be a cast-iron investment.'

'Two million for a tiny cottage is ridiculous.'

'Oh babes, why not?' She sounded so disappointed, he could hardly bear it. 'You earn a fortune. Your bonus is massive.'

This had him up and pacing again, stretching the cord of his desk phone as far as it would reach. 'Massive? My bonus is pitiful. A million quid, two million quid in a good year, how far d'you think that goes? For starters there's Julie's alimony. Three hundred grand and school fees for the boys on top.'

'Poor thing.' Francesca's voice took on a softly sympathetic tone. 'So sad you loathed her.'

Ivan had never let on, but actually he'd been fond of Julie. She'd been a real brick through those dreadful early years when all the old-style merchant bankers had looked down their noses at him, wincing when he used the wrong knife and fork at client lunches, raising an incredulous eyebrow when his pronunciation let him down. Forehead, forrid. Hotel, 'otel. Valet, vallit.

Who the fuck cared? And yet the snotty accents, the nonchalance of their frayed shirt-collars and those old public school jokes had created a gulf that no boy from a Swindon comprehensive could ever hope to cross.

Ivan had hated their idleness, too. While he worked until eight every night, they would casually leave the office at two on a Friday afternoon, drawling, 'Sorry old fellow, have to get to Gloucestershire in time for drinks. Staying with the St Clair-Gaskells. Know them by any chance?' Of course Ivan never knew any St Clair-Gaskells. The question was asked only to reinforce the chasm of class that yawned between them.

Then, quite suddenly, he had been liberated. The old merchant bank was taken over and its hierarchy had felt the boot up their overbred bums. And as the big bastards from Wolkenbank came in and shook the place up, Ivan had felt at home at last. The Wolkenbank culture was not a nurturing one, it was sink or swim. He was a good swimmer.

But while his star had waxed at Wolkenbank, so Julie had also waxed after the birth of their second son. She'd had to go. The newly successful Ivan Straw needed a glamorous wife to entertain his growing client list, not some plump frump. Francesca had come along at exactly the right time, though he'd learnt fast that young wives needed a lot of money if you were to live up to their and their Daddy's expectations.

'Are you still there, babes?' Any minute she'd start on about a swimming-pool at their place in the hills above Grasse. Christ. Refurbing the house, buying the mews, digging a pool, he'd need to trouser something a lot longer than a two-million-pound bonus to pay for that lot.

'Got to go. Talk about it later.' As he put the phone down, he noticed the fine tremor in his hand. Those bastard pills. They kept him on an even keel emotionally but he hated the side effects. Perhaps if he didn't have to worry so much about money his symptoms would improve.

Money. Wolkenbank would never pay more than a few million. Piss in the wind. His eyes flickered across to the rain-swept view from his window. Serious money was what he needed, and at the party last night he'd glimpsed how he might get it.

Ivan had been thrilled when he'd got the invitation. Jules Dix was a successful player in the hedge fund world. The whisper on the street was that he'd been bought out by one of the Russian billionaire boys, but this evidently hadn't stopped him throwing his annual party, his thank-you to those who had co-operated with him in one profitable way or another over the past twelve months. Modest wine, an unostentatious venue, no big-name speaker, yet for the handful of City professionals invited, it was unmissable. Ivan had met Dix occasionally, had slipped him a few bits of inside information, but this was the first time he'd been asked to the party.

Before going in, he'd smoked a quick cigarette in Berkeley Square. Sod the drugs, a fag was the best mood stabilizer he knew. Looking towards the Mayfair side-street known as Hedge Fund Alley, he had watched Dix arriving at the unobtrusive club where the party was being held. The sight had him grinding out his cigarette in disgust. Poseur. What was the point of driving that crap little car when he could be in a Maserati? And why ever did Dix prat around in chinos and a jumper when he earned fifty million quid a year?

Once inside, he forgot to be supercilious. Moving between the club's heavy leather sofas were some of the richest men in London. He ignored the hangers-on. Bankers, accountants, the odd spook who'd retired into the twilight world of corporate investigations. Ivan wasn't interested in men on the take. He wanted men on the give.

He was watching a muscle-bound, black-clad man standing below an over-lit Stubbs and wondering whom he was protecting when suddenly the minder moved aside to reveal the much shorter man behind him. Ivan felt his heart thump with excitement. So *that* was Dix's new Russian investor! He was across the room like an eel and within moments was looking down into the small black eyes of Platon Dyengi. The Russian's handshake was a warm, fleshy clamp.

'Ivan Straw, Wolkenbank.'

'Ivaan? *Vui Russki?*'

'Pure English. Swindon, I'm afraid. My mother was a romantic.'

Ivan didn't need to ask anything about Dyengi. Everyone knew the story. Born to poverty in the Urals, he had got rich during the Gold Rush days when Russia was selling herself off to the highest bidder. He'd grabbed at the chance to rape and pillage his motherland's assets. Flying from city to city to keep ahead of the opening markets, Dyengi had bought up shares, companies, commodities, buildings, whatever he could get his hands on. In a few brief months, he had sprinted from the poverty line into the billionaires' enclosure; then, keeping his head well below the political barricades, he'd quietly moved everything out of Russia.

Although Dyengi was known to be obsessively secretive, Ivan had heard the gossip in the City. Once safe in Western Europe, the man had settled down to playing multiplication games with his money. Offshore funds, third world gaming, global trade finance, occasionally tarts or drugs, the Russian was said to keep his billions on the move and always working for him.

As soon as they started talking, the minder moved back in front of them to protect Dyengi and block him from view. Ivan dived in straight away, alluding to a couple of very private deals that he'd heard whispers of. The black eyes stared back unmoved.

'So?'

'Look,' Ivan tried again. 'I hear about more takeovers than all this lot put together.' He waved a hand towards the guests in the room behind them. Lowering his voice, he went on, 'So far, all I've told Dix has been chicken-feed. But if the hedge fund pays me real money I'll put you on the track of some decent deals.'

A thin smile appeared on Dyengi's face and hung there throughout the rest of their brief conversation.

'You bring deal. Then we see. *Ubiraisya*,' Dyengi added quietly to the man guarding him. There was a touch on Ivan's elbow and before he knew what was happening he'd found himself ejected from the position below the Stubbs as the minder blocked him off from any further conversation with the Russian.

He left the party soon afterwards and had been thinking about it ever since. *You bring deal. Then we see.* Ivan was determined to bring Platon Dyengi a deal, a bloody good deal.

'Oh shit!' he said aloud, looking down at his hand. He'd been chewing a finger absent-mindedly and had ripped a piece of skin from the nail bed.

The pain brought him sharply back to the present. He was in his hard-fought-for corner office on the twenty-second floor of Wolkenbank's London headquarters and he was supposed to be planning a meeting with some small-time chief executive who wanted his help with an acquisition. He felt a little smile crossing his face. Small-time didn't need to mean unprofitable. *You bring deal. Then we see.* If he was going to stand a chance of a legover with the Russian, this Alan Dove and his ambitious plans might be as good a place as any to start.

His thoughts were interrupted by a call from his secretary. 'Taxi's here, Ivan, you'd better get going. Pneumatech's office is miles away, over in Covent Garden.'

In the cab, Ivan flicked through the notes that one of Wolkenbank's analysts had prepared for him.

21 January 2005

DR ALAN DOVE, CHIEF EXECUTIVE, BIOSCIENCES PNEUMATECH PLC

Studied Medicine at Southampton University, won highest academic prize two years running.
Successful career in the NHS; specialized in gastro-enterology.
By age 30 he was Senior Registrar at one of the big London teaching hospitals.
Abandoned medicine in 1990 to found Pneumatech Biosciences plc.

Ivan gazed out of the window as the taxi crawled along the Embankment. Brave decision that must have been, leaving a safe job to start a whole new career in business. Why had Dove done it? Money. Of course. What other reason could there be?

Dove took three research scientists with him when he left the National Health Service.
By 1995 they had two lung drugs on the market and turned in their first profit.

That was impressive. Five years from start-up to profit was bloody good going in the biotech industry. Those scientists must have brought some well-developed research along with them. Ivan approved of that. No point in seeing your money-spinning ideas frittered away by the NHS monolith. Much better to take all the cash for yourself.

As at 13 Jan 2005, Pneumatch's market cap was £450 million.

Ivan skimmed down the list of figures that showed what he already knew. It was a small but profitable company. From an initial conversation with Alan Dove over the phone, what he also knew was that Pneumatech's Chief Executive was an ambitious businessman with his eye on expansion.

F-ACE plc. Also in the biotech sector.
Specialist in skincare and cosmeceuticals.
As at 13 Jan 2005, F-ACE market cap was £400 million.
Chairman: Jock Hillyard, ex Brigade of Guards.

Dove had said he wanted to combine F-ACE with Pneumatech, that the two businesses were a brilliant fit, but that there was a problem he'd like to discuss if Ivan would come and see him. Running his eye down the numbers, Ivan couldn't immediately see what that problem might be. The businesses were of similar size and profitability; it looked as if all that was needed was a simple merger. Ivan didn't do simple mergers. There must be more to it than that.

'Here we are, guv.' The taxi-driver had pulled up outside a modern, steel-pillared building on Long Acre. 'Have a nice day,' he added cheerfully as Ivan got out.

One of those mother-hen types ushered him up to the Chief Executive's office. 'Dr Dove will be with you in a moment. Do make yourself comfortable, Mr Straw.'

Comfortable? The room was like a flipping operating theatre. Ivan had a quick scan round for clues to Dove's personality. The walls were stark white, bare of anything except for one large frame holding an impressive number of certificates from Southampton University's medical school. An immaculate sheet of polished marble presumably served as a desk, and there was a set of bookshelves on which were propped a photograph of a pedestrian-looking woman and some heavy-looking reference tomes. Apart from these and a few chairs, the room was clinically empty.

For some reason, Ivan had drawn a mental picture of Alan Dove as being a tall, bearded boffin, and he was momentarily taken aback when the man himself walked in. Short and broad-shouldered, he had a peculiar rolling gait which Ivan guessed must be due to the disproportionate length of his back compared to the stumpiness of his legs. The poor chap had a face like a bespectacled gargoyle. He must have found it bloody hard to pull the birds.

Casting around for a friendly subject to start with, Ivan nodded towards the photograph on the bookshelf, taking in the large nose and the brown, cow-like eyes. 'Nice-looking woman. Your wife?'

'Oh yes, that's Juliana.' Dove hardly glanced at the picture. 'She used to be my secretary. Now can we get down to business?'

Making a mental note not to bother with small-talk in future, Ivan switched on a more serious expression. 'So, Alan, you want to merge with F-ACE. It makes strategic sense, and combining the two firms would take you into a whole new league size-wise.'

'And it's only the start of my growth plans.' As he said this, Dove's fleshy lips broke into a grin. It was only there for a moment but it made him look boyishly excited. Small man, big ambitions. Ivan felt a sudden rush of optimism. There were fees to be made here.

'Have you approached F-ACE yet?'

'I met the Chairman but I didn't get very far. One of those tall army types. He made it abundantly clear he thought that both I and my idea of a merger were a waste of time.' Dove took off his thick glasses and began to rub them vigorously with a cloth. His face looked vulnerable without them as he peered across at Ivan. 'Jock Hillyard, he's called. D'you know him?'

'Not personally, but I can guess the type. Army haircut, polished shoes and six foot of pig-headed arrogance in between.'

'You've got him exactly, the conceited bastard. An agreed merger would be impossible. Even if Hillyard begged me, I couldn't work alongside him.' Dove hid his weak eyes behind his pebble glasses again. 'I'm going to have to make a hostile bid for F-ACE, but I don't see how I can afford it.'

'I understand the problem. F-ACE's market value's four hundred million quid and there'd be a bid premium on top of that. You'd never able to raise that much either in cash or Pneumatech shares.'

Dove was looking at him steadily. 'So is there *any* way of doing it?'

Ivan gave a slow nod. 'You've come to the right person.'

THREE

Mary plodded around the edge of the field known as Ladyleaze, about half a mile away from Trister. Head down, she was only vaguely aware of a chilly east wind blowing her hair into her eyes and the occasional struggle through patches of sticky mud where the farm tractor had turned too close in to the hedge. Time. Time was the problem. Never enough time to get everything done. She was trapped on the twin hamster-wheels of office work and domestic drudgery.

Weekends when she'd been able to read serious books or to swap ideas and silly jokes with her husband felt light years away. Recently, her conversations with her family seemed to have degenerated into endless petty demands.

'Grace has lost her hockey boot. D'you know where it is?'

'Can you sew in this name tag for me, Mummy?'

'I can't find any clean socks, Mary. And the laundry basket's overflowing with Grace's dirty clothes.'

She had heard her own replies becoming equally petty. 'Just stop nagging me, can't you? Grace is a day-girl now, remember? The school doesn't do her washing any more. Or her ironing, or her mending for that matter.'

Stumbling over a tree-root, she stubbed a toe painfully and found herself almost in tears of self-pity. It was just all too much. She'd spent the entire day cooking for the freezer and now she should be getting ready for her only night out in ages.

Instead, she was having to trek all over the farm to find Guy because he hadn't bothered to take his mobile. It was maddening how thoughtless he could be. He'd promised to be back half an hour ago, and she couldn't go off leaving Grace all alone in their huge house.

Still, at least her daughter was happy, and so was her father-in-law. Mary remembered how Sir John's face had lit up on finding her sitting with Grace at the kitchen table that afternoon when she had brought her back from St Blaise's. She'd immediately broken into a near-hysterical litany of her troubles.

'I simply couldn't leave Grace at school. She was unbearably miserable. Oh God, I don't know what to do now. And there's the Partner meeting tonight.'

As her voice tailed off, Sir John had leaned down to pat her hand. 'Don't worry, Mary, I've an easy answer to this. Didn't want to interfere before. The thing is, boarding made a man of me. Made a man of Guy too. But we don't want Gracie made a man of, do we? It's quite simple. Gracie stays here with me. Bangers and mash every night, eh? Bangers and bacon for breakfast too if you like.'

Grace had been immediately enthusiastic. 'That's brilliant, Grandpa! Of course! Why didn't we think of it before? You can be my nanny when Mummy and Daddy are working.'

Sir John had nodded seriously. 'About time you learned about the countryside, too. Hardly know a tern from a tit, do you? You're a Kersey, Grace, and a Kersey needs to know three things. His manners, his breeding and his farmland. Your manners are sound and I'll be able to teach you the other two in the evenings after school.'

'But won't it be a bore for you?' Mary had asked. 'Having Gracie here's going to disturb your peace and quiet.'

'Not a bit of it.' He had looked almost bashful. 'As a matter of fact, the evenings can be a little solitary with you away in London and Guy in Cambridge.'

Solitary? The word had shocked her. It had never occurred to her that her father-in-law's weekday evenings at Trister might feel lonely. 'Well, if you're absolutely sure,' she'd said quickly, 'it might just be the perfect answer.' Mary remembered that she'd felt a rush of optimism. If Sir John looked after Grace in the evenings, he wouldn't be alone and her daughter could give up boarding entirely.

'All settled then, eh, Gracie?'

And so it had been settled, and the arrangement had worked out well. Everyone was happy. Everyone, that was, except her.

If only Guy would help more. Morosely, Mary pushed a dead branch out of the way, ignoring the soft *tick-tick-tick* of a wren disturbed by the noise. Whenever she thought of asking her husband to take on one of the myriad jobs that needed doing at Trister, he never seemed to be around. He was always just on his way out to give a lecture, or rushing off to research some ancient Greek poet in the Cambridge University library. It wasn't as if being a Fellow of Pentecost College was exactly a high-earning job. She brought in ten times more than he did. Her shoulders sagged as another wave of self-pity washed over her.

As she was trudging on around the field, a cock pheasant erupted at her feet in an artillery barrage of offended squawks, making her leap in surprise. She stopped to watch its whirring flight away across the farmland that undulated towards the horizon, punctuated at intervals by the spires of village churches standing out dark against a flaming sunset. Calmed by the homely beauty of the Suffolk landscape, she found herself noticing the hedgerow beside her, where grey puffballs of last year's Old Man's Beard were jewelled with scarlet hawthorn berries, dusty blue sloes and the dark purple of a few wizened blackberries. Peeping out from below the hedge she caught a glimpse of primrose yellow. The promise of spring.

Surprised by a sudden joy, Mary started walking again, briskly this time, pulling the sharp scents of the evening field deep into her lungs. Of course she could make things work. She just needed a bit more planning and some self-discipline. That was all.

It wasn't long before she heard the sound of men's voices floating through the twilight. They were shouting and joking like schoolboys.

'Would you mind peeing in that hole and not down my boots?'

'Sorry, my aim's gone. I used to be able to drown a flying wasp.'

'Smells like the bogs at Bertie's, but will it work?'

'Course it will.' Mary recognized Sir John's voice. 'Badgers always leave. I would too, lot of men pissing on my head.'

'Funny thing, urine,' she heard her husband cut in conversationally. 'Animals make it a language of their own. Now the hare, for example, uses a technique called "retromicturation".'

'Silly ass my son is. What he means is that hares piddle backwards. Reads too many books, that's Guy's problem.'

Rounding a corner of the hedge she saw them, her husband, her father-in-law and four of their neighbours, all crowded together and urinating vigorously into the entrances to a badger sett.

'*Cave muscas*!' Guy was the first to spot her.

'Oh, very droll,' Mary said. 'And I do realize that a *musca* is a fly, in case you were wondering,' she added, fighting a flash of irritation with her husband's endless Latin quips. 'Aren't you coming in? It is my night off the domestic leash. And besides,' she lowered her voice, 'your father looks cold.'

Guy was at Sir John's side in an instant, arm protectively around his shoulders. 'Come on. Let's get back to the house.' Touched as always by Guy's solicitous love for his father, Mary's annoyance vanished. As they strolled across the fields towards Trister, the men exchanged jokes while Mary's mind drifted back to that evening in Cambridge when she had first seen just what a good son her husband was.

She and Guy had been exact contemporaries at Cambridge University, though at different colleges. They had met by chance at a lecture on Judaism and Hellenism. Mary had been waiting in a virtually empty seminar room in the Classics Faculty when Guy had come in, glanced around, caught her eye and had slipped into a seat next to her.

'You must skip a lot of lectures,' was the first thing he said. 'I've never seen you here before.'

The lazy smile, that hair flopping over his strong nose, something about him had taken her breath away. Instead of making a nonchalant reply to show how cool she was, Mary had found herself trying to impress him with her views on the overlap between Classical studies and her own subject, Theology. 'St Paul was a Roman citizen and Christ Himself was probably fluent in Greek,' she remembered saying earnestly.

'So you're a member of the God squad, are you?' His laughing eyes had looked deep into hers, flirting, challenging. 'Good. You can keep me on the straight and narrow path. Let's go out for a drink as soon as this lecture's over.'

In a very short time they had become inseparable. They had studied together, got drunk together, danced together and slept together. Whenever Mary thought of her undergraduate days, they seemed to have passed in a glorious haze of sunshine, laughter and love. Halfway through their third year, Guy had proposed to her and they had begun to plan a six-month honeymoon. They would make their way slowly round the Mediterranean exploring Graeco-Roman remains, finding occasional work whenever they ran out of money. They would joke and read, they would make love under olive trees, and only when they got back would they think about doing anything more serious with their lives.

When she saw their exam results pasted up outside the Senate House, Mary had thought that life couldn't get any better. Not only had they both got First Class degrees, but Guy had won a prize of quite a large sum of money for gaining the top Classics result of his year. That evening was etched into her memory. They had been wandering hand-in-hand down King's Parade towards Guy's college, Pentecost, bickering gently about where their honeymoon was going to start.

'Don't be silly, Mary, of course we must go to Athens first. It's where everything began.'

'It may be where *your* everything began, but mine started in Jerusalem. If we go there first, we can move on north through Syria and see Damascus.'

'Tell you what.' Guy stopped outside Trinity. 'Let's toss for it. Heads for Jerusalem, tails for Athens.' Feeling in his pocket, he found a coin and spun it in the air saying, '*Iacta alea est*,' as it tumbled among the cobbles.

'Do try and get your Latin right,' Mary remembered joking as they bent down to see which way the coin was facing. 'That's money, not dice. And you've thrown it so badly I can't see which side's up.'

The Porter from Pentecost found them there, squabbling happily as the daylight gradually faded into dusk. 'Mr Kersey!' They both looked up as he hurried towards them. 'I was told you were out here. There's been a phone call. You'd better come along to the college.' The message was a simple one but it had changed their lives. Guy's mother Jane had felt tired that afternoon, had gone up to bed for a rest and had never woken up. It was the first time Mary had seen Guy cry.

Within a couple of weeks it became obvious that their honeymoon dream was over. Sir John slipped into a period of deep mourning and needed Guy, his only child, to help him through it. Trister needed them too. Guy's parents had managed to scrape by, using buckets to catch the drips where the roof leaked and ignoring peculiar smells from the aged drains, but the house couldn't be allowed to decay any further. Trister was a voracious heritage and wanted urgent attention.

Guy and Mary had shouldered their responsibilities without a fuss. Guy's prize-winning degree brought him an immediate offer of postgraduate work at Pentecost, while Mary found herself a graduate trainee role at Lock Chase and set about earning enough money to keep Trister standing. Now, as she watched Guy steering his father home through the deepening dusk, Mary had a fleeting regret for the carefree honeymoon that they'd never managed to take, but she knew they'd done the right thing. Sir John had eventually recovered from the shock of his wife's death, and while Trister would always need money spent on it, at least its structure was sound. Without Guy's support and her income, both man and house might have collapsed.

As they crossed the four-arched brick bridge over the moat, light spilled out on to the courtyard that opened up in front of Trister and Mary felt as if her home was throwing out its arms to welcome them. It was, as Sir John so often pointed out, one of East Anglia's more perfect medieval manor houses, having been built by a fifteenth-century Kersey using the local silvery-red brick hung on a timber frame. Mary loved the irregularity of Trister's H-shape, whose two wings didn't quite match each other, and whose oak front door had been set off-centre to allow for the oriel window that provided light for the Great Hall. As they walked inside, Mary felt a wave of affectionate responsibility for the house. She loved Trister and it was where she felt at home. It gave her the odd twinge of guilt that she also found the Kerseys a great deal more lovable than her own family.

'A decent bloodline, Kersey. Quite sound, according to Debrett.' Mary had never forgotten and had still scarcely forgiven her mother's reaction thirteen years ago when she had made the long trek to her parents' icy house on the western flanks of Dartmoor to tell them that she was going to marry Guy. 'Pity it's such a recent baronetcy. Seventeenth-century, isn't it?' Lady Emma had added from the comfort of nine centuries of unbroken descent through the Earls of Ivybridge.

'Really, Mother, you *can't* talk like that nowadays. Peerages, ancestry, it's all irrelevant.'

'No need to chew my head off, Mary. Good breeding is never irrelevant. But actually the real problem with the Kerseys is not that they're *parvenus* but that they're Protestant. A mixed marriage is so uncomfortable.' Lady Emma pushed her heavy auburn hair back from a face that still bore the marks of great beauty. 'I don't suppose you could get Guy to convert?'

'No Mother, I *don't* suppose I could get Guy to convert.'

'Shame really. Though converts never understand the important things about Catholicism, do they? The Immaculate Conception. Transubstantiation.' Mary's mother had shaken her head dismissively. 'By the way, your poor father's very distressed. He's had to go off to polish his pyx again.'

Mary's father Leo was also of an old Catholic family, from whom he had inherited a set of the miniature chalices used secretly by priests during the great persecutions. She was used to his vanishing to seek spiritual comfort from this collection.

While her older brother and sister had conformed, married well and settled near her parents in Devon, Mary had troubled her father greatly, firstly by fighting for an academic education instead of the finishing school that he had planned for her, and now through the even worse offence of loving an Anglican.

After a sharp but inconclusive argument with Mary about whether a convert could ever be classed a 'proper' Catholic, Lady Emma had suddenly brightened and said, 'But of course there is one consolation. You'll be marrying a *really* good house.'

Her relationship with her parents had been strained ever since. Mary paid them a duty visit twice a year, during which she invariably found herself pointing out how wrong they had been about her 'mixed' marriage. On one thing her mother had undoubtedly been right, however. Mary had indeed found herself married to 'a *really* good house'. But Trister was also a burden, and at times she was glad to escape.

Slipping a double rope of pearls round her neck, she pulled on the elongated Chanel cardigan that she'd bought as an extravagant Christmas present to herself. She loved the way the olive green cashmere brought out the copper lights in her auburn hair, while its length conveniently disguised both her stomach and the fact that her favourite grey suede trousers had bagged irretrievably at the bottom. If she looked at herself sideways in the mirror, stood on tiptoe and sucked her tummy in as hard as she could, her size actually seemed quite reasonable. She turned to look at herself full on. Rather broader in the beam that way.

Grabbing her copy of the *Iliad*, she slipped down the main staircase and popped her head round the library door. Grace was sitting by the fireplace listening while Sir John swapped stories with his neighbours. She went over to kiss her daughter before asking her father-in-law, 'Any idea where Guy is?'

'Stepped outside, I think.'

'Will you say goodnight to him from me? I must rush or I'll be late.'

Mary huddled her coat around her as she hurried towards the old barns at the rear of the house, now used as garages. She stopped suddenly. Just ahead of her, a long shadow had stirred. She gave a little gasp of fear before the figure moved under a light and she could see who it was.

'Goodness, you gave me a fright. Whatever are you doing here?'

'I escaped for a breath of fresh air. And to tell you to drive safely.'

Mary felt her face soften as it still sometimes did when she looked at her husband. Tall and lean, his dark forelock flopped forwards over the beaky Kersey nose, which he bore like some heraldic badge. He was smiling now, a rare change from his normal expression of pensive gravity.

She reached for his hand. 'You're sure you don't mind me sloping off tonight? It took me an age to plough through the *Iliad* and I'm desperate to hear what Meg has to say about it. And then the inside of her house is so bizarre. That dining-room floor! It always cheers me up to see it.'

'Don't be silly, of course you must go. I'd come with you if I could but I really must stay with Father. You know he gets the glooms after too much port.'

She stroked her husband's arm, moved as always by his protective care for his father. 'Actually it's lucky you can't come. You'd only show off and no one else would dare say a thing.'

'Mary! That's jolly unfair. I've had years of practice listening to undergraduates talking rubbish about Homer and as a matter of fact I'm famously patient and encouraging.'

'A termagant, more like. And Guy,' she added seriously, 'you will make sure Grace gets off to bed at a reasonable time, won't you?'

'I'm not sure why you think I'm such a complete incompetent. We'll be fine. And if you get one of your mad urges to use your phone while you drive, do be careful. It's illegal, you know.'

Preferring not to answer rather than to lie, Mary climbed up into her old Land Rover and blew a kiss though the window, struggling to wind it up as she drove off.

The book club meeting was being held in Meg Dewey's house. Melbury was only ten miles west of Trister as the crow might have flown, but Mary knew it would take a good twenty minutes to get there along the twisting Suffolk lanes. With a guilty glance to check for blue flashing lights in her rear-view mirror, she pulled out her mobile and switched into her Lock Chase voicemail to return some calls.

'Hi Sven, sorry I didn't get the chance to see you last week when you were over. We have the latest statistics on the Interchange fee and I'm getting it all sent over to you. Let me know if you need anything else.'

'Rob, it's Mary. Could you check we sent the Interchange stuff over to the Stockholm office, please? Sven's waiting for it urgently.'

After listening to a long message, Mary pressed the Forward key on her phone. 'This is Mary forwarding a message to the whole Cirrus Bank team. Our client announced record profits last week and as you'll hear, he wants to thank Lock Chase for the part we played. Since every bank in the world seems to be making record profits, I'm not sure we can take *that* much credit, but I want you all to know the Chief Executive thinks you're doing a great job. Well done, everyone.'

West Hall, on the outskirts of Melbury, was an old house, seventeenth-century or earlier. As she pulled up on the gravel drive Mary wondered, not for the first time, how Meg Dewey had got planning permission for the extensive and eccentric remodelling of the inside of the house. Probably Meg hadn't bothered with anything so tedious. Perhaps she'd bought her way out of any trouble.

For Meg was rich. She was very rich indeed, though no one was quite clear where her money came from. The general assumption was that either she or her husband had inherited a fortune.

FOUR

Meg Dewey lay stretched out on a sofa, admiring the way the curves of her body surged voluptuously under the velvet of her dress. As she waited for the book club members to arrive, she sipped from a glass of sieved white peaches in champagne which a maid had just brought into her study. It was quite her favourite room.

Dominating it was an outsize 1920s stainless steel desk on which squatted three telephones – one silver, one anthracite and one clear Lucite. Around the walls hung her collection of suicides. There was a large Gertler, whose death had been a head-in-the-gas-oven job, and two paintings by Nina Hamnett. She had flung herself from a window, dying impaled on the Notting Hill railings below. There were also several pictures by Christopher Wood, who'd managed a quicker death under a train at Salisbury station.

Meg was idly wondering whether a Van Gogh would be a good investment when her silver telephone rang. It took incoming calls only and automatically recorded them.

'Hot news Meggy!' Meg smiled as she recognized the voice, 'I was interviewing a senior manager from LloydCurtis this afternoon. Heavens, he was indiscreet! You'll never guess what he told me.'

'No need to keep me waiting.'

'Seems his boss has been a bit of a clever boy. He's selling out to Doverwhite in exchange for a three-year rolling contract as Executive Chairman. *And* with options at the pre-deal price. The shares are bound to rocket when this gets out.'

'Great!' Meg winced as she pressed the cold metal of the telephone to her ear. 'I'll tuck away a line of LloydCurtis shares right now and then deal on Doverwhite.'

'Fantastic. You're having your book club lot over tonight, aren't you?'

'Yes, and they'll be here any minute. I'd better rush.'

Meg switched to the anthracite handset – outgoing calls only, untraceable, recording optional. She made two rapid calls, the first to a broker at his home in north London. The second call was to a number in Surrey.

'Dix? It's Meg Dewey here. Listen, Doverwhite's buying LloydCurtis. Looks good to top two hundred pence per share. It's only at one-sixty now so you might want to take out a little forward contract.'

'Hey, thanks, Meg.' He sounded annoyingly offhand when she was passing on such a good tip. He'd been grateful enough in the past, but that was before some filthy rich Russian had poured a fortune into Dix's hedge fund.

'I'll want twenty per cent of your net profit,' Meg reminded him. 'And a case of Pétrus,' she added. He could certainly afford it. 'Magnums, and a good year please, none of your afterthoughts.'

'As if.'

The calls were invigorating. She pushed the blonde curls back from her big forehead, collected her notes and walked out of her study, waiting until she heard the door locking automatically behind her. As she was crossing the hall, she paused to listen. A car. No, two cars pulling up on the gravel outside. When there was no ring on the doorbell, she opened the front door a fraction. Mary Kersey and Urban Palewski were standing talking together. Interesting.

She put her ear to the door and closed her eyes in concentration.

Mary had been hoping to catch a quiet word with Urban at the book club meeting. He had told her he'd be driving over from the Martello tower near Lowestoft where he spent most of his weekends, and she was delighted that they had happened to arrive outside Meg's house at almost the same time. There was something bothering her.

'Urban, can you hang on a second?' She stirred the gravel on Meg's drive with her foot, not quite sure how to start. 'I'm worried.'

'What about?' He moved closer, looming over her in the semidarkness.

'About this potential biotech client I've seen on the sales pipeline. Lock Chase helping with the integration of Pneumatech and F-ACE. I don't think we should touch it.'

'For goodness sake, why? It could be a huge case.'

'Because the whole takeover of F-ACE smells fishy. It's all been so fast and there were those stories in the papers. We're supposed to work to the highest ethical standards.'

'Lock Chase is a business, Mary. We can't be purists all the time.' She found Urban's even-mindedness much harder to deal with than if he could just violently disagree with her. 'Alan Dove seems to be a decent man and besides, from what I saw in the press, it was F-ACE that messed up. Pneumatech seem to have come along as a bit of a white knight and I really don't see why we shouldn't work for them.'

The way Mary interpreted the newspaper reports was rather different from Urban's bland acceptance that all had been well.

She'd seen the nuances. Pneumatech may have been a knight, but she didn't think it had been a white one. She was wondering how far she could push her objections when Urban put on his most emollient voice, as if she was some child to be soothed.

'Maybe it would help if you understood the business issues better. If you're in the office on Monday, I'll take you through the whole piece and the kind of work we'll be doing if we get the go-ahead from Pneumatech.'

'Sorry, I can't. I'm flying to Washington first thing. Cirrus want me to look at an acquisition target called NuAge Bank. Stupid name, and I hope I can talk them out of buying it. NuAge seem to make their money forcing dodgy home loans on to impoverished sub-prime borrowers. I'll be back in the office on Wednesday if that helps?'

'Wednesday?' Urban's face was in shadow but Mary could imagine the raised eyebrow. 'Why aren't you getting the red eye back on Monday night and coming in on Tuesday?'

'Well, I will if I can get away in time. But I'll probably have to go straight into the City when I land and then . . .' Mary bit her tongue, forcing herself not to confess that she was rushing back to be in Suffolk on Tuesday. It was parents' evening at Grace's school and Guy was insisting he couldn't make it because of some college feast, so she had to be there. But she was blowed if she'd let Urban, or anyone else at Lock Chase, know about her domestic problems. She had her career to think of and they'd think she was a lightweight.

'Mmm. See you Wednesday then.' There was a pause. 'And Mary. It would be helpful if you got to know the Doves personally once they've moved into White Gables. Pneumatech could be an important client.'

Mary felt that this was really heaping coals of fire on her head. It was bad enough that Lock Chase was taking on a client she didn't approve of. The fact that the client had bought a weekend house whose land bordered Trister was uncomfortable, but at least she'd assumed that she could keep well out of Dr Dove's way. Now here was Urban trying to manipulate her into befriending the man.

Just then, she noticed that Meg's front door was open a crack. Had she been standing behind it listening? Not that it would matter; Meg was a housewife, not a businesswoman. A car drew up on the gravel beside them and immediately the front door was thrown wide open. 'Darlings!' Meg stood in the doorway, arms held out in welcome. 'What are you two doing skulking about? And here's Peter too. Come on in and have a delicious Bellini.'

'Bless you my child, make it a huge one please.' Father Peter Cromwell's yellow hair emerged from his Morris Minor, followed by a short, round body dressed, as always, in clerical black. 'I've just got back from a conclave in Bristol. Concelebration with the Anglicans. Very dry.'

'Bristol?' Mary gave him a peck on the cheek. 'Was it held at Clifton Cathedral?'

'Clifton!' He glared at her in shuddering disapproval. 'Have you ever seen it? As a carpet warehouse quite delightful, but as a sermon in concrete unspeakable. A dreary barn, like so many of our churches. And when you think of all the ravishing Perp. and Dec. that the Protestants nicked.'

'Would *I* like to be ravished by Perp and Dec?' Meg could never bear to be left out of a conversation for long.

'I'd no idea you were interested. Where to start?'

Knowing her parish priest's passion for medieval architecture, Mary smiled as Peter stood, oblivious to the cold, and waved an arm extravagantly in front of him. 'To find the *perfect* Perpendicular church one treks up to Norfolk. St Agnes, Cawston.

Flawless. And then there's Salle with that divine little Lady Chapel tucked away in the attics . . . oh dear, the list is endless. And me with only a red-brick box for Our Blessed Lord to live in.'

'I think it's a very good thing that we Catholics only have modern churches,' Mary said firmly. 'It means we can concentrate on prayer and redemption instead of having to worry about leaky belfries and rotting rood screens.'

'You must get quite enough of that at Trister,' laughed Meg, ushering them indoors.

All the female members of the book club were wearing trousers that night. Few women who had eaten at West Hall wore a skirt there a second time, the dining-room being floored entirely in mirrored glass. This reflected back the silver-lacquered walls and ceiling so that Mary always felt she was being fed inside a hollowed-out diamond.

'Where's Dominic, Meg?' Mary asked, lowering herself gingerly onto a spindly Rennie Mackintosh chair.

'He's port-tasting in Lisbon. Very young port. It's got so much tannin, he says it's like sucking iron filings and he has to go to the dentist as soon as he gets home to get the black scraped off his teeth.'

'And how is the wine trade?'

'I've no idea,' said Meg cheerfully, pouring a golden green wine into her glass. 'It keeps him happy and he gets me good booze. Do you like this Gewürztraminer? I should really be giving you authentic Greek wine but I'm too kind. Oh goody,' she added, 'grub's up.'

The dining-room doors swung wide and Meg's idiosyncratic interpretation of Trojan War food was brought in. A roast saddle of hare oozed purple blood into a celeriac and potato purée, while hecatombs of plump snipe sat on deep-fried bread, their long beaks skewering their little bodies. To these were added a Greek salad and a two huge bowls full of buttery rice.

The usual chatter about horses, schools and neighbours started up while everybody ate. Determined to get rid of the roll of fat around her middle, Mary picked austerely at a few strands of shredded carrot until the smell of the fried bread overcame her. Eating two slices guiltily fast, she couldn't help wishing that she was more like Meg, noisily sucking up snipe brains next to her and apparently with no qualms at all about feeding her greed.

There was a large pile of clean bones in front of Meg when she put down her fork, saying loudly, 'Shut up, everyone. I'm starting now.' Waving her copy of the *Iliad*, she announced, 'This is my favourite book in the world. I first read it when I was a teenager and I've read it at least once a year ever since.'

After the first few sentences, even the hungriest had stopped eating and for the next twenty minutes the group sat transfixed as Meg took them through the history, the characterization and the linguistic brilliance of Homer's poetry. As Meg finished her talk, Mary fleetingly wondered why she chose to hide such a good brain behind that eccentric exterior. The discussion that followed stayed focused on the subject for longer than usual before it fragmented and slid from literature to local gossip and inevitably to the local hunt.

'Have you met that artist yet? I saw him out hound-walking.'

'Mmm. Such a shame he's gay.'

'There's nothing wrong with being gay, is there, Mary?'

'Nothing at all that I can see.'

'Mary! You're an RC! Your lot thinks faggots should be burnt alive.'

'Only if they're made of wood. But why don't you ask Peter? He's the priest.'

'Mary's quite right. Show me anywhere in the Bible where Christ says it's wrong to be gay.'

'Well, I suppose you know best. And I only meant it was a shame the artist's gay because he's ravishing. Face like a fallen angel and a body to die for.'

'He rides like a dream, too. Even impresses the Master.'

'Sounds divine. What do you think, Meg?'

Mary knew that Meg was invariably bored by horses and hunting. 'Far too *sportif* for me,' was the brisk reply. 'But I do rather like the sound of our other new arrival, Dr Dove. I love that ugly, dominant type. He's your new neighbour, isn't he?' she added, turning her large blue eyes on Mary. 'Know anything about him?'

Mary was momentarily nonplussed, prevented from saying what she suspected about the man by the Lock Chase code of absolute client discretion. After a short hesitation she muttered, 'I haven't met him.'

Meg was still looking at her quizzically when someone else said, 'They've got a lot of land. Hell if they stopped the hunt from crossing it.'

'Even more hell if Blair really means to ban hunting.'

'Don't be silly. They may have passed a bill but they'll never actually stop us. Apart from anything else, Blair would need to recruit an entire mounted police force. They can't exactly follow us over the fields in Panda cars.'

Later on, despite the chilly night, Mary drove home with the windows open, breathing in the fresh, loamy smells of the fields. Turning up the long drive that led to Trister, the Land Rover's lights picked out a badger rolling along like a little Sherman tank. Guy or Sir John would have shouted at her to drive faster and try to run it down, but Mary was squeamish about killing animals. She stayed in a low gear until it had lurched off into the darkness.

A few minutes later she was pushing open the heavy door to her bedroom. Guy looked up from the book he was reading. 'How was your evening?'

'Fascinating. I was impressed by how well Meg knew the *Iliad*; she's cleverer than she pretends. Did you have a good time?'

'Rather too good, I'm afraid. I'll have a terrible head tomorrow morning and I'm lecturing on Aristophanes at nine. You're off to Washington, aren't you?'

'Yes, I need to be away by seven. A flying visit, but you know how I love going to the States. So much energy. Freedom from all our stupid inhibitions about class and race.'

'No history worth speaking of. Modern life at its most execrable.'

'I just don't know how you can say that,' Mary couldn't stop herself from snapping back. 'You've never even been there.'

'Sorry, port talking.' Guy's gentle answer was a reproach in itself. 'Time to turn the lights out?'

Later, as Mary drifted off to sleep, she thought about the next morning. It would be getting light as she left. Rising sun on cobwebs. The craggy backs of a few dry cows, monochrome *îles flottantes* in a chest-high mist. Birdsong. A clean smell.

She woke with a start, realizing that she hadn't even finished the Our Father, let alone the Act of Contrition she meant to say after that grumpiness with Guy. Taking up where she had left off, she prayed, 'And lead us not into temptation, but deliver us from evil.'

FIVE

'You pathetic flake!'

Walking past Spider Wood's office, Mary could hear her voice quite clearly through the closed door. No doubt she was shouting at some poor consultant whose work hadn't come up to her absurdly exacting standards.

'How many times do I have to tell you? Validate the frigging data!'

She peered through the glass panel in Spider's door to spot which unfortunate victim was getting a tongue-lashing. At first she could only see the huge, grainy photographs of derelict industrial landscapes that were hung on the walls, but then Spider came into view. Although she'd never been particularly close to the only other female Partner in Lock Chase's London office, Mary couldn't help admiring her beauty. She looked like some green-eyed Nefertiti with that black hair swinging straight as polished basalt around her elegant cat's neck. And how could anyone be bad-tempered when their mouth was cut like a fat pink orchid and their legs were so impossibly long?

'If you don't have that analysis complete and on my desk by seven tomorrow morning, I'll tell Urban to put you on the planned exit programme!' Spider made the Lock Chase method of gently easing out the bottom decile of underperformers sound like a lethal injection. 'Now sod off out of here!'

Before Mary had a chance to move, Spider's door flew open

and one of the firm's recent graduate hires came stumbling out. Putting out a hand, Mary stopped him. The poor boy looked as if he was going to cry.

'What's up, Daniel?'

Spider's furious face appeared over his shoulder and for a second Mary felt as if she'd distracted some icy-eyed predator by offering herself as prey. 'I'll tell you what's up. You may be happy with this shitty standard of analysis, but I'm not prepared to put up with it.'

Mary was tempted to make some equally angry answer but she made an effort to control herself. After all, it was perfectly true that she was a far less demanding Partner than Spider. She believed in letting her teams cut a few corners so they could leave work at a reasonable time each day. Spider, on the other hand, was a purist. A consultant working under her had absolutely no time for a life outside Lock Chase, and judging by the hours she spent in the office, neither did she. Mary thought that Spider was a workaholic slave-driver, and she knew that Spider thought that she herself was lazy and slapdash.

As she stood facing Spider, her hand protectively on Daniel's arm, Mary was relieved to see the anger vanish from her face to be replaced by a rueful smile. 'With my temper, it's me that should be the flipping redhead, not you.'

Thankful that Spider's flare-ups were usually as fleeting as summer thunderstorms, Mary returned the smile. 'I've got a few minutes; why don't I come in and see if this guy's as bad as you think?'

Spider raised a black eyebrow before nodding slowly. 'Why not? We're talking about cranes, mind. Proper gritty industry, not one of your pansy banking clients.'

Pushing Daniel ahead of her, Mary followed Spider into her office and slipped into a seat at the end of the table while

Spider spoke to her waiting case team as if nothing had happened. 'Get a move on. I need that ten-slide pack for my presentation to the Rimini board tomorrow and it's already well past seven. It's going to be a long evening.'

Clearly used to her irascibility, the team's leader resumed the review at the point where Spider's sudden fury had broken it off. 'We were on the Pathfinder slide, making sure we're all agreed on the key messages.'

'Shoot.'

'Basically Rimini's a nice, solid company. Balance sheet healthy, costs well controlled, margins stable. But here's the problem.' He indicated a line on the slide. 'Profits are flatlining and there's no growth left in the business. We've boiled it down to three questions. One, can they expand overseas? Two, can they grow by acquisition? Three, can they diversify into other businesses?'

'Let's start overseas.'

An experienced member of the team took over. 'No go, I'm afraid. They won't cross the Atlantic. Burnt their fingers badly on a Californian joint venture a few years back. North Africa and the ex-Soviets look pretty dodgy too. Transportation's difficult, million quid cranes go missing and it's really hard to get paid.'

Mary saw the panic on Daniel's face as the team leader turned to him. 'Want to take us through acquisitions?'

'Of course. I, er . . .' She threw him what she hoped was a reassuring smile and was relieved when he found his stride. 'Four players dominate the European heavy lifting sector. One of them will always be there when there's something big and complicated that needs a crane. Bridges, buildings, ships, the London Eye, whatever. We've taken Rimini's competitors apart and looked at them every which way. Similar market shares, lots of family shareholdings. In summary, it isn't going to be possible for Rimini to grow by buying any of its direct competitors.'

With a brief nod in Daniel's direction, Spider turned back to her team's leader. 'So is there anything they *can* do?'

'There's good news on the diversification work stream. We've been looking at earth shifting, tunnel boring, that sort of stuff and we reckon they use the same skills that Rimini already has in the crane business. We're still working on the market share data but so far it looks like there's no dominant players.'

'Hmm. So no obvious acquisitions.'

'Sure, but they can start up new divisions. Earth-moving, for example. Great marketing potential there. Rimini Makes The Earth Move For You. What d'you think?'

Mary's snort of laughter got a cold look from Spider. '*I* think you haven't got time to frigging joke. We've taken fifteen minutes just to get through the summaries. Let's get to the meat.'

Having seen Daniel through his successful re-entry into Spider's meeting, Mary got up to go. She knew what would come next. Spider would keep the team there for hours as she ripped into any slide that showed the slightest lack of clarity or logic, covering it in thick red ink. Each red line could mean hours more work before Spider was satisfied and on a night like this, none of them would be getting much sleep.

As she moved towards the door, she glanced at Daniel's face and saw his eyes following her anxiously. She paused, holding the door-handle. She was busy herself and wanted to leave the office at a reasonable hour, but she couldn't abandon the poor boy without a word of comfort. He was probably facing his first all-nighter, and who knew what kind of mood Spider might be in by the end of it?

'Can you spare me Daniel for a few minutes?'

'Sure.' Spider was so intent she hardly glanced at them as they left.

'Look, Daniel,' Mary said once they were out in the corridor, 'you mustn't get so worried. Consulting isn't that complicated. In fact it should be simple, *really* simple. When you get confused by some complex problem, just take it back to the four "C"s you learned in kindergarten. Now what are they?'

The boy was silent.

'C'mon you idiot. Give me the four '"C"s.'

'Customers, Competitors, Capabilities, Costs.'

'Well done.' Mary hoped she didn't sound patronizing. 'And while you're at it, remember there's a fifth "C", Cynicism. We don't take our client's word on *anything*. We validate every single thing he says about his business.' Mary tried to imitate Spider's voice. 'If he just wanted to have his golden words fed straight back up his frigging arse he'd have hired one of our competitors.'

Her mimicry drew a smile from the young consultant. 'Thanks, Mary. Really thanks.'

'No problem. Now get back in there and show Spider what you're made of.'

'I will, and I really appreciate you taking the time to sort me out. I guess you're really busy yourself?'

'I'm seriously busy,' Mary smiled wryly. He could have no possible idea what a nightmare it was trying to juggle career, marriage and a child.

'Your clients are all in financial services, aren't they?'

'Yes, and the sector's growing like mad. Takeovers, mergers, I can hardly keep up with it. The bankers all seem to believe they've found this New Paradigm. It's the Great Moderation. No more Boom and Bust. They think nothing can ever go wrong for them again.'

*

What an excellent banker he was. Ivan Straw peered at himself in the newly installed onyx and crystal Art Deco mirror in his black-tiled bathroom. Pneumatech's takeover of F-ACE had been brilliant. A textbook BOOB job. Borrow, Offload, Obliterate, Buy.

Alan Dove hadn't been able to afford F-ACE when it was trading at four hundred million quid, so Ivan had got the share price battered down till Dove had been able to pick the company up half price. The whole job had only taken a few weeks, and by the end F-ACE had been gagging for Pneumatech to take them over. Sodding genius.

He stretched out his jaw so that the electric razor would run smoothly up his neck. He didn't like the thing, but he'd had to give up poncing around with a brush and shaving soap after the tremor had made his razor slip once too often. He paused to admire the narrow lines of his face. What a handsome sod. Pushing the heavy, dark hair back off his forehead, he examined his temples. No signs of receding. Good. Ivan switched on his razor again. Pneumatech, Wolkenbank, Dix and his Russian investor, they'd all got what they wanted. The perfect BOOB job. He grinned at himself in the mirror, remembering.

With Platon Dyengi as backer, Dix's hedge fund had massive financial clout. Riding on the back of it he'd gone in big. No point in arsing about with little deals. The hedge fund had borrowed thirty million quid's worth of F-ACE shares from various dopey pension fund managers and had immediately offloaded them on to the market for thirty million in cash. That had gone straight into an offshore account, earning a nice bit of interest while he'd got down to the fun part. Obliteration.

He'd made sure he kept Dove right away from any negotiating with F-ACE. Ivan didn't know the man that well and hadn't wanted to risk him coming over all ethical. In the event it had been easy. Dove had seemed almost embarrassed. 'I, er ... the thing is, I think I told you that I didn't really get on with Hillyard.'

As soon as he met Jock Hillyard, Ivan saw exactly how he might have patronized Pneumatech's ugly little Chief Executive. He was one of those tall, flash-looking military types and he played a barbed game. Ivan had been having a day of mild depression and his reactions were slow.

'Tell me about yourself, Mr Straw. I always like to know what kind of animal I'm dealing with.'

'I'm an investment banker. Wolkenbank. Mergers and Acquisitions.'

'Yes, yes. I can read that off your business card. What I want to know is your background. School. College. Regiment. The kind of thing that makes a chap who he is.'

There was no way Ivan was going to own up to Swindon, or to the fact that he'd started work as a bank clerk straight from school and had never been to university, let alone the army. He hadn't confessed but he knew he'd sounded weak and evasive.

'It's been very pleasant to meet you,' Jock Hillyard had said after a short and uncomfortable conversation. 'But I can't imagine why my company would dream of agreeing to be taken over by Pneumatech. F-ACE is not for sale.'

The second meeting had gone rather better. Ivan had made sure of that.

One of the Sunday papers had carried a story claiming that there were serious errors in F-ACE's last set of accounts. It had been a typical Friday night drop, given to just one journalist to ensure a prominent position as an exclusive. Over the following days, more unpleasant little newsbites had popped out, each more damaging than the last.

By the time Ivan saw Hillyard again, the F-ACE share price had fallen by a quarter. It seemed that every time the 'funny accounts' story began to die down, another well-sourced rumour would stir it up again. Ivan was impressed by how well the man was standing up to the pressure.

'Absolutely no problem at all. Just a misinterpretation. Blown up out of all proportion by the press.'

'Your share price has taken a hammering, hasn't it? Market cap down below three hundred million. Pneumatech is still very keen to come to an agreement with you. It'd make a lot of sense to both sets of shareholders.'

'I thought I'd made myself perfectly plain.' Hillyard's voice had risen aggressively. 'Your plan to take over F-ACE is not acceptable.'

Ivan had persisted. 'Don't you think we should at least talk about the potential benefits? You wouldn't want your shareholders finding out you'd turned down a great opportunity without even bothering to look at it.'

That shot had gone home. Hillyard had looked nonplussed. Ivan could see he was wishing that the Pneumatech approach would just go away but that he didn't quite have the courage to end their talks there and then, just in case his shareholders found out and kicked up a stink. Eventually Hillyard had settled for prevarication.

'Look, Straw. I'm up to my ears at the moment. Why don't we meet again in a few months' time? See how things are going then.'

The next story had broken in the papers two days later. 'F-ACE shares plummet in kidney scare.' It had been a real corker.

Troubled bio-technology company F-ACE, currently fighting accusations of publishing misleading accounts, suffered a further massive

fall on the stock market today. Well-sourced rumours state that
Phase 3 clinical trials of its much-hyped anti-wrinkle cream have
been dogged by unexpected side effects. Blood has been found in
routine urine samples taken from volunteers trialling the cream.
It is feared that the skin-cream may cause kidney damage in suscep-
tible individuals.

Ivan had sat back and watched the story take off. Blood, piss,
drugs companies, it was a journalist's dream. As the F-ACE share
price went into freefall with every new rumour, he was astonished by how long Hillyard held out. It was another two weeks
before the call came. When Ivan was shown into Jock Hillyard's
office he was pleased to see how much less of the posh
guardsman there was about him.

'Oh, good morning, Ivan. Kind of you to drop by. Things have
got very nasty here recently. My board are even threatening to
vote me off,' he had said, shaking his head in disbelief. 'I just
can't understand how all this has happened. And so *fast*.'

He'd let the silence run until eventually Hillyard had
attempted a chummy smile. 'Think we might be prepared to
talk to you chaps about a deal after all.'

Ivan patted eau de cologne around his neck and gave an
approving nod at his reflection in the mirror. Hillyard's reputation had been completely buggered but everyone else had
got what they wanted. Pneumatech had taken over F-ACE and
Wolkenbank had raked in a decent fee for managing the
takeover. Dix's hedge fund had sold their borrowed F-ACE
shares for thirty million quid and had only had to pay half
that when the time came to buy them back. A fifteen-million-
quid profit from his BOOB job: Platon Dyengi should be pleased
with *that*.

Ivan himself hadn't come out of it empty-handed either. He'd made a packet out of some quiet share-dealing on his own account. In fact he'd managed the whole thing brilliantly. Fast, secret, lucrative. Fucking perfect.

SIX

Urban winced as his office door slammed shut. He didn't need to look up to know that it was Spider who had come in and that she was in a bad mood. It was too early in the morning for this.

'You're late.'

'You wouldn't frigging *believe* it! I've got half an hour with a client this morning and my idiot case team have left a bloody great brick for me to show him. Thirty slides when I told them I'd need ten, absolute max. Apparently the bastards ran out of time. They slipped out to stuff their faces with pizza when they should have been here working. And I don't give a rat's tit that they stayed up most of the night.'

Tired of hearing Spider work herself up into one of her rages, Urban interrupted roughly. 'Put a sock in it, for heaven's sake. If you can't control your case teams by now, that's your problem. I want to talk to you about our new client, Pneumatech. I'm going to lead the case and I'd like you to be Second Partner.'

'Work with you? Hey, Urban, that's nice. We haven't worked together for an age.'

Spider was grinning at him, her temper forgotten in an instant. He caught himself noticing how lovely she looked when she smiled. Perfect teeth, wide mouth, ivory skin. Luckily, she wasn't his type at all. He made it a point of principle to view any sort of physical relationship in the office with the horror of incest.

He flicked his eyes down to the papers on his desk. 'Pneumatech's a biotechnology outfit. It develops drugs for lung problems. They've just bought a company called F-ACE, skin care specialists. You probably saw it in the papers?'

'I skimmed the headlines. Rumours about dodgy finances, wasn't it? Doesn't sound like our ideal client.'

'Oh, I think it's all right. Pneumatech snapped F-ACE up on the cheap but the CEO assures me it's fundamentally sound. Mary asked the same question, actually. Mind you, she tends to think every takeover's dodgy.'

'Mrs Whiter-Than-White's always setting herself up as the guardian of our morals. You're pretty pure yourself, Urban, so I guess if *you* say it's sound, then it's sound. What's the case?'

'Post-merger integration.' Urban's mind wandered back to his first meeting with the new client. 'I had quite a fight with the Chief Executive. He couldn't see he'd risk losing his best people if he just slashed costs and rammed the two companies together. I should probably warn you, Dr Alan Dove's seriously driven. He's not going to be an easy guy to work with.'

'Dr Dove?' Spider's green eyes widened and two small pink patches appeared on her normally pale cheeks. 'What's his background?'

'Is that relevant?' Getting no answer, Urban went on, 'Dove founded Pneumatech about fifteen years ago. Hit a little jackpot with his very first business. Before that he was a doctor, specialized in gastroenterology. Why do you want to know?'

'It's always useful to have some background before you meet the client.'

'Oh, I don't think you'll need to meet Dove, just sanity-check our work for him. I'll be his main contact. In fact he seems to have taken rather a shine to me. He's asked me to dinner at his house tonight.'

Without a word, Spider got up and went to the door. 'Hang on,' Urban called her back. 'There's something else I want to talk through with you.'

He watched while she came back and perched herself on the edge of his desk, swishing her long legs impatiently. 'I can give you five more minutes, so shoot.'

'I want you to run the Mardi Gras event. Everyone worked really hard last year and we all deserve a break.'

'Me? Organize some idiot party? You're having me on!'

'I mean it, it'll do you good. Your human skillset's crap.'

'Crap? That's not going to help me beat my confidence problem, is it?'

'Don't be silly, Spider. You're the most self-confident woman I know.'

'Honestly, I'm a *femme sérieuse*. This party stuff scares the shit out of me.' Urban smiled. She had to be joking. He didn't believe she'd been scared of anything in her life.

'Get Mary to run the party,' Spider went on. 'You're always over the moon about her people skills, though personally I think she's a flake.'

'Leave Mary alone. You're running the Mardi Gras event and that's it. If you need any help, I'm here. Unless you think I'm a flake, too.'

'OK, I'll do it. But I'm going to give you enough frigging flakes to last you a lifetime.' Her face was stern but her eyes were laughing at him. Funny how he'd never really noticed them before. The irises were black-rimmed, like a cat's eyes.

'Meg? It's Mary.'

In her Suffolk study, Meg smiled into the clear Lucite handset – domestic calls, incoming and outgoing, recording optional.

'Mary, darling! How wonderful to hear your voice. What's up?'

'Well, I'm really sorry but I don't think I'm going to be able to get to the book club meeting this weekend. You see, there'll be a mountain of ironing, I've hardly had a moment with Guy and really I don't think I should leave Grace.'

'You haven't read the book, have you?' Meg could always tell when Mary was fibbing. Catholic guilt sounded loud and clear in her voice.

'Oh dear, is it that obvious? I'm seriously too busy to read it.'

'Well, I wish you'd come anyway. I'll hate it if only horsey people turn up. They'll only rabbit on about this wretched hunting ban, which can't come fast enough as far as I'm concerned.'

'I feel awful saying it, but I rather agree.'

'Talking about hunting, have you heard about your neighbours down here?'

'The Doves, you mean?'

'Exactly. You know their land's bang in the middle of the hunt's Saturday country? So the Master himself called round and met Mrs Dove, down from London to brief the builders. Full make-up, London clothes and some sort of foreign accent.'

'She's from Luxembourg.'

'Oh, well, that explains a lot. Apparently she was very pleasant but she said her husband wanted to have the entire estate landscaped and she was sure he wouldn't let them hunt there in case the young planting was damaged. Our revered hunt Master just made a little bow and left, couldn't trust himself to speak. But *whatever* can they be planning to do? Lakes, d'you think?'

'You'll have to ask Urban. He's going to some black-tie bash they're giving tonight.'

'*Such* a glamorous life you all live. Dominic and I are having fish and chips, can you think of anything duller?'

LOUISE PATTEN | 57

'A takeaway Chinese and a desk full of work's a pretty dreary prospect.'

After they had both hung up, Meg picked up the anthracite handset – outgoing calls only, untraceable, optional recording.

'Thank goodness I caught you. Didn't you say you were going to dinner with Alan Dove tonight, the Pneumatech Chief Executive?'

'Yes, I was just leaving. They live in sodding Westminster, hell to get to. I'm going to be screamingly late.'

'There's someone I want you to pump. Urban Palewski. I've told you about him, remember? He heads up the London office of Lock Chase and I'm sure he'll have been asked because Dove's a client. Lock Chase don't work on little things, so there must be something big coming up with Pneumatech. Or maybe it's about the F-ACE takeover.'

'There was a funny smell about that deal, didn't we think? Anyway, of course I'll interrogate Mr Palewski. Nice to meet one of your friends for a change.'

'Be subtle, won't you? He's very smart. He weekends in Suffolk too, don't forget. In a Martello tower near Lowestoft.'

'Lucky man. And don't worry, Meggy. Subtle's my middle name.'

SEVEN

Urban could hardly see what he was eating. An avalanche of stubby orange canna flowers had been poured over the ivy leaves that trailed right down the centre of the table, while between them, rivers of kumquats flowed artlessly from a pair of heavy silver cornucopias to cover almost every inch of the highly polished mahogany. He supposed that the extravagance of the decoration, the silverware, the ranks of wine glasses, were all meant to display Alan Dove's success. Even the food seemed to have been chosen for the expense of the ingredients rather than the comfort of his guests' stomachs.

Forcing down a complicated first course of lobster and black truffles in some kind of pepper jelly, Urban knew he was going to have serious indigestion. The conversation was pretty indigestible too. Juliana Dove kept breaking off in mid-sentence to point out an empty water glass or an unfilled plate to one of the staff.

'And so, as I was saying,' she turned back to him after yet another interruption, 'I was sent away from Luxembourg when I was only nine years old to get an English education.'

Urban felt a sudden spark of interest. 'I came to England as a child too. Didn't you miss your parents terribly?'

'My mother I missed very much.' Her big brown eyes were staring at him and for the first time he felt he had her full attention. 'But my father? No.' Her face was serious. 'Papa was a big man, always angry. He would lose control of his temper and lash out with his fists.'

'How terrible!' Urban started to say, 'And did he. . .' but he had lost her again.

'No, no! The toast *there* for Lord Pimperne.'

'So you were sent to school in England?' he prompted when she had focused back on him again.

'I went to Beverleigh, in Kent. After the homesickness passed, I was very happy there. I learned colloquial English, I learned deportment and I learned to type.'

'I'm sure that was very useful.' Urban's smile was wasted on the back of her head.

'The red wine *now* please. No, don't wait for the meat course. I'm sorry, you were saying something?'

'I was asking whether you found typing a useful skill.'

'Very! My first job was working for Alan.'

Urban glanced down the table at his host. 'He's an impressive man, your husband. Did you know him when he was working in medicine?'

'No, it was when he started Pneumatech that he needed a secretary. Then, after a while, Alan wanted a wife. I had no husband and we made a good match.'

Urban made a quick calculation. Dove must have been in his thirties when he married her and she'd presumably still have been very young. Perhaps as well as a husband she'd found a replacement for her violent father. 'And Alan,' Urban found himself saying his thoughts out loud. 'Does he ever lose his temper?'

'Alan?' She looked at him in astonishment. 'Never. He would *never* lose control of himself.' Juliana stood up suddenly. 'Will you excuse me? I must tell the cook something.'

After the discontinuities of his first-course conversation,

Urban turned with some relief to talk to the pretty redhead on his other side, who was showing off a lot of bosom.

'Amy Flower.' The hand she thrust out was surprisingly cold. 'I write for the *Daily Business*. Senior correspondent actually.'

Five minutes later, Urban was wishing that he was still stuck with Juliana Dove. Amy's career had begun as a doorstepping journalist. According to her, there'd been no local murder so shocking, no private grief so terrible, that she would not intrude with her questions.

'Tenacity, Urban, the secret of my success. I started out leaning on doorbells. Rape victims, bereaved parents, anyone'll give you an inside scoop if you hang round long enough looking sympathetic.'

She seemed far too sweet and bubbly for such cold-heartedness. Urban didn't believe a word. 'You're joking, surely?'

'Like hell I am. And it's just the same now I'm working in the City. Show me a sacked executive or a shamed auditor and I'll screw a story out of him. Everyone talks in the end.'

Was it his imagination or was she pressing her arms to her sides to deepen her cleavage? 'So tell me, Urban,' she was leaning in closer. Her breath smelt of fresh toothpaste. 'How long have you known Alan Dove?'

'Oh, not that long.'

'Did he invite you because of Pneumatech?' Those wide, sea-blue eyes were charming.

'Probably.' She giggled up at him, flirting openly even though her boyfriend was just across the table.

'So is he a Lock Chase client?'

'What?' Suddenly her eyes looked more cunning than appealing.

'Come on, Urban, I'm not an idiot. Alan Dove must be a client to have invited you to a private dinner like this.'

She was very good, but not good enough to catch him out. 'Actually, Amy, the Doves and I live quite near each other in Suffolk. A beautiful county, do you know it?'

'Haven't been there for years.' There was a slight pause before she went on, 'So if you aren't going to tell about Dove, who else are you working with?'

Urban turned on what he hoped was a charming Slavic smile. 'I'm really sorry but I'm afraid we never talk about our clients or they wouldn't trust us any more, would they? Now let's talk about you. And your boyfriend, tell me about him.'

'Tim?' Urban saw with relief that he'd diverted Amy from her third-degree interrogation. 'That's him over there.' She indicated the clean-featured man sitting on the other side of Juliana Dove. 'We've being going out for ages. Tim's a Tory MP and he chairs the Commons Select Committee on Health. That may be as far as he's going to get. His moral stances get in the way of his ambition.'

'What sort of moral stances?'

'Well, prisons for one. He's always banging on about prison reform and it makes some of his constituents quite shirty. If he loses Somerset South West, he's going to have to look for a safer seat and I'm not sure he's going to get one unless he stops being so wet.'

'But surely if he's prepared to sacrifice his career for something he feels strongly about, that's rather impressive, isn't it?'

'Bugger impressive. If he'd seen as many murderers and perverts as I have he'd soon want them banged up in shitholes for life.' Seeing Amy's blue eyes widening, Urban wondered what was coming next. 'You're brilliantly persuasive, aren't you? That's why you're a genius at your job. So tell me, how should I persuade Tim to be a bit less rigorous for the sake of his career?'

Flattered, Urban did his best to advise her. At least it would keep her mind off Lock Chase.

'I think that when people have a really deep-rooted belief in something being right or wrong, you can't change it. Tim seems an upright kind of man. His fundamental beliefs are his core. If he had to compromise them it would probably break him. I know I'd never change my own core beliefs.'

As soon as the words came out of his mouth, Urban regretted them. Amy swooped. 'So what are these core beliefs of yours?'

Aware of the danger of making an enemy of an influential journalist, he was trapped. 'I believe that totalitarian states are evil and that democracy is good,' he said slowly. 'I've seen both systems. I'm Polish. My parents smuggled me out when I was a child.'

'Good God! Can you remember anything about it?'

Urban looked away. Her gentle voice came back to him. *Ave Maria, gratia plena. Ave Maria, gratia plena.* Those were the last words of his mother's that he'd heard as he was bundled into the boot of a Trabant. She was tiny, with huge dark eyes and curly brown hair, and he'd thought her the most beautiful woman in the world. Closing his eyes, he could see her standing by the car, tears streaming down her face. And behind her his father, tall, hawk-featured, an arm protectively around her shoulders, staring down at him, willing him to be brave. As the boot lid slammed shut, he could still hear his mother praying.

Urban opened his eyes to see Amy Flower staring into his face.

'Can you remember it?' she prompted.

Apart from that last image of his parents, it was only the smells he remembered. Dust, engine oil, burnt rubber. A break as he was wrapped in a tarpaulin and carried on to a boat. Then more darkness as he was shut in the engine room and was again alone with the smells of dust, oil, perished rubber and a little later his own vomit as the boat pitched and rolled across the Baltic.

'No,' he forced the word out. 'I remember nothing.'

'So what happened to you?'

'My parents had arranged for me to be taken to Oxford, to stay with a generous and wonderful man. Poor Professor Fowler, he'd expected to have me for a month, two at the most. He hadn't dreamed he'd be lumbered with me for life. My father and mother had an escape route arranged, you see. They were to follow me.'

'Did they make it?'

'I waited.' Urban closed his eyes again. He could still see the long Oxford garden with its herbaceous borders and its scattering of apple trees. He had stood there day after day, staring north-eastwards, towards Poland.

'And?'

'They never came,' he said bleakly. 'I was told years later that my father was with the Resistance. He and my mother were shot by the Russians shortly after they got me out. I don't even know where their bodies are buried.' With a shake of his head, he fell silent.

'I'm really sorry.' To his great relief, he saw that the hard blue eyes had softened. 'My parents got themselves lost along the way too, but I've found ways to get over it.'

'I suppose you mean that time heals.'

'Oh, bugger that, I mean having fun! Stuffing my face with food, getting wasted, and I'm mad about old cars.' The eyes slid away from him. 'Poor me. So many lovely games but only a journalist's salary to play them with.'

EIGHT

A shaft of bright spring sunshine lanced down through the high Victorian vault at the heart of the Houses of Parliament. Sprawled along a green leather bench, Amy could hear the tail-coated attendant phoning up to Tim's parliamentary office. 'Is that Mr Cusack? Miss Amy Flower's waiting for you in the Central Lobby, sir.'

Even at a fast trot, Amy knew it would take Tim a good five minutes to get from his eyrie above St Stephen's Entrance. Today she had to wait seven minutes until he emerged on to the marble floor, out of breath.

'Sorry, Amy. Bumped into our Chief Whip. Couldn't get away.'

'Never mind, darling, you're here now. Any chance of a cup of tea? I'm on to a story and I need your help.'

Tim grabbed her hand. 'I'm starving. Let's go and have a plate of chips in the Members' cafeteria.'

'Can't think of anything more romantic.'

Amy was in a tearing hurry to chase up her piece and as soon as they'd put their plastic trays down at a free table she got straight to the point. 'Angel. I want you to do something for me. It's about Alan Dove.'

'Nice chap, I thought, very direct. We had a fascinating conversation about whether the Hippocratic Oath applies to modern medical ethics.'

'Yes, sweetest, another time. I'm trying to get some legs on to a story. It seems Dove may have had a dodgy legover with a hedge fund while he was buying a company called F-ACE and I need to know all about it.' She sucked mayonnaise off an underdone chip and gave him one of her best smiles. 'I'd love the inside scoop.'

'For heaven's sake, Amy.' He'd put on that annoyingly strait-laced look. 'I can't just go about getting privileged information and passing it back to you.'

'Oh, rubbish. Don't be so pompous. All I'm asking you to do is find out anything you can about the F-ACE takeover from whichever Select Committee looks at that kind of thing. That's not a lot to ask. I'd do the same for you, sweetness, now wouldn't I?' She licked her fingers and stared at him. 'Just do this for me now and I'll think of something lovely to do to you later.'

She'd hardly bothered to lower her voice and Tim was blushing like a schoolboy. 'Well, all right, I'll ask around.'

Knowing that he always kept his word, she was on her feet in an instant. 'Thanks, darling, and now I must scoot. Got to meet a man with a leak.'

'You sweaty hog, Guy,' said Sir John. 'Fancy festering indoors on a lovely March day.'

Mary stayed curled up in her armchair by the fire while the strings of her husband's upbringing pulled him politely to his feet. 'We *have* been outside this morning,' Guy said mildly. 'We walked right down to the end of the drive to pick up the papers.'

'Not even a pipe-opener. You need to get a good pull of Suffolk air into those lungs of yours.'

'Is Grace with you?' Mary put down the *Daily Business* and

tried to remember whether she should be nagging her daughter about her weekend homework.

'She's helping out down at the dairy. I had to come in to call the flesh van. Cow died in the night. Mastitis, poor old girl.'

'Father, don't you think you should put on something a bit warmer?' But Sir John wasn't listening. Pausing only to kick a threadbare Persian rug out of his way, he hurried back out into the open air. Mary saw the little frown on Guy's face as he shut the morning-room door.

'If your mother was still alive, she'd have made him put a coat on,' she told him. 'You're a wonderful son, but you aren't his wife.'

'You're right, of course.' With a sigh, he picked up a bundle of files while Mary went back to the newspapers.

After several minutes of peace, Guy said abruptly, 'Why does our Bursar want to invest so much of the college's money in commercial property?' Struggling to stay with the thread of a complicated article on China's population, Mary ignored him. 'He says we can't lose,' Guy went on regardless. 'The British economy's stable.'

Mary put down her paper sharply. It took her an age to get back into a story once her concentration had been broken. This time, she forced herself to swallow her annoyance. She was starting to feel embarrassed by how often snapping at her husband featured among the sins she murmured to Peter Cromwell in the confessional box. 'Are you going to do anything about it?' was all she said.

'I'm dragging myself along to a seminar on college funding. Boring subject at the best of times and it's being held in that dreary hall of Newnham's. It smells of broccoli and female high-mindedness.' Guy turned back to his files.

Mary abandoned Chinese demography as her eye was caught by a headline.

Daily Business   *Saturday 19 March 2005*

Questions raised over Pneumatech takeover.

The Financial Services Authority is considering an investigation of share price movements in the period prior to Pneumatech Bioscience's acquisition of F-ACE, according to informed sources. The City watchdog is thought to be concerned by reports of hedge fund collusion and the creation of an improper market.

Significant volumes of F-ACE stock were reportedly shorted immediately prior to the circulation of negative rumours about the company. There was a fifty per cent fall in F-ACE's share price on the back of these rumours, and Pneumatech was able to buy the company for £200 million, less than half its former value.

Pneumatech's Chief Executive, Dr Alan Dove, was unavailable for comment.

For once the interrupter rather than the interrupted, Mary said, 'Listen to this! It's about our neighbour, Dr Dove.'

Mary read the story to Guy, who said vaguely, '*Quocumque modo rem.*'

'Horace?'

He looked up. 'Oh, well done! "*Make money no matter how.*" Did you know who wrote it or was that a guess?'

'More of a fifty-fifty bet. Your quotes are always either Horace or Catullus.'

'I'll catch you out with someone obscure next time. But I really can't understand what Alan Dove is supposed to have done. All this business about hedges and shorting.'

'I've explained it to you before, Guy. You never listen.'

'I'm listening now,' said her husband. 'Hedge funds are some sort of investment trust, aren't they?'

As Mary swivelled round in her comfortable old armchair, she noticed the stuffing oozing out of its cracked leather and sighed. More expense. 'Well, yes,' she said, 'they do buy shares in the normal way. But the big difference is that they also *sell* shares they've borrowed. That's what shorting means. They hope that the share price will fall so they can buy back the borrowed shares for less than they sold them for.'

'And if the share price goes up instead of down?'

'Then the hedge fund would lose a lot of money. And I mean a *lot* of money. They have very rich investors and they place huge bets for them.'

'Arabs, d'you mean?'

'Arabs, Russians, Americans, anyone with a lot of millions to invest. People who would get seriously nasty if their money was lost. That's why the shadier hedge funds manipulate the market to make absolutely sure that any share they've shorted *does* go down rather than up.'

'What an awful world you work in. This business sounds like straightforward thievery to me. Why do people do it?'

'For heaven's sake Guy, you know exactly why. Money, power, status.'

'Well, I don't want any part of it and I'd rather you didn't either.'

'There are a lot of things I'd rather not do.' Mary couldn't keep the irritation out of her voice. 'But I have to do them if the bills are going to get paid.'

She knew what Guy would do. His preferred tactic was always to ignore her and change the subject when she became 'tiresome' as he called it.

'Come on, lazybones. Let's walk up Neat's Hill,' he said. There! She was right.

As she put her newspaper down, Mary's eye was caught again by the headline, '*Questions raised over Pneumatech takeover.*' Heaving herself out of her chair, she said, 'I wonder what Alan Dove's doing about this.'

NINE

'*Investigation. Collusion.*' Dove shook his head in despair as he hunched over the newspaper article on his desk. How *could* they write this about him? He'd like a few words with the evil-minded, ill-informed cow who had written this rubbish. Why did he assume it was written by a woman? Because it was always women who had it in for him. It had been like that since his school-days.

When they chose to send him to Hawley-Wilson Comprehensive, his middle-class, intellectual parents could have had no idea of the damage their left-wing enthusiasms would do. He tried never to finger the scars of his school years, but occasionally they would open and weep of their own accord.

'Aaah!' A wild scream as he plodded towards the pool during those compulsory swimming lessons. 'Here comes Fatty Four-Eyes! Run!' Shrieks of laughter, nubile arses, flying legs scampering away from him. Early adolescence, when the longing for a girlfriend had been at its fiercest. The impossible agony of swimming trunks. Blonde hair, a girl towering over him, tits shoved teasingly into his face and then, 'Gross! Fatty's got a stiffy! Look, everyone!'

It wasn't his fault that he was so short, or that his eyes bulged. And he'd been precociously clever, a bully's dream. It was always the girls at Hawley-Wilson who'd been the cruellest. The boys had hidden his books and put drawing-pins on his chair, but it was the girls who had hurt him when he'd sat on one. 'He's only pretending! He can't feel a thing through all that blubber.' A burst of giggles. Girls. He had yearned for them, feared them, hated them.

Turning away from the *Daily Business*, his eye was caught by the photograph of his wife. That stiff smile always amused him. Juliana hated having her photograph taken. With a sigh, he pushed himself up from his chair and straightened his shoulders. Better find out what was going on.

As he opened his door, the phone rang. 'Chief Executive's office, Miss Wilson-Smith speaking,' he heard his secretary say. After a short pause she said abruptly, 'I'm sorry, but you can't talk to Dr Dove. He is in conference.' She put down the handset with some force and turned to him.

'Well, I must say, some of these journalists can be extremely offensive, they really can.' Sadie shook her permed curls at him. 'Teenage scribblers the lot of them. Don't you agree, Dr Dove?'

His secretary's stalwart support was calming. 'So who's managed to get here for the meeting? And by the way, I do appreciate your giving up your Saturday to come into the office.'

'It's my pleasure, Dr Dove. Everyone you asked for is on the way.' She ticked off the list on her fingers. 'The Chairman has driven up from Surrey and is already in the building. Mr Straw is only coming down from Kensington, so he should be here shortly, and the lawyer's on call if you need him.'

Dove had scarcely got back into his office when his Chairman barged in. 'Morning, Alan. What have you been up to then, eh? Doing a bit of insider trading?' Gregory Loach marched over to Dove's desk and threw the file of assorted papers he was carrying into the centre of its pristine marble surface.

Being fanatically tidy himself, Dove found Loach's tendency to walk into his office and strew his papers about almost intolerable. He had to remind himself that while his Chairman was rough-tempered and had the sensitivity of a block of granite, he was also an incurious man who preferred his golf to his work. Loach rarely questioned the way he ran Pneumatech, which was precisely why Dove had chosen him as Chairman when he floated the company.

'Good of you to come in, Gregory,' Dove murmured. 'Sorry to have to bother you at the weekend but we must put out some form of response to these hacks. Coffee?'

'A tea, please, Alan. Milk and sugar. And a biscuit if you have such a thing.'

Sadie disappeared to bring the Chairman his tea and a double espresso for Dove, and moments later Ivan Straw arrived.

'Ah, Straw, there you are,' said Loach. 'Pull up a chair. Bloody journalists, eh? What do you think we should do?'

'I suggest you put out a straightforward denial. As a matter of fact I've been working on something you might use. Shall I read it out?' Straw made it sound as if his draft was the result of hours of careful thought, but Dove guessed that he'd scribbled it out in the back of a taxi on his way to the meeting.

It was clear that Loach wanted to get back to his golf in Surrey, and Straw's simple denial was soon agreed to. Dove said little during the brief conversation. Resentment festered inside him. The press release achieved nothing. He wanted a retraction, a full apology from the anonymous bitch who had slandered him. Twenty minutes after the meeting had finished, Dove was calming himself by clearing some paperwork. Assuming everyone would long since have left to continue their interrupted weekends, he was surprised when Ivan Straw slipped in and quietly closed the door.

'That was a fun meeting, wasn't it?' Odd how the banker's smile never reached his blank green eyes. 'That press release was a perfectly sensible response to start with, but I think we need to make sure this story gets killed until it's very dead, don't we?'

Resenting the over-familiar tone, Dove replied curtly, 'You have a suggestion?'

Straw leant over until he was almost breathing into his ear. 'Setting aside today's little fuss, you're good at acquisitions, aren't you?' Dove pulled back involuntarily from the smell of stale cigarettes, but Straw either didn't notice or didn't care. 'You seem to be doing a good job of slotting F-ACE in with the original Pneumatech business?'

'Early days yet, but yes, it's going well. I hadn't fully realized what we could do when we put Pneumatech's scientists together with F-ACE's products.' Dove could feel the excitement rising as he talked. 'It means creams that really reduce wrinkles, and we may be close to developing a depilatory cream that removes unwanted hair permanently!' He paused, the enthusiasm dying from his voice. 'Of course, those *bastards* on the City papers will never give me any credit.'

Straw homed in even closer on Dove's ear. 'I suggest,' his whisper was sibilant, 'that to silence today's little contretemps for good, you need to make F-ACE look like piss in the wind. Take over something *really* big. That'll make the market look up to you. No one will remember any hiccups there may have been on the way.'

For the first time since he'd read the *Daily Business* that morning, Dove relaxed. The bold move. Redouble the size of Pneumatech. The world would have to look up to him then. He nodded slowly.

Straw's narrow face was deadly serious. 'I'll start looking on Monday.'

*

Meg was re-reading *Orlando* when the silver telephone rang.

'A little nugget for you. That Pneumatech takeover was a BOOB job, and you'll never guess which hedgie was behind it.'

As Meg listened, she felt her face harden. 'So *that's* what happened to F-ACE, is it? I'll kill that bastard Dix and his sodding hedge fund. After all the tips I've given him, he bloody well should have cut me in. He's too busy sucking up to his new Russian investor to remember his loyal supporters. *Shit*!'

'Keep your hair on, Meggy. I wish I hadn't told you now.'

'Sorry. I'll call you back when I've recovered my temper. I'm buggered if we're just going to let Pneumatech drop.'

Frowning, Meg replaced the silver handset and switched on her computer.

'I hear Dix made a lot of money for you out of the Pneumatech deal.' Ivan Straw spoke carefully. This was the first time he had managed to get through to Platon Dyengi on the phone.

'Was good. You bring me another now?'

'The first sniff of a big one.'

'No tell on phone. You come to villa Majorca. I hear you have nice wife. Bring her.'

Staying with the Russian! Ivan tried to keep the excitement out of his voice. 'That would be great.' He wanted to go on talking but the line was already dead.

TEN

So this was how bureaucracy worked. Urban had been kicking his heels for twenty minutes. Always punctual, he'd arrived at the Treasury's headquarters in Whitehall a few minutes before three and had been sitting on a bench in the marbled reception hall ever since. Occasionally the receptionist would glance across at him and say, 'I'm sure Mr Elginbrode won't keep you much longer,' but he didn't believe her any more.

He'd made a detailed inspection of the multi-coloured lights incongruously stacked at the top of the grand staircase, had twice read through Her Majesty's Revenue and Customs' statement of Purpose, Vision and Way, and had been reduced to watching the ebb and flow of civil servants when he became aware of the slight figure standing in front of him.

'Mr Palewski? Aiden Elginbrode.'

Everything about Elginbrode seemed anonymous, Urban thought as he followed him up concrete stairs and along windowless corridors. Mid-brown hair, unremarkable clothes, forgettable face. As they sat down together in an office looking out over the Whitehall rooftops he noticed that even the man's voice was self-effacing.

'I'm most grateful to you for sparing the time to come and see me. I wanted to talk to you about an assignment that Lock Chase might undertake.'

'I should probably tell you straight away that we do virtually no consulting work in the public sector.'

'Because you think us timorous?' That half-smile gave Elginbrode an impish look; Urban found himself warming to the man. 'That's rather why I called you. I'm nervous. There's a worm in the economic bud. If it continues to grow unchecked, I fear that it will eat the heart out of the City of London.' Having no idea what Elginbrode was talking about, Urban stayed silent. 'I refer, of course, to the hedge fund industry. It has been allowed to spawn into what one might term a global casino. It gambles with billions and fixes the odds on every game.'

'That sounds extraordinarily corrupt,' said Urban, still not clear where the conversation was going.

'Corrupt?' The diffident manner vanished as Elginbrode leant forward across his desk. 'A handful of people are making *fortunes* by manipulating the markets. One day the world's financial system will come to a shuddering halt unless they are controlled. And d'you know the worst thing?' Urban shook his head. 'The industry's an offshore free-for-all. They don't even pay tax!'

'But surely the authorities keep an eye on them?'

'Hedge funds are entirely, ah, unregulated.' Elginbrode had recovered his hesitancy. 'And that rather brings me to the point of our meeting. I'm trying to build an argument strong enough to persuade Ministers to introduce regulation and I believe that Lock Chase could help me.'

Urban was still perplexed. 'I don't quite understand why you need help. Surely the government would want to regulate anything with such a huge influence on the economy?'

'Influence. Ah yes. Influence. You've hit on the word exactly. Where so much money is involved, one is fighting vested interests and that's my problem. Many powerful institutions and individuals benefit from the status quo. The case for regulation needs to be incontrovertible. I'm looking for an adviser who is both ethical and discreet and who understands the financial system.'

Urban smiled. The answer was obvious. 'Mary Kersey. She's very busy at the moment, but I know she'd make time for this. She's ethical, she's discreet and she's a Partner in our Financial Services practice. It's right up her street.'

'A woman?' A crease appeared on Elginbrode's pale forehead. 'Hmm. I'm not sure. I'll be asking my adviser to look at every company takeover that might have the whiff of a hedge fund hanging round it. There are some unpleasant people involved. They won't appreciate having their wings clipped.'

'Oh, don't worry about Mary,' Urban said. 'I'm sure she knows how to look after herself.'

'You're such a slimeball.' Spider was pacing around Urban's office, legs swishing angrily against the lining of her scarlet skirt. 'I crapped a lizard over the Mardi Gras event! I got the best feedback ratings ever and all you can do is gripe because I went over budget.'

He sat back in his chair, trying to keep the amusement off his face as he waited for her fury to vanish like it always did, as suddenly as it had erupted. Watching her pounding up and down, he caught the surprisingly feminine scent she always wore and wondered idly what it was.

'Urban! Are you listening to me? Did you just ask me in here to give me grief about a party? OK, so it did cost a hundred and thirty K and the budget was a hundred, I do admit that. But it was a success. It *was* a success. Wasn't it?'

It suddenly occurred to him that Spider's self-confidence might not be as cast-iron as he had always assumed. Surely it was insecurity he'd heard in that anxious inflection? 'Let's just set the thirty off against your bonus this year and say no more about it.' He paused, realizing that she was actually looking quite upset. 'Joke! It was a *fantastic* event, Spider, one of the best ever, and there I was thinking a skiing trip would be boring. I had a lot of snow when I was a child, you know.'

'You don't say so?' Her frown dissolved into a wide smile. 'And didn't you have some Escape from Gdansk drama? I don't think I ever heard that story before, or the one about the mad professor.'

'Now that's a bit unfair. Professor Fowler was very sane. Taking me in was probably the only mad thing he did in his life, and just because the Commies had once let my father visit Oxford. He said my dad was one of the most brilliant linguists he'd ever met. Oh, God. What a waste.' He looked at Spider ruefully. 'See? At least I talk about my past, which is more than you do.'

'*Touché*. Though my childhood was just dull, you know.'

Urban waited. Was Spider finally going to tell him about her background? She didn't go on, and eventually he said, 'Well, nothing about the Mardi Gras event was dull. In fact it was brilliant. Everyone had a great time. Even Daniel came back cheerful. Quite an achievement, seeing how you've been killing him.'

'He's just idle, that boy. He'll be grateful to me one day. I've taught him to love facts and to work his balls off, the perfect recipe for a useful life. But thanks, Urban, it's not often I get any praise from you. Was that all you wanted to say? You know there's a Pneumatech team meeting in ten minutes.'

'Actually it's Pneumatech I need to talk to you about.' Urban motioned Spider to sit down.

'There's nothing wrong, is there? The work *is* going ahead?'

Urban wondered why she'd bothered to ask. It was his job to worry about keeping the business coming in, not hers. 'Of course it's going ahead. It's just there's a small complication. The

Treasury have asked us to look at whether hedge funds should be regulated.'

'How incredibly boring. Which poor Partner's going to be running that case?'

'I'm getting Mary to do it. She knows all about financial services, and let's face it, she's pretty keen on rectitude.'

'She's a frigging do-gooder, that woman. Don't you think she should be adding value to her bank clients instead of brown-nosing bureaucrats? And anyway, why aren't the Treasury using accountants?'

'Accountants have conflicts of interest and the Treasury trusts Lock Chase's reputation.' Urban allowed himself a small smile. He'd been immensely flattered when Aiden Elginbrode had told him that. 'Anyway, Spider, the reason I'm telling you this is that the Treasury want us to have a look at every recent acquisition where there've been odd share price movements. The Pneumatech/F-ACE deal's on the list. That's all you need to know.'

'OK, so now I know.'

'And by the way, if you ever meet him, don't mention hedge funds to Alan Dove. He's spitting tacks about that story in the *Daily Business*. Took it as a massive personal insult.' As he was speaking, Urban happened to glance over at Spider. She was staring blankly ahead as if she were miles away. 'Spider?'

'Nothing.' She swept out, as usual banging his office door shut behind her.

ELEVEN

'Hey, Ivan, I really think I'm going to enjoy myself.' Francesca pressed herself against his side. 'This is a *nice* way to travel.'

'It's all so bloody effortless, isn't it?' Ivan could hear the yearning in his voice. 'This is what real money buys. Remember what I've said, won't you, doll? If we play our cards right, Dyengi might get me a top job at Dix's hedge fund. And *then* we'd have some serious money. A bit more than the few pissy millions I'm earning at the moment, anyway.'

He could see that his young wife was childishly thrilled by the Citation X parked on the runway right in front of them. Ivan was excited too. He'd have to watch it. Too much adrenalin could tip him into an episode of hypomania. But it was hard not to feel exhilarated when he was almost touching proper money. He was sick of scraping a pittance from investment banking. A million, two million, what use was that? The big hedge funds, they were a different league. Working for one of them, he might be looking at fifty million quid in a decent year. If he could just get the Russian to wangle him a place with Dix, he'd be made.

Platon Dyengi had sent a car for them, as fast, black and discreet as its chauffeur. What with the television, the mildly pornographic DVDs, the drinks and the cigars, the journey from Kensington through the Friday afternoon traffic seemed to have taken no time at all, and suddenly there they were at the airport's discreet entrance for private jet passengers. No crowds, no queues, they hardly even had to get out of the car to show their passports. It was indeed 'bloody effortless' and it did indeed cost serious money. But then Platon Dyengi's money *was* very serious.

'Welcome, welcome, my dear!' Ignoring Ivan, Dyengi hurried down the steps from the plane to grab Francesca's hand. 'Aah, but you look wonderful. I see you will not be too hot.'

Ivan watched approvingly as his wife allowed her suede jacket to slip back off her shoulders to show what was underneath. Her bosom was just contained inside what looked like a simple silk scarf tied casually across her chest and around her waist. This was, as Ivan knew, two grand's worth of brilliantly constructed *trompe l'oeil* with much artful sewing supporting Francesca's superstructure, to which the Russian's eyes were glued. Ivan couldn't blame him, his wife's breasts were fault-less. He should know. He'd paid for them.

Dyengi steered Francesca up the steps to where his wife was waiting, squinting down at them in the April sunshine. 'And so this is Anya, who is my wife.'

Dyengi was clearly still on his first marriage. Short, square and middle-aged, Anya Dyengi was no hourglass beauty, more a well-stuffed sausage from chin to knee. She smiled calmly at Francesca and Ivan guessed that she was used to dealing with her husband's amusements. 'Welcome. Come inside.' Anya waved them through into the plane.

Having expected extravagance and luxury, the interior of the private jet was deeply disappointing. The armchairs were uphol-stered in something that felt unpleasantly like plastic, while the walls and floor were covered in a cheap laminate.

Ivan searched for something polite to say. 'Interesting. What style have you had this done in?'

'*Shtoyest* "style", *Anya?*'

'*Moyushchiysya.*'

'Oh, but that's not *fair*,' Francesca's voice purred softly. 'If you speak Russian, Ivan and I won't understand a word. What did you just say?'

'I tell Platon the style of plane is washable.'

An hour later, Mach 0.85 over the Loire Valley and Ivan could see exactly why the Citation's interior was *moyushchiysya*. Blue-black globules of caviar spattered the walls, flicked there by Platon, who seemed to be seeing the world as one huge vodka-fuelled joke. An empty bottle of Starka rolled about on the floor until it was eventually collected by the muscle-bound minder, who otherwise sat mute and stern on one of the side seats. Ivan scarcely touched the vodka. His doctor was always warning him about alcohol, the risk if he took it with his pills. Drink could tip him either way, depression or elation. He wasn't taking any chances this weekend.

It was dark when a convoy of armoured cars swept them through two sets of security gates and into the Majorcan compound. Anya stumped straight off to bed and Dyengi vanished almost immediately afterwards, leaving the Straws to be served a solitary dinner by a fleet of silent staff. Ivan didn't care. He'd had a tiring week. He was looking forward to a long sleep and then a leisurely chat with his host.

'Good morning sir, madam.' Ivan screwed his face up as a beam of sun shot into his eyes. 'Breakfast is on your balcony. Mr Dyengi asks you to join him at the jetty in an hour. He will be taking you out on his boat.'

Platon's boat turned out to be a hundred-foot Pershing with its own helicopter perched on the aft poop. Guests were already milling about on the sun deck, drinking champagne, but there was no sign of either of the Dyengis to make introductions.

LOUISE PATTEN | 83

Ivan and Francesca were forced to stand around on the fringes of conversations and hope to be included.

'Darling, I must tell you! Charles has won a simply massive out-of-court settlement on the Rookley divorce case. He's taking all of us to Palm Beach for a month on the back of it, the nannies too.'

'Bought them in Singapore. Cost me twelve mill, but I'd promised the old girl some decent stones.'

'We've been staying in an absolute *palace* in Queensland. It was bloody hot, but mercifully even the outdoor pool had air-conditioning. Icy mist sprayed above the water the whole time. Heaven! I hated coming back.'

Like squabbling starlings falling silent when a hawk flies over, there was a sudden hush as Platon Dyengi appeared. The chatter started again almost immediately as he was surrounded and subsumed into the crowd of his guests. Ivan cursed under his breath. He had no chance of getting near the Russian, let alone having a quiet chat with him.

Apart from opening a window on how the world's richest lived, the weekend was a waste of time. Ivan found that every moment was spent in mass entertainment with a shifting group of people he dismissed as Eurotrash. They lunched on the Pershing, jetskiied all afternoon and had dinner with fifty others in a nearby hotel. Next morning, they were driven halfway across the island for a lunchtime drinks party before hurrying on even further to eat seafood at an outrageously expensive restaurant on the coast.

Dyengi threw the occasional word at Ivan and stroked Francesca whenever he came near her, but she was only one of many beautiful women trying to get his attention. Not until Sunday afternoon, when they were on the doorstep of the villa and about to leave, did Ivan manage to get Platon alone. The conversation was brief and uncomfortable.

'Look, I hope you don't mind my raising this but I'm really keen to get a job with Dix. I'm fed up with Wolkenbank.'

'Ivaaan.' The Russian growled his name like a threat. Two security guards who'd been standing by the waiting car immediately moved closer. 'Is holiday.' Dyengi's dark eyes were chilling. 'You want advice? Send more deals. Big deals. If good money, maybe we see. If not . . .' Still holding Ivan's eyes with his own, Dyengi slowly drew his finger across his throat before turning back into the house.

Ivan stared after him, shocked. Had he just been threatened? He couldn't believe it. Dyengi must have been joking. Surely? Obviously. His approach had been bad timing. Russians were notoriously volatile. He was sure to invite them again. There'd be another opportunity in another of his villas. In the meantime he was going to take the Russian's advice. He'd be chasing up Alan Dove and a few of his other clients as soon as he got back. He'd make sure he slipped Dix a really big deal.

TWELVE

'Thank you, Mary, delicious sandwiches.' Getting up from tea in Trister's kitchen, Sir John walked out into the dusk, calling over his shoulder, 'Milking time! Coming to help, Gracie?'

Her daughter jumped up from the table and was halfway out of the door after him when Mary said, 'But darling, I've hardly seen you. Why don't you stay in now and we can have a chat? Like we used to? You know Daddy and I have to go out to dinner tonight, so we won't get a chance to talk later.'

'Sorry, Mummy. Grandpa's showing me how to do the iodine on the cows' udders.' Pulling on her gumboots Grace was gone, racing to catch up with her grandfather.

Mary was left alone with the washing-up and the sad thought that this was a punishment for working such long hours. Grace saw so little of her that she seemed to be growing away from her own mother. She picked up a plate. Three sand-wiches left. Better finish up that cucumber one before it went soggy. And one of the chicken sandwiches was losing its filling. She ate it absently, overcome by a sudden jealousy for her father-in-law. Always stuffing Grace's head with grand ideas about her Kersey antecedents. She'd never dream of pushing her far-higher-born Ivybridge ancestors down the child's throat.

Collecting up the mugs, Mary knew she was being idiotic.

She couldn't manage without Sir John's help. But still, Grace needed something else to think about. A pony, for example. As she finished clearing the table, she saw there was only one sandwich left. Silly to leave it.

That evening, she and Guy were going to dinner with the Blythe Vale Hunt's Master of Foxhounds. Guy had been moaning about it all day. 'Whatever cognitive organ our MFH may possess, it doesn't reside in his head. I can't stand an evening talking about hunting and listening to all that bravado about who's going to go to jail for breaking the ban. And even worse, the wine's preternaturally filthy.'

'I'm not wild about hunt dinners myself. But still,' Mary squared her shoulders, 'supporting the local hunt's our duty. And besides, I want to find out about getting Grace a pony. We *are* going to get her a pony, aren't we, Guy?' she added, seeing his raised eyebrow. 'Please. It'd be so good for her.'

'All right. All right. I know that look of yours. We'll go tonight if you really want to, and we'll get a pony for Grace if you *really* want to. Just don't expect me to do any unspeakable equine activities.'

'No hacking, tacking or plaiting. I promise. And Guy,' she smiled up at him, 'it's sweet of you to agree.' Peter Cromwell would have given her a pat on the back for that, Mary thought as her husband wandered out of the room. She'd been making a real effort to be more amiable after the scolding she'd had at her monthly confession that morning.

'Bless me, Father, for I have sinned.' She had knelt as usual in curtained darkness, looking through a small metal grille at Peter, who was sitting, brightly lit, on the priest's side of the confessional box.

'May you make your confession with a humble and contrite heart.'

'It's Mary and I'm at my wits' end.' She saw Peter nod, but as he didn't say anything, she went on. 'Guy's driving me mad. I know I don't see him often enough because I'm working so hard, but that's really not my fault. And when I do see him, he can be so irritating and I'm finding it incredibly difficult to stop myself being grumpy. We used to be so happy,' she added wistfully.

'Every time you come to confession you complain about your husband!' Peter's usual discreet murmur had vanished and Mary hoped there was no one else in the church to hear his sudden angry bark at her. 'You've got to snap out of this! Your marriage is a sacrament and you must try harder to make it work.' His voice sank back to its normal confessional hush. 'Now go home and be nicer to Guy.'

Peter had given her a longer than usual list of penitential prayers and Mary had been quite ruffled by his ferocity. Normally he was the gentlest of confessors. As she left the church, she had resolved to do as he said. She *would* be kinder to Guy.

That evening, she took real trouble over her appearance. Instead of the comfortable trousers and jacket that she would normally have worn, Mary chose a dress she knew Guy liked and put her hair up into the sort of wispy bun that he'd loved all those years ago when they'd been carefree undergraduates together. The effort was well worth it when she came downstairs and saw how her husband's eyes crinkled into a smile of approval. 'You look lovely,' he said, putting an arm round her. 'Far too pretty to waste on our MFH and his hunting friends.'

Minutes after arriving at the cold house in whose warm stables their host spent most of his time, Mary bumped into Anna-Clare Francis, the small and whip-thin District Commissioner of the Blythe Vale Pony Club. Not being particularly horsey herself,

Mary didn't know Anna-Clare well and was rather afraid of showing her ignorance about ponies in front of such an expert. 'I'm so glad to see you here,' she started. 'The thing is, I'm looking for a first pony for my daughter Grace and I wonder if you might know of something suitable.'

'Age?' Anna-Clare fired at her, giving Mary the feeling that she'd been hauled up in front of her headmistress.

'Well, I'm not really sure.' Mary clutched her glass of over-chilled and syrupy Pinot Grigio and hoped she didn't look too vague. 'We want one that's safe, but not too decrepit.'

'I meant your daughter's age, not the pony's.' The District Commissioner smiled suddenly, showing very irregular teeth that somehow made her look quite human. 'You'll want something the right size for her.'

'Sorry, I was being an idiot,' Mary laughed. 'Grace's coming up to twelve, though she's still quite a beginner at riding. As a matter of fact it's her birthday next month and a pony would be the perfect present if I could find one in time.'

'A novice twelve-year-old. Let me think.' Anna-Clare stood frowning to herself for a couple of minutes, then gave Mary a decisive nod. 'Dimple! She's a lovely little Exmoor, the ideal pony for your daughter, and I know the Smythes are looking for something bigger for Jenny. You'll presumably have lots of grazing and shelter at Trister. Plenty of room for two.'

'Two?' Anna-Clare must have misheard her. 'But I'm only looking for one.'

'Mary!' Once again, it was like being in front of the head-mistress. 'You *couldn't* keep a pony on its own! They're herd animals. They get terribly lonely if they don't have at least one friend.'

'Oh, I see,' Mary said weakly. 'I didn't realize.'

'Don't worry. I'm sure I can find you a field companion.'

'Oh thanks. Thanks awfully.' Mary tried to sound both grateful and nonchalant, though she did wonder how Guy would take to the idea of *two* ponies.

'Naturally Grace will be joining the Pony Club. You'll need a trailer to bring her pony to our meetings.'

Mary took a slug of the vile wine. One pony had somehow become two, plus a trailer which she would have to learn how to tow. And how was she going to find the time to drag Grace and the pony all over Suffolk to Pony Club events? She had a sudden fear that Dimple and Dimple's friend would turn out to be yet another exhausting responsibility.

'I'm sure you know how to ride, Mary,' Anna-Clare was saying. 'Why don't you hunt?'

Fortunately she was saved the embarrassment of trying to explain her equivocal views on fox-hunting by the arrival of Dominic and Meg Dewey.

'Hi, everyone! So sorry we're late. Dominic's plane was an hour delayed.' Mary felt as if the whole room had warmed up as Meg undulated in with her husband fluttering darkly behind her like a little pet bat. The party immediately sat down for dinner, and Mary was soon laughing with the rest as Meg shouted down the table on the subject of Alan Dove and his landscaping.

'Have you seen that bloody great lagoon he's having dug? Going to be used for fishing and water-sports apparently.'

'And what about the house? Idiotic name, White Gables. Not a gable in sight.'

'The White's accurate. They've just had it painted.'

'Wait till they've had a bit of rain and the lichen starts growing. They'll have to call it Green Gables.'

'Bet they leave before the lichen. They won't settle in here. They don't hunt.'

Mary bent towards Dominic Dewey, sitting in silence next to her. Keen to avoid the interminable subject of hunting, she said, 'I do wish you'd join the book club. Why don't you?'

'Heavens, no!' He glanced across at his wife and lowered his voice. 'Meg would never let me. She likes to compartmentalize her world and keep me out of bits of it. In fact there are *huge* chunks of her life that I know nothing about.'

'How extraordinary. I don't suppose there's anything about Guy I don't know.'

'Ah well, a bit of secrecy's fine with me. The wine trade's a funny business and Meg's not exactly a Leontes. Never minds if I've had a drop too much at a wine-tasting and had to sleep on a friend's floor,' Dominic giggled. 'Or even in a *very* generous friend's bed. And I'll be sleeping on the floor here if we don't go home soon. I've just flown in from Adelaide and my nights and days are *utterly* confused.'

Much later, Guy and Mary were standing side by side looking up at a clear, moonless sky. Peter's words in the confessional box came back to her. 'Your marriage is a sacrament and you must try harder to make it work.' Mary said slowly, 'I need to talk to you, Guy, a proper talk. I'm finding it really hard looking after Trister *and* Grace *and* working all hours.' Sniffing the damp, weedy smells from the moat, she added, 'I wish I had even one minute each day just to stand and breathe like this.'

'*Pecunia non olet.*'

'Catullus,' Mary said automatically.

'Vespasian! *Money has no smell.* Knew you'd never get that one!'

Mary felt that her resolution to be kinder to Guy was being unfairly tested. Why couldn't he ever take her seriously? Had he even bothered to listen? 'I mean it,' she tried again. 'I'm absolutely knackered and the work's still piling up. Urban's even got me running a whole new case for the Treasury.'

'Interesting?'

'Eye-opening. But there's a mass of research to do, as if I hadn't got enough on my plate.'

'Then why don't you do something less exhausting?'

'How can I? We need the bloody income.' Mary bent down and threw a pebble into the moat, watching as the circle of ripples briefly rubbed out the reflection of the stars. 'Now go home and be nicer to Guy,' Peter had told her. She mustn't start getting annoyed with him again. Taking hold of Guy's arm, she said, 'Ignore me. It must be tonight's inferior wine talking.'

'I'm not going to ignore you. What you've told me about the world of business hardly instils a feeling of confidence. I'm bound to say that for all its faults, at least *my* world's a decent place.'

'I'm afraid your world wouldn't exist without my world to pay for it,' Mary sighed. 'And I can't see how I'd find anything that'd pay me as well as Lock Chase does.'

'Do try to be rational. You'll never know what jobs are about if you don't look.' Guy turned to face her. In the dark, she could just make out his perennially grave expression and that floppy forelock of hair. She resisted an unexpected urge to push it back out of his eyes. 'Now I come to think of it, there was a charming woman who helped us find a new bursar for Pentecost. Mrs Scott, she was called. Quite a senior figure in the headhunting world, or so she implied. What was her Christian name? Beth. That was it, Beth Scott. Why don't you go and see her?'

'D'you know something . . .' she reached up to kiss his cheek, 'I might just do that. I'll call her next week.'

Urban looked around at his fellow Partners. 'Questions, anyone?' It was one of their regular meetings, and he'd just concluded a brief presentation on the integration of F-ACE and Pneumatech.

'You said this case was nearly finished, but can we get any more out of the client?' asked one of the junior Partners.

Urban allowed himself a quick smile before reverting to his preferred air of measured calm. 'Well, this is absolutely not for definite, but I've been there a couple of times when the Chief Exec's had his investment banker in. A guy called Ivan Straw, from Wolkenbank. They're planning another acquisition. A really big deal this time. If it happens, we'll be in line for a massive piece of work. Any thoughts welcome.'

There was the usual clamour of advice as everyone tried to get their own opinion heard, and it was some time before Urban could cut through the noise. 'Please! Let's think about what we can do that's practical. What about you, Mary? The Doves are your neighbours in Suffolk. You said you'd get to know them.'

'I'm not sure I should. Now I've started this hedge fund work for the Treasury, that F-ACE takeover's bang on my radar screen of deals to take a look at. Is it ethical to be working for a client I might end up investigating? I really don't think so.' Urban clenched his fists under the table. Sometimes Mary's principles could be seriously annoying.

'You don't think so, don't you?' Urban's irritation was knocked into the shade by Spider's white-faced anger. 'Well, you listen to me. While you're arsing about with bureaucrats we're adding real value to this client and we are *not* pulling out of Pneumatech. You're a real lightweight,' she added furiously, 'intellectually, at least.'

Urban was astonished by Mary's self-control. 'I'll just go on with my research and then we'll see who's right,' she said calmly, but he couldn't let it go like that. Managing a group of talented mavericks was like herding cats. He had to keep them working as a team, which meant he couldn't possibly let Spider get out of line like this.

'We'll take a five-minute break. Spider, I want to talk to you.' Urban turned his back on her and strode ahead to his office, closing the door firmly after she'd followed him in.

'What the *hell* was that about?' He kept his voice cold. 'How dare you be so rude to Mary, and in front of all the other Partners? I tell you, Spider, she's worth ten of you. Haven't you even noticed how she's built up our banking sector practice? That's not a lightweight in my book. And you might do me the courtesy of looking at me while I'm talking.'

Spider slowly turned to face him, though she didn't meet his eyes. The blood had drained from her face, leaving it oddly grey and drawn. Good God, he hoped she wasn't going to faint.

'I'm sorry, Urban. It wasn't about Mary at all.'

He wasn't going to let her off that easily. '*Sorry*! I wish you damn well were sorry. And if it wasn't about Mary, then what was it?'

Hell! Now the corners of her mouth were trembling, he'd never seen her like this. 'It was just . . .' She paused. 'It was just my frigging temper.'

As she stood in front of him, dark head drooping like some exotic lily, the fight all gone out of her, he felt an unexpected urge to look after her. 'Look, Spider, we need to have a proper talk, see what I can do to help you. Why don't you come and stay with me in Suffolk one weekend?'

Spider managed a weak smile. 'Separate rooms?'

'Separate floors.' Urban regretted his impulsive invitation almost immediately. He'd always kept Lock Chase and the rest of his life far apart. Still, it was done now. He'd have to make the best of it. 'How about some time next month? There's a meeting of our local book club coming up, you'd enjoy it. And actually, Mary's a member. If you saw her away from the office, you might get to know her better.'

A few minutes later, they were back in the Partner meeting. Urban was glad to see Spider nodding an apology to Mary.

At the end of the meeting, he said, 'Well, thanks, everyone. Let's hope the Pneumatech deal happens and that we get a lot of work out of it, the sales pipeline's looking a bit thin. And by the way,' he added, 'I know I don't need to tell you, but no talk about what Dove might be planning. It's probably huge and it's certainly secret.'

'I have something very interesting and very secret to tell you.'

'Tell me news! I am in villa Andorra and is silly boring.'

Ivan was relieved. It was a long time since Platon Dyengi had taken one of his calls. He'd been forced to contact the Russian via the hedge fund and could never be sure that Dix wasn't privately taking the credit for his careful snippets of information.

'Well, I only have one story, but it's a great one. Remember Pneumatech and the F-ACE deal?'

'*Da*. I always remember where I make money.'

'This is another takeover. And it's so secret, even the Pneumatech board haven't discussed it yet.'

'You ring to tell me you know secret or you ring to tell me secret?'

Ivan could hear the impatience in Dyengi's voice and hurried his words. 'Sorry, Platon, sorry. No, I'm ringing to tell you that Pneumatech are planning a US acquisition. A big one. A billion dollars, maybe more. I've found Alan Dove a target and I'm working on it right now. I'll let you know when to buy shares.'

There was a silence from the other end of the line, then the Russian growled, 'Is good, Ivan. Keep telling me. If it turns well and make me money, then we attend to you.' A quiet laugh was followed by, 'If it lose me money, we attend to you too.'

The line went dead.

THIRTEEN

There was a spring in Mary's step as she weaved her way through Shepherd Market. Early lunchers were already sitting at outdoor tables, enjoying the May sunshine. Arriving at Mumford Scott, she paused to admire the bow-fronted house whose white façade was punctuated by window-boxes ebullient with multi-coloured miniature roses. She felt a surge of optimism. When she had contacted Beth Scott, the headhunter had surprised her by immediately agreeing to meet. That must be a good sign. Maybe she already had the ideal job for her?

Mumford Scott's interior was just as pretty as its exterior, with flowers everywhere and comfortable chintz armchairs to wait in. Mary was only there for a couple of minutes before a smiling girl was holding a hand out to her. 'Mrs Kersey? I'm Mrs Scott's assistant. It's two flights up to Beth's office so we can go in the lift, unless you'd rather take the stairs?'

Mary said ruefully, 'Lift, please.' She was seriously out of condition and didn't want to arrive hot, fat and flustered to meet this top headhunter.

She realized she needn't have worried as soon as she met Beth Scott, who looked as if she took the lift too. 'Mary! I'm delighted to meet you.' The expression on Beth's round face made Mary feel as if she truly meant it. She relaxed happily into another chintz-covered chair, certain that she was going to enjoy the meeting.

'Now I know lots about you from the CV you sent me, so why don't I tell you about Mumford Scott?' As Beth brushed a strand of dark blonde hair back off her forehead, Mary noticed what a piercing blue her eyes were. 'For starters, there never was a Mumford. You see, Mary . . .' She glanced sideways as if about to tell a deep secret and checking that no one else could hear. 'When I set up my business I picked it at random out of the A to Z. It's *de rigueur* for a search firm to have two names. Egon Zehnder, Spencer Stuart, Russell Reynolds. Whereas the top consulting firms tend to have one name, don't they? Bain, McKinsey, Boston. In fact Lock Chase is a bit of a binomial oddity.'

'Binomial. No wonder my husband liked you. I don't suppose you remember Guy? He's a fellow of Pentecost, you found them a Bursar.'

'Guy Kersey, of course! How's he getting on?'

Beth's chatter was somehow both reassuring and encouraging. Mary found herself telling her all about Guy, and then about Grace, Sir John, Trister and the impossibility of maintaining a huge house and a family with virtually no help and while working full-time.

'Good gracious, you poor thing!' The sympathy in Beth's blue eyes made Mary want to lean forward and hug her. 'I absolutely *must* help you. But listen, if I'm going to find you a wonderful new job I need to understand more about what you actually do, because your CV's a bit short on facts. Can you give me a real example of a client and the kind of thing you're advising them on?'

'Oh dear, that's going to be difficult.' Mary felt herself blushing. This woman really wanted to help her, how could she explain without sounding as if she didn't trust her? 'You see, Lock Chase has this code of absolute discretion and . . . um . . .' Her voice trailed off into an uncomfortable silence.

'Don't look so glum.' Beth's giggle was infectious. 'Everyone tells headhunters everything. We're even more secretive than you are. And seriously, I can't help you unless I know more. Isn't there just one of your clients you could tell me about?' She leant forward and touched Mary's hand as if she were making a solemn pact with her. 'No one will hear a word about it from me, I swear.'

After a brief tussle with her conscience, Mary decided it would be all right if she told Beth about the Treasury. It wasn't as if it was a commercial client, and besides, there was something about the headhunter that made Mary feel as if she could trust her completely. Beth sat in silence, holding her gaze with those amazing blue eyes while Mary told her how the Treasury were worried about the destabilizing effect of hedge funds on the economy and about the part she was playing in developing a case for regulating them.

'I know it sounds dull, but it's actually really interesting work. You'd be amazed what goes on around the average takeover.'

Beth went on looking at her. Mary was sure that she was being evaluated and prayed that she wouldn't be found wanting. Eventually Beth nodded once, firmly. 'I can trust you. I'm going to tell you something you may find helpful in your inquiry. Have you heard of a company called F-ACE? Bought by Pneumatech earlier this year?'

Fortunately Beth didn't seem to expect an answer, because she went on immediately. 'I interviewed a man called Jock Hillyard recently, he used to be Chairman of F-ACE. He told me there were some very funny goings-on when they were taken over. You might want a chat with him.'

'Thank you,' Mary said. 'That's really helpful, I'll get in touch with him.'

'A pleasure.' Beth glanced down at her watch and gasped. 'Heavens! Is that the time? I must whiz. I've really enjoyed talking to you.'

'And about my moving jobs?'

'Of course, of course! Some non-executive directorships, perhaps. And you'd be brilliant running strategy for a big corporate. I'll keep my ears open.'

'Bless me, Father, for I have sinned.'

'May you make your confession with a humble and contrite heart.'

'It's Mary again, Peter. I've done my usual list of sins, but I've also taken a serious dislike to someone at work. She was really rude to me the other day. I managed to keep my mouth shut, but in my heart I hate her.'

'Hatred is a terrible sin, Mary. It eats away at your soul. Offer this small trouble up to Almighty God, and when you next see this woman, turn the other cheek as Our Blessed Lord would have done.'

'You're right, of course,' Mary sighed through the metal grille that separated her from the priest.

'And how are you getting on with Guy?'

'Better, I think. I took your advice, and I'm trying really hard to be nicer and to see more of him. I've even been to a headhunter to ask if she could help me find a less demanding job.'

'And do you think she will?'

'No, I doubt if anything's going to come of it. I've thought about the meeting and I'm afraid she's one of those people who just can't help being nice, but it doesn't lead to anything.'

FOURTEEN

Dusk was falling when Urban swung his battered truck off the road and on to the long, sandy track that led down across the heath towards the low Dunhithe cliffs and the sea. He was glad it was such a beautiful evening. The setting sun had striped the underbelly of the clouds in glowing fuchsia, while a little breeze twirled the sand up into dust devils and twitched at a line of scrawny trees. Although it was May, the leaves were only just opening along their crabbed branches.

As they neared the cliffs, the track bent sharply left past a church, once significant, now abandoned to the encroaching sea. Its massive tower gaped open to the sky but the stone and flint walls were still intact. As they swung by, he turned to catch a glimpse of its intricate rood-screen through the glassless east window but his eyes never got further than Spider on the passenger seat beside him. She had cupped her hand out of the truck as if to take hold of the salty breath of heath and sea. Her head was thrown back, her lips parted in a half-smile.

He was taken aback. He'd never seen her looking so fresh-faced and rosy-cheeked. It was lucky she was angular and that he only liked girls with curves, otherwise he might find her attractive. As he turned his attention back to driving, he came to a decision. For the next twenty-four hours he was going to concentrate on Spider. His news could wait.

Alan Dove had caught him as he was leaving the office.

'I have Dr Dove for you, Urban.'

'Damn, I was just off. You'd better put him through.'

'I've found my acquisition target.' As usual, Dove had launched into what he wanted to say with no polite preamble. His voice sounded excited. 'It's a great opportunity. I'll need your help.'

'Can you tell me what it is?'

'Skinshine Corporation.' Urban was pleased that Dove didn't bother to remind him about confidentiality any more. 'A pan-American chain of beauty salons. We'll be able to sell F-ACE's products direct into the US market!'

'How much are you paying?'

'We're still negotiating, but Straw thinks they'll settle at one point one, maybe one point two billion dollars.'

Urban's heart sank. The sum was ridiculous. Pneumatech could never raise that kind of cash. Before he had time to make the point, Dove was speaking again. 'This'll be a big move into cosmeceuticals and lung drugs won't fit any more. I'm selling my Lung Division to pay for Skinshine.' You had to hand it to Dove, it made complete strategic sense. 'I'll need you to do a formal valuation of the Lung Division and I want you to validate the logic of the two deals for my board. And you can help me plan the integration of Skinshine as well.'

Urban had a struggle to keep his voice calm and professional as they said goodbye. This was fantastic. Months of work and right up Lock Chase's street. He'd wanted to cheer as he hurried off to meet Spider at King's Cross.

He drove on in silence, fast, leaving a high trail of dust floating behind the pickup. Eventually coming to an area of marsh and water, Urban had to slow right down to negotiate the wide puddles and the shifting drifts of fine sand across the track. 'Dunhithe Broad,' he said, raising his voice against the noisy engine and the rush of wind. He glanced at Spider again. She was still smiling.

A pale shape lifted itself clumsily off a post and flapped slowly away.

'Barn owl, see its white tummy?'

Now she was laughing at him. 'I've never thought of an owl having a tummy. Never thought of you being a naturalist either, come to that. I thought you were urban.' A moment later they were over the cattle grid and passing his sign.

'Isn't that Russian writing? I thought you hated them.'

'Russian? You must be joking! That's Polish. It says "*Strefa Zdekomunizowana*", which means "Communist-free zone". I like to keep the bastards out.'

His Martello tower was surrounded by three acres of sheep-cropped grass. In the sudden quiet when he turned off the engine, he could hear the gentle tearing sound of grazing. Spider had slithered out of the truck and was staring round her at the curly white blobs, all methodically going about the business of eating.

'Oh, aren't they enchanting! Do they have lambs?'

'Actually most of these sheep are still technically lambs, though they've already got to the big, fat, silly stage. I suppose we'd never eat them if they stayed skinny and charming, would we?' He swung Spider's bag out from the back of the pickup. 'It must be said, they're extremely efficient lawnmowers for the absentee landowner.'

'That's enough frigging natural history for one day. Give me the low-down on this weird tower thing we're staying in.'

'It was built to protect you English from Napoleon. A worthy cause.' Opening the heavy front door, he ushered her through the massive walls and into a bricklayer's paradise of arches and vaults. 'This was once the powder magazine. I've made it rather nice, don't you think?'

He looked proudly around the large, circular ground floor, which he had converted into a haphazard but comfortable space, laid out in concentric circles. The outer rim was the kitchen. An inner circle was formed by a crescent-shaped counter, which served as both breakfast bar and elongated dining table as necessary. In the centre of the room were a pair of comfortable-looking leather sofas and an untidy pile of books and 78 rpm records.

'Do you want an immediate drink or shall I show you your bedroom first?' asked Urban, suddenly formal, embarrassed at having brought a woman he worked with into his private sanctum.

Spider seemed completely unaware of his discomfort.

'Well, I'd like to go upstairs except there don't seem to be any.'

'A cunning secret to keep invaders from taking over the whole tower. You see that cupboard? Turn the handle.'

Spider did so, and the door swung slowly outwards to reveal a staircase built right inside the walls of the tower itself. He led her in a gentle spiral up past the first floor where his own bedroom, bathroom and study were and on to the second floor, into which they emerged from another cupboard.

'Oh, wow!' whispered Spider.

Originally this had been the open roof of the Martello tower, enclosed with high, protective walls. Urban had had it glassed in to create a circular room, apparently open to the stars just appearing in the sky. He saw Spider examining the skylight, on which he had stencilled the words '*Cave Vespertiliones*'.

'So what the hell kind of language is that?'

'Spider, really! I can't believe you never did Latin at school.' Urban cursed himself as her face closed. The whole point of this weekend was to get to know her better; he'd need to take things very gently.

To cover his mistake, he went on, '*Cave Vespertiliones* means "Beware of the bats". When I moved in there was a colony of pipistrelles lodging here. A neighbour said that all I had to do was leave a light on and they'd move out. So I did, and they did. But every few months, they try to make a comeback. They hurl themselves at the glass roof and one or two always get in through that skylight if it's left open. Then they beat themselves to death on the glass ceiling trying to find their way out again. It makes me feel guilty so I try to discourage my guests from opening the skylight. There's a perfectly good window which they can open if they want to and the bats never come in that way.'

'Bats do *not* sound great. They get tangled in your hair, don't they?' Spider tossed her head in an uncharacteristically female gesture. Urban watched as her hair swung obediently back to her shoulders. It was like heavy black satin. 'Still, they're not as bad as spiders,' she added.

Urban smiled at her. 'I rather like spiders.'

'You must be mad! What's nice about them?'

'Oh, I don't know, maybe I feel sorry for them because they're persecuted. People destroy their webs, and then the spider has no means of catching food to get the energy it needs to spin a new one. The poor thing's doomed to die of starvation. I'd have thought you'd be fond of your namesakes,' he added.

'I wasn't called Spider after the creepy-crawlies. No way. It was a name I picked up at university. They thought I looked like Spiderwoman.' She grinned at him. 'Can I get on with unpacking my stuff now?'

Taking the hint, Urban backed out of the door saying, 'See you downstairs. Put on something warm and we'll have a walk along the beach before we eat.' As he vanished into the wall, it occurred to him that since Spider was a nickname she'd picked up at university, she must have another Christian name and he'd no idea what it was. It was a ridiculous thing not to know about her and he was tempted to go straight back and ask. But then he heard her whistling to herself and decided that for the moment he wouldn't risk doing anything that might disturb her happy mood. He'd find out Spider's real name some other time.

When she emerged back through the door in the wall, he was making cocktails. 'Try this. It's my version of a G & T.'

He watched in amusement as Spider knocked her glass back. 'Fuck a duck, Urban, what the hell's this?' she spluttered.

'The gin is replaced by Polish vodka, straight out of the freezer, and the "T" is tea. I use chilled Earl Grey, but Lapsang Souchong is nice too. You can add lemon if you like.'

'No thanks, I'll have it straight.' Spider sipped a second glass cautiously. 'Kicks like a goat, but it's delicious. I'd better have something to eat before I drink any more or I'll get completely legless.'

'There's a stew in the oven. Let's walk down to the sea while it warms up.'

A few minutes later as they stood on the shoreline, Spider surprised him by saying dreamily, 'This reminds me of the place where I was the happiest I've ever been. I was born near the sea. We lived on the backwaters a couple of miles from Frinton. Every afternoon, my mother would collect me from school and we'd go and have tea in our beach hut. Hard-boiled eggs and peanut butter sandwiches. Winter and summer, we'd always go there.'

He watched her as she stood in silence, staring out at the breaking waves. Something about her caught at his throat, some sudden vulnerability in the turn of her mouth. 'We moved away when I was eight.' Her quiet voice hardly carried over the hushing of the sea.

'And did you ever go back?'

Had she forgotten he was there? 'No, I never went back.' Turning abruptly, she hurried off towards his tower.

Watching her struggling up the slippery stones, Urban felt a sudden unease. In the office, Spider was a powerful force. He thought of her as a colleague, almost as a man. But now she looked strangely defenceless, slithering clumsily on the shingle, head down, shoulders hunched against the sea spray. Whatever could be the matter? Baffled, he plodded slowly after her.

When he got back to the tower, he found that she'd already vanished upstairs. As he waited for her to reappear, he wandered distractedly round the kitchen, putting plates out and laying the end of the counter with knives and forks. That unexpected glimpse of fragility beneath Spider's self-confident exterior had unsettled him. How would she be when she emerged from the door in the wall? How should he behave? He'd had a long week and he wasn't sure how he would cope if there were any histrionics.

The staircase door flew open suddenly. One look and he could see that she was back to normal. Urban felt his face relax into a smile of relief. 'Hey, something smells good!' Her voice sounded cheerful again too. 'Can we eat right away? I'm seriously hungry.'

'Of course, and d'you want to watch a film afterwards?' Urban decided that watching a movie would help them both unwind, and besides, he always liked the chance to show off his hi-tech DVD system.

'Sure, what've you got?' As she was asking the question, he pushed a button in the wall. A panelled cupboard slid open to reveal a flat screen and his precisely catalogued collection of old films. 'I don't believe it,' Spider giggled. 'You're a closet cinema buff!' She knelt down to look through the hundred or more carefully labelled cases. 'St Trinian's, I haven't seen this for years,' she said a moment later, sitting back on her heels. 'Why don't we forget the dining at the table bit and have a slob night? We can eat off our knees while we watch this.'

The film turned out to be a great choice. They sat next to each other on one of Urban's leather sofas, eating stew with baked potatoes and drinking burgundy. The more they drank, the funnier the film seemed, and Urban felt quite exhausted with laughter by the time it was over. He made some coffee to help them sober up, after which Spider insisted on helping him to clear up.

While she was washing the plates he said idly, 'I wish Professor Fowler had sent me to a school like St Trinian's.'

'Really?' Spider handed him a glass to dry. 'I thought you were happy at Winchester.'

'I suppose I was. It's just their expectations were so high because I had a scholarship. I felt I had to work really hard all the time, so I never gave myself the chance to mess around and have fun.' It occurred to Urban that this would be a good time to try to get Spider to open up a bit. 'So what about you?' He tried to make his voice sound casual. 'It's perfectly normal to tell people where you went to school, you know.'

'Oh, that's just crap.' Spider began to scrub fiercely at the pan he'd used to heat the stew in. 'And fuck this for a game of soldiers. Don't you think you should get a dishwasher?'

Urban assumed that she'd ignore his school question, but after another effort with the scouring pad she said, 'It *is* crap telling everyone where you went to school. All it does is reinforce people's prejudices. If I said I'd been to some select girls' public school like Mary lardy-arse did, you'd assume I'd got where I am through a great education, not my brilliant brain. Or supposing I'd been to a bog-standard comprehensive? You'd think I was Rock of Gibraltar-sized chippy and an ambitious geek.'

Spider handed him the pan, now shinily clean, and turned to face him. 'So that's why I keep my education to myself. It's just one fewer pre-judgement for people to make about me. But as it happens and since you ask so nicely, after we moved away from the sea I was sent to a suburban London grammar. All I ever did at school was work, just like you. I didn't get pissed or smoke my first fag till I went to university. Satisfied?'

Urban was quite satisfied, he decided later that night after they had climbed the staircase to their separate bedooms. He'd managed to get her to talk about her upbringing, and maybe now she'd started she would feel able to tell him a lot more about herself.

The next morning he was out on the sheep-speckled lawn, enjoying the way the sea reflected back the sunlight in dazzling, dancing shards, when Spider came up and stood beside him. 'I'm starving again. It must be all this fresh air.' He looked at her in surprise. Cheeks flushed, hair ruffled by the salt-scented breeze, she had lost all the immaculate office veneer that he was used to. Urban resisted a sudden urge to put a friendly arm round her shoulders as they walked back towards his tower.

The downstairs room was full of the smells of coffee, bacon and toast, and one end of the crescent-shaped counter had been laid for breakfast. There was even a little posy of wild flowers peeping over the rim of a milk jug.

'Hey, you're so domesticated! Do you clean and sew as well?'

Pouring out mugs of coffee Urban said, 'I'm afraid not. I'm looked after by the lovely Sarah Scammell. She takes care of the tower, the food, everything. I don't know what I'd do without her.'

'Young, is she?'

'Technically, Sarah's very young. About sixteen, I should think.'

'Some poor child crawled out of her bed to make your breakfast? That's gross!' Spider looked as though she was about to storm out of the door when he put a hand out to hold her back. She jerked her arm away crossly.

'For goodness' sake, I said she was *technically* sixteen. Sarah Scammell was born on the 29th of February, so she only gets a birthday every four years. It's her little joke to say she's a teenager but I suppose in reality she must be about sixty. Does that make you feel better about eating her breakfast?'

Spider gave him a wry smile as she sat down at the counter. 'You're a real shit,' was all she said as she started to eat.

They passed the morning in idle companionship, admiring the water-clock on Southwold pier and laughing at the names of the beach huts, before driving on to lunch on seafood in Orford. Urban kept meaning to have a serious conversation, but somehow the time never seemed quite right. In the afternoon, they visited the fifteenth-century church at Blythburgh and gazed down over the estuary.

'So that's the River Blythe then, is it?'

Urban propped himself comfortably against a wall and turned to look at her, suddenly taken by the perfect regularity of her face in profile as she gazed out towards the sea. 'You'll find everyone at the book club tonight talking about the Blythe Vale. It's the name of our local hunt. Apart from Parson Woodforde's diaries, no one will be interested in anything else.' He shifted his position so that he was once again staring out over the salt marshes that guarded the banks of the Blythe estuary. He felt very relaxed with the sun-warmed stones against his back. The smells of bladderwrack and warm sludge drifting up from the marshes and the keening of the seabirds were oddly soporific.

He pulled himself together. At this rate he'd never get round to having that talk with Spider. Perhaps he'd do it better if he was moving. 'Come on. Let's go back and inspect my sheep.'

As they wandered across the grass beneath his Martello tower, Urban was wondering how to start Spider talking when she said unexpectedly, 'I always feel safer when I'm near a front door.'

Keeping his voice carefully neutral, Urban said, 'And why's that?'

'My parents' marriage was shit.' Spider stopped walking and looked up at him. 'They fought all the time. Their worst rows were when they'd been out drinking. If things were really bad, my mum would give Dad a "pavement rocket". That meant she stood right outside the house where they'd been partying and gave him hell at the top of her voice. One step down was the "car rocket". That meant she'd not lay into him till the drive home. The mildest level was the "bedroom rocket". Indoors was somehow OK. If the outside world couldn't hear them I felt it might not be real.'

Urban held back from pushing Spider to tell him more about her parents. Instead, he pointed to a little niche above the front door of his tower, from inside which a pair of stone angels looked benevolently down at them, wings outstretched. 'You can always feel safe when you come through this door,' he said quietly. 'It's "*pod aniolami*". That means "under the angels". They protect me and anyone who comes here.'

'Know something? I do feel safe here,' Spider startled Urban by saying a little later when they were sitting companionably drinking mugs of tea and eating Sarah Scammell's walnut cake. 'But since you're going to drag me outside again, I suppose I'd better think about having a bath. Who's going to be at this book club thing tonight?'

Urban put down his cup of tea and stretched out his long

LOUISE PATTEN | 111

legs in front of him. 'Well,' he said, 'the meeting's being held at Peter Cromwell's presbytery, so obviously he'll be there. You'll like Peter. He's a Catholic priest, mad about medieval architecture, looks like a dwarf daffodil.'

'Sounds gay to me.'

'That's irrelevant, as you'll see when you meet him. Everything's irrelevant except his faith. He's worldly, but he's also entirely holy. Oh, and he's Mary's confessor too.'

'I can't believe her sins are a bundle of laughs.' As Spider said this with a smile, Urban decided she wasn't being malicious. 'Who else?'

'Well, Meg will be there for certain, Meg Dewey. A bit of a mystery, Meg is. Rich as Croesus but no one has any idea where her money comes from. She's pretty if you like scale in a woman. Blonde curls, blue eyes, that sort of thing, oh and an amazing, um, posterior.'

'For Christ's sake, if you mean her arse why don't you just say so? And why's it so amazing?'

'It sort of trembles along behind her as if it had no connection at all to the rest of her body.'

Spider snorted with laughter. 'So, we've got a fag and a fat hag so far, can't wait. Does Meg have a hunky husband?'

'Not exactly. Dominic's built more along the lines of her midmorning snack. Small, expensive and rather delicious.'

'Urban! I'd no idea you could be such a bitch. And I don't believe a word you're saying. I bet they're all really normal, boring people. You're just trying to big them up so I don't crap around and say I won't go out to their dreary dinner. You are, aren't you?'

'I think I'm describing them rather accurately, actually. To continue, there's Mary of course, and her husband Guy. He teaches at Cambridge, a Classicist. Knows everything you ever wanted to know about obscure Greek poets.' Seeing Spider's raised eyebrow he hurried on. 'He may be a little prolix but Guy's a decent chap. Very straight, very English. You'll like him, honestly.'

'Right. So we've got the fag, the fat hag, the fat hag's bag, plus we've now got meaty Mary and the Greek nerd. Honestly, Urban, it can't get any better, can it?'

'Depends how keen you are on horses. The rest are the hunting contingent. Conversation restricted to all things equine.'

'Mary, thank goodness you're here. I need help!' Peter Cromwell grabbed her arm and dragged her into the hallway. 'There's an infestation of horsewomen in my kitchen. Is Guy with you?'

'He's just parking. Urban's here too, so there'll be lots of people to protect you. He's got Spider Wood with him, she's very pretty.'

'Hey, thanks Mary,' said Spider, coming in behind her with Urban.

'I'd have said beautiful.' Peter held out a hand. 'Early Balenciaga?'

Mary was constantly astonished by the eclectic range of her parish priest's knowledge, but Spider seemed to take it as normal. 'Balenciaga rocks,' she nodded enthusiastically. 'Schiapparelli too. And I'd fuck a rat for early Chanel.'

'You mustn't blaspheme, Spider!' Urban sounded horrified. 'He's a priest!'

'My dear man, blasphemy means taking the Lord's name in vain,' said Peter firmly. 'There's nothing wrong with a good old Anglo-Saxon word. Now will you please come on through to the kitchen and rescue me from the eternal nag talk.'

'And you can stop looking like you've got a turd under your

nose, Urban,' Spider said as they all followed Peter. 'If my language is OK with a frigging priest then it should be OK with you!' Mary didn't think she'd ever heard Spider giggling like that.

She'd no idea Spider could be so consistently pleasant either, Mary thought a little later. She had smiled enthusiastically while Peter explained to the group why he found the Parson's diaries so charming. 'They're such a measured, unselfconscious study of ordinariness in Georgian England. Imagine one of those muddy, rural landscapes. Woodforde is that shadowy, clerical figure almost lost on the horizon.'

Spider had even laughed out loud when Guy chipped in with one of his obscure jokes. 'Given the amount of offal he got through, one might say that he was extispicious.'

The biggest surprise had come when towards the end of the evening Spider slipped round to sit next to her. 'Urban says I need to apologize, Mary, and he's right. I was really rude to you the other day and I'm sorry.'

Even if Peter hadn't told her to turn the other cheek, Spider looked so rueful that Mary would have forgiven her immediately. 'Oh please, let's forget it. It was pretty unreasonable of me to say we should stop working for Pneumatech and I'm probably wrong about Alan Dove anyway.'

'No. You're probably right.' Spider was silent for a moment. 'Hey, let's not talk about him. Tell me about your kid.'

'Gracie? Oh my goodness, she's turned into exactly the kind of horse-mad obsessive that Peter loathes. We gave her a pony a couple of weeks ago. Actually two ponies, because Dimple needed a companion. It was her birthday and it was absolutely brilliant. A complete surprise. She burst into tears when she saw them, and I was almost in tears myself! Though I must say, Dimple's adorable and Grace's already managing her really well, though she's not tried jumping yet.' She pulled herself up. 'Oh dear. I'm turning into a horse bore myself.'

Spider was looking at her thoughtfully. 'I've read you all wrong. You don't talk about your kid much so I reckoned you just dumped her while you were working.'

'Dumped her? God no, I'm always sneaking off to Suffolk to see her.' Mary couldn't resist adding, 'I keep quiet about my family in case anyone at Lock Chase thinks I'm a frigging light-weight.'

'*Touché*!'

Spider was looking at her from those astonishing green eyes and grinning. Mary wanted to go on chatting, but Urban came over and interrupted them. 'Just the pair I was looking for.' Mary glanced around. There was no one nearby except Meg, who'd been unusually quiet all evening and now seemed to be dozing. Even if she was awake, Mary guessed that she was well out of earshot.

Urban said quietly, 'I've got some great news about Pneumatech. Looks like it's catching fire at last. Can you come outside for a minute and I'll tell you about it?'

FIFTEEN

The sunny weather continued the following day, lighting up the yellow concrete cobbles of Meg's new path. 'I think I've finally exterminated every blade of grass in the garden now the Yellow Brick Road's finished.' This was shouted over her shoulder to Dominic, who was some distance behind her.

'Oh, shit!' Meg turned to see him struggling with the hem of the scarlet silk dressing-gown that he was wearing while carrying two Moser hock glasses, a corkscrew and a bottle of chilled wine. 'And why the murderous hatred for a bit of good old English lawn, I've never understood.'

'So dreary, so predictable, so depressingly, eternally *green*. I like proper colour in my garden, like this, for example.' Meg waved an arm in front of her to where the yellow path ended in a broad crescent of silver and gold bricks, on which stood a little brass table and two fatly cushioned iron chairs.

Plumping herself down while Dominic uncorked the wine, Meg admired the latest addition to West Hall's garden. Where the brick crescent ended, a flower-bed extended several feet back to a high, protecting wall, itself obscured by a riot of blinding yellow where forsythia had been interplanted with laburnum to provide a continuity of brilliant colour.

'This is my money-bed, Dominic, the gardeners have just finished planting it out. A bit hard to see now, though there's a little clump of penny-cress coming up already. And I think those yellowy leaves might be moneywort. I've had lots of golden rod and marigolds put in, and something called bald-money. Looks like superannuated cow parsley but I had to have it for the name. The twiggy thing down there is an *Eleagnus* "Quicksilver". Filthy smell but it's a good colour, silver leaves, gold flowers. Oh, and crown imperials. They stink too, but I'm planning to divide them and get lots of half-a-crown imperials.'

'Oh, ha ha,' said Dominic, handing her a glass of wine. 'And have you put in any windflowers, as in sailing-close-to-the?'

'Very bitchy, dear, and no I haven't.' She looked at him speculatively. 'You do know, don't you, that if I hadn't come to the rescue and married you, you'd be one of those sad camp boys, lurking round the edges of seedy parties in south London? See what you've got instead. Lovely fresh Suffolk air, lovely money and best of all, lovely me.'

'I like the last two very much, but I've never been entirely sure about the Suffolk piece. I know it was the scene of your happy childhood years and all that, but don't you feel we might have lived in this backwater for long enough?'

Meg took a deep breath and thought about moving. It might be a nice idea but it would be complicated. Not yet, she decided. Shaking her head, she said, 'I've still got a few more memories to re-live,' and drained her glass. 'I know it costs a million pounds a bottle, but this hock tastes like gnat's piss. Far too subtle. You can give me some more, though, and I'll see if it improves on acquaintance.'

Her husband was refilling her glass with a pained look when the sound of a telephone bell rang loudly across the garden. 'Oh, one of mine! Must rush.' She hurried back down her golden path.

Unlocking her study, Meg grabbed the silver phone. As soon

as she heard the voice, she said, 'About time! Why didn't you call earlier?'

'Your messages are getting so abstruse it's taken me all morning to work out who it was from.'

'Safety first! You never know what bugger might be listening.'

'Language, please! So why were you calling?'

'To brag. I was at a book club meeting last night and I overheard hunky Palewski telling Mary Kersey and some doll-face that Pneumatech's catching fire.'

'Cool! I bet Brother Dove's planning another acquisition. A dog always returns to his own vomit.'

'Exactly,' Meg said, but she didn't smile. 'I'm still cross that Dix and his horrible hedge fund didn't tell us about F-ACE. We could have made a lot of dough out of that one.'

'Cheer up. Maybe we should stay away from hedge funds altogether if they're going to be regulated.'

'Oh bollocks to that, Captain Sensible. It all sounds like political posturing to me. There are way too many vested interests making fortunes to kill that cash cow.'

'You're probably right, Meggy. Bankers, brokers, the guys investing the man in the street's pension, they've all got their fingers in the pie. And as well as that, the hedgies stuff handfuls of spare cash up all the right charitable and political bottoms.'

'So let's just make our own money, and it's Pneumatech I'm interested in right now. Find out what you can, will you? If Lock Chase think it's catching fire, I want to buy shares before it starts blazing. Don't leave any stone unturned.'

'Don't you feel virtuous that we went to early morning Mass?' Mary asked Grace. She started up the Land Rover and put it into first gear a great deal more carefully than usual.

'Father Peter said how nice it was to see us in time for the first hymn. D'you suppose he notices how late we usually are?'

'Oh dear, he probably does. What was he saying about Dimple?'

'He said he'd come to Trister and bless her and Binky if I wanted them welcomed into the parish. Though honestly, I can't believe Dimple's only been with us for a fortnight. I feel as if I've known her for ever.' As the car began to creep forwards, Mary had to concentrate too hard on her first experience of towing a trailer to reply. Grace chattered on happily. 'And Binky's so good, isn't she? I think she likes pottering around keeping Dimple company. I did worry that Bink might mind when we left her behind today but she just stared at us and then went back to eating.'

Having successfully negotiated a right-hand turn on to the main road, Mary began to relax her grip on the steering-wheel. 'So they were a good birthday present, were they, darling?'

'The best ever! And I bet Dimple's going to be brilliant when we get to Pony Club. Um, but Mummy . . .' Mary caught a hint of anxiety in her daughter's voice. 'You will stay and watch, won't you? Just in case I can't manage. This first time, I mean.'

Mary completely sympathized. She was feeling a bit shy herself. All those non-working, horsey mothers, whatever would she talk to them about? 'Of course I'm staying. I can't wait to see the pair of you in action.'

Arriving at the muddy field marked 'Blythe Vale Pony Club', Mary successfully passed the nightmare test of reversing the trailer into a narrow space between two professional-looking horseboxes. After Grace had trotted off on Dimple, she pulled out her BlackBerry. She needed a few minutes to gather her strength before joining the Pony Club mothers.

Subject: Jock Hillyard

Hi Bella

Re my meeting with Hillyard tomorrow afternoon, could you dig out the file on the F-ACE acquisition for me? Also I'll need to take that little voice recorder. Can you make sure it still works? Thanks.

Mary

As she pressed the Send button, Mary glanced across the field to where children, ponies and parents were milling around. She could see Grace on the edge of the group and thought she was looking back at her accusingly. Guiltily, Mary leaped out of the car. She might not know a soul and she was embarrassingly ignorant of Pony Club etiquette, but Grace needed her support. She'd just have to force herself to join in.

Half an hour later, Mary was enjoying herself hugely and couldn't imagine why she'd felt so shy. She hadn't realized that Anna-Clare Francis would be there, and the District Commissioner had roped her into helping straight away.

'Lovely to see you, Mary. Would you mind giving us a hand setting up the obstacle course?'

Other mothers had quickly included her too. 'Excuse me, could you hang on to Etty for a minute while I do up her girths?'

'You're Dimple's new owner, aren't you? She's a nice little pony and such an old friend. What's your daughter called?'

Dimple turned out to be an immediate passport into the group. As a Pony Club veteran, everyone knew her, and Mary was delighted to see that Grace was soon joining in with the other children as they chatted about their ponies.

'You're really lucky having Dimple! She's brilliant at anything where you have to go steady.'

'Alfie's a nightmare. He gets so excited in the races, I can never stop him.'

'I hope we're in the same team for the dressing-up race. Mayfly loves Dimple so she'll stand next to her for ever while I get my clothes on.'

Eventually the games started. As she watched seventeen excited children bending round poles, dropping balls into buckets and urging recalcitrant ponies past obstacles, Mary could see why Dimple was so popular. Her rump might be large and her coat rough, but her mealy muzzle and floppy lower lip were enchanting. She was calm and gentle, didn't barge the other ponies, and although she seemed to come last in virtually every race, the huge smile was never off Grace's face.

Mary hardly managed to get a word in on the drive back.

'Wasn't Dimple wonderful? Loads of people recognized her, I didn't feel like a stranger at all.'

'Did you see, Mummy? She didn't even flinch when I walked her past the umbrella. That's a *really* good sign.'

'Actually I think I could have won the egg and spoon race if I hadn't dropped my egg. And didn't Dimple stand quietly while I picked it up again?'

As they arrived back at Trister, it occurred to Mary that it was nearly four hours since she'd even thought about Lock Chase, her marriage, housework, or any of the other worries that normally nagged at her.

SIXTEEN

'We haven't got any other private equity outfit interested, but Churngold Capital are keen. Your Lung Division's just the kind of business they buy.'

Dove felt a surge of excitement. Straw was moving fast and seemed to be doing a great job. 'Any news on Skinshine?'

'We're pretty close on price now, but we shouldn't talk about that over the phone. Any chance of you coming over to Wolkenbank?'

'I'm in the car on my way to see some headhunter at the moment. I don't want to piss her off by chucking at the last minute, you never know when you're going to need them. But I'll come straight on to the City afterwards.'

He was hardly through the door of Mumford Scott when a smiling girl was standing in front of him. 'I'm Mrs Scott's assistant. She's two floors up, so shall we take the lift?'

'I'd prefer the stairs,' Dove grunted.

Halfway up, he suddenly felt his heart thumping. It certainly wasn't that he was unfit, it was something about that nubile bottom climbing the steps ahead of him. Hawley-Wilson. Plodding up to the art room behind a group of girls. One of them turning. 'Fatty! You were looking at my butt, weren't you? Here's something to take your mind off it, you perve.' She had spat on him, and then they were all spitting, the stuff was all over his glasses, he couldn't see. When he'd finally made it to the art class, the girls were all giggling and the teacher had scolded him in front of everyone for being late. She'd been a woman too. He tried to force the memory out of his head, but he was in a bad mood when they reached the second floor.

'Alan, how delightful to meet you.' As Dove returned the handshake, he was taken by the expression in Beth Scott's blue eyes. She was trying to charm him. Women. They were all the bloody same. 'I know you're pressed for time,' she was waving him into a chair, 'so shall we get straight down to business? Could I suggest that you tell me a little about Pneumatech and we'll see how things go from there?'

Nosy headhunters. He wasn't having any of *that*. 'I didn't come here to tell you about my company. You asked me here to listen to what you think your firm can offer.'

He watched the woman closely as she went into her sales pitch. Quite a sweet face. Perhaps he'd been a bit rough. 'But that's *really* enough about my company,' she said after a few minutes. 'Now do tell me about Pneumatech. Are there any areas where you might be needing help? Are you planning to get rid of any executives? Or perhaps you are thinking of recruiting in new areas. Overseas perhaps?'

That last question was a lucky one; he might get a bit of free advice. 'Well, there's one thing you could tell me. I'm always hearing that compensation rates are higher in the US than here. Is that true?'

The woman had briefed herself well. Quite impressive, as a matter of fact. She gave him a good idea of comparative British and American salaries in the biotechnology industry. 'That's very interesting. And are the comparators the same in other sectors? Retail, for example?'

She was helpful on that too, though Dove guessed that the

information she gave him was no more than he could have learned from reading the American business news. He'd had enough. Forcing what he hoped was a pleasant smile he began to get up, but Beth Scott put a hand out to stop him.

That sunny expression of hers had switched to something like commiseration. 'One of my researchers showed me such a horrid article about Pneumatech. Collusion with hedge funds, wasn't it? You must be hoping this Treasury inquiry's not going to investigate your company.'

Dove felt his jaw drop.

'You haven't heard about it, then?' she prompted him.

'Heard about what?'

She leaned forwards, propping her round face on one hand. 'In confidence, Alan, I had a charming woman in the other day. Mary Kersey she was called, a Partner with Lock Chase. She told me the Treasury have called in her firm to help build a case for full regulation of hedge funds and she's leading the work. There.' She was smiling at him again. 'I always keep an ear open for news my clients might be interested in.'

Dove was furious. Enquiries, investigations; all his plans could collapse. He had to see Straw. 'I'm not one of your clients, Mrs Scott, and if you'll excuse me, I'm extremely busy at the moment. I'll show myself out.' Leaving her standing in the middle of her office, he was up and out of the door without a handshake or even a 'thank you'.

Despite his hurry, as he walked out of Mumford Scott and looked around for his car, Dove felt a shiver of excitement. Just round the corner was the discreet, double-fronted house that he occasionally visited. He was briefly tempted to ask Cyril to leave him in Shepherd Market for another half hour, but just as quickly decided against it. Being with a tart was really no more exciting than the perfunctory sex he had with Juliana.

He knew it was entirely his fault. He didn't allow himself to let go sexually. Ever.

He was on the phone to Straw as soon as he was back in the car. 'Ivan? Dove here.'

'Are you on your way over to Wolkenbank?'

'Yes, but there's something I've got to tell you straight away. Those government *bastards*,' he spat the word out, 'you'd think they had something better to do with their time, wouldn't you? I've just been at Mumford Scott.'

'A good source of high-quality gossip.'

'That makes it even worse because it's probably true. Beth Scott told me there's going to be a full inquiry into hedge funds. Apparently they've even hired Lock Chase to help. Consultants! What a bloody waste of time and taxpayers' money that will be. And supposing they stir up the F-ACE takeover story again?'

'Hmmm.' There was a long pause from the other end of the line. Eventually he heard Straw say, 'Probably a storm in a tea cup. Still, I'll put a few feelers out. We don't want any bureaucratic nonsense coming along to disturb your big acquisition, do we?'

Mary was used to being kept waiting whenever she went to see her client at the Treasury, but she still couldn't stop herself arriving on time. It was half an hour before she was at last in the glassed-in office tucked away in a corner high above Whitehall. As she pressed the switch on her pocket tape recorder, Aiden Elginbrode leant forward to catch Jock Hillyard's clipped accent.

There was a damned funny smell about it. Press leaks, bogus stories. At the time I was too caught up in the whole thing to realize what was going on but I can see it clearly now. Short sellers move in, share price manipulated down, F-ACE in chaos and forced to sell out to the first half-decent offer that came along. We were screwed. I beg your pardon. We were sabotaged.'

'And do you know who was behind this sabotage?' Mary's voice came in.

'*I'm damned sure that snake from Wolkenbank was at the heart of it. Ivan Straw. Pal in the City tells me he's in cahoots with a hedge fund, Dix Associates. And then there was Dove.'*

'Dr Alan Dove?' Mary remembered that she had wanted to get the name quite clear on the tape. '*D'you think he was involved?'*

'*Stands to reason. He wanted F-ACE, I wouldn't sell it to him. This way, he got what he wanted, and damned cheaply too.'*

As the tape finished Mary looked eagerly across the table. 'So what do you think? Is this enough to string them up?'

'Alas, no.'

Used to his taciturn style, Mary said eagerly, 'But Aiden, even though it is circumstantial, the circumstances are pretty compelling, don't you think? I mean, it's pretty clear. Dove worked with his banker and some creepy hedge fund called Dix Associates. They manipulated the share price of F-ACE down so far that Dove could afford to buy it and they all made shed-loads of money.' She allowed a smile to flit across her face. 'I *told* Lock Chase we shouldn't be working for Alan Dove. The man's not ethical.'

'You may think that, but you can't prove it, can you?'

'Well, that's something you could help with. Any bank's going to talk to the Treasury, aren't they? I thought you might put out a few feelers. At Wolkenbank, for example?'

There was a long pause before Elginbrode nodded in agreement. 'I'll see what I can do.'

Folder:	Inbox
Message status:	Opened
To:	Ivan Straw
From:	Supervisory Office, Frankfurt
Subject:	Treasury query

Mr Straw,

This office received a call today from a Mr Aiden Elginbrode of
the UK Treasury. As part of a routine investigation concerning
the hedge fund industry, he is interested in your client
Pneumatech's acquisition of F-ACE. Specifically, Mr Elginbrode
was querying the involvement of Dix Associates.

The Treasury are using the consulting firm Lock Chase to
support their work in this regard. You may expect to be
contacted either by the Treasury or by Lock Chase.

Should you be so contacted, please cooperate fully with any
inquiries. Please keep this office informed and included on
copies of all e-mails, letters and other communications relevant
to this matter.

Supervisory Office
Wolkenbank

How the *fuck* did they find out about Dix? Ivan Straw kicked
his office desk hard. As he did so, hopelessness leapt suddenly
out of her lair to grab his throat. The Russian would be livid;
secrecy was an obsession with Dyengi. Ivan's bright vision of a
fifty-million-pound job seemed to vanish in a dark mist.

He recognized the symptoms. Nicotine would help. He had

to smoke his unfiltered cigarette down so far that it burnt his lips before he was sufficiently in control of himself to ring Alan Dove.

'Alan. Ivan here. I've got a quick question for you.'

'Fire away.'

'You told me Lock Chase are helping the Treasury look at hedge funds.'

'Of course, yes.' Ivan heard Dove's voice tightening with anxiety. 'Why? Why are you asking? What's happened?'

'Nothing at all's happened, Alan, nothing at all. I was only wondering if by any chance you'd picked up the name of the Partner at Lock Chase who's leading this work for the Treasury?'

'Yes, I did, as a matter of fact. It's a woman. Lives at Trister, a big house near us in Suffolk. Mary Kersey, she's called.'

'Mary Kersey. Trister.' Ivan wrote the names down on a piece of paper and tucked it carefully into his wallet. 'Thanks, Alan.'

'Just one thing before you go,' Dove said as Ivan was about to ring off. 'Remember I told you I thought Theodore Stevens should stay with the Lung Division when we sell it?'

'Theodore Stevens. Who the hell's he?'

'One of my non-executives. The thoracic surgeon, lung transplants and that sort of thing.'

'Of course.' Ivan remembered now. 'You thought a buyer might pay more for your Lung Division if a medical big-hitter like Stevens was part of the deal.'

'Exactly. Anyway, I wanted to let you know I've spoken to him now and he's perfectly happy to step down from the Pneumatech board when the Lung Division's sold.'

'That's good news,' said Ivan. 'How did you manage it?'

He heard Dove give a short laugh. 'Money, obviously. I told him he'd make a nice little pile if he sticks with the private equity buyer till they sell the Lung Division on again.'

SEVENTEEN

Amy Flower lowered herself into the squashy grey leather of the Mercedes 280 SL's driver's seat. The engine coughed twice to clear its throat as she backed carefully out of a redundant boat-house in Twickenham. Edging out into the Friday evening traffic, she inhaled deeply. She adored the nostalgic interior smells of a classic car. An exotic, indefinable essence of old leather, ageing carpet and hot engine oil. And there were undernotes of some old-fashioned scent like Mitsouko. For the hour it took her to crawl to the M3 she sniffed and meditated. Tim Cusack. She'd only agreed to spend this weekend in his constituency because she'd been pissed.

He had taken her to Club Gascon, her favourite restaurant in the entire world. 'Pity Smithfield's such a bugger to get to,' she had said over her third glass of Calvados. 'If it was closer to the paper I'd be in here every day.'

'Then you'd get fat. And men wouldn't ogle you and drive me absolutely insane with jealousy. In fact, darling Amy, that reminds me. Are you quite sure you wouldn't like to move in with me? Handsome, upright and about-to-be successful MP, what more could a girl want?'

She had looked speculatively across the table. He was some-times good for a story, he quite often made her laugh and he was great in the sack. It was the about-to-be-successful bit she wasn't so sure of. She hadn't dragged herself up from the gutters of the local newspaper world only to shack up with a no-hoper. Then there was the constituency. If she moved in with him, she'd have to spend time in Somerset South West being charming to a lot of dreary party workers.

'Tell you what, darling,' she had said after a few moments' thought. 'Get me another glass of this apple juice and I'll come down to your cottage one weekend and give the constituency thing a try-out. What do you say?'

'Hooray! You'll love it, Amy, and more importantly my voters will love you.'

Once they had negotiated a date, he'd said, 'I'm afraid you'll have to wear boring clothes. Skirts and things, if you don't mind? My constituents are pretty conservative in the clothing department.'

Remembering this at the last minute, she had shoved an old denim skirt into her suitcase as she was leaving, already half-regretting a wasted weekend. Amy felt better when the suburban snarl-ups were behind her and she was on the motorway. She put her foot hard on the accelerator. The old Mercedes was taut to drive and clung to the road as Amy swung in and out of the fast lane, tailgating whenever she could to add to the excitement.

Once she was past Basingstoke and on the A303, the traffic grew thinner and she sat comfortably at ninety. Occasionally a car in front annoyed her and she would accelerate fast up to a hundred and twenty, to sweep past with a blare of the horn and a flash of lights. She stopped once, just before Mere, to fill the car's tank and to drink a cup of excruciating coffee. By the time she came off the A303 at Ilminster it was nearly ten and she was getting tired. She hoped Tim would have a decent supper and a large bottle of wine ready when she arrived.

Turning off up the short, muddy track that led to Tim Cusack's rented cottage, Amy parked in the most sheltered spot she could see and climbed stiffly out. For a moment she stopped to listen to the silence of the countryside, then she leaned back into the car and pressed the horn several times, shattering the quiet and bringing Tim out of his cottage at a run.

'For God's sake, Amy, don't do that! You'll wake the Thompsons' baby. They're constituents. I can't afford to alienate anyone at the moment.'

'And hello to you too. Nice to see you after a four-bloody-hour drive.'

It turned out that Tim had already eaten and there was nothing but eggs, bread and a bottle of filthy red wine that he had won in a raffle. The next morning Amy woke up hungry, hungover and in no mood to enjoy the constituency day that Tim had planned for her.

'Rise and shine, darling!' He woke her with a mug of tea and a plate of digestives. 'We'd better get going. The bring-and-buy's right on the other side of the constituency.'

'Fuck off. I'm not coming to your buggery bring-and-buy. I'm tired, I've got a headache, I'm hungry and I *don't* call biscuits a proper breakfast.'

By the time Amy had grumpily climbed into the crumpled denim skirt and had brushed out her Titian hair, it was well after nine-thirty. Then they got stuck behind a tractor and arrived at the village hall too late for Tim to open the bring-and-buy. That meant he had to stay on to draw the raffle instead, and Amy thought she was going to expire from boredom as he dragged her from stall to stall, stopping for a chat at every one. Though she had to hand it to him, he could certainly turn on the charm for the old ducks.

Once they had finally got away from the bring-and-buy, Tim took her into one of his Conservative clubs where she found that she was expected to drink sweet sherry with the wives while Tim stood at the bar talking politics with the men. After that, she went on strike.

'Oh, come on Amy, I'm kicking the first ball at Bridgeford Town Football Club. You'll enjoy it.'

'You must be joking. I've tailed along after you like a flipping poodle. I've listened to fatuous old harridans prattling on. I'm pissing well bored out of my head and now you want me to watch you berking about with a ball. No way! You can stop and get me something to eat from that shitty-looking kebab joint over the road, and you can take me back to your cottage. I'm going to have a kip and then a walk and I don't care what you do.'

So while Tim went back to Bridgeford alone, Amy was left with her bad temper and her kebab.

Feeling a bit better after some food, she sat down to read through the letters that Tim had left in tidy piles on his worm-eaten desk. Amy had a sudden fond thought that Tim would never have dreamed of reading someone else's personal papers and so it hadn't occurred to him to lock them away. What a dick. She herself wouldn't dream of *not* reading personal papers, given the chance, and was soon chuckling over the problems he had had to deal with at his MP's surgery. Christ, they moaned a lot. Poor old Tim.

Having skimmed through his constituency correspondence, Amy unearthed something else. She knew that as Chairman of the House of Commons Select Committee on Health, Tim had a full-time clerk to provide advice. And here was this clerk's background briefing on passive smoking, a subject Tim's committee seemed to want to opine on.

She expected it to be dull, but she hadn't got anything else to read.

The Chairman may wish to consider the appointment of Mr Theodore Stevens, FRCS, as an expert adviser for the Committee. Mr Stevens' reputation as a thoracic surgeon is unparalleled. Furthermore, he has written a number of relevant and well-received papers on the subject of passive smoking and related issues of lung damage. In considering his possible appointment it should be noted that Mr Stevens receives certain moneys as a Non-Executive Director of Pneumatech Biosciences plc, a company specializing in the research and development of pharmacological products for use in the treatment of lung and other diseases.

Perhaps it wasn't that dull after all. Amy read on more carefully.

The Chairman should, furthermore, be aware that this company may be subject to investigation in relation to its acquisition of a company named F-ACE. It is believed that certain financial bodies known as hedge funds may have played an inappropriate role in this acquisition. As you may be aware, the Treasury has initiated a comprehensive study into the possible regulation of hedge funds.

She pulled out her notebook.

During preliminary discussions with Mr Stevens, I raised this issue with him. In seeking to reassure me, Mr Stevens told me, in strictest confidence, that he had been informed by the Chief Executive of Pneumatech Biosciences plc, Dr Alan Dove, that the division of that company dealing with research into lung disease, being the area in which Mr Stevens has specific expertise, would shortly be sold. Mr Stevens understands that he will cease to be a Director of Pneumatech at that point. His connection with the parent company being thereby severed, Mr Stevens feels that any potential conflict of interest would be avoided and that it would, therefore, be appropriate for him to assist your Committee.

Fucking hell! So Dove was flogging off his Lung Division, was he? Now why would he want to do that?

By the time Tim got back from the football match in Bridgeford, Amy had tidied up all his papers and put them back in neat piles on his desk exactly as she had found them. She even had a cup of tea ready for him and listened patiently while he rabbited on about his constituency until she could stand no more of it and hurried him off upstairs to play muff-diving.

As she steered the little Mercedes back towards Twickenham the following day, Amy reflected that Tim's life in London was a lot more fun than the version she'd seen in his constituency. She wouldn't be going down there again if she could help it. Still, she'd brought back a useful souvenir.

The call came though that night. 'You've no idea what I've found out about Pneumatech! We need to go in deep.'

Meg pushed herself upright from the sofa where she had been lazing and put down a glass of Madiran. 'What's up?'

'Dove's only flogging off his entire lung drug business!'

'Inter*esting*. I'll bet he's selling his Lung Division to fund something mega. Keep your ear close to the ground and we'll make loads more lovely dosh.' Meg felt a rush of excitement. She was going to invest *very* heavily in Pneumatech. This could be another gusher.

'You sound in a good mood. Has Dominic been pouring wine down your gullet or something?'

'How did you guess?' Meg waved the bottle cheerfully at the telephone. 'As a matter of fact, I'm celebrating. Remember Seachest?'

'That was a stinker, wasn't it? Didn't you buy on the back of a take-private that never happened?'

'Well, it's happening now, the announcement's tomorrow. I bought at thirty-two and they've finally sold out at fifty-seven. That's another few millions under the bed!'

'I hope you were careful.'

'Of *course* I was careful,' Meg replied crisply. 'I bought the shares through all our different nominee companies, like I always do. The trades can't possibly be traced back. No nosy authorities sniffing around that I've heard about.' Stretching widely, she stood up. 'Calloo, callay! I'm off to fetch another bottle. Happy days and cheers to Seachest!'

Dyengi was furious. 'Why you not tell me about Seachest? You say you don't know? *Obmanschik*! You cheat me?'

'Look, Platon.' Ivan tried to keep his voice calm. 'I just didn't hear about Seachest. These private equity buy-outs are secret as hell. No one hears about them except insiders, and I can't be on the inside track of *everything*. Frankly, I think I've done pretty well. I've passed Dix the scoop on three deals recently and I rather assume you'll have made a bob or two out of them unless his hedge fund was asleep on the job.'

'They are awake.' Dyengi flipped in an instant from fury to friendliness. 'You make me good money, Ivaan, I like.'

'Well, I've more to tell you.' Cradling the phone close to his ear, Ivan said quietly, 'Remember Pneumatech?'

'You tell me they will do deal. It happen now?'

'Soon, but now's the time to buy.' Ivan caught himself fiddling with a packet of cigarettes on his desk. Sodding smoking ban.

It was one of his agitated days. 'Some group of nominees bought a big stake this morning and I'm worried the story might be getting out. The world's full of leaky buggers.'

'So what is deal? You know what they do?'

'I'm Pneumatech's banker, Platon, I know *exactly* what they are going to do. Sell off half the company in the UK and buy a business called Skinshine in the States. They're looking to make five hundred and twenty million sterling from the sale and spend eight hundred on the purchase. There are going to be some fat fees for me in that lot, I can tell you.'

'And we turn me a nice profit too. I tell Dix to buy right now.'

'And you'll think about a role for me going forward, Platon?' He watched his left foot jiggling restlessly. Perhaps he'd feel better if he stood up.

'*Morzhit byt*, Ivaan, perhaps I do. You screw up Seachest, but mainly you done good.'

With Dyengi in such an amiable mood, Ivan hesitated to tell him the bad news, but then decided that it had to be said. He sat down again. 'We have a potential complication. There's something I need to tell you about.'

There was a grunt. He took the plunge.

'The Treasury's investigating hedge funds. I wouldn't have bothered you, but I hear it's getting serious. Not just taxation but full regulation. Your business with Dix would be completely buggered.' He had to move the phone away from his ear at the eruption of incomprehensible Russian fury. When it was over, he added, 'The inquiry'll be unstoppable unless someone shuts it down.'

'Is many strings I can pull.' Dyengi's voice was calm again, and very cold.

'Well, you could start with Lock Chase. You know how much the government relies on these bloody consultants. There's a woman called Mary Kersey who's leading the Lock Chase work for the Treasury. I've heard she's a real pest.'

'You tell me about this woman then I tell you what you do.'

EIGHTEEN

Mary had run out of excuses.

'Look,' Urban put on that commonsense voice of his. 'I know that not all of our clients meet your exacting standards but we do have a crust to earn. All I'm asking is that you offer the Doves a bit of dinner at Trister. They are your neighbours, for goodness' sake.'

'I really resent you asking me to prostitute my own house, and I don't at all see why I should entertain Alan Dove.' She'd feel guilty later, but she couldn't help being snappy. 'The former Chairman of F-ACE told me Dove's takeover of his company was improper.'

'I wouldn't have thought he was exactly an unbiased observer, and I reckon Dove's perfectly straight. Anyway, I wouldn't be asking you if it was trivial. Pneumatech's a big client, so Dove's important to us. And besides . . .' Urban added the irrefutable point. 'We all think the economy's running on borrowed time, don't we? We're facing an almighty correction, and when it comes, if we don't have enough work to go round we'll have to start laying off consulting staff. Not a nice thing to have on your conscience.'

So Mary had telephoned Juliana Dove and a date had been fixed. 'I hope I'm going to get a huge pat on the back for this,' she said glumly to Urban the Friday before the dreaded weekend.

'The loathsome Doves are coming to dinner tomorrow night, which means I'll have to waste the entire day cooking.'

Urban smiled benevolently down at her. He was always nice when he'd got his own way. 'You're being very good about this. I promise it won't be forgotten.'

'Oh well, at least Meg and Peter are coming along to give me moral support.' Mary started off down the corridor. 'I'd better get to the AGA-face. Wish me luck!'

'*Powodzenia!*' she heard Urban call after her retreating back.

Peter Cromwell was first to arrive, wearing a long black cassock and looking rather like a daisy with that round face and yellow hair poking up from his white dog-collar. 'I had a straight choice between going home to change and being late or turning up dressed like this and adding a touch of elegant sanctity to your gathering.' Glancing around he added, 'But how divine everything looks. I don't think I've seen Trister by candlelight before.'

It had been a lovely day, and Mary had left the windows open so that the scents of summer could drift inside the house. A late sunbeam lit up pieces of seventeenth-century Kersey silver which glowed softly along the length of the dining-room table. These were interspersed with far older silver bowls from Mary's own family, holding the deep scarlet rose of no known name that flowered rampantly in the walled garden. She couldn't stop herself smirking as Peter praised the grace and restraint of her table.

'Ravishingly pretty. Well done, dear. It'll be a lovely evening.'

As they sat down to dinner, Mary feared the evening was going to be anything but lovely. Alan Dove was not an easy conversationalist. Searching for a way to entertain her unwanted guest, she launched into a description of Dimple. 'You've no idea how sweet she is. I'm forever sneaking down to her field to slip her an apple. She makes this endearing noise when you feed her.' Dove's glasses flashed blankly as she ended with a limp imitation of the pony's breathy whicker. Not an animal lover then.

She switched to the dull conversational harbours of Trister, White Gables and Suffolk life and found the tactic surprisingly successful. Dove was immediately interested in the house, and wanted to know all about the Kerseys and their ancestry. 'It must be wonderful to live surrounded by your own history.' He gestured at the centre of the table. 'Is this the family silver?'

Mary had a sudden urge to make it clear that she wasn't just some lucky appendage of the Kerseys. She had her own ancestry too. 'As a matter of fact the older pieces are mine.'

'Yours?'

'My mother passed them on to me. Her brother's the Earl of Ivybridge.'

'Good heavens!' She really had his attention now. 'That's a *very* ancient family. The seat is Brink Castle, I believe? Is it still inhabited?'

'It's a bit crumbly, but my uncle lives there. Even if the castle fell down, I don't think he could bear to leave the family chapel. There are centuries of ancestors in the crypt.'

'You're all Catholics, aren't you? How impressive to have stuck with your religious principles for so long.' Dove said this with such frank respect that Mary found herself thinking that if she didn't distrust his business scruples so much, she might actually quite like the man. A moment later, she changed her mind. She couldn't believe what she had heard and had to ask him to repeat it.

'I said, I've been told you're carrying out an investigation into hedge funds for the Treasury, Mary. Is that right?'

Shocked, she was saved from having to reply by her waitress, the wife of a local pig-farmer, whom Mary had coerced into helping out that evening. Bustling across with a serving plate, she nudged Dove playfully with a fat elbow. 'One of my Tom's piggies this is. Sweet thing she was, we called her Rosie. Learned to come to her name. Bright little piglet, bless her. Made lovely crackling too, hasn't she?'

Alan Dove took only the tiniest slice of Rosie while Mary took far too much. This sage-scented porchetta was one of the best things she cooked, and pork crackling was one of those unctuous, fatty and utterly delicious things that she just couldn't resist. She grabbed the opportunity of turning away from Dove to talk to Peter on her other side, and by using the excuse of checking things in the kitchen, she managed to avoid any more conversation with him until dinner was over.

Catching the eyes of her female guests, Mary took them upstairs to her bedroom, leaving Guy to usher a token bottle of Fonseca round the table. Juliana Dove shut herself firmly in the bathroom while Meg stretched out on Mary's bed. 'Lovely evening, darling, and I've had wonderful gossips with Peter and Guy. But I haven't had a chance to talk to Dr Dove yet. You will introduce me?'

'Of course.' Mary lowered her voice, as she wasn't quite sure how soundproof the bathroom walls were. 'Though he's not the easiest of men to talk to.'

Meg smiled a sphinx-like smile and murmured that she was always interested in powerful men. 'So unlike my own dear Dominic,' she added maliciously.

It was some time before Juliana emerged, preceded by violent blasts of scent and wearing so much eye make-up that it wasn't immediately clear how she was able to see. Following her guests down the wide oak staircase, Mary was stopped by Alan Dove, who was standing alone in the Great Hall gazing up at the medieval stained glass which still survived in the oriel window.

'Beautiful glass. I imagine that's the Kersey family crest, is it? I like the blue.'

'And irreplaceable. I think the recipe for that deep azure was lost some time during the Black Death.'

'The Black Death,' he repeated slowly. 'Yes. We never had the chance to finish our conversation. Your hedge fund inquiry. I wanted to say something.' Imagining she caught a hint of menace in the flash of those pebble glasses, Mary shivered. In a low voice, Dove went on, 'There are a lot of peculiarly vicious wasps in that particular apple-cart. Be careful you don't find yourself getting stung.'

'Mary darling, there you are!' Meg interrupted them brightly.

Remembering that Meg had asked to be introduced to Dove and delighted to have the chance to escape, Mary muttered, 'I don't think you've had the chance to talk to my friend Meg Dewey yet, have you, Alan? I'll leave you two together while I go and get some coffee. Join us in a minute.'

Mary moved away, but was still in earshot when Meg began to talk. She thought how very peculiar Meg's voice sounded, almost as if she were simpering. 'Dr Dove! I'm *so* thrilled to meet you. Actually, I'm a small shareholder in Pneumatech, a *very* small shareholder of course.'

That was a surprise. She'd never imagined Meg having anything to do with shares. Standing poised in the doorway, Mary wondered if her conscience would allow her to stay and eavesdrop. No, of *course* she couldn't. Listening in to other people's conversations was a despicable thing to do. She hurried on into the Long Library.

A couple of hours later, Peter's voice came from the depths of a plush-covered sofa. 'Well, actually I thought she was rather lovely, and very serene considering her upbringing. The poor woman told me she'd been sent away to board in England when she was only a child. A violent father, apparently.' Mary, exhausted, was listening while Guy, Peter and Meg conducted a post-mortem on the evening. 'And wasn't she glamorous in that pink pussy-cat blouse?' he added.

'Peter! You *couldn't* think she was glamorous. She had enough make-up on to insulate an attic.' Meg sounded really cross. 'And as for him, I couldn't get him to say a word. In fact I thought he was bloody rude. He barely talked to me.'

'Well, that's odd, Meg, I can't imagine anyone not wanting to talk to you. Perhaps he's just shy with women,' Guy said kindly. 'Actually I rather took to him. A little one-track-minded on the subject of business, but once we got on to scientific research funding I found him very interesting. He thinks Southampton's got a more innovative medical school than Cambridge and explained why as well. Rather persuasively in fact. I'm bound to say I've often wondered whether we weren't rather sitting back on our scientific laurels.'

Peter stretched and yawned widely. 'Oh, excuse *me*. Too full of delicious food, and wasn't the waitress heaven? I thought I was going to die laughing when she started talking about udder infections as she was passing the cream round. Mary, my angel, you are *quite* brilliant in the way you manage your staff.'

'If only I had any,' said Mary wryly.

'So what did you think of your new neighbour then?' Meg asked her.

'I think he's overwhelmingly driven. I've seen other busi-nessmen like him. They climb far higher than one thinks possible, then when eventually they trip up on their own hubris, they fall faster and much, much further than one expects. And no one likes them enough to put out a hand to stop them crashing to the ground.'

'Very wise, dear.' Peter yawned widely again. 'Talking of falling,

I must fall into bed. I've been shattered by my priestly duties today.'

As they waved their friends off across the bridge, Guy put an arm on Mary's shoulder.

'I'm bound to say it's rather a relief to speed the going guest.'

Tired and with an incipient headache from too much red wine, Mary replied sharply, 'You may be relieved but how do you imagine I feel? I did all organizing, *and* the cooking.'

With a very audible sigh, Guy took his arm away from her shoulder and walked back into the house without a word, leaving Mary to stare down into the cold waters of the moat, torn between self-pity and exasperation with her husband.

NINETEEN

'Yes, a lot of nominees have been piling into our shares recently,' Alan Dove said smugly. 'I've no idea who they are, but it's great to see we're broadening our investor base.' As they finished the normal business of the meeting, he smiled around at his board members. He'd already talked to each of them privately and expected his announcement to be a formality. But even so, he was excited.

'The final subject for today's meeting is strategy,' said Gregory Loach. What a misery the Chairman was. Never a smile on his face. 'Over to you, Alan.' He even managed to make those few words sound grumpy.

'Gentlemen.' Dove started quietly, his head bent down over the neatly stacked papers in front of him. 'I've always been ambitious for Pneumatech. I want to make the company really big, and I've found the way to do it.' He looked up suddenly. 'We're going to carry out two simultaneous deals, one sale and one purchase. We're going to double the size of Pneumatech overnight.'

Although everyone knew the outline of Dove's plans, doing the two deals at the same time was new to most of them. A babble of comment erupted round the table. 'Quiet, PLEASE!' roared Loach. 'We are not children. Let the Chief Executive finish what he wishes to say.'

In the silence that followed, Dove placed his stubby fingers on the table in front of him. 'We are going to purchase Skinshine Corporation. A thousand upmarket beauty salons across the USA. The company was founded by two brothers, Bill and Charlie Arbchecker. They're in their sixties and they want to get out of the business and have some fun. They like my plan to retail F-ACE products through the Skinshine chain and they are prepared to sell us their company for one point two billion dollars. That's eight hundred million pounds.'

'We'll have to keep a close eye on the exchange rate.' What a fatuous thing to say. Dove ignored his Finance Director's interjection.

'To raise the money to pay for Skinshine we're going to sell the Lung Division. A private equity firm wants to buy it, Churngold Capital. They're talking five hundred and twenty million pounds.'

'There's a big gap there, Alan,' his Chairman interrupted. 'If you sell the Lung Division for five twenty and buy Skinshine for eight, you'll need to raise two hundred and eighty million pounds. You can do that, can you?'

Loach was peering down the table at the Finance Director, who gave a movement of his head which could have been either a nod or a shake before saying, 'Well, Chairman, we've got two hundred million pounds' worth of banking lines. As for the other eighty, credit's cheap and money's easy to get, but I've no guarantees.'

Dove cut across the sudden hubbub round the table. 'We have other sources of finance! I'd be grateful if you'd let me continue.' His Finance Director was so wet. He should have realized he'd have to do everything himself. Dove made a mental note to call Straw as soon as the meeting finished.

'We'll need to get shareholder approval for the two transac-

BAD MONEY | 146

tions,' he went on firmly, 'and fortuitously our Annual General Meeting is due to take place in three months.'

'Remind me what date the AGM is?'

'The eighteenth of October.'

'Ah, Alan . . .'

Seeing Stevens trying to cut in, Dove held up a hand to silence him. 'Just let me finish, Theodore. The consultancy firm Lock Chase have been working for me to validate my logic. I have invited them here to make a presentation to the board and I believe that they are waiting to come in. Now, questions?'

'Well, yes, Alan, I do have a question. It's about risk.'

Risk? What did Stevens know about risk, Dove thought crossly, before admitting to himself that the surgeon must think about it every time his scalpel was poised to make that first incision into a breathing human body.

'I'm worried about you doing these two deals at the same time,' Stevens went on. 'I'd feel a lot happier if you could get the Lung Division sold and have the cash safely in the bank before you go off and buy this new company. Otherwise you might find yourself committed to spending a fortune in America and then something going wrong with the sale in England.'

Dove tried to stop himself frowning at Stevens. Why was he asking questions? He thought he'd got the man on side when he'd told him how much money he could make from a private equity buyer.

'There's another thing, Alan. This Churngold Capital that you say is going to buy the Lung Division. I've been finding out about these private equity firms. I'm told they promise you the earth when they're interested in buying your business, say yes to everything you ask. But at the first sniff of a problem they change their minds and say no.'

Before Dove had time to reply, Loach came to his rescue. 'You're making some valid points, Theodore, but why don't we listen to the consultants? They may answer your questions.'

'For goodness' sake, what's up, Spider? It's only a client presentation. You're jittering about as if you were nervous.' Urban had meant his comment as a joke, but she seemed to take it seriously.

'Of course I'm not nervous, you mad idiot. I just hate being pissed about. They told us to turn up at this board meeting at ten-thirty and we've been farting about waiting for nearly an hour now. Gregory Loach must be a useless Chairman to let them run so late.' He noticed she had a way of flicking her fingers when she was disturbed, like a cat unsheathing its claws. 'You shouldn't have made me come to this presentation. I've never even met this lot,' she grumbled.

'But Spider, we agreed. You're the scientist. It's much better that you do it, just in case there are any detailed biotech questions,' he replied patiently.

'I haven't done any science for years.'

It was when she said this that the penny dropped. It was obvious now. She was scared she might be asked some impossible technical question. Looking round for something to distract her, he noticed a man who walked past them, froze as he saw Spider and very obviously came back for a second viewing. Once Urban started looking he saw that several other passers-by also paused to stare at her.

'Have you noticed all these guys eyeing you up? Who do you fancy?'

For some reason she seemed to find this funny. 'None of them.' Looking up into his face, she became serious again.

'What about you, Urban? What kind of women do you like?'

'Me? That's easy. I've always gone for girls with a bit of shape to them.'

'You mean tits and bums?'

'Exactly. It's probably Oedipal.'

'Your mother was curvy then, was she?'

'Very.' *Ave Maria, gratia plena*. He could still hear the words quite clearly, but these days he had to concentrate hard to see his parents' faces. 'I wish I had a photograph.'

At that moment, an innocuous-looking woman came scuttling out of the Pneumatech headquarters. 'Mr Palewski? Miss Wood? I'm Sadie Wilson-Smith, Dr Dove's personal assistant.' She held out a hand. 'The board is ready for you now if you'd like to come up?'

As they were shown into the boardroom, Urban was astonished to see Spider slipping quietly into a chair. Normally she'd be rushing round introducing herself, shaking hands with everyone, cheerful and slightly aggressive. She must be *very* nervous. Touched by the thought that she needed protecting, he moved in front of her. He wasn't having her troubled by introductions if she didn't want them.

It quickly became clear that Pneumatech's famously ill-mannered Chairman didn't intend to make any welcoming remarks, so Urban got going by himself. 'Thank you for the invitation to present our findings to you. I'm Urban Palewski and I'll be talking to you about the acquisition of Skinshine Corporation and its integration with F-ACE. With me is my colleague Spider Wood who's going to talk about the divestment of the Lung Division.'

He could see Spider looking uncomfortable as the eyes of the Pneumatech board rested on her, so he dived straight in. For twenty minutes he held their attention. He took them right through the logic of the merger before concluding, 'Our view is that Skinshine is a great acquisition and a fair price. With the innovative beauty products you have in F-ACE, you could double your profits in three years.' He glanced across at Spider. 'And now I'm going to hand over to my colleague who'll cover the sale of the Lung Division.'

Spider's presentation was clinically competent. She took the board through each of the division's drugs, commenting on their value in the light of probable competitive and technical developments before moving on to an assessment of the Lung Division as a whole.

'Our view is that five hundred and twenty million pounds is a sound number, but biotech companies are notoriously difficult to value. Some new wonder-drug could wipe one of your cash cows off the face of the earth. On the other hand there could be millions in one of the drugs you have under development. Your scientists are really pushing the genomic envelope, but we haven't put a penny of value in for their work because we think it's too speculative. So there you have it. We've done all the analysis we can. Five-twenty looks like fair value but you might be kicking the hell out of us for getting it wrong in a couple of years' time.'

As soon as she had finished, Urban was on his feet again. 'And now I'll be happy to take any questions.'

Spider looked at him in surprise. She must have caught the 'I'. As he motioned to her to sit down, she threw him a look of such gratitude that he was almost sorry when his chivalrous intentions were ruined by Gregory Loach.

'No time for questions, we're running late as it is.'

Urban glanced across at Alan Dove to check whether his client was happy for them to leave, but Dove wasn't looking at him. Because of his thick glasses it was hard to be certain, but he appeared to be staring at Spider, whose face was turned away from him. As Urban collected up his papers, he saw Dove getting up and moving slowly round the table towards her. Spider leapt up and hurried out of the boardroom without saying goodbye to anyone.

'The board meeting just finished.' Dove launched into the phone call without even a hello. 'I need to talk to you.'

'Well, good afternoon, Alan.' Ivan threw his legs up on his desk. He'd got to know Alan Dove well in the last few months. When he was this abrupt it usually meant he was on weak ground, trying to bully himself into a stronger position. 'What's the problem?'

'The good news is the board's given me the go-ahead on both deals. The bad news is there may be a problem with money. We have bank lines of two hundred million but we need an additional eighty and my Finance Director's messing me about. I thought the cash was in the bag, but now he's saying the banks might not play ball. Wolkenbank can lend us eighty million quid, surely? I'm putting enough bloody business your way.'

No chance, Ivan decided immediately. Wolkenbank very rarely lent money. They preferred to make their profit out of fees from doing deals, not interest on loans. Eighty million wasn't a lot, but the Wolkenbank credit committee would need a very strong argument and his own total commitment before they'd even consider making a loan to some mid-cap company in a risky sector.

Ivan wasn't about to put his neck on the line for Dove. If something went wrong and the bank lost even a fraction of their eighty million pounds, he could say goodbye to his bonus.

He'd rather see the whole Skinshine transaction collapse. Though if there was any chance of that happening he'd make damn sure the Russian had sold his holding of Pneumatech shares first. He shuddered to think what Dyengi might do if he ever lost him money.

On the other hand, he did stand to make a *very* fat fee from both the Skinshine purchase and the Lung Division sale. Ivan would be doing everything he could to help Dove get the funding he needed. It just wouldn't be coming from Wolkenbank.

'I'm sorry, but it's an absolute no-go. I wouldn't even ask. What we *really* need to do is pay eighty million pounds less for Skinshine.' As he was speaking, various ideas revolved in his head. Share-price manipulation? Another BOOB job? Tricky. Skinshine was a big company and the US authorities were tough on insider trading. One little slip and they'd slap him in jail. 'Sorry, what was that, Alan?'

'I said that if we can't pay less for Skinshine, we might be able to raise eighty million pounds more from the Lung Division.'

Ivan swung his legs down off the desk and reached for a pad of paper. 'Go on.'

'Lock Chase gave me the idea. When they valued the Lung Division, they didn't include anything for our genomics research, and that could be worth not millions but *billions*. We should be able to get Churngold Capital to increase their bid by a measly eighty million pounds.'

Ivan scribbled a few lines on his notepad. As he did so, he noticed that his hands were quite steady. Amazing. Just two days off the tablets and the tremor, that hated side-effect of his medication, had gone. He'd have to start taking the pills again straight after he'd done what he had to do; he knew he couldn't live a normal life without them. But just now, he needed the accelerated reactions that the early stages of hypomania always gave him.

'So what do you think, then?' Dove prompted.

Ivan's first instinct was that Dove was madly optimistic to suppose that any private equity firm would increase a sum they'd offered to pay for a buy-out. It was usually the other way round. They put in a high initial bid to see off any competition and chipped away at the price afterwards. But then strange things did sometimes happen when private equity firms were really keen on a deal. There was also the not unimportant point that Wolkenbank would be paid a percentage of the transaction size. He would get a bigger bonus selling the Lung Division for six hundred million than for five-twenty.

'It sounds like this is something we should meet to talk about, Alan. I can get myself freed up any time that suits you.'

'I've got a meeting in the City at three. I'll get Cyril to bring me straight on to you afterwards.'

'Sure. See you later. Oh, and by the way,' Ivan was careful to keep his voice casual, 'have you heard anything more about that Treasury inquiry? We wouldn't want any new stories about F-ACE coming out to muddy the water, would we?'

'I've heard nothing new, though I did meet that Lock Chase woman, Mary Kersey. She was very pleasant, as a matter of fact, not at all grand. I hadn't realized that her uncle is the Earl of Ivybridge.'

An aristocrat, was she? Not just an interfering bitch but a sodding toff as well.

'As a matter of fact,' Dove went on, 'I told her to be careful of the hedge fund industry. I tried to warn her off, though I don't suppose she paid any attention.'

Upper-class cow, Ivan thought as he put the phone down. She needs something a lot stronger than a verbal warning.

TWENTY

Mary was hurrying along Piccadilly when her phone rang. 'Is that you, Bella?' she shouted against the whine of two empty bendy-buses crawling past her up the slow incline to Piccadilly Circus. 'Hang on, can you? I'll try to find somewhere quieter.'

Turning up Dover Street, she dived into a doorway and pressed the handset to her ear but the line had gone dead. She was still peering at the tiny screen when a text message popped up:

2pm meeting cancelled. Sorry short notice. Refixed next week. Bella.

Mary leaned back in the doorway and sighed with relief. She'd been worried about this meeting. It was with a potential new client and she hadn't had a moment to prepare for it.

Finding herself with this gift of a free hour in the middle of her working day, she decided to walk back to the office rather than taking a taxi. It would do her good to get a bit of exercise. Strolling up Bond Street, she paused to admire a jeweller's mirrored window display and caught sight of her tired face reflected back from among the diamonds. Hell's bells, what a mess she looked.

A few yards further on, a sign caught her eye. It was a message of irresistible temptation above an elegant blue door. *Fast Track Makeover: Manicure, pedicure, mini-facial. One hour.* Just one little hour's indulgence. Her midriff would still be fat but at least her extremities would be presentable. With no more than a moment's pause, Mary pressed the lacquered brass bellpush. The door swung open.

'Good afternoon, madam.' The voice was a gentle purr. '*How* may I help you?'

'I don't suppose you could do me a one-hour makeover? Now, I mean.' Feeling thick carpet under her feet, smelling rich scents, hearing the murmur of leisured voices, Mary felt an uprush of guilt. This wasn't her world. She ought to get back to work. Turning, she was about to walk straight out again but it was too late.

'But of *course* we can, madam. It will be our pleasure. Come this way and I'll give you a robe to change into.' The receptionist gave Mary an encouraging smile and moved off down a softly lit corridor. Mary followed and was lost.

Cuddled in a turquoise towelling dressing-gown, she noticed the sign. 'No mobiles please.' After a moment's hesitation she reached into her briefcase and switched off her phone. Bella invariably knew where she was and whom she was meeting, and in between meetings, her mobile was always on. Mary had sometimes thought that Lock Chase might just as well have her microchipped and be done with it. Now, for the first time in years, no one knew where she was and no one could get in touch with her. Even though it would only be for an hour, she felt gloriously, irresponsibly liberated.

The beauty salon kept its word and it was indeed almost exactly an hour later that Mary stepped back out on to Bond Street. She felt wonderful. Her nails were varnished and her face glowed as if it had been polished too. Walking on air past boutiques and couturiers, Mary vowed to herself that she would simply make time in future for a regular beauty treatment. She had quite nice hands – maybe a manicure every fortnight? And a pedicure. Definitely another pedicure.

It wasn't until she had crossed Regent Street that she realized her phone was still switched off. Her immaculate fingernails seemed to glint knowingly as she pressed the button on the side of her mobile. Immediately it sprang into life. The message light flashed and the screen glowed with a text message.

Ring husband. Accident. Where are you? V worried. Bella.

For a whole minute the world stopped. People pushed past her, a motorbike roared by, but Mary stood frozen with fear. Accident. Not Grace. Please God, please. Not Grace.

Her phone rang. 'Mary? Hello?'

'Oh Guy! What's happened? Where are you? Is it Grace?'

'. . . On my way to . . . ambulance . . . I can't . . .' The line went dead.

Mary's hands were shaking as she dialled Guy's number, but the call switched straight through to his answering service. She started to run.

As she reached Wardour Street, Guy rang again. 'Just listen in case I get cut off again. Reception here's appalling. Gracie's fallen off Dimple. I'm in the ambulance taking her to hospital. We don't know how bad it is yet. Can you . . .' The line went silent.

'Which hospital?' Mary screamed into her phone. Passers-by turned to look at her then hurried on their way.

A taxi swerved then jerked to a halt as Mary leapt out in front of it, feverishly waving her arms.

'Blimey, lady, you trying to kill yourself?'

'My daughter's had an accident! Can you take me to the station?'

'Which one, lady?'

Mary stared at the driver, white-faced. 'Oh God. I don't know. I don't know which hospital they've taken her to. It'll either be King's Cross or Liverpool Street. Which is quickest from here?'

'Hop in. There's roadworks all round King's Cross so I'll take you to Liverpool Street. Do my best to get you there as quick as we can.'

As the taxi pulled away, Mary's mobile rang again.

'Guy?' Mary's voice was high and panicky.

'Spider. Bella just told me about your kid. Is there anything we can do to help?'

'Help? Oh yes.' Mary forced herself to concentrate. 'Could you give Bella a hand dealing with my meetings until I'm back? I don't know how long I'll be away because I don't know how badly hurt Grace is. Christ, I don't even know *where* she is. I feel like I'm in some kind of nightmare. I don't even know which hospital she's going to.'

'Hospital? She's going to hospital? Shit, poor kid. Listen Mary, don't think about work, I'll get everything sorted.'

'Thanks so much. I'd better get off the line in case Guy's trying to get through.'

'Sure. And look after yourself.' Spider hung up.

The conversation had helped Mary to calm down, so that when Guy rang again she could ask quite clearly, 'Which hospital are they taking you to?'

'All the way to Ipswich, I'm afraid. You'll need to get a train from Liverpool Street.'

Mary breathed a silent prayer of thanks for the roadworks which had diverted her taxi to the right station.

'I'm on my way there now. Any news?'

'It looks like concussion. The ambulance men have put her

in a neck brace but that doesn't necessarily mean anything. Just get to Ipswich as soon as you can and try not to worry.'

'This is ghastly. I feel so dreadful that it's happened the only time I've ever, ever turned off my phone.'

'Mary!' Guy sounded as if he was struggling to control his voice. 'It was an accident. It wasn't your fault. Just get to the hospital. I'll ring if I have anything to tell you.'

Mary subsided into the corner of the taxi and prayed. Twenty decades of the Rosary passed as she stared blindly out of the grubby windows of a train and then of an Ipswich taxi. She clutched her phone like a crucifix the whole way, but it stayed silent. She hadn't dared to call anyone in case it stopped Guy from getting through to her. She was at the doors of Ipswich Hospital when she finally heard it ring.

'Mary?' Guy's voice was oddly muffled. 'I'm at the hospital and I'm not supposed to be using a telephone. Where are you?'

'I'm here, at the hospital.'

'Will you come and find us? We're in Casualty. Grace has just this minute come back from X-ray and I can't leave her. She's a bit muddled.' Guy must have heard her sharp intake of breath because he hurried on. 'They're going to keep her in overnight but they say she'll be fine. She's hit her head and sprained her ankle, but no bones broken.' Guy's voice sounded high with strain. She wondered if he was keeping something horrible back from her as she rushed to the Accident and Emergency department.

A nurse was waiting for her there, but despite the soothing words she murmured as she showed her to Grace's bed, Mary wasn't at all prepared for the bandages wrapped around Grace's head, or for the smears of dried blood on her cheeks, or for the drip going into her arm. Worst of all was the sound of her daughter's confused voice.

'Trotting out. Bang.' Horrified, Mary looked across the bed to where Guy was sitting white-faced, stroking Grace's hand. The corners of his mouth moved in an attempt at a smile. 'Dimple,' Grace muttered, then suddenly she was shouting, 'Dimple! Mummy, Dimple!'

A kind-faced young doctor hurried over and told them not to worry, that this wandering talk and sudden agitation often happened with concussion. Guy also did his best to be reassuring. 'She's been like this for a while. I know she sounds awful, but actually she's a lot quieter than she was when we first got here.' Sure enough, Grace's fits of shouting gradually died away, and as they sat silently watching over her, she eventually fell into an apparently peaceful sleep.

'She'll be fine now.' The doctor was back again to check on her. 'We'll keep an eye on Grace down here for another hour or so, then we'll move her up to the children's ward where she can stay until we're sure she's safe to go home. There's a vending machine along the corridor,' he added. 'I'm sure you could both do with a hot drink.'

A few minutes later they were sitting together on a pair of hard chairs just outside Casualty, clutching plastic cups of coffee. Guy, who had seemed so calm, suddenly crumpled. 'Oh God, Mary. Oh God. It was terrible.'

Reaching across to take her husband's hand, Mary said gently, 'Can you tell me what happened?'

Staring into the grey puddle of coffee at the bottom of his cup, Guy said, 'I was in my study. Working on Hesiod. The first thing I knew was when I saw Father.'

His voice broke. Mary waited patiently until he was able to go on. 'He was running up from the Triangle. Running. He looked like an old man. Head down. Arms flailing. Legs all jerky. He was shouting for me, "Guy! Guy!" Of course I rushed straight out. Father almost collapsed in my arms. His face was quite blue. He was gasping for breath. He managed to pant out, "Gracie. Get an ambulance!" So I dashed inside and dialled 999. By the time I got outside again I could see him trying to run back down to the Triangle. I caught up with him and told him to stay at the house so he could direct the ambulance. Then I went on. And found Grace.'

His voice cracked again, and Mary said soothing words to him as if he were a child. 'Calm down. Grace is fine now. Don't talk if you don't want to.'

'But I must tell you.' Guy looked up at Mary, his face drawn. 'I found her curled up like a baby down under the blackthorn hedge. She was moaning, so at least I knew she was alive. That idiot pony Binky was careering round shrieking her head off. I was worried she was going to charge into Grace. And Dimple.' Guy fell silent.

'Dimple? Dimple's all right, isn't she? Grace couldn't bear it if anything happened to her.'

Guy put a hand on her arm. 'There was no hope. She'd snapped her foreleg clean through. It was a terrible mess, there was nothing anyone could do.'

'Dimple,' Mary whispered.

Guy closed his eyes. 'The vet shot her.'

TWENTY-ONE

A disembodied voice from the intercom buzzed in his ear. 'Churngold Capital is up on the sixth floor, Dr Dove. Mr D'Arby will meet you outside the lifts.'

Down on the ground floor, the metal door of a two-man lift opened in a series of jerks. Dove peered inside. He hated these old rattletraps, and besides, it would do him good to walk up. He'd probably get there quicker too. As he started a fast climb up the stairs, Dove reflected that the building was just what he'd imagined. Known to be one of the more reticent players in the notoriously secretive world of private equity, Ralph D'Arby had clearly eschewed the normal City statement office block in favour of this anonymous building on Kingsway. Even the entrance was discreet, squeezed between a low-cost gentleman's outfitters and a pizzeria.

When he emerged from the stairwell he was relieved to find himself in the recognizable comforts of corporate civilization. There was D'Arby, expecting him to come out of the lift, looking so effortlessly elegant, suit flawless, tie straight, white cuffs just showing. Dove felt a twist of envy. However expensively he dressed, he could never get his stumpy-legged, broad-shouldered body to look like that. D'Arby turned his head and switched on a wide smile as the fire door to the stairwell sighed shut.

'Alan, there you are! Welcome to our humble abode.'

The office into which he was ushered reflected Churngold

Capital's culture of understatement. It was a large and comfortable room but quite bare of the normal corporate trophies. Nor was there anything on show that even hinted at the enormous wealth that Ralph D'Arby was known to have amassed from the business.

'So, Alan,' D'Arby said once they were seated round his faux-ivory coffee table. 'You've sent us an Information Memorandum. We've read it, we think your Lung Division is worth five hundred and twenty million pounds, and we thought you were happy with that number. But now you reckon it's worth more, so here I am to listen to you.'

Dove leaned forwards in his chair. He felt confident, he felt optimistic. He couldn't imagine D'Arby disagreeing with him. 'Frankly, Ralph, we got our Information Memorandum wrong. We didn't include a proper valuation of the pipeline. We've some research just waiting to be translated into profitable drugs and quite frankly, it's astonishing.' Dove paused for a comment or a question but D'Arby stayed silent. 'What I'm about to tell you is highly commercially sensitive. It must remain absolutely secret, you understand?'

Seeing Ralph nodding, he continued quietly, 'We're way ahead of the curve in genomics research, *way* ahead. I'll give you an example. One of my researchers is an asthma specialist and he's had a breakthrough. He's pinpointed specific, individually targeted cures for around forty per cent of all asthmatics, imagine! It's not just asthma cures, either.' Dove reached into his briefcase. 'I've brought along a summary of some of the more exciting areas of our research.'

As D'Arby took the papers from him, Dove added, 'I'm tempted to say you should double what you're offering for the Lung Division but all I'm asking is that you raise your offer from five twenty to six hundred million. Otherwise . . .' Dove hoped the lie wouldn't be obvious. 'I'll have to pull the whole sale and start again.'

'Oh, you don't need to do that, Alan. I'd like to stay in the game. Your firm's got a good track record in drug development and I'm ready to believe there could be value in your research pipeline.' There was a flash of his white teeth. 'I'm happy to look at these papers, but I'll need another financial evaluation if I'm going to make a higher offer.'

Dove was elated. 'Of course, no problem. Lock Chase did the first valuation for me, so it makes sense for them to do this one. I'll get on to them straight away.'

He jogged happily back down the stairs. Six hundred million for the Lung Division sounded like it was in the bag. And tomorrow he was off to Washington for the shopping trip of a lifetime.

The heat made him gasp as he emerged from the plane, all the other passengers having been held back so that the handful travelling First Class could disembark in comfort. Despite the temperature, Dove almost ran down the aircraft steps. He loved visiting America. He felt great.

Smiling broadly, he climbed into a waiting Lincoln towncar. With a short halt for customs formalities, he was driven across to a far corner of the airport where, alone in the wavering heat haze, a six-seater stood ready to fly him down to Skinshine's Lynchburg headquarters. As his car drew up beside the Arbchecker corporate jet, two crisply shirted men emerged cool and smiling from the cockpit. Each wore the badge of a retired US Air Force pilot.

Inside the little plane Dove found Thomas Butler, his expensive City lawyer, sweating heavily in one of the fawn leather armchairs. Since the documentation for the Skinshine deal had all been agreed already, his presence wasn't strictly necessary, but Dove was keen to have him at the signing of the deal to support his personal prestige with the Arbchecker brothers.

'Afternoon, Alan. Pleasant flight across the pond?' Watching his lawyer mopping a sweaty brow with an already damp handkerchief, Dove felt rather pleased with himself. He wasn't sweating at all. 'Unbearably hot, isn't it?' Thomas Butler went on. 'I've just got off the plane down from Boston. It was a lot cooler up north, I must say.'

Dove was about to reply when one of the pilots popped his head round the cabin door. 'Wheels up in five. Flight'll take around twenty minutes. I should get your seat belts fastened. Turbulence reported. S'gonna be a bumpy ride!'

The pilot vanished, and almost immediately the plane's engines started up and with them the blessed relief of the air-conditioning. The lawyer was obviously used to being flown around in company jets. Dove watched as Butler tightened his lap belt then leaned behind him to pull a shoulder strap out of the top of his seat, fastening it down by his right hip.

Dove himself, unused to private planes, had a moment's embarrassment while he fumbled to clip the shoulder belt in place and felt only fractionally more secure when he was strapped in. The plane suddenly shot forward and within seconds was airborne, in what felt like a vertical take-off. Abandoning any attempt to look calm, Dove grabbed his armrests, leant back against the headrest, closed his eyes and begged to a God he didn't believe in.

The plane accelerated into turbulence worse than he had ever dreamed of. They bucked and bounced along an invisible roller-coaster, tossed sideways in sudden cross-winds, taking throat-tightening plunges, then leaping like a bronco over fantasy jumps. Dove opened his eyes just once during the flight. Glancing down, he saw enormous patches of sweat spreading right across the front of his shirt despite the air-conditioning. He closed his eyes again and waited for death.

'Here we are guys, not such a rough ride after all!'

Dove slowly opened his eyes to the cheery words of the co-pilot as they taxied down to the parking area for private planes. At least he had managed not to be sick and he didn't think he could possibly look as bad as Thomas Butler, who was staring glassy-eyed at him across the aisle. The plane's engines were abruptly switched off and the southern heat began to seep back into the icy interior. Dove's legs felt like jelly but his voice was firm. 'Not a word of this to the Arbcheckers. We're here to do a deal. We don't want them to think we're wimps.'

His lawyer managed a slow nod in agreement and stood up shakily. 'Agreed. But on one condition. We go back to Washington by car. I'm never stepping into one of these flying coffins again.'

Dove had the uncomfortable feeling that he wasn't looking his best when he stepped down on to the tarmac of the little airport to be greeted by his hosts, and he was relieved to see that the pair looked quite as shambolic as he felt. Bill and Charlie Arbchecker stood side by side. He had been briefed that two years in age divided them, but it looked as if little else did. Both had receding russet-coloured hair, big bellies, rumpled, loud-checked suits and broad smiles.

'Alan! Hey! Great to see you!' A hearty slap on the back from Bill and a gorilla handshake from Charlie almost took Dove's still wobbly legs out from under him.

'And you must be Al's lawyer, huh? Howdy.'

That evening, the Arbcheckers took them to the reconstructed colonial town of Williamsburg for dinner. Staring out of the windows as the limousine slowly progressed down Duke of Gloucester Street, Dove loved the place on sight. The villages near White Gables might be more beautiful than the brick and clapboard of Williamsburg, but he found them muddled and unhygienic, their streets and houses twisted into irrational shapes. Williamsburg, on the other hand, was thoroughly clean and comprehensible. Its streets were laid out in a grid, its houses were uniformly rectangular. He smiled at his reflection in the tinted glass of the car windows as an unexpected thought jumped into his head. Juliana would like this place.

Over a heavily old-world dinner of oysters and hotpot in one of Williamsburg's historic inns, Dove raised the question of exactly when his acquisition of Skinshine should become irrevocable. In the negotiations so far it had been assumed that the deal would be conditional only on approval at the Pneumatech AGM. Dove had, however, taken some notice of Theodore Stevens' words at that last board meeting. It *was* risky to sign a binding agreement to buy Skinshine before he was absolutely certain of getting the money to pay for it from the sale of his Lung Division.

'You see, Bill,' Dove tried to make his voice casual as he said the words, 'it really would suit me better if we could make the deal irrevocable on the successful sale of my lung business rather than having the AGM as my cut-off date. There's no risk involved from your point of view,' he added hurriedly, seeing Bill Arbchecker's eyes narrowing. 'The sale's absolutely in the bag. I've got a big private equity house gagging to buy my Lung Division, it's just a question of timing.'

As Dove's voice tailed off, Bill continued to stare coldly at him for a couple of minutes. Then his mouth opened and shut like a steel trap, letting one word out.

'No.'

There was not a trace of a smile.

Taking his cue from his older brother, Charlie added, 'The

deal goes unconditional at your AGM or we pull out. Right now.'

Clearly trying to be helpful, Thomas Butler chipped in, 'Well, it might at least be worth considering Alan's suggestion. I'm sure we could alter the legal agreement to give you sufficient comfort.'

Bill Arbchecker cut across him as if he didn't exist. 'When I need advice from the hired help, I'll send out for my own attorney.'

Charlie picked up the Arbchecker baton. 'So is the deal still on or do we quit?'

For a long moment, Dove was silent. He wanted desperately to buy Skinshine, but on the other hand he felt a tug of anxiety. Supposing the deal with Churngold Capital *did* fall through. Where would he be then? How could he pay for Skinshine without the sale of the Lung Division?

Looking across at the stony stares of the two Arbchecker brothers, his heart sank. There was absolutely no way the brothers were going to agree to his acquisition being conditional on the sale of the Lung Division. He was going to have to bite the bullet one way or the other. Take the risk or quit.

He knew the answer. There had never really been a question. Pulling out was unthinkable. He would look a complete idiot. The Chairman of his board would be impossible, Ivan Straw would despise him. And worse than that, he'd lose the chance of transforming his company, of becoming a real player in the business world. In the *global* business world. He needed to do this deal. His desire for it was visceral. And after all, he could still pull out any time up to his AGM if anything did go wrong with the Lung Division sale.

'You'll have an unconditional offer on the day of my Annual General Meeting.'

The deal was signed the following morning. Celebratory photographs were taken of Alan Dove and the Arbchecker brothers standing together and shaking hands, all squinting into the strong sunshine. With the formalities over, Alan Dove took the Skinshine corporate jet back up to Washington to catch his return flight to London.

The signed papers went to Washington by road. Pneumatech's expensive City lawyer was sticking by his resolution to stay away from small planes.

TWENTY-TWO

With one arm around Grace, Mary smiled at her husband across the mound of earth over which Peter was praying.

> *Fresh and green are the pastures*
> *Where He gives me repose.*
> *Near restful waters He leads me*
> *To revive my drooping spirit.*

It had been entirely Guy's idea to have a funeral ceremony for Dimple. While Mary was still with Grace in Ipswich Hospital, he had cast his High Anglican principles aside and asked Peter Cromwell to hold a Catholic service over the place where the pony had been buried. Guy had even gone to the trouble of planting a weeping birch, whose young branches drooped over Dimple's grave.

> *Eternal rest give unto her, oh Lord,*
> *And let perpetual light shine upon her.*
> *May she rest in peace.*

Grace was looking peaceful too. Mary had Peter to thank for that. As they were on their way down to the field, Grace had suddenly said, 'You can't *know* that Dimple's in heaven. Anna's mummy doesn't even believe it exists. She says when you're dead, you're dead. Supposing it's true?'

'Of course it isn't true,' Mary had said firmly. 'Is it, Peter?'

'My dear Gracie, what a daft idea. Jesus brought lots of people back to life, didn't He? That was to show us that everyone can come alive again after they've died. Can you think of any of them?'

Grace glanced up at him. 'There was that little girl, wasn't there? Jesus said *Talitha cumi* and she hopped off her deathbed.'

'Well done! Anyone else? What about someone who stinketh?'

'Lazarus!' Grace actually giggled.

'There were rumours going round that the people Jesus brought back to life weren't really dead. So with Lazarus, Jesus waited till his body was decomposing in the heat.'

The words took Mary's mind back to a conversation she'd had with Guy. It was the day before she brought Grace home from hospital and he had rung to tell her they'd buried Dimple in a sheltered corner where the pony had liked to stand and daydream. 'I hadn't realized you were going to bury her so quickly,' Mary had said. 'I don't suppose you had a look at her foreleg to see if there was any sign of a bullet wound? Grace is still insisting she heard a shot.'

Guy's answer had been eminently reasonable. 'I think that's extremely unlikely. Gracie was very confused, and besides, people don't wander around firing off guns at passing ponies. And as it's been so hot, Dimple's body was already starting to decompose when we buried her. I'm afraid I didn't get close enough to do a post-mortem.'

'And then Jesus brought Lazarus back to life.' Peter's words brought Mary back to the present. She noticed the gentle sweetness of the priest's smile as he looked down at her daughter and added, 'I think your friend Anna's mummy is rather silly, don't you? Of course there's a heaven.'

'And Dimple's in it,' Grace had said firmly.

When the service was over, Grace hung back to wait for her father and grandfather, who were making slow progress up from the field. Mary walked on ahead with Peter.

'You're a true godsend. It was so kind of you to hold a service for an animal.'

'Saint Francis would have done it, so I don't see why I shouldn't. And talking of God's creatures, how are you getting on with the lovely Spider? I seem to remember you disliking her.'

'Spider?' It hadn't been much more than a month ago, but so much had happened since that book club meeting at Peter's presbytery, Mary felt as if years had passed. 'She's been so helpful since Grace was hurt, I've completely changed my mind about her.'

'And Guy? I think you've changed your mind about him as well.'

Mary looked at Peter thoughtfully. He was extraordinarily perceptive, and she was indeed feeling quite differently about Guy. When she'd been rushing around trying to combine eleven-hour working days with managing a household, it had some-times felt as if her husband was just another burden, wanting to talk to her, claiming her attention when she had a hundred and one other things to do. But Grace's accident had forced her to take time off work. Without the constant pressure of Lock Chase, she'd had the chance to see her home life more clearly.

'Guy's been wonderful, helping out, fetching and carrying, he does things without my even asking.' She stopped to look at Peter. 'Grace's accident has given me time to think, and I've realized something.'

'Go on.'

'All those times when I've been irritable with Guy, I thought it was his fault. He never listened, he never helped, he was always coming out with those Latin quips of his. But now,' Mary scuffed a toe around in the grass, embarrassed. 'Now I think I was wrong. I've been so tired and cross all the time, and Guy's been the only person I could take it out on.'

'Have you told him?'

'I haven't, actually.'

'Well, I think you should.'

That afternoon, when Grace and Sir John had gone off to the dairy together, she took Guy down to the moat. As she watched the sunshine dancing on the water, Mary thought how difficult it was to apologize. Still, it had to be done. She turned to face her husband, and as she looked at his familiar face, she noticed that faint worry lines had crept around his eyes and under the hair that flopped over his forehead. The words suddenly seemed very simple.

She reached out to take his hand. 'I'm not very good at saying sorry, but I am, truly. I've been vile to you. I don't know how you've put up with me.'

'Well, you have been a bit crotchety, but it's quite understandable.'

She couldn't let him make it so easy for her. 'I've been a lot worse than crotchety. I've been exhausted and bad-tempered, and I've let myself take all my tiredness and irritability out on you, when you're the man I love most in the world. You've been so patient, why didn't you tell me?'

Guy looked embarrassed. Mary understood how hard he found it to talk about intimate things like emotions, but she had to clear the air. 'Go on, why didn't you tell me I was being so impossible?'

'Well, I suppose you've often seemed too busy to talk.' There was a pause. 'And I just thought it was easier if I slipped off to Cambridge and kept out of your way.'

'So that's why you were never around to help.'

'You never asked me to.'

Mary felt a smile twitching the corner of her lips. How typical of a man. Why hadn't he seen what needed doing rather than waiting to be told? But she wasn't going to say that. Things were going to be different between them, and from now on, if she wanted him to do something for her, she wouldn't expect him to guess, she'd just ask. There was another thing she'd decided. She would be back in the office the following week and she was determined to keep her hours under control. A proper work–life balance. That was what she'd have.

Pulling Guy's head down to her, she kissed his mouth. 'Shall we go upstairs?'

'*Da mi basia mille.*'

'I'll give you a billion kisses if you want them.'

Much later, Mary was lazing in a hot bath when Guy put his head round the door. 'Hurry up and get ready. There's a book club meeting tonight.'

Wiping bubbles off her face, Mary looked at him in surprise. 'But we can't possibly go. I haven't even read the book.'

'I should think not.' He walked across and held out a towel for her. 'Primo Levi's far too depressing for you. We'll just go along and listen.'

Mary wasn't used to Guy being assertive. 'What about Grace?'

'She's getting stronger by the day and it'll do Father good to look after her. You get dressed while I make sure there's something for them to eat while we're out.'

'*What* did you just say?' The words were muffled by the big bath towel that Guy was hugging round her.

'Don't sound so surprised, I do manage to feed myself quite often, you know, I simply read a recipe. Any literate person can cook.' He unwrapped the towel and looked at her. 'And you need to eat more, Mary. I don't think you've had a proper meal since Dimple died.'

As Mary was tugging on a pair of jeans, she noticed something strange. Guy was right. The waistband was distinctly loose.

They hardly talked on the drive to Urban's Martello tower, but Mary occasionally reached across to stroke Guy's hand, and when they arrived she sat close to him on the sheep-cropped grass in the shadow of the tower. Above their heads, dusk-hunting birds chittered after gnats, while beyond the shallow cliffs the sea could be heard softly slapping against the shingle beach. Urban had provided an extravagant picnic, but liking the feel of her loose trousers Mary ate carefully, while only half-listening to the book club's analysis of Levi's Auschwitz autobiography.

'Bother!' Peter began scratching a leg vigorously. 'Can we go inside now, Urban? These mosquitoes think I'm manna from heaven and I've had enough of this dîner sur l'herbe experience, delightful though it has been.' As he stood up, he pointed to one of the picnic baskets. 'Guy dear, would you help me carry this in?'

With Guy's height and Peter's lack of it, they were a lopsided sight as they walked back to the tower, the wicker basket swinging between them. The rest of the group followed, gathering up plates and glasses that were scattered over the grass.

Urban waited for Mary, who had lingered to admire the first stars pricking through the violet sky. 'You're back in the office next week, aren't you? I'd value a bit of your female intuition on something Alan Dove's asked us to do.'

'Alan Dove? I'm not sure I could be impartial.'

'I'd really like you to know what you think. I trust your judgement.'

Even though she knew that Urban was an arch manipulator, Mary felt ridiculously flattered. 'Well, if you're sure you want me, I'll be there. I've got masses to catch up on and I'll need to double-check with Bella, but I'm pretty sure I've some time free on Wednesday morning if that suits you?'

'I'll make sure it does.'

'By the way, what does Dove want you to do?'

'Well, it's really very unusual. You know he's selling his Lung Division? We've done a sale valuation and we've even presented it to his board. But now he's . . .' Urban stopped abruptly.

Mary looked back at him questioningly and saw Meg coming up behind them. It was surprising how silently such a big woman could walk.

Wednesday's meeting had a frosty start. There was no sign of Mary, and Urban was drumming his fingers on his desk when Spider sauntered in, late as usual.

'What happened to *you* yesterday?' He didn't even wait till she'd closed the door. 'There I was in Alan Dove's office for a key meeting and you send some pitiful excuse at the last minute and don't turn up. Gut ache indeed. Gut ache, my giddy aunt. I've never heard you say your guts ached in all the years I've known you.'

Instead of apologizing, she eyed him coolly. 'That shows how little effort you've made to get to know me in all those years, doesn't it?'

Urban was astonished. It was such an extraordinarily unfair thing to say. He was saved from having to answer by Mary bursting in, flustered and apologetic.

'Oh, I'm *dreadfully* sorry. The trains! I've had to come up from Cambridge. Guy insisted I had dinner with him last night.'

'Don't worry. Here, let me tidy you up.' Spider leant across and tucked an escaping label back into the collar of Mary's jacket.

'Thanks. And don't you look fantastic?' Mary was smiling at Spider as if she was suddenly her best friend. 'That dress gives you great curves.' So that was it, thought Urban. Spider was dressing differently. He'd wondered why he'd been feeling faintly disturbed by her recently. His mind wandered back to the previous week.

She'd been walking towards him down the corridor, her body silhouetted against the low-energy lighting that came on in the evenings. It was extraordinary, but she seemed to have changed shape. If she hadn't spoken, he'd have assumed it was someone else. 'Christ, Urban. Don't you even have a life? This is the third night running I've been in the office with you.'

'Hypocrite. Since you've been in the office too, you can't have a life either.'

'My work is my life,' she had said sententiously. 'And I'm frigging starving. Let's send out for a giant pizza and give ourselves a break.'

Eating and joking in his office, he had unintentionally touched her hand for rather too long, and suddenly it was as if she had turned to ice. He was used to her sudden outbursts of temper, but that leap from teasing laughter to cold formality had been very disconcerting. Just like now. He had no idea why Spider should be so chilly towards him.

Urban spoke uncharacteristically sharply. 'You women are incredibly unprofessional. One of you tips up late and the other doesn't even bother to tip up at all to a crucial client meeting.' Frowning at them, he went on, 'Since you've both finally deigned to appear today we'd better get started, but don't expect me to forget this come appraisal time.'

Mary raised an eyebrow, while Spider just stared blankly at

him. Neither said a word, and Urban began to feel a bit foolish. Realizing he'd better take a lead, he held his hands up in mock surrender. 'Oh, all right. That was over the top and I apologize. I'll even kiss and make up with you two witches if you'll let me.'

'As long as you promise you'll hate every minute of it.' Mary was smiling now. Reaching up to grab his shoulders, she pulled him down towards her and kissed him three times on alternate cheeks. Urban felt his heart give an odd leap when Spider offered him her hand and an ivory cheek. He brushed it gently with his lips.

Harmony restored, he said, 'So let's get down to business. Alan Dove's had an indicative offer of five hundred and twenty million quid for his Lung Division. We carried out a valuation and that figure seemed perfectly fair. Now Dove's suddenly come back and asked us to value it at six hundred million. He says we should have included a price for their genomics research.'

He could see Mary putting on that firm-jawed look of hers. 'I can't believe you're even *dreaming* of rolling over for Alan Dove and saying you got the first valuation wrong.'

'It's not quite as straightforward as that.' Urban ran a hand through his hair. This was going to be a difficult decision. 'My guess is that Dove can't make the sums work. If he buys Skinshine for eight hundred million and sells the Lung Division for five-twenty, he'll have to raise just short of three hundred million quid. That's one hell of a pile for a company Pneumatech's size. On the other hand, if he can get six hundred million for the Lung Division then he's only got two hundred million to find and that's presumably do-able. Silly sod. He should have got the Lung Division sold and the funding safely in place before he had a pop at Skinshine. The question is, are we going to help Dove out of the hole he's dug for himself?'

Spider seemed to be making a close study of her elegant hands. 'What happens to our client if he can't sell the Lung Division at all? What then?'

'To put it bluntly, if Alan Dove can't sell it, he's totally screwed. He's committed to buying Skinshine.'

'He can't be,' put in Mary. 'He'll need his shareholders to agree first. The deal will be conditional on that. The same'll go for selling his Lung Division.'

'You're right.' Urban nodded. 'Of course you're right. He'll need to get formal approval for both deals at his Annual General Meeting. Mid-October I think it is.'

'So he can wriggle out of buying Skinshine any time until his AGM, but after that he's stuffed if the Lung Division isn't sold?' Spider was still examining her hands as she said this.

'That's about it.'

Urban asked Mary what she thought.

'Ethically I think we should refuse to help. I could easily live with the collapse of Dove's reputation on my conscience.' As Mary paused, Urban was aware of Spider staring at her, tense and alert. 'On the other hand, he *is* a Lock Chase client and I suppose we should at least understand what he's asking.'

'You're the scientist, what do you think, Spider?'

'Sorry, Urban, miles away. What were you saying?'

'This genomic stuff. Should we have included it? Is it worth another eighty million pounds?'

'The value question's very difficult. They have a couple of brilliant scientists on board and their work could be worth a fortune one day. But whether you'd put a value of eight hundred million, eighty million or eightpence on their research up to now, I couldn't say without having a look at it. The whole field is just too new.'

'And what exactly is this "whole field"?' prompted Mary.

'It's the Book Of Life, every single human gene decoded. Theoretically it's medical Nirvana, but there's a bloody great problem and I'd be surprised if Dove's cracked it.' Spider leaned forward to emphasize her words. 'A human genome uses one hell of a lot of terabytes. Real progress needs awesome computers and I doubt if Dove's researchers have got that kind of capacity.'

'But is it impossible?' asked Mary.

'No,' Spider said slowly. 'Not impossible.'

Urban ruffled a hand through his hair as both women looked at him questioningly. 'Let's take this one step at a time. I'll tell Alan we're prepared to look at his research, and once we've done that we'll decide if we can sign up to his six hundred million figure. How much time d'you think you'll need, Spider?'

'I work all hours.' She smiled across at him. 'So it won't take long if I get a move on.'

TWENTY-THREE

One Saturday afternoon, Mary unexpectedly found herself with time on her hands. Grace had gone to see a school friend and Guy had taken the opportunity to go to Cambridge for a few contemplative hours in the University library.

Mary decided it was finally time she got to grips with her daughter's bedroom. Normally she would have bullied Grace to put her own clothes away, but she'd been very gentle with her since the accident, as a result of which there was now such a mess of clothing strewn across Grace's floor that it was quite hard to get the door open. Mary found the quiet folding and sorting surprisingly therapeutic and worked her way methodically across the floor.

At the bottom of a pile in the far corner of the room she found the bag that they had used to bring Grace's clothes back from the hospital. Gingerly she pulled out a T-shirt. Seeing dried blood on it, Mary shivered and threw it straight into the rubbish bag. She was about to do the same with the jodhpurs, which she had pulled out next, but then she paused. Grace might want another pony one day. It was silly to throw them away.

She went through the jodhpur pockets, expecting to find the normal litter of sweet wrappers from the toffees that Grace was always sharing with Dimple, but to her surprise they were almost empty. There was just one piece of paper, which Mary unfolded.

Four words were written in careful block capitals. KEEP AWAY FROM HEDGIES.

Mary stared at the note. Hedgies. Hedge funds. From nowhere, Alan Dove's words came back to her. 'There are a lot of peculiarly vicious wasps in that particular apple-cart. Be careful you don't find yourself getting stung.' As she remembered what he'd said, everything suddenly seemed to fall into place. The hedge fund inquiry was looking at Pneumatech, potentially jeopardizing Dove's huge American deal. He'd hoped to scare her with that talk about vicious wasps, but she hadn't stopped helping the Treasury and so he'd tried something stronger. Gracie *had* heard a shot. Alan Dove must have fired at Dimple and then put this note in her daughter's pocket. To warn Mary off.

She slumped down on Grace's bed, horrified. What a wicked man, and to think she'd even helped him. Only last week she'd agreed to that second valuation going out. Too late to try to stop it. Dove would have the report in his hands by now.

Once again, D'Arby was there waiting for him as Dove emerged from the stairwell.

'Delighted to see you again so soon, Alan. Unusual for us to have our vendors round here quite so often,' he added, as he led the way through Churngold Capital's reception area and into his office. 'There was something particular you wanted to tell me that couldn't be said over the telephone?' D'Arby sat back, leaving the question hanging in the air.

'You got the Lock Chase analysis safely, did you?' Dove caught himself bending forward. It didn't do to look eager. He forced himself to lean back and relax.

'Yes indeed. It tied in absolutely with what our technical advisers said. Essentially both firms were polite about your current drugs but iffy about the value of your genomic research. Could be this, could be that. That's the trouble with these consultants. They put in so many "ifs" and "buts" it's hard to work out if they're actually giving you any comfort at all.'

'Well, I'm glad the two lots of analysis agreed, at any rate. Does it bring you any closer to the six hundred million pounds I'm asking for the business?' He couldn't stop the words coming out in a rush. 'You see, Ralph, the fact is I'm in rather a hurry to complete. I'm buying a terrific company in the States and the Lung Division sale's paying for it.' He paused. 'Obviously I could just borrow the money, but this way saves having to raise a lot of debt.' Dove knew he was a bad liar. Of course he couldn't raise enough debt. He felt his eyes sliding away guiltily and hoped the lie wasn't visible behind his thick lenses.

D'Arby didn't rush to reply, and Dove felt himself shifting in his chair. Eventually D'Arby seemed to make his mind up. 'I appreciate you being so candid, Alan, and I'll help you out.' Dove's heart leapt. 'Let's agree the six hundred today and move to Heads of Agreement as soon as possible. If we get our lawyers straight on to it, I don't see any reason why we shouldn't have something signed by the end of next week.'

'The end of next week? That's fantastic! That'll mean I can get the announcement out in plenty of time ahead of the AGM in mid-October.'

'Hang on, Alan,' D'Arby interrupted. 'Our agreement will be subject to due diligence. If the due dilly throws up anything we don't like, we'll be able to pull out with absolutely no recourse. You do understand that?'

'Of course, yes!' Dove had a sudden vision of his board members' faces when they heard about this triumph. He couldn't wait to get on the phone. 'Let's shake hands on it and I'll put my lawyer to work straight away.'

'No, we won't shake hands just yet, that's asking for trouble. We'll shake hands when the due dilly's done and the whole deal's cut and dried. Look, Alan, I admire anyone who's built a great business from nothing like you have, but you've never sold a business before.' There was a pause. 'You'll have something to announce by the end of next week, but in reality what we've got is an expectation of a deal, not the real thing. Savvy?'

'Of course, and don't worry. Until the AGM, everything's conditional from my side too.'

Mary sat facing Aiden Elginbrode in his office. KEEP AWAY FROM HEDGIES. The note lay on the table between them, its black capitals still clear despite the many hands Mary had passed it to.

Guy's initial reaction had been shock. 'I can't believe it! Someone must have – my God! Someone put this in Grace's pocket while she was unconscious. It's almost unthinkable!' He had rapidly moved on to fear. 'This is a threat, Mary. There's someone out there who'll do anything to stop your Treasury work. Someone who cares more about money than a child's safety.'

'I think someone shot at Dimple and that's why she broke her leg. Gracie's always said she heard a bang.' After a pause, Mary had added, 'Alan Dove tried to warn me off when he came to dinner.'

'No.' He had shaken his head firmly. 'Not Alan Dove. You can't seriously think a man like him would attack a young girl on a pony.' Mary had indeed thought that, but as she had no proof she had held her tongue. 'It'll be some stranger from that shady world you're investigating. You could be in real danger. In fact I'm wondering whether you shouldn't resign from Lock Chase altogether.'

His concern had been touching but irrational. She'd recovered from the shock of Grace's injuries and Dimple's death, and now that she was back at work she felt strong and capable again. 'I'm a big girl, Guy,' Mary had smiled. 'Not quite as big as I used to be, but I can still look after myself. And anyway I can't possibly resign,' she hadn't been able to stop herself adding. 'We need my salary, remember?'

Guy had shaken his head, clearly unconvinced, but all he had said was, 'Will you at least get Urban to find some way of protecting you?'

'I'm going to talk to him the moment I'm next in the office. Promise.'

Spider had been with Urban when Mary had walked in, waving the piece of paper. 'Just look what I found in Gracie's pocket!' She had slapped the note down in front of them. 'Hedgies. Hedge funds. It's a threat.'

'Whatever are you talking about?' Urban's voice had been kind but firm. 'I can't understand a word you're saying.'

Taking a deep breath, Mary had explained that she'd found the note in the pocket of Grace's jodhpurs, unworn since Dimple's death. 'Someone shot at Gracie's pony then put this note in her pocket and I can guess just who it was. Alan Dove wants me to stop working with the Treasury. He thinks he can frighten me off.'

Like Guy, Urban hadn't been convinced. 'You're understandably sensitive, Mary, it's absolutely to be expected. That ghastly accident was a terrible shock to you. But the thing is, Dove's a client. We've worked for him for some while now and there's never been any sign that he's not just a normal, decent, upright bully.'

Neither woman had smiled. Mary wasn't listening any more. 'Alan Dove did this and I'm going to prove it.'

Spider had followed her out of Urban's office. 'D'you really think Dove shot your kid's pony?'

'Yes, I do.'

'Well, I believe you. I want you to know that. It's about time that arsehole got his comeuppance.' There had been a pause between them, then Spider had added, 'By the way, you've lost weight. Suits you.' Mary had been left smiling at the compliment while Spider had stalked off down the corridor, her black hair flicking behind her like the tail of a cat.

Both Guy and Urban had been acting obtuse about Dove, but Elginbrode had to believe her. Pushing the note further towards him, she looked straight into his eyes. 'So you see it *has* to have been him. He must think I've got too near the knuckle. I'll bet he's terrified in case the finger gets pointed too publicly at Pneumatech and it ruins his ambitious little games. It's obvious. Alan Dove showed his hand by warning me off when he came to dinner. I didn't take any notice, so he upped the ante.'

Elginbrode nodded thoughtfully but said nothing.

'All I want is the chance to prove the case against Dove. Surely you can help me? After all, it's virtually part and parcel of the work we're doing for the inquiry anyway, isn't it?'

Elginbrode pursed his lips and finally spoke. 'I'm afraid I've just been informed that the hedge fund inquiry is going to be deferred.'

It took a moment for his words to sink in. 'You mean,' stammered Mary eventually, 'you mean after all our work? After all the proof we've got? All the insider trading, the market manipulation, the concert parties? But it's an obscene industry!'

'Certain *very* powerful people don't want to see the hedge fund industry being regulated. And they don't just have power, these people have influence and money. Everyone who can be bought has been bought, and with more than enough cash to kill any inquiry stone dead.'

May was shaking her head in astonishment. 'I simply can't believe it. Surely there's someone somewhere who can't be bought?'

'Oh, indeed. Yes indeed. They'll have been silenced by platitudes. "It's a global industry, so if we regulate it here, the hedge funds will simply move elsewhere." "The City of London will lose out and some foreign rival will benefit." Very effective arguments.'

'But that's ridiculous. If we all followed that logic, no one anywhere would ever stand up for their principles.'

'Indeed.'

There was a long silence, during which Mary found herself struggling with unexpected tears. Eventually she broke it by saying so quietly that it was almost a whisper, 'My daughter could have been killed. The pony she adored is dead. Alan Dove's a monster. Couldn't you help me nail him?'

'I can see no reason why I should not.' Elginbrode was a dry and intellectual man. Mary had rarely seen him smile, but when he did the effect was captivating. 'You must understand that I have to be a little circumspect.'

She returned the smile and nodded eagerly as he went on, 'Naturally I have access to the share registers of listed companies. And in special circumstances there are other sources available to me. Telephone records, bank account details, and so on.' Elginbrode stood up, always the way he indicated that a meeting was over. 'You may rest assured that I'll be keeping an eye on the activities of Dr Alan Dove and his company.'

TWENTY-FOUR

The City clocks were chiming seven as Ivan Straw hurried along Threadneedle Street. Head down, he shouldered his way between the shoals of half-awake traders hurrying to catch the opening markets. He hated September, holidays over, weather cooler, days shorter. And he loathed early morning starts, struggling out of bed when his blood sugar levels were at their lowest and the black dog was waiting to grip him by the throat. A shag sometimes helped lift his spirits, but this morning Francesca had turned a sleepy back when he'd tried to feel her up.

Sodding market announcements. Always so bloody early. He wouldn't even have time for a fag. Buggeration. Fuck everything. Nearly there. Better try to pull himself together. He managed to raise his eyes from the pavement just in time to see Alan Dove's driver pulling up at the narrow passageway which led down to the Livery Hall. Stupid dick, coming in that huge car. Ostentatious pile of crap. He forced a smile.

'Morning, Ivan! Everything set?' You had to hand it to him, Dove looked bloody calm for a man who was about to unleash news of two massive deals on an unsuspecting financial world.

'Fine, fine.' Ivan managed to squeeze the words out, hoping that he wouldn't be expected to say anything else until he'd got some caffeine into his system.

The smell of soup from long dead dinners met them as they walked inside. In the far corner of the chamber where he had sat through so many City presentations, Ivan spotted Pneumatech's advisers drinking coffee together. Only after he had burnt his mouth on one cup and was half way through a second did he have enough of an energy surge to join them. Advice was flooding over Dove as lawyers, spin-doctors and accountants tried to prove their worth.

'We're expecting a really big turn-out,' said an eager-looking young PR adviser. 'There was a rumour going round the City last night that this was a not-to-be-missed presentation!'

'I've brought along a summary of the Heads of Agreement with Churngold Capital in case you need to refer to it. My team were up all night finalizing the documentation.' What a tit Thomas Butler was, Ivan thought. Always puffing up how hard his dreary law firm worked.

'We spoke to Skinshine yesterday evening.' That was the PR shoving his oar in again. 'They've confirmed they're happy with the final announcement and they'll put out their version when the US markets open. You may want to have a quick glance at what they're going to say. I've got it with me here.'

A woman's voice broke through. 'Dr Dove, we've got a lot of people arriving now. We've moved them into the Great Parlour till you're ready for them.'

Ivan caught Dove's elbow and muttered, 'Good luck up there. Sock it to them.'

'Right between the eyes,' Dove replied as he made his way on to the platform.

Ivan glanced at his watch. Exactly seven thirty. These Livery bods were good time-keepers even if they were filthy coffee-makers. As a gilt clock chimed the half-hour, the chamber doors were flung open and a stream of people pushed their way in. From where he was standing, Ivan counted nearly fifty analysts, all grabbing seats and copies of the Stock Exchange announcement that had been left on each chair. As he watched them skimming through the pages and saw their looks of amazement, he felt a moment of quiet triumph. It was he who had masterminded the Skinshine deal, and none of these bastards had had the first bloody idea about it. He was a sodding genius.

A hush fell over the room as Dove stood up to speak. Ivan was surprised to hear how calm a presenter he was. Balls of steel. There was even a small ripple of applause when he revealed the sale price of the Lung Division. There had been a broad consensus in the City that it was worth between four-fifty and five. Six hundred million quid was way beyond anyone's estimates.

As the analysts rushed back to their desks, so the financial journalists began to straggle in. Seeing that Dove was immediately surrounded by his corporate hangers-on, Ivan slipped out for a smoke. It was raining as he got out on to the pavement, but he didn't bloody care. That first drag of nicotine deep into his lungs lightened his mood as much as a whole skyful of sunshine. He had just smoked his first fag down to the stub and was thinking about having a second when his mobile rang. It was one of the Wolkenbank traders, giving him an update on Pneumatech's share price. Having listened to the news, he hurried back into the Livery Hall and elbowed his way through to Dove's side.

'Your announcement's hit the markets like a bombshell. Your stock's up bloody forty per cent and rising.'

For a second Dove stared up at him, a wide grin splitting his fleshy lips. Ivan thought that if it had been his company's share price taking off like that, he'd be capering about all over the place, but Dove always seemed to keep himself under iron control. The smile was swiftly gone.

'Great news,' was all he said. 'Now let's see if I can wow the scribblers.'

Ivan could see from the speed of pencils flashing across notepads that the journalists were indeed wowed. He watched Dove give another calm performance, and when he had finished, quite a few hands shot up with questions.

'Alan, the Skinshine deal sounds really interesting but aren't you afraid that e-commerce will ultimately destroy the retail environment?' This came from an earnest girl in the front row.

'If you mean the internet will stop women from going to shops, I wish you'd let my wife know.' This raised a ripple of laughter. 'But the point is, you can't have a beauty treatment over the web. All round the world, the number of per capita visits to the beauty parlour is rising. Our deal will take advantage of this trend by offering the world's most advanced cosmeceuticals in those beauty salons. It's "win-win-win". Great for F-ACE, great for Skinshine, great for our customers.'

'Dr Dove, some of those F-ACE products you told us about sound like fairy tales. Are you really telling me I'll never have to dye my hair again?' Another ripple of laughter passed round the hall. The journalist asking this question had unkempt, greying hair that looked as if it hadn't seen shampoo, let alone a dye bottle, for some considerable time.

'Madam, within a few years we'll have you wearing your long golden hair like Lady Godiva.'

'Never been starkers on a horse in my life, never been to Coventry in my life either. Still, I get your point. My readers will love this.'

After several more questions along these lines, Ivan's attention had begun to wander when a woman with startlingly red hair and great knockers stood up. 'Amy Flower, *Daily Business*. Can you tell us why you decided to execute two such big transactions simultaneously? It's fairly risky that you're selling half your company. But it feels *extraordinarily* risky that at the same time you're buying a huge new business in the retail sector which you've never worked in and on a continent where you've never operated before.'

Ivan felt his hands clenching. Amy Flower was clearly a bright bird. Would Dove be able to handle the exocet she'd fired at him?

'My board have pondered long and hard over these deals, Amy. We came to the conclusion that the sale of the Lung Division makes sense because it will no longer fit within the group and we have a buyer prepared to pay us six hundred million pounds. Birds, hands and bushes come to mind, I think. As for the Skinshine acquisition, we are buying a ready-made sales outlet in the world's biggest beauty market for the world's best beauty products. If I were to offer you the secret of eternal youth, wouldn't you grab it with both hands?'

That was good, bloody good, thought Ivan. Someone shouted from the back of the Hall, 'We all know Amy's already found *that*. She's really eighty-five!'

Ivan watched as the redhead tried to return to her point, but the mood was broken and Dove sensibly called an end to the meeting. 'I'm afraid we're out of time, hope you got what you came for.'

Ivan moved to Dove's side as he stepped off the dais. 'Well done, mate.'

'Thanks, Ivan. I could do with a coffee.'

As they walked back down the length of the hall together, Alan Dove pointed to a woman sitting on her own, apparently absorbed in the press announcement. 'Whatever's Mary Kersey doing here?' he asked.

'So that's Mary Kersey, is it?' Ivan scanned her face to make sure he'd remember it. Snub nose, coppery mop, she didn't *look* like a toff. 'Not a lot to write home about face-wise, is she?'

'I think she's rather charming. Lovely grey eyes. But Ivan . . .' There was a note of worry in his voice. 'Do you think she's here because of that Treasury report on hedge funds?'

'No, I don't. It's been put right back in its box.' And she should be back in her box too, the aristocratic cow. Why the fuck was she here?

Dove was talking again. 'No hedge fund inquiry? Good gracious. I thought it was a certainty. Why ever was it dropped?'

'Oh, there are ways.' Ivan looked away to hide a smirk. He'd done his own bit with the Kersey woman, and he could just imagine the strings that had been pulled by the Russian and his contacts. 'Best not to ask.'

While they were drinking a celebratory cup of tepid coffee, Ivan's mobile flashed with a message. Having read it, he barged through the gaggle of advisers and extracted Dove to give him the news. 'I've just heard from the dealing room at Wolkenbank. Your share price is still rocketing up. The world's thrilled with your twin transactions.'

Ivan didn't add that one Russian billionaire would be particularly thrilled. Dyengi was already happy about the pony. 'The *loshad* die? You shoot good, Ivaan,' he had said. And now there was Pneumatech, the Russian would be dead pleased. On Ivan's advice, Platon Dyengi had piled into the shares and after today's announcement he'd be sitting on a fat profit, with more to come when the deals got formal approval. He'd give Dyengi the nod to get out of Pneumatech a few days after Dove's AGM. All the fat should be in the share price by then.

A little later that morning, Meg Dewey was lolling in front of her computer idly scanning the business news. 'Well, stuff me for a mushroom,' she said aloud, sitting bolt upright as Dove's announcement caught her eye. The Pneumatech share price was surging upwards. Bugger. She should have bought even more when it was cheap.

Meg leaned over to pick up the anthracite handset and made two brief calls. 'Our stake in Brother Dove's outfit's worth twenty million and rising. I don't want to lose a penny of it, so keep your ears pinned back, will you?'

Having printed off the text of that morning's announcement from Pneumatech, she stretched out comfortably and started to read carefully through it.

'What a bollock boring job this is,' Amy Flower sighed, doing a cat stretch in front of a *Daily Business* computer screen. Hot-desking in one of the paper's glass-walled cubicles, she was trawling through each mention of Pneumatech in every publication in the world. Dove had slid too smoothly over her questions that morning. There was a story to be found if only she looked hard enough, and so she'd fallen back on good old-fashioned investigative journalism. A bit of information here, another bit there, and suddenly they melded together and gave you a piece that none of your competitors had spotted.

The only problem with good old-fashioned journalism was that it needed lots of good old-fashioned work before you got the sniff of a story, and Amy was bored. She knew about Pneumatech's huge investment in computer systems courtesy of *Technology World*. She knew from *Recruitment Quarterly* that Dove had a new Head of Public Relations. All doubtless very interesting to someone, but Amy couldn't see how any of it could be of the least use to her.

She was just thinking about wandering down the corridor for a cup of coffee when her eyes flicked over an article in

Consultancy Forum. 'Bingo!' she breathed as she scanned it. 'Flaming bingo!'

Consultancy Forum was a serious magazine full of worthy articles on new management tools and techniques. The only spot of levity was a gossipy column called *The Consulting Room* and there was the piece she was looking for.

> *The Consulting Room hears that Lock Chase is firmly ensconced in Pneumatech and the lead Partners have been nicknamed 'Beauty and the Beast'. The Beauty is raven-haired Spider Wood, the Beast is Urban Palewski, head of the London office of Lock Chase and a devastatingly handsome heartbreaker.*
>
> *Will Beauty get her Beast? Watch this space. True to form, the reticent Lock Chasers refused to comment when we called them.*

Amy was delighted. That Pole had been dead sexy. High cheekbones, slanting brown eyes, dark, feathery hair. She dialled the Lock Chase number.

'Amy, of course I remember meeting you. Dinner at Alan Dove's house, wasn't it?'

She decided that the best way with Urban Palewski was to play it straight, which obviously meant inventing a story. The *Daily Business* was running a series on the world's top strategic consultancies, she extemporized. Could she interview Urban, either on or off the record?

'I'm really sorry, but it has to be no. We never talk about our clients and we never talk to the media about our business. It's our firm's policy and very tightly adhered to.'

There was a note of such finality in Urban's voice that she didn't bother to press him any further. With a sigh, she said goodbye as nicely as she could manage and hung up. She'd have to try the woman with the silly name.

Amy had a story planned for the beautiful Miss Wood, but it was with no expectation of success that she again rang the Lock Chase number.

'Spider Wood.'

'Oh hi! My name's Amy Flower and I was hoping you might be able to help me. Maybe meet up for a chat or something? I'm a financial journalist on the *Daily Business* – you may have read some of my stuff.'

'I may have done,' came the unhelpful reply.

'The thing is, Spider, I'm really keen to move into consultancy. I've always been interested in business but I sort of slipped into journalism by accident. I've got a First in Modern Languages,' Amy hoped the lie sounded fluent, 'and of course I've learned a huge amount about the business world from writing about it. My contact book's as long as your arm.' At least that part was true.

'Sounds interesting,' the answer came after a long pause. 'How do you think I could help?'

'Well, I've obviously talked to loads of consultants as part of my job but I've never really asked what it's like to be in the business. I mean, what's it like for women? Do I have the right skills, that kind of stuff. So maybe I could buy you lunch some time? The only thing is,' Amy added for authenticity, 'I'd be grateful if you didn't mention this to a soul. I wouldn't want anyone on the paper knowing I'm thinking of leaving or they'd all be after my job like bloody piranhas.'

'That's OK, I won't tell.' There was another long pause. 'I'm pretty tied up at the moment but I've got a window free for a lunch next month. Would the nineteenth of October work for you?'

Amy leafed quickly through the pages of her diary. She noticed that Pneumatech's Annual General Meeting was on the

eighteenth of October and guessed that Spider must be tied up
with her client until then.

'The nineteenth of October would be perfect. One o'clock?
There's a great Lebanese place under the old Enron building.
We won't be recognized. No one eats there on a midweek
lunchtime.'

'Suits me fine – see you then.' Spider had hung up, leaving
Amy to wonder whether Miss Wood could possibly have believed
her story, and if not, why in the world she'd agreed to meet her.

Still pondering this, Amy ambled happily down to the paper's
rest area. Such an inappropriate name, she thought. Its big sofas
saw all the real action at the *Daily Business*. This was where journalists would trade facts with each other and swap nuggets of
unprintable business gossip. Here flirtations were started and
secret meetings fixed, sometimes purely for lust, more often to
get another toehold on the slippery ladder leading to the Editor's
chair.

Disappointed at finding nobody there, Amy curled herself in
a corner of the largest sofa and began to flick idly through the
pages of airbrush in *Cheese!*.

'Well, bugger me,' she muttered to herself. 'I've spent the
whole morning trying to get a bead on the bloody man and
now I can't get away from him.'

The magazine had fallen open at an article on Juliana Dove,
with a photograph of her in her bedroom. Amy peered at it.
Mrs Dove looked rather sweet with that bovine face and those
huge brown eyes. Rather like a Jersey heifer. Though it was odd
to see a cow dressed in what appeared to be a ribbon-trimmed
meringue.

The Cheese! *team were thrilled to be invited into the gracious
Westminster home of Dr Alan Dove. Dr Dove is the well-known*

businessman, while top London hostess Juliana Dove hails from Luxembourg. As our pictures show, no expense was spared in creating a beautiful atmosphere of authentic elegance in the couple's charming house. Fashionable London queues up to be invited, attracted by the thrilling mix of top people always to be found there.

We hear that some famous politicians find the welcome at the Dove's division bell house so charming that they often 'drop in' between votes to take 'pot luck' at Juliana Dove's generous table. But there is room for only sixteen at a crush in Juliana's divine dining room. Cheese! is all agog to see what she can do on a larger canvas when she throws her circus-themed party later this month!

TWENTY-FIVE

There was a knock on Alan Dove's dressing-room door. He didn't look around when it opened, as he was concentrating on fighting the last pearl stud into his stiff white shirt, made to measure, as were most of his clothes. Off-the-peg shirts that fitted his thick bull's neck and shoulders were always too large for the rest of him.

Once the stud had been subdued, he turned to look at his wife, admiring her long satin dress, the colour of morello cherries. 'You look very nice,' he said, and indeed she did. Cunningly constructed and with a built-in brassiere, the dress lifted and separated Juliana's lavish bosoms, nestled between which sat the ruby and diamond pendant he'd given her on their tenth wedding anniversary. There were faint red marks where it had chafed her skin.

'Could you do up my zip, Alan? I can't reach to the top.'

She turned round, allowing him to see the pallor of her broad back and shoulders, normally modestly hidden under one of her old-fashioned blouses. How beautiful the translucent effect of skin never exposed to the sun looked on a well-built woman like his wife. As he pulled up her zip, he gave a brief caress to the nape of her neck and had to resist an urge to kiss the creamy flesh of her throat. They were in a hurry.

'I think I have all the details of this evening planned properly.' Juliana sounded calm and competent. 'The theme is original and I've kept the cost inside your budget. Naturally I'll take care of the Royals and our other VIP guests, but is there anyone else you'd like me to pay special attention to?'

He looked up sharply and their eyes met in his cheval glass. In the mirror, steamy from his recent bath, he caught himself with an expression which he tried never to show. He looked anxious. Juliana had seen it too.

'My dear, is anything wrong? Your business? I thought everything was going so well for you?'

Dove smiled briefly and shook his heavy head. 'Everything's going fine. This is my night of triumph.' He paused. Nothing to worry his wife about, but still, maybe she could help. 'Perhaps you could turn the charm on for a chap called Ralph D'Arby? He runs Churngold Capital. You'll remember, that's the private equity firm buying our Lung Division and there seems to be a bit of a delay in signing the deal with them. It'll soon be the end of September and I was hoping to have everything tied up by now.'

'Of course I'll talk to him, Alan. And I'm so sorry if this deal is making you anxious.'

He tossed his head as if to throw off any residual cares. 'I'm sure there's absolutely nothing to worry about, the sale's all but closed. I've never had better press, share price still soaring, my board eating out of my hand. No, Juliana,' he concluded firmly, 'there's nothing, absolutely *nothing*, to worry about.'

Guy and Mary were getting ready in the cramped bedroom of their Battersea flat.

When she had opened the invitation to Juliana Dove's party, a horrible grinning clown had leapt out of the envelope at her, showering the kitchen table with glitter. Mary's first reaction had been to throw the thing straight into the bin.

Convinced that Alan Dove was behind the event that had hurt Grace and killed her beloved Dimple, Mary had never wanted to see him again unless he was behind bars. But after a few minutes thought, she realized that she'd be more likely to get him behind those bars if she accepted this ghastly invitation. She might just find out something at his party, when he was off his guard. With a small sigh she had retrieved the invitation from among the kitchen rubbish.

'Damn and blast!' Guy exploded as he struggled with his bow tie. 'I hate dressing up as a penguin. Just remind me why we're going to this wretched affair?'

'Do be fair. I go to Cambridge dinners for you.' Mary turned to watch him fight a recalcitrant knot. 'And Guy, you know *exactly* why we're going.'

'Because you think Dr Dove's a pony killer, I haven't forgotten.' His tie subdued, he turned to look at her, a slow smile crossing his face. 'I'm bound to say you do scrub up well. I wish you'd wear revealing clothes more often.'

'I'm not showing too much up top, am I?' She felt herself blushing like a schoolgirl. 'I'm sensitive about over-exposure.'

'I can't imagine why you should be.'

'Did I never tell you?' Mary said. 'In my formative years I always had to say goodnight to Grandmama Ivybridge before I went out. One evening I was wearing a top that might conceivably have shown my navel if I'd raised both arms above my head. She took one look and made me go back and change. I've never forgotten it. "You look inexpressibly vulgar in that revealing article," she said. "There are *some* parts of your anatomy which should be seen *only* by your husband." I've never flaunted my midriff since.' Looking down at how the grey silk of her dress hung straight to the floor instead of straining across her middle as it would have done only a month or so ago, she added cheerfully, 'Though now I've got so much thinner, I'm tempted to try a bit more flaunting.'

'Mary, my love, the world's loss is my gain. I can't tell you what it means to me to have exclusive viewing of your tummy. I believe it's the secret of our happiness.' He gave her a hug. 'Though I did like you with a bit more padding – you're getting awfully thin.' Stroking her arm, he added meditatively, 'Why don't we skip the party and have a huge plate of pasta and an early night instead?'

'No, I've got work to do,' she said firmly. 'Tomorrow, perhaps?'

It was raining heavily when they climbed out of a taxi at the top of the long, concrete ramp that ran down to the entrance of Tate Modern, where the Doves' party was being held. Hand in hand, they splashed between a line of spluttering torches, scarcely noticing the pair of baby elephants shivering miserably with their minders outside the glass entrance.

Once inside, they stood recovering their breath and taking in the extraordinary sight in front of them. The contents of an entire circus seemed to have been transported into the Turbine Hall. Everywhere they looked there were jugglers tossing balls, stilt-walkers covered in gold body-paint, and women in spangled leotards contorting themselves. A troupe of acrobats padded about on their hands, their feet floating surreally among the faces of the Doves' guests, while miniature ponies in silver harness and feathers were led around the edges of the party, occasionally slithering on the polished flooring and dropping little piles of dung.

'This must be costing an absolute fortune,' Mary said in astonishment, 'unless Dove's paying for it through some dodgy tax break. Oh good, just what I need,' she added as a clown approached them carrying a tray of multi-coloured cocktails. Despite the layers of pancake make-up, he managed a dismissive look when Mary asked what the drink was.

'It's a Rainbow, madam. Vodka jeujed up with fruit purée. Very fashionable on the scene, a Rainbow is.' Mary reached out to take a glass, but Guy shook his head in horror. With a swing of his baggy blue-and-white-striped hips, the clown moved off, leaving Mary shuddering with repressed laughter.

'I don't think we're smart enough to be Scene,' she said, taking her husband's arm. 'Shall we wander round being unseen instead? I might overhear something useful about Dove.' They strolled off through the party, catching scraps of conversation.

'. . . Shame he never got that peerage. He'd been trying to get up the PM's back passage for years, sponsoring all those city academies and what-not. No one told the poor old sod he should simply have given the Party a bung. The widow's livid, so I hear.'

'. . . Louboutin, who else? Look, the fur runs right under the instep. Shame I can't wear them more than a couple of times, everyone will have seen them. I'll pass them on to my Bratislavan if they fit her, though she's a giantess. So used to the little Filipinos, weren't we? We'll have to get longer beds for these new au pairs.'

'. . . I told him he was an old-fashioned fool. Borrowing up to the hilt's the name of the game these days. Cheap debt, asset prices rocketing, there's no way you can lose.'

'Would you like a drink?' A tiny waitress was standing in front of them, staggering to keep hold of a jeroboam of champagne and a tray of brimming glasses.

'Yes please,' Mary said, putting down the Rainbow, which had turned out to be quite disgusting.

Guy also took a glass. Seeing him about to prop an elbow against a scantily draped female statue on a marbled column, Mary said urgently, 'Be careful!' but it was too late.

The statue squealed loudly. 'Excuse *me*, Mister!'

'I do beg your pardon!' Guy, his elbow covered in chalk from

the Living Statue's feet, stepped smartly backwards. There was
a loud curse from behind him, and they both swung round to
see a short, dark-eyed man glaring at them, champagne dripping down the huge diamond studs in his white shirt-front. 'I'm
so sorry,' Guy said hastily. 'Coppelia here gave me a fright when
she came to life.'

It was over in an instant. Four huge minders surrounded the
man, jostling Guy roughly aside as they moved their client away
to somewhere safer. Mary stared after them, frowning. 'I think
that was Platon Dyengi you bumped into. He's one of those
oligarchs.'

'Platon? Not much of the Platonic vision there, by the looks
of him.' As Guy was busy brushing chalk off his sleeve Mary
didn't bother to mention the tall, thin man she'd seen hovering
behind Dyengi. It was Ivan Straw, Dove's banker. Presumably
the financial brains behind Alan Dove's slimy deals.

She persuaded Guy to stay on for another two hours at the
party, drinking champagne and eating from an extravagant
buffet. But despite chatting to business acquaintances and
shamelessly eavesdropping on strangers' conversations, Mary
picked up nothing of any interest about their host. 'I think I've
drawn a blank here,' she said to Guy eventually, 'and my feet
are starting to hurt. Shall we go?'

'Yes, please,' he said fervently, and grabbing her arm he began
to steer her through the guests and circus entertainers towards
the doors.

'Hang on,' Mary said as they passed a sign for the cloakrooms.
'I'm just going to dive in here. Won't be a minute.'

When she came out again she found Guy standing waiting
for her, a thoughtful look on his face. As they emerged into the
rainy night, he said carefully, 'Rather an odd thing. Alan Dove
came up to me while you were in the Ladies and said how very

sorry he'd been to hear about Gracie. He sounded genuinely upset. I really do think you're wrong about him.'

Was it possible? Might it have been someone else entirely who had caused Grace's accident? The thoughts flickered through Mary's mind as they hurried up the long ramp towards the cab rank. As they climbed into a taxi, she felt her jaw clenching. Impossible. 'How could I be wrong?' she said, as soon as Guy had given the driver their Battersea address. 'First, Alan Dove warned me, second, he's got a motive, and third, it couldn't have been easier for him to slip across the fields from White Gables. For heaven's sake!' Mary stopped herself. 'Sorry, I didn't mean to be sharp. But who else could it have been?'

TWENTY-SIX

Urban was rather sad that the Pneumatech work was finishing. Sharing a client case with Spider had been fun. She was bright, she'd made him laugh, and she looked great in those new clothes of hers. There'd been the odd occasion when he'd found himself wondering if perhaps she was his type after all. He'd squashed that thought very fast. He liked women to be feminine, vulnerable. And besides, Spider was a colleague.

He was bent over his computer when he heard her coming into his office. 'Hi, Urban. How's our favourite client?'

'Dove just told me he won't need our help after his AGM, the arrogant bastard,' he grumbled at his screen. 'If you ask me, he's on a major ego trip. You worked your butt off doing that valuation, didn't you?'

'I know a shitload more about genomics now, that's for sure.' Spider sounded very cheerful. He looked up. She was wearing another new suit, a soft sort of olive colour, tightly nipped in at the waist.

It occurred to him that he was staring at her, and he quickly bent his head back down to his computer screen, muttering, 'I guess the Lung Division is Churngold Capital's problem now, not ours. Last time I spoke to Dove, he said they were keen as mustard.'

Urban didn't look up again until he heard his office door slam.

*

'Ralph? Alan Dove here.'

'Alan, hello. How are things going?'

Alan Dove frowned into the telephone as he tried to work out how far he could push D'Arby. 'I was calling to ask you the same question. Not that I'm worried,' he added hastily – he wouldn't want the man to think he had him over a barrel. 'I'd just feel more comfortable having the sale of my Lung Division all sewn up before the Skinshine purchase goes for approval at my AGM. It's on the eighteenth, if you remember.'

'That soon, is it?' Dove didn't believe that Ralph D'Arby could possibly have forgotten the date. He'd reminded him often enough. 'I don't think we'll be quite ready by then. I like to get my investors absolutely comfortable before I sign a deal.'

'But surely you've had plenty of time to get that done by now?' Dove tried to keep any hint of anxiety out of his voice.

'It's a slow old business. The billionaires who manage their own money move pretty fast, but my most loyal investors are American pension funds and Middle Eastern investment offices. They like to take things at a sensible pace, particularly when there are aspects that are a tad outside our box, like your Lung Division.'

'Outside the box? My Lung Division? But you've always said it was Churngold Capital's typical pharmaceutical investment. "Plain Vanilla" were your exact words.'

'Ah, but that was when we were offering five-twenty. Six hundred million and a pile of blue sky research is a different kettle of fish altogether. That's the piece I have to get my big investors happy with.'

'So who are these people? Would it help if I talked to them myself?'

'Talk to my investors? You must be joking!' Dove could hear

the incredulity from the other end of the line and wished he'd kept his mouth shut. 'Jedd Fontaine, sitting in Geneva with a pool of petrodollars he cares for like a triage nurse. He'd think I was trying to slip something past him if I even hinted you wanted to contact him.'

'OK, it was a silly suggestion.'

'And the Montana Teachers and Lecturers Society, I suppose you'd want to talk to them too?'

'Please forget it, Ralph. I've never even heard of them.'

'You'll know them as MOTELS. Jo-Marie Cary's their Chief Investment Officer, and she'd have my balls if I lost a cent of MOTELS money on a dodgy investment. And as for talking directly to a man whose company I'm thinking of buying? She'd think I'd gone stark staring mad.' There was a long pause which Dove didn't even try to break. Eventually D'Arby said, 'Any other suggestions?'

'Not suggestions, exactly,' said Dove carefully, 'but I do have a couple of interesting bits of news that came out in the press over the last few days.' Without giving D'Arby the chance to stop him, Dove immediately began to read from the press cutting in front of him.

'*The long-awaited House of Commons Health Committee investigation into passive smoking has finally been announced, coinciding with the appointment of Theodore Stevens FRCS as expert adviser to the Committee.*

'*As one of the world's foremost thoracic surgeons, Mr Stevens is well placed to comment on every physiological aspect of nicotine inhalation.*

'*The Committee is expected to hold its first sitting before the House rises in December.*'

'You ought to be pleased with that, Ralph. You get Stevens when you buy the Lung Division.'

'*If* we buy the Lung Division.'

D'Arby still sounded grumpy, but Dove knew the next piece would pull him round.

'*Pneumatech has won the prestigious Pharos prize for research in the emerging field of pharmacogenomics. The company was judged Outstanding in three of the five categories used in assessing entries for the award. These were: Degree of innovation; Use of leading-edge technology; Commercial potential.*'

'Commercial potential?' D'Arby's voice suddenly sounded a lot more cheerful. 'That is rather good news.' There was another of his pauses, then he said, 'Look, Alan, don't get me wrong. I like your business. I'm moving things along as fast as I can, but I do *hate* to be hurried. Makes me nervous.'

On October the eighteenth, Ivan Straw wasn't at all nervous. He had no doubt that the Skinshine transaction would be approved at that day's Annual General Meeting. After that, come hell or high water, Dove had to buy the US company, which meant he'd have to pay Wolkenbank a seven-figure fee for handling the purchase.

Francesca would be getting some bloody great diamonds come Christmas. She deserved them, and her daddy would be pleased to see his little girl in some decent ice. Ivan would be buying a present for himself too. A pair of Purdeys, maybe? An apartment in some liberal country for when he fancied something even younger than Francesca?

If the Lung Division sale also went ahead, he'd be looking at shed-loads of bonus. He could buy cars, holidays, ten-year-old girls, whatever he bloody well liked. But Ivan wasn't entirely sure that the Lung Division would sell. The suits at Churngold Capital were taking their time. Dove would be a hero if it did fly, but completely stuffed if it didn't.

Ivan didn't really give a toss either way. He'd be happy with the bonus he'd get from Skinshine. And he'd get a pat on the back from the top guys that would do his career prospects at Wolkenbank no harm at all. That was if he stayed. Things were going well with the Russian. Ivan was expecting Dix to call him with an offer of a job at the hedge fund any day now. Dyengi himself had actually phoned to talk about it.

'Maybe is time soon now you join Dix. You done well, Ivaan. You tell me good deals and you stop Kersey woman investigation.'

'I really put the frighteners on her. I pointed her out at Alan Dove's party, remember? She looked quite haggard.'

'What is 'aggard?'

'Thin.'

'She was fat.'

'Not nearly as fat as she used to be, the interfering cow. *She* won't be troubling us any more.'

'She better damn not.'

That phone call had tipped him into dangerous territory. Euphoria, a massive high, that feeling that nothing could go wrong. Luckily he'd spotted the symptoms, taken a pill, had a fag, brought himself down to safer levels. He had to keep himself stable. The two deals weren't done yet, and the Russian was holding a sodding great stake in Pneumatech. If the Lung Division sale did go arse-first, it would knock the shit out of the share price. He'd have to make sure Dyengi had advance warning to punch the sell button long before the market knew. Ivan would be sticking to Dove like a rash.

With this in mind, he made sure that he shared Dove's car for the short drive from Pneumatech's headquarters to the hotel where the AGM was being held. 'Bloody good press you had this morning, Alan,' he said as he climbed in. 'Even the City diary vipers think Skinshine's a great fit with F-ACE. Any news from Churngold Capital, by the way?'

'It's all going fine. I'm in close touch with Ralph D'Arby. He's one of those people who hates being hurried, but really it's just a question of crossing T's and dotting I's.' Dove sounded very sure of himself, bloody cheerful in fact. 'And the share price just keeps on rising. D'you know something, Ivan? I totted up the value of my options last night, and as long as the share price holds up till I can cash them in, I'm going to be a multi-million-aire!'

Ivan felt a flash of jealousy. *He* was the one who had found Skinshine, *he* had masterminded the deal, *he* should be the sodding multi-millionaire. Fortunately they were just arriving at the AGM venue, so he was saved the trouble of having to congratulate Dove on his potential wealth.

In its brochure, the hotel described itself as 'A charming home-from-home where guests are met with a welcoming smile.' 'Change that to "welcoming smell",' Straw muttered, as the pair of them made their way down a gloomy corridor to the Function Suite where the AGM was to be held.

Pneumatech did not believe in spoiling its small shareholders with food and wine at its Annual General Meeting, and not many turned up when nothing better than weak coffee and a few biscuits were on offer. Casting his eye around, Ivan thought that if you excluded the camel-train of corporate advisers sitting at the front and the smattering of City bods poised for a quick getaway at the back, there were probably no more than twenty shareholders there. He took a seat to one side of the room so that he'd be able to watch both Pneumatech's board up on the platform and also the audience.

As he glanced down to the back of the room, his eye was caught by the pretty redhead who had just slipped in. Amy Flower. The name suddenly came to him, a journalist. Tight top, nice tits, he was thinking, when the clock flipped to the hour and Gregory Loach stood up to introduce Dove and the rest of the Pneumatech board.

It was the usual rubbish. Slick presentations from management and amateur questions from shareholders. Ivan let his mind wander. He only vaguely heard, 'I have received over one hundred and fourteen million proxy votes in favour of the motion and fewer than twenty thousand against,' but he was certainly concentrating by the time Loach said, 'I therefore declare the motion *carried*.'

Carried! So it was done. Dove had to buy Skinshine now, and one sodding great chunk of bonus was in the bag. Grinning happily, Ivan glanced around the room and noticed the redhead slipping out. As she left, she revealed the woman sitting behind her. He felt his broad smile slipping. Mary sodding Kersey. What the hell was she doing there? She was starting to make him nervous. Guilt touched his elbow. It couldn't be about the pony, he'd covered his traces too well. Something new with the Treasury? Couldn't be. That inquiry was completely dead. But he was going to have to find out.

As Loach was making his closing remarks, Ivan slid down the room and into the empty seat next to her. 'Ivan Straw.' She touched his proffered hand as if it were a snake. 'I saw you at Alan Dove's party. A jolly affair, wasn't it?'

'Very. Now if you'll excuse me?'

Ivan stayed firmly in his seat, blocking Mary in.

'Now this isn't a place I'd expect to meet you,' he said casually. 'Does Lock Chase normally send its Partners to AGMs?'

The woman was trapped and she looked furious. 'I can't see that it's any business of yours why I'm here, but *some* of us remember a very bad smell around Pneumatech's last takeover. We're watching in case the same stink's hanging round this latest escapade. Now if you'll excuse me.'

Ivan leant back hastily as Mary Kersey forced her way past him. He stayed where he was. He couldn't believe it. The bloody woman was still prying. After what had happened to her daughter, she must have the hide of a hippopotamus. From nowhere, a childhood rhyme leapt into his head.

> I shoot the Hippopotamus with bullets made of platinum,
> Because if I use leaden ones his hide is sure to flatten 'em.

Platinum bullets. Now there was a thought. Looking down, he saw his hands trembling. He needed a fag.

TWENTY-SEVEN

Meg leaned gloomily on the open window of her study. No more sunshine this year, and what a miserable time to be alone in soggy Suffolk. Dominic was in South America on one of his buying trips. He'd phone occasionally to cheer her up with descriptions of the blue skies of the southern hemisphere. At West Hall, the equinoctial gales had torn off all but the most tenacious leaves, and the rank smell of decay hung like a mist in the cold air. Even the gardener's bonfire bore the sweet scents of death in its drifting smoke.

Shivering, Meg slammed the window shut. Could she stand the rusticating boredom of another English winter? Was it really worth hanging around to see if her gamble on Pneumatech shares would come off? She could keep an eye on the equity markets just as well from somewhere sunny.

The silver phone rang. 'I've just got back from lunch.'

'Lucky bloody you. I had yesterday's stew reheated.'

'Meggy! Shut up and listen, I haven't got time to chat. My lunch was with a deep-throat informant. Pneumatech's going belly-up. We've got to get out right now.'

'Blimey, are you sure? The share price is still powering up after yesterday's AGM.'

'Yes, I am sure. Abso-bloody-lutely sure. Dump the whole lot. I'll ring again as soon as I can, just sell!'

The moment her caller had hung up, Meg picked up the anthracite phone and started to dial.

Less than half an hour later the silver phone rang again. 'Have you sold?'

'Yes I have, I got rid of the lot. But I really hope you haven't made a mistake. The share price keeps ploughing on up. Mind you, we made one hell of a profit. Would you believe we've cleared eighteen million?'

'Shit!'

'Swear box,' Meg's words came automatically.

'Bollocks!'

'Don't be silly. Seriously though, I've been thinking. We've got thirty million quid stashed away already, so we've nearly fifty with the Pneumatech profit. That's plenty to keep us going. It might be time to join the navy and see the world.'

There was a laugh from the other end. 'The Atlantic and the Pacific weren't terrific, were they, Meggy?'

'And the Black Sea isn't what it's cracked up to be. I know, I know. I just think we've got enough. Some day the hounds of hell are going to chase us and I don't want to be around to hear them baying. Besides, I've had enough of looking for happy childhood memories down here. In fact I'm really pissed off with sodding Suffolk.'

'Now who's swearing? But maybe you're right. Let's have a conflab about it. Meantime, I must go and get my head down. I'm going to be Dr Dove's nemesis and I do feel a tad guilty about destroying the man. But then if I don't wield the sword myself, my source'll only go and tell someone else, so I might as well take the glory.'

Meg felt her spirits lift. 'Eighteen million quid's profit *and* you trash Alan Dove. That'll teach him to treat me like a half-wit.' Putting the phone gently back in its silver cradle, she went out, her study door locking automatically behind her. As she went upstairs she started singing.

We joined the Navy to see the world.
But what did we see? We saw the sea.

Mary took a surreptitious peep at her watch. Quarter to four. An east wind was blowing, combined with a depressing drizzle of rain. Her feet were cold and damp, and she'd been standing around in this stable yard since before two. She'd had no idea that buying a pony from the Master of the Blythe Vale Hunt would turn out to be such a very serious business.

Guy had surprised her by suggesting that their daughter needed another pony to stop her moping, and had volunteered to ask her himself. He'd reported back to Mary, 'Grace liked the idea. She said it would stop poor Binky neighing all the time and that she'd lost her best friend too.'

'Well done, Guy! I'll get the word out that we're looking.'

The Master himself had telephoned, interrupting their Sunday lunch. 'Hear you're after a pony,' he'd said in his usual direct way. 'My youngest has grown out of Minim. She's a girl's pony, just the ticket for Grace. Come over to the kennels and try her. Better make it quick though, Minim's a star out hunting and there'll be a lot of people after her.'

Overhearing Mary's half of the conversation, Grace had started hopping around her whispering loudly that they could go on Wednesday. It was a half-day holiday. Somehow Mary had found herself being pushed into agreeing to view Minim. Wednesday, nineteenth of October, as she noted on the kitchen calendar. More than a little equivocal about the morality of fox-hunting and nervous that he might quiz her about why she never rode out with the Blythe Vale, Mary had been relieved when the

Master had added, 'Can't be there myself I'm afraid, but I'll make sure my kennel huntsman looks after you. There's nothing about horses that Charley doesn't know.'

The moment Minim was led out of her snug little stable Mary could see why the Master had said she was a girl's pony. 'Oh!' Grace had breathed. 'She's a palomino! Isn't she beautiful?'

Mary thought the combination of a golden body and silver-white mane and tail gave Minim the air of a film star with a bad fake tan, but she was certainly in great shape. As Charley explained, her breeding was pure Arab on her sire's side, which gave her that fine bone and the endurance to carry Grace for a whole day's hunting. Minim's dam was a Connemara. 'Rochestown Muffet's her name and this pony's typical of the foals she throws. Small, quiet, very steady with hounds.'

Mary's hope had been that if they couldn't keep off the hunting motif they might at least get the business of trying out Minim over reasonably quickly. Unfortunately Grace and Charley took the afternoon's work very seriously. Minim was lunged at walk, trot, canter, and over a set of low cavaletti jumps. She then stood patiently while Grace and Charley went over every point of her body from ear to ergot. After more than an hour of this, Minim was tacked up. Grace rode her at a cautious walk, in a more confident rising trot, and finally in a triumphant canter which ended with her popping straight over the line of cavaletti with Grace not even losing a stirrup in the process.

It had got very cold and Mary was aching to go home, but it wasn't the end of the try-out. Grace pulled out her copy of *The Manual of Horsemanship* and Charley patiently answered her questions about feeding, bitting, shoeing and other equine minutiae that Mary had never even heard of. With nothing else to do, she pulled her BlackBerry out for what felt like the hundredth time that afternoon and saw that at least there was something new to read.

Date: Wednesday 19 October

To: Mary Kersey

From: Elginbrode, Aiden

Subject: Share movements

Mary,

On the subject under discussion when we last met, my office has detected some unusual movements on that company's share register.

You might wish to come and see me when I will be happy to take you through the changes in share ownership which have caught our attention.

Kind regards

Aiden Elginbrode

HM Treasury

Subject under discussion. That company. How typical of him to be so cautious about putting Pneumatech's name in writing. She sent Bella a message asking her to fix a meeting with him as soon as possible. A glance at her watch showed it was four o'clock. Only fifteen minutes had crawled by since she'd last looked. She was just starting to think that her feet would never thaw when she saw Charley making his way across the cobbled stable yard. Thank the Lord, they must have finished.

'All done, Mrs Kersey.' Charley beamed at her. 'Anything you'd like to ask about the pony?'

Mary was about to gabble that there was absolutely nothing she needed to ask except how soon she could go home, but then she pulled herself together. *Caveat emptor.*

'Does Minim have any faults?'

'I'm afraid she does, Mrs Kersey, yes.'

'Oh dear.' Catching sight of Grace's stricken face behind Charley's shoulder, Mary was tempted not to go any further. But supposing Minim's fault was dangerous? She'd have to ask.

'So what exactly is the problem with Minim?'

'She farts.'

'She *what*?'

'She farts, Mrs Kersey. She's the most terrible farter I've ever come across. She can frighten the life out of you when the hunt's all silent on a still morning, waiting for the whimper of a hound. Always does it when she goes back in her loosebox too. I'll show you if you like.'

Charley was right. The moment her headcollar was off, the pony loosed off a tempestuous volley of wind. Fighting to keep a straight face, Mary asked, 'Is that it? I mean is that her only fault?'

'That's it, Mrs Kersey. Nothing else wrong that I'm aware of.'

'Gracie?' The grin was enough. Turning back to Charley, Mary held out a hand. 'We'll take her then.'

At eight o'clock that evening, Amy Flower was sitting alone at a table for two in the Churchill Room of the House of Commons. It was the gloomiest place in the world in which to have been abandoned, with nothing to look at except portraits of past premiers and the handful of lone guests who had also been deserted by Members of Parliament summoned to vote. For entertainment, there was only the monotonous bell and the television sets hanging around the walls and showing the word

'DIVISION' in stark black letters on a grey background. At least Tim was one of the first back from voting, breathing heavily from his fast trot along the corridors.

'I'm sorry, this is really tiresome,' he said as he sat down. 'There are going to be at least three more votes, I'll be stuck here all evening.' A white-aproned waitress appeared with melon and Parma ham for Amy and an unspecified terrine for Tim. He peered at her plate. 'The food's wholesome here but it's pretty basic. And a table at Wilton's left going begging.'

'Oh, don't worry, it couldn't matter less. I'm still stuffed from lunch, anyway. Lebanese mezze with a brainy woman. Seriously pretty, too.'

'Not as pretty as you, couldn't be.' She could hear his voice soften and felt a fleeting guilt at what she was going to do. 'Who is this paragon?'

Amy grinned at him. 'Now I couldn't possibly tell you that, could I? Never reveal my sources. Let's just say my column tomorrow should be a bit of a whopper. It'll ruin a man's career and it might fuck up a whole company if I'm lucky. What a score that would be!'

'For heaven's sake, Amy! Don't you worry about the morality of ruining people's lives with what you write?' He was so noble. Now she didn't feel guilty at all.

'I'm a journalist, you dick-head. Why in hell should I be interested in morality?'

Tim was still looking at her, but he obviously hadn't been listening. Abandoning his barely tasted terrine, he had tugged a small box out of his pocket. 'Hey, just a second,' she started to say, but he wasn't to be stopped.

'Amy, will you please marry me? Chuck in the *Daily Business*, come and live in the constituency. You know I love you, don't you? As a matter of fact . . . oh *shit*!' The division bell started to ring again, loud and persistent. 'If I run now I should be first through the lobbies. And you will say "Yes" when I get back, won't you?' He hurried out of the Churchill Room, leaving the little box sitting on the table like an aide-memoire.

Despite that promise to run, it was nearly ten minutes before he came back, giving Amy plenty of time to work out her lines. 'Bloody hell, you've been an age,' she said as he sat down.

'So sorry, darling Amy, I was as quick as I could be. Were you OK?'

'I've had hours of excitement. I went along the corridor for a pee and as usual they'd run out of loo paper. I came back along the Terrace and said hi to a few dreary hacks. Then I started jotting down some thoughts for a leaving piece.' She motioned towards the notebook in front of her.

'A leaving piece?' Amy heard the surge of happiness. 'So you *will* give up work and marry me! Oh, that's wonderful. Wonderful.'

As he started to fumble with the little box, she leaned across the table to put her hand over his.

'You're an angel to want to marry me, but the thing is I'm not ready to settle down yet. I'm planning on a bit of travel before I get too old to enjoy it.'

'You haven't met someone else, have you?'

'Of course I haven't, you berk. You're the only guy who gets a flash of my tarantula.'

She caught Tim's uneasy glance towards the next table and wished she'd spoken a bit more quietly. She'd meant to leave him, not to embarrass him. He grabbed her hand. He was obviously going to try again.

'I don't think I can live without you any more. If you really want me to, I'll give up politics, abandon my constituency. I'll even go round the world with you if you want me to. But please marry me.'

Amy gently recovered her hand. 'That's sweet of you, Tim, but you'd be miserable out of England. And your constituency'd be devastated if you left them. In fact I'll bet you get an increased majority at the next election.' She sipped at the thin Burgundy, then looked at him steadily over her wine glass. 'I'm sorry, but it's definitely a No.'

She watched while Tim fingered the unopened box, then slowly put it back into his pocket.

TWENTY-EIGHT

Daily Business   *Thursday 20 October 2005*

Doubts over Pneumatech Lung Division sale
By Amy Flower, Senior Correspondent

Questions have been raised about the value of Pneumatech's Lung Division, up for sale to pay for the company's much-heralded US$1.2 billion acquisition of Skinshine plc.

Lead bidder for the Lung Division is secretive private equity group Churngold Capital, understood to have made an initial offer to Pneumatech of £520 million for the business, subsequently hiking their offer up to a weighty £600 million.

This £600 million valuation relies on speculation that leading-edge research will soon pay off. Pneumatech was recently awarded the prestigious Pharos prize for discoveries in the emerging field of pharmacogenomics and was particularly cited for the commercial potential of its work.

But doubts about the value of this research have been raised by sources close to the company. Experts predict that it will take a decade of high-energy information technology investment to produce the necessary 'bioinformatic' capabilities needed to develop commercially viable drugs from this as yet untested field.

If the sale of the Lung Division to Churngold Capital were to collapse, it is not clear how Pneumatech would finance the Skinshine

acquisition, irrevocable since Pneumatech's AGM two days ago.
No one from Pneumatech was available for comment last night.

Alan Dove was just about to shout to his secretary to get hold of Churngold Capital when his phone buzzed. 'Mr D'Arby for you.'

'Ralph! I was just going to ring you. You've seen the *Daily Business* this morning? I don't believe it! I simply don't believe it! However did she get hold of this stuff?'

'I was rather hoping you could answer that one.' Dove was taken aback by the anger in D'Arby's voice. 'Frankly I'm livid about the publicity. I think I've told you how important discretion is to my business.'

'I understand that, Ralph, and I've absolutely no idea where the leak could have come from, no idea at all.' Dove shook his head in perplexity. 'Obviously a few people know about your involvement, my board, Lock Chase, Wolkenbank, the lawyers. But where that technology stuff came from is an absolute mystery. It's all *cobblers* as well.' He took a deep breath. 'Cobblers,' he repeated quietly. 'My scientists have all the computer capacity they need and they're convinced that they're on the edge of a breakthrough. I can assure you that whenever those guys have talked about breakthroughs in the past, they've always delivered.'

'That may all be true, but I can't buy your Lung Division unless my investors are on side. They'll see the story in the *Daily Business* and frankly, Alan, it doesn't look good. I've already had Jedd Fontaine on to me. Talk about Jumpy in Geneva, he even accused me of putting his clients' money into a scary biotech play. *Me!*' The voice was suddenly furious. 'I'm one of the most cautious buyers in the entire private equity world.'

Dove could hear the phone ringing in his outer office and he could see from his screen that the Pneumatech share price was all over the place. He had to buy some time. 'Look, Ralph, I've a hell of a lot on my plate just now. There'll be journalists, analysts and every other sort of low-life trying to get hold of me. But I'll tell you now the story's *crap*.' He took another long, slow breath. Keep calm. Stay in control. 'I'm going to ring the *Daily Business* and I'll get the story retracted. That'll calm your investors down, won't it?'

'OK. I'll keep out of your hair until this afternoon.' Dove was relieved to hear D'Arby recover his normal urbanity. 'Come over for a chat then, will you? Shall we say two-thirty?'

His desk phone was ringing again the moment he put down the receiver. 'Mr Straw for you, Dr Dove.'

Straw had been on to him already that morning. It had been very early, before either of them had seen the papers. The banker had been ridiculously agitated about a series of offshore nominee companies which the previous afternoon had all sold their entire holdings in Pneumatech. There had been absolutely no warning, and Straw had had no idea who the ultimate owners of the shares might be. Dove couldn't understand why his banker had been so concerned over what was doubtless just a bit of profit-taking.

Now Straw was on to him again and sounding quite panicky. 'I've read the *Daily Business*. Alan, you've got to tell me! Is there any risk of Churngold pulling the plug on the Lung Division deal? Tell me, for fuck's sake!'

Dove had to speak quite sharply to him. 'Pull yourself together and listen. I've just been on the phone to Ralph D'Arby and I'm going over to Churngold Capital early this afternoon to make sure we're all straight. Everything will be fine, Ivan. There's nothing to worry about.'

'Ring me the minute you get back.' Straw was being absurdly aggressive, but he had slammed the phone down before Dove had the chance to tell him so.

The combination of D'Arby's anger and Straw's aggression flustered him. Dove forced himself to sit quietly and ignore the ringing telephone until he felt his normal optimism returning. This was all a storm in a tea cup. The technology story was rubbish. The Lung Division was a great business. Churngold Capital would certainly buy it.

During the morning, he watched the screens carefully and was glad to see that Pneumatech shareholders appeared to be echoing his sanguine view. The share price had the odd jittery moment, but it been unpredictable since those big sales yesterday. Just after two, sick of fielding calls from journalists, exhausted by a rally of angry questions from his Chairman, Dove abandoned his office for the drive to Churngold Capital.

At exactly half past two, he arrived at the top of the stairwell. He'd found the last couple of flights a struggle. No time to take any exercise. Dove paused just inside the fire door. Ralph D'Arby would be waiting by the lift, and he didn't want to be seen panting. Having recovered his breath, he was about to push the door open when he heard D'Arby's voice.

'Don't get me wrong, private equity's a great business. And thanks to this benevolent government I pay less tax than even the workmen on my Sussex estate. I'm just a touch worried.'

'You, worried?' The voice was young and female. 'But you always seem so calm.'

'This boom's getting to me, it can't last. Bust will come as night follows day and I'm afraid the next bust'll be a big one. That's why I'm making sure I've got my investors completely on side before I sign this deal, I need them to stick with me through the dark times. If they're not happy, I'll pull out.'

'Does the vendor know that?'

'Good God, no. What's the point of frightening him off? We have a little motto here. We always say Yes unless we say No.'

Dove pushed the door open. D'Arby looked faintly embarrassed when he saw him. 'Alan, hello. I was just giving a bit of homespun advice to my rookie here. Come along, we're using our meeting room today, not my office.'

'So, Alan,' he started, with none of his usual preliminaries. 'You seem to have steadied the share price today. Sometimes these stories can tip a company over the precipice, can't they? Very irresponsible our newspapers can be.' There was a pause. 'Any luck with the *Daily Business*?'

Dove could see from D'Arby's frown that his expression had given him away. 'Bloody blocking secretary wouldn't put me through to the editor,' he mumbled.

'That's a shame, Alan, a real shame. You see, a full retraction might have calmed things down. We've had a lot of calls. Our investors have read the Amy Flower piece and they're not pleased. The story gives the impression that we're over-paying for a risky business that's engaged in highly speculative research.'

Dove panicked. He'd overheard D'Arby saying he'd be prepared to pull out if his investors weren't happy, and he was running out of time. 'Over-paying? All right then, if we can sign today, I'll drop back to the five-twenty you first offered.' As he said this, Dove held on to the arms of his chair. Five-twenty for the Lung Division would mean he'd have to find another eighty million to cover the Skinshine purchase.

D'Arby was tapping his fingertips together as a slow smile crossed his face. And so he bloody well should be smiling, Dove thought as he watched him. Five-twenty was a great offer. Churngold Capital would be paying a fair price for the Lung Division's current drug business while getting all of their ground-breaking research for free. He held his breath as D'Arby first raised an eyebrow and then slowly nodded. Dove's breath came out in a fast exhalation. It was going to be all right.

There was a tap on the meeting-room door, followed by D'Arby's secretary peering round it. 'Sorry to bother you, but Jo-Marie Cary's on the line from Montana. Shall I put the call through to you in here?'

'Yes, do. Stay here, Alan. No reason why you shouldn't hear what she has to say.'

'Ralph?' Dove thought that Jo-Marie's Brooklyn accent sharpened the name into an accusation.

'Jo-Marie! Good to hear from you, how's the weather out there?'

'Snowing. I'm calling about this press report. Let me remind you that the Montana Teachers and Lecturers Society does not, repeat *not*, sanction any speculative investments in our placements with private equity firms. This applies to Churngold Capital as much as to anyone else, Ralph. I'm not picking on you personally. I took a moment to get a report done on pharmacogenomics and the related field of bioinformatics before calling you. I have the data in front of me right now. Your proposed investment is way out of line.'

Dove thought with amazement that given the time difference, Jo-Marie and her team must have started work at about five that morning in order to have had time to get a research report done. The teachers and lecturers of Montana were certainly lucky to have her looking after their pension fund.

She hadn't quite finished. 'Ralph? You still there? You're outside the guidelines. You gotta pull out of this or I kick up a stink. Understood?'

Dove opened his mouth to speak but was silenced by D'Arby's fierce shake of the head. 'Understood, Jo-Marie, understood. Thank you for your call,' he added, but she had already gone.

Switching off the speaker-phone, D'Arby gave a resigned shrug of his shoulders. 'I'm afraid the time has come to say "No".'

Dove felt his mouth fall open. This couldn't be happening. 'What d'you mean? What the hell do you mean?'

'I'm really very sorry, but you heard what Jo-Marie said. It's a great shame. I like your Lung Division business Alan, really I do, but Churngold Capital isn't going to buy it.' Dove sat, dumbfounded. 'Stay here for as long as you like,' he heard D'Arby saying. 'Do use the phone if you want to,' he added, edging towards the door.

'But our agreement!' Dove managed to stutter. 'We've signed Heads of Agreement! You *can't* pull out now. You've *got* to buy the Lung Division.'

D'Arby turned back from the door to face him. 'Sorry, old man, but that won't work. Remember we only signed subject to due diligence? We could always pull out if there was something we didn't like in the due dilly. It just so happens that something we didn't like turned up in the *Daily Business* this morning so we're pulling out. No recourse. Sorry, Alan, but there it is.'

Urban Palewski was alone in his office when Dove's call came through.

'Thank God you're there! I'm in the car on my way back from Churngold Capital. They've pulled out and I've got to find another buyer for my Lung Division. I may need to go as low as five hundred, so I can't use your six hundred million valuation or it'll look like a fire sale. You'll have to do me a new one. I want you to say that it's worth a minimum of five-thirty. And you must give the business a stronger write-up. Lay it on with a trowel.'

Urban waited in silence as Dove fired orders at him.

'And this has to be kept quiet, understand? The whole world's after me, listen!' Urban could hear a faint ringing in the background. 'That's Ivan Straw trying to get me on my other line. He'll be desperate to know how I got on with Churngold Capital, but I'm not telling him a bloody thing till it's too late for him to trade.'

Picking up a pencil, Urban began to take notes so that his thoughts would be clear once Dove was prepared to listen.

'No one's to know about this till after the Stock Exchange is closed, understand? The last thing I need is any leak this afternoon. There'd be panic selling of my shares and I'd be accused of stoking up a disorderly market.' There was a pause, followed by an angry shout. 'Urban? I want you to get started on this work for me. Right now!'

'Just a moment, Alan,' Urban said into the sudden silence. 'It's not as easy as that. Lock Chase has done two valuations for you already and we did them in good faith. We valued the Division at what we genuinely thought it was worth, and we've written a description of the business as we believe it to be. I don't see that anything will have changed sufficiently to make us alter our opinion.' Dove was trying to interrupt but he wouldn't let him. 'Do please hear me out. One of my colleagues did most of the work on the last valuation and I need to see what she thinks. We'll get back to you shortly.'

'You'd better be back with a Yes,' was all he heard before the line was cut off.

Urban immediately dialled an internal number. 'Spider, have you got a moment? There's a hurricane blowing up at Pneumatech and they want our help again.'

Urban turned his head as he heard the door. He opened his mouth to say something and forgot to shut it. Spider was wearing a simple cream suit, cut in some cunning way so that it emphasized her figure. Her hair shone like the black jet around her neck, echoed by the slight gloss of dark tights and a pair of black patent leather stilettos.

'What's up, Urban? You look like you're catching flies.'

Urban was embarrassed to have been caught staring at her. Pressing his lips together, he pulled his face back behind a façade of formality and tried to think of something sensible to say.

'So what does dear Doctor Dove want from us now?' She might look astonishing but she sounded quite normal.

'Believe it or not, he wants us to do yet another valuation of his Lung Division.'

'The guy's a complete dick.'

'He may be a dick, but he's a client and he's in trouble. Churngold Capital has pulled out, presumably because of the papers this morning. Dove's going to have to find a new buyer fast so he can pay for Skinshine. Otherwise, he's up shit creek without a paddle.'

Urban glanced up and caught Spider staring at him, eyes wide, lips parted in a faint smile. The moment she caught his eye, the shutters came down and she turned her head away.

'So what do you think we should do?'

'I think we should tell him to fuck off,' Spider said calmly. 'I didn't mind re-doing the first valuation after he told us all that stuff about their genomic research. What my team wrote was as near the truth as we could get. But I'll be buggered if I'm going to sign off on some fantasy of a shitty little sales pitch just to get Alan Dove out of a tight spot.'

He nodded thoughtfully. 'You're right, we probably should turn him down, but are you quite sure it's what you want me to do? We might be helping to destroy not only the man but also his whole business.'

Eyes hard, Spider nodded at him. A moment later she left the room. Gazing after her, he murmured, '*O tiger's heart wrapped in a woman's hide.*' Then with a shrug, he picked up his phone to relay the decision to Alan Dove.

Sauntering past the Bentley showroom on Berkeley Square to eye up the latest arrival, Amy Flower felt her mobile vibrating in her pocket. She listened with growing excitement as her deep insider passed on another Pneumatech exclusive. She checked her watch. Nearly four. She'd have plenty of time to get the story written before the paper went to bed. But still, there was no point in taking any risk on missing the deadline. She waved frantically to flag down a passing taxi.

On the drive back to her office, Amy glanced out of the taxi window and saw that she was actually passing the angular steel pillars of the Pneumatech building. She'd love to know what was going on in there.

TWENTY-NINE

Alan Dove was trying to think.

Sadie called through to say that Ivan Straw wanted to talk to him urgently. 'Tell him I'm still with Churngold Capital.' He checked his watch. Just gone four o'clock, another half hour till the Stock Exchange closed. He wasn't telling anyone anything until then, especially a banker like Straw who wouldn't think twice about telling all his friends to sell out of Pneumatech. 'I'll talk to Urban Palewski if he calls, but no one else.'

He had just bent his head to rest it on his knuckles when the phone rang again.

'I have Mr Palewski from Lock Chase for you.'

It was a short, angry conversation. Afterwards, Dove sat immobile, staring blankly at the wall opposite his desk. All his optimism drained away. D'Arby, Palewski, he'd thought they admired him for building a great business from scratch, liked him even. But no. When the chips were down they wouldn't support him. Voices from the past jangled in his ears. 'Here comes Fatty Four-Eyes! Run!' Nothing had changed. He was still the ugly runt from Hawley-Wilson Comprehensive.

As he was sinking his head into his hands in despair, he caught a glimpse of his wife's photograph. Juliana. How soothing her placid face was. Those brown eyes were never judgemental. She'd always accepted him for what he was. Thinking of her, he remembered. Tonight's dinner. Black tie, show-business guests, he'd forgotten all about it. He reached across his desk and switched through to his private line.

'Juliana? Something's come up which I need to deal with urgently. I really am extremely sorry, but I won't be able to get away for the dinner.' As he spoke, he felt a sudden spasm of pain in his gut. All this stress was doing him no good at all.

His wife's steady voice was immediately calming. 'Don't worry, your business must of course come first. But I can't talk for long, Alonso is here to put up my hair.'

Dove had a vision of the nape of his wife's neck, exposed fat and creamy when her hair was pinned up. If only he was sitting by her side, telling her his problems. Just the thought of it was relaxing. 'Thanks for being so understanding, Juliana, and I hope you have a very pleasant evening.' He hung up and sat quietly in his office. He felt in control again, capable of thought and decision. A few more minutes and he was clear about what needed to be done. Pushing himself up from his marble desktop, he went out in search of his secretary.

'Ah, Sadie, there you are. I'm going to have to call an emergency meeting. Can you get hold of as many board members as possible? I suppose the lawyers and Wolkenbank will need to be here too. Let's aim for a seven o'clock start. Warn everyone that we may be going on late. I'd better call the Chairman myself.'

He had to steel himself as he heard Loach's number ringing. He wasn't expecting much sympathy from this quarter, and after he'd explained about the collapse of the Lung Division sale, his Chairman's first words proved him right. 'Christ, man, you've ruined the company! And don't expect me to stand by you, I'll not be having my reputation smeared by your idiocy!' Loach had yelled. 'Why the hell didn't you let me know sooner?'

Determinedly holding his voice steady, Dove explained that

he'd only recently got back from seeing the private equity firm and had been trying to get the wheels in motion to find another purchaser for the Lung Division. 'I haven't been able to make a lot of progress so far, but it's early days. We need the board meeting to agree a holding position. And we'll have to decide what we tell the Stock Exchange.'

'No! We must avoid an announcement at all costs. We'd look like madmen, agreeing to buy a company we can't pay for.'

'I think we should discuss it with the board, Gregory. I'm asking our advisers to attend. They'll be the ones to help us decide about the announcement.'

Dove was held up by a last-minute telephone call. It was nearly ten past seven by the time he got down to the boardroom and found everyone else sitting around the long table, waiting for him. Despite the short notice, the whole board had managed to get to the meeting and at the far end of the table he saw that both Ivan Straw and the lawyer, Thomas Butler, had made it too.

'This is a bad day for the company and for us.' Loach was speaking almost before Dove had sat down. 'I'm glad you've all made it here, particularly you, Theodore. I understand you were dragged out of the theatre.'

'Not exactly, Chairman, I was in an operating theatre when Sadie rang but only as an observer. Very dull it turned out to be. A routine bronchial arterial embolization. None of the blood and fireworks I'd been expecting.'

'Quite.' Loach looked vaguely queasy. 'We'd better get down to business. As I said, it's a bad day for the company. I'll let the Chief Executive explain the situation to you.'

Dove knew that apart from Loach, neither his board members nor the advisers had yet been told what had happened. It would shock them, but he decided to come straight out with it. He'd had too long a day for prevarication.

'Late this afternoon, Churngold Capital withdrew from purchasing the Lung Division. I did everything I could to get Ralph D'Arby to change his mind, I even offered to reduce the price, but he was adamant. The *Daily Business* has frightened his investors off.' Glancing down the table, he happened to catch Ivan Straw's eye. The banker's face had turned quite grey. 'The timing of Amy Flower's piece this morning has a whiff of malignancy about it.' Dove kept his voice soft. 'Had it appeared the day before the AGM, or even on the morning of the AGM itself, we could have postponed the shareholder vote. But as it is, we are committed to buying Skinshine. And as we do *not* now have a buyer for the Lung Division, this board has to decide what course of action to take.'

Stevens was shaking his head. 'You told me I'd be making a fortune from these private equity people. I've even put down a deposit on a boat, non-refundable. Will I get compensation?'

Loach cut in before Dove could answer. 'Don't be an idiot, Theodore, we're *all* in trouble. Pneumatech may be on the edge of bankruptcy, and no money left to compensate anyone. Now get on with it, Alan. How do you propose to get us out of this mess?'

Determined to stay in control, Dove went on calmly, 'We need to find a buyer for the Lung Division before we have to pay for Skinshine.' Struck by a sudden thought, he looked at his lawyer, sitting glumly at the bottom end of the boardroom table next to the ashen-faced Straw. 'Or can we find some legal loophole to get out of buying Skinshine?'

Thomas Butler's reply was immediate. 'No chance, the agreement's watertight. Whatever else happens, you'll have to buy Skinshine. And indeed,' he added, 'the Arbcheckers are not unknown for their aggression in matters of litigation. They'd eat you for breakfast if you played fast and loose with them.'

'This is dreadful! Absolutely dreadful!' Loach's sudden outburst caught Dove by surprise. 'I'll not stay and see my name dragged through the mud. I'd rather resign my position immediately and be done with it. I'm out of here.' Grabbing his briefcase and leaving the usual litter of papers scattered about, Loach stormed out of the boardroom, slamming the door behind him.

'I apologize, the Chairman's been under a lot of pressure lately, health problems I believe,' Dove improvised. Glancing around the table, he saw that Straw was not only white-faced but now also appeared to be swaying in his chair. Hypoglycaemia, he thought, his medical training coming back to him. Carbohydrates, and fast. 'Let's have a short break while I ask the Company Secretary to arrange some food. We'll make more progress if our stomachs aren't growling at each other.'

Dove didn't complain when Straw immediately lit a cigarette. This and the takeaway pizza which arrived shortly afterwards seemed to flip him straight from silent lethargy into noisy action.

'I'll get back to Wolkenbank straight after we've finished here,' Straw insisted. 'I can research all night and start contacting potential purchasers first thing in the morning. I'll definitely find you a new buyer!'

Straw's energy burst continued in the debate over whether they should put out a Stock Exchange announcement, and Dove was astonished at the passion with which his banker fought against it. 'We'd be mad to put out an announcement now! The share price would go into freefall!' Straw was almost shouting and was hammering his fist on the table to emphasize his words. 'And I'll *never* find another buyer unless we keep the whole business of the Churngold Capital pull-out under wraps! For God's sake, we mustn't tell the City a thing!'

'I'm not sure we can keep this a secret for long, Ivan.' Dove kept his voice very calm, thinking that the ferocity of Straw's arguments bordered on the irrational. 'Too many people are going to know about it.'

'Then at least give me a night to work on it! Whatever you do, you *can't* make any announcement till tomorrow!' Was the man suffering from a destabilizing sugar-rush after that hypoglycaemia, Dove wondered? Or was there some sane reason for his wanting to hold the bad news back from the markets? If so, he had no idea what it might be.

Straw's ranting was eventually cut short by the lawyer. With an immovable gravity, Thomas Butler insisted that any material fact likely to cause a major shift in the share price had to be made public without delay. It was the law, and that was that.

Butler's words allowed Dove to shift the debate on to what the announcement might say. Having lost the argument about putting nothing out at all, Straw persuaded the board that they should at least be as circumspect as possible in what was said. After a certain amount of wrangling, the anouncement was drafted to confirm that *one* of the bidders for the Lung Division had indeed pulled out, but leaving the implication that this was not the *only* bidder. It was with the greatest reluctance that Thomas Butler could be persuaded to agree to this.

'If we aren't lying outright, we could certainly be accused of withholding material facts,' he said. 'God help us if there's another leak and the City learns we've been economical with the truth. The share price will nose-dive and our reputations will all be in the soup.' Despite his reservations, the announcement was duly dispatched, to arrive with the Stock Exchange for release first thing the following morning.

'At least it's Friday tomorrow,' Dove said, trying to cheer

Straw up. 'Maybe everyone will be too busy planning their weekend to notice our piece of news.'

Daily Business   *Friday 21 October 2005*

Pneumatech Lung Division sale collapses
By Amy Flower, Senior Correspondent

Private equity firm Churngold Capital has pulled out of the bidding for Pneumatech's Lung Division, leaving the company high and dry.

Pneumatech was depending on raising cash from the sale to fund its ambitious US\$1.2 billion acquisition of American beauty retailer Skinshine Corporation. The offer for Skinshine went unconditional at the Pneumatech's AGM earlier this week. Churngold Capital was the only remaining bidder for the Lung Division and their withdrawal leaves Pneumatech with a £600 million hole to fill.

Chief Executive Dr Alan Dove, who just three days ago hailed the simultaneous acquisition of Skinshine and divestment of the Lung Division as 'a spectacular double whopper', now finds himself caught in a spectacular double whammy. Will a white knight ride up with the £600 million Dove needs for his overvalued Lung Division or will shareholders have to cough up to save the company from an inglorious trip to the US courtrooms? No one from Pneumatech was available to answer this thorniest of questions.

Ivan Straw's hands were shaking so badly that he had to hold his arm still in order to light a fresh cigarette from the stub of the one he'd just finished. Although he was expecting it, the sudden ringing of his phone made him leap.

'Ivaan! I am angry! You lose me much money.'

'It wasn't my fault. Dove didn't tell anyone till after the market closed last night. I couldn't do a thing.'

'And worst,' the Russian spat savagely, 'you lie to me, Ivaan! Hedge fund woman is not stopped.'

Ivan's heart sank. Mary bloody Kersey.

'How do you know?' As he asked the question he heard the tremor in his voice. He took another deep drag on his cigarette.

'I have high up friend in Treasury. Good friend who tell me.'

The Treasury. Mary Kersey. Ivan was hit by a sudden idea. He recovered his nerve fast. 'I've got it! We know the Kersey woman's mad keen to get hedge funds regulated, and we know the Treasury's been looking at Pneumatech. And don't forget that Mary Kersey works for Lock Chase, and Lock Chase have been helping Dove.'

'So what you say?'

'She had a reason and she had access to all the information. Platon! It was Mary Kersey who planted those stories in the *Daily Business.* It's obvious. It was all her fault!'

'Then she lose me much money. This I hate. Ivaan. You listening?'

'Yes, Platon.'

'You fail me once with this woman, now you do it right. I don't care how. You just shut her mouth closed.'

THIRTY

Mary walked faster, wishing that she'd turned straight back inside the Treasury building the moment she'd spotted the man standing on the corner of Parliament Square. She could have made some excuse to the receptionist, popped back up to talk to Aiden Elginbrode, had a cup of coffee with him in his office, until the coast was clear. She looked nervously back over her shoulder. Yes. There was that narrow face, bobbing between the heads of the other pedestrians about fifteen yards behind her. If only the Monday morning traffic in Whitehall wasn't so heavy, she'd run across the road to see if he followed her. There was Nelson's Column up ahead – surely she'd be able to lose him in Trafalgar Square? Or maybe she should jump into a taxi and throw him off that way? Mary hurried on.

Waiting to cross Cockspur Street, she glanced over her shoulder again, then turned to look more carefully. She could see no one but strangers. He wasn't following her after all. How ridiculous. Why ever would a man like Ivan Straw be stalking her? She was imagining it. Maybe she was feeling irrational because she was tired with all the work that had been piling on her recently. And also she was anxious about passing on to Urban the conversation she'd just had with Aiden Elginbrode. Mary walked on slowly, knowing that actually she wasn't being ridiculous at all. Those cold eyes of his. She remembered the frisson of fear when she caught him watching her from behind a bookstall at Liverpool Street station that morning. She was sure she'd glimpsed him on Saturday too, slipping between the shoppers in Halesworth. There was no doubt about it. Ivan Straw had been following her.

'Can I tell you something weird?' Mary couldn't stop herself from saying, the moment she was in Urban's office. 'You know Ivan Straw, Dove's banker? He's started stalking me.' The words sounded silly, even as she was saying them.

Urban raised an eyebrow. 'Are you sure?'

'It must be coincidence.' Mary tried to shrug off her fear. 'Don't tell Guy, will you? He's been a bit worried about my personal safety since Grace was hurt.'

'Of course not.' Urban's voice had a soothing note to it. He probably thought she was being completely mad. 'But to be honest, Mary, I'd have thought Straw had other things on his mind at the moment. Did you see the weekend papers?'

'About Pneumatech? Thank heaven you and Spider refused to do another valuation for Dove, otherwise we'd be being hauled over the coals along with his other advisers.'

'I couldn't believe it!' Urban ran a hand through his hair, ruffling it into untidy dark waves. 'That statement implying there were other buyers. How could Pneumatech think they'd get away with it?'

'I blame Dove's arrogance.' Mary decided that wasn't entirely fair, and added, 'Though he can't have dreamed that the *Daily Business* would come out the very same morning with a piece saying there were no other bidders.'

'How d'you think the paper got on to the story so fast?'

'Well, that was actually what I wanted to talk to you about.' Mary was relieved to find the conversation drifting naturally towards the questions that Elginbrode had suggested she asked.

'I went to see Aiden this morning,' she said carefully. 'We talked about Pneumatech. He's pretty sure someone with inside information talked to that journalist on the *Daily Business*.'

'Amy Flower?'

'That's the one.' With a prayer to St Stephen for courage, Mary took the plunge. 'Aiden said only a tiny handful of people could have given her the facts for her piece on Thursday. Which private equity firm was involved. The bid size. The technological detail. Her second article was suspiciously accurate too. Who told Amy Flower that Churngold had pulled out? That they were the sole bidder for the Lung Division? Aiden thinks only Alan Dove could have known all that. And us.'

Mary looked across at the deep frown on Urban's handsome, hawkish face. 'What the *hell* are you talking about?'

'I'm sorry. I wish I didn't have to say this, but it does look as if someone from Lock Chase has been talking to Amy Flower. Dove would hardly have leaked all that information to her himself, would he? And there's something else. The timing.' Mary looked down at her hands. This was even harder than she had expected. 'It seems like some sort of vendetta. That first article came out just *after* the Skinshine bid went unconditional, when Dove no longer had any option but to buy the company. And then the second article. What was the point of someone briefing Amy Flower about Churngold Capital pulling out? Because it made absolutely certain that Dove was stitched up before he had time to find another buyer for his Lung Division.'

There was a long silence between them before Mary added evenly, 'You know something, Urban, I wanted to bring Dove down myself. For what he did to Grace. But someone else seems to be doing it for me. You understand what I'm saying, don't you? The only people who had all the information that was leaked to Amy Flower were you and Spider.' There was another pause before she had the courage to add, 'And it wasn't you, was it?'

For a moment, he stared blankly back at her as he registered what she was saying, but then he was leaning across his desk, his face rigid with anger. 'I can't believe you're saying these things. I thought you and Spider were friends now.'

'And so we are. This hasn't got anything to do with friendship, it's about right and wrong.' Mary returned his stare. 'There's been something strange with Spider and Pneumatech all along, hasn't there? Skipping meetings with Dove. Odd silences. I've seen it myself and so have you.'

Urban slumped down in his chair and put his head in his hands. He didn't move for a long time. At last, he looked up and nodded. 'I'd swear by anything that she's straight. But yes. There has been something weird with her and the Pneumatech case. I can't really believe she'd go leaking stuff to the papers and I can't imagine why she might want to. But it's possible.' He sighed and straightened up. 'What do you think I should do?'

'Couldn't you just ask her?'

'Well, it's not quite as simple as that.' Mary had to wait for what seemed like an age before Urban said quietly, 'You're right. I'll ask her.'

'There's something else.' Mary needed a lot of willpower to pass on the other thing Elginbrode had told her. 'A group of nominees dumped a pile of Pneumatech shares on the nineteenth of October. That's the day *after* the AGM but the day *before* Amy Flower's first piece appeared. Maybe whoever's behind those nominee companies knew the leak was coming and sold out before the share price collapsed. That's insider trading. I think you should ask Spider if she had any nominee accounts.'

Urban's chair squeaked on the floor as he thrust it backwards.

'Point one, I'll talk to Spider right now. Point two, there's *no way* she'd have done anything dishonest.'

Without another word, he strode out of his office, slamming the door behind him.

'I'm really sorry, babes, I'm having a bugger of a time.' As he lit a cigarette he saw that the Virgin and Child on his ashtray was lost under a mound of stubs. 'This Pneumatech business is a complete cock-up and I can't get away till it's sorted.'

'Oh, Ivan.' He could just imagine that sexy pout of hers. 'I don't *want* to go to France on my own.'

He had a sudden idea. 'Francesca, listen. Why don't you take your father? He loved the house in Grasse last time he came.'

'Well, I suppose that might work.' Her voice brightened. 'And I could always take him down to the coast for some shopping. I'll call him now and ring you right back.'

When the phone rang again a few minutes later, he didn't wait for his PA to answer it. 'Hi doll, did you get hold of your daddy?'

'Who my daddy?' The voice was quite the opposite of Francesca's soft purr. 'Mr Dyengi tell me to ring you. He say you must deal with Mrs Kersey quick. When you see man in black coat, is me. I am watching you.'

That skulking figure he'd half-seen behind him, always there at the turn of his head. Not some pill-begotten nightmare then.

'I'll get it done as fast as I can, for fuck's sake!' Ivan stumbled over the words in his fear. 'And just bloody leave me alone. Christ!'

Chrystus, I'm doing this badly. Urban looked miserably across his office at Spider's blank face. She had listened to him in icy silence, her expression growing ever more glacial, until he found himself stumbling over his words like a nervous teenager.

'Spider, you *must* understand why I have to ask you this. Please. You knew all about the Churngold Capital offer and you were the only one of us who really understood the technology. And you must admit you've been a bit odd about Alan Dove, skipping meetings with him, blanking out when someone talks about him. All I'm asking for is a simple answer. If you say you had nothing to do with those press leaks then that'll be the end of it. I promise I'll believe whatever you say.'

There was a long silence after he'd finished speaking. Spider's expression was unreadable, but he could see her alternately flexing and clenching one of her hands as if she were thinking about hitting him. When finally she spoke, her green eyes still gave nothing away.

'Yes. It was me. I talked to that *Daily Business* journalist, Amy Flower.'

Although Urban had been half-expecting, half-dreading the answer, when it came he felt shock and surprise. Trying not to show this, he said nothing, waiting for her to speak again.

'I guess I'd better show you something that'll explain things,' she went on eventually. 'Not now. Not here in the office. Can you come round to my place this evening?'

Urban couldn't prevent a sharp intake of breath. No one had *ever* been to Spider's place. Like so many things, she kept her home life private. He had a vague idea that she lived somewhere in Pimlico but that was all he knew. He hoped he sounded calm. 'It can wait till then, of course. What's your address?'

Having fidgeted through a profitless afternoon, Urban decided to walk to Pimlico, thinking that a fast stride down through Mayfair and across Green Park and Victoria would clear his head for whatever ordeal lay ahead. Spider had given him no hint of what she was going to show him, and despite the walk, when he reached the tall, white houses of St George's Square, he could feel his heart thumping with anxiety. Having found Spider's ground-floor flat, Urban made himself pause on the doorstep and take a few deep breaths before ringing the bell.

The door opened slowly and he walked into an airy room which opened directly into a high-walled garden at the back. 'I had to have some space outdoors for my boys,' was the first thing that Spider said, leaving him dumbfounded by the idea that she was secretly married with children. Then a wail from just by his left ankle made him jump, and he bent down to stroke the Siamese cat winding sinuously round his ankle. 'This is Greymalkin,' said Spider. 'He's a real sucker for men. Always trying to slip off with the milkman, aren't you?'

Another yowl came from behind the door and a second Siamese slid into view. 'What a beauty! I'll bet you're Paddock.' Urban found himself stroking the two cats, both purring with the high-decibel roar of their breed.

'Think you're bloody clever guessing his name, don't you?' Spider's voice was quieter than usual, and he looked up from the cats to see her smiling.

'It wasn't exactly difficult. There's something very witch-like about you. Of course you'd have a couple of Familiars hanging about.'

'Fair is foul and foul is fair.' As she said the words, her expression changed to the blank stare that Urban saw so often. 'Rather a good theme for this evening. I wish I didn't have to do this, but I owe you some sort of explanation. Sit down and I'll get some wine. Red OK?'

When Spider came back, he was sitting on her white sofa, a cat perched on each knee, their chins pointed to the ceiling in ecstasy as he rubbed their throats. Urban stood up politely, forcing both cats to jump down on to the floor where they began to wash vigorously.

There was a thick A4 notebook under Spider's arm. 'Is that what you want to show me?'

'Pour the wine while I find the right place.' She bent her head low over the journal so that a curtain of black hair hid her expression from him. 'What a load of adolescent tripe this is. Hospital, hospital, hospital.' Spider flicked over the pages. 'I think this was about when it started. Yes. Read from here.'

Putting the open diary in his hands, she walked across the room and curled up in an armchair to watch him.

<u>Monday</u>

'How's the bowels?' Mrs Delaney called over to me as soon as I woke up. She's really embarrassing, and anyway how would I know how they were when I'd only just woken up? I said they were fine, thank you, and then asked her about her glands. Big mistake. She was still telling me about her goitre thirty minutes later, not a great start to the day.

Then I was told I couldn't have any breakfast because I was going down to X-ray and they wanted my stomach empty. It's terrible when they do this. I lay there absolutely starving while everyone else was eating toast and boiled eggs. I waited and waited, and eventually a porter came to get me at half past eleven, by which time my stomach had cleaved to my backbone. He took me to X-ray down in the basement and they X-rayed my head! I tried to tell them that the one bit of me there's definitely nothing wrong with is my brain, but the X-rayer just said it was what was written down for me so I had to have it.

It took forever, ENDLESS waiting in those horrid, smelly green lino corridors, and when I finally got back to the ward, lunch was over and I was so hungry I started to cry.

Nurse Joyce was on duty, thank goodness. She's from Great Ormond Street and she wears a striped pink uniform instead of the horrible grey the Hammersmith nurses wear. She got me some biscuits but I felt very weak and shaky until suppertime. Dr Dove came round in the afternoon.

Urban's mouth fell open as he read the name. He glanced across at Spider but her face revealed nothing. She motioned him to go on reading.

He gave me his creepy grin. I don't like his mouth, his lips are so fat and damp-looking. I told him it was disgusting that they had X-rayed my head and that if I was ever going to get better I needed proper food. He just laughed at me in his nasty way and said I could wait. I wanted to cry again, but there's something about Dr Dove that makes me want to fight, not cry. I think if he saw me crying he'd think he had won some battle.

Tuesday

Last night Mrs Amato died. I don't know why people always have to die in the night. It wakes us up because the nurses pull up the metal bars on the bed frame of the person who has died. I thought the bars were to stop you rolling out of bed when you were having a fit or something. I can't see why they think that someone who's just died is going to start rolling around all over the place. If you haven't been woken up by the crash of the bars being pulled up, the next thing they do is rattle the curtains round all our beds. Then they push the whole bed with the corpse on it out of the ward. The beds are really heavy metal things with creaky wheels but the noise doesn't matter because we're all awake by this stage anyway.

I liked Mrs Amato. She said she'd teach me Italian.

Saturday

What a horrible, horrible night. I was really ill, my temperature went right up and I was very sweaty. Our beds have this horrible thick plastic mattress cover, and mine has a ridge right down the middle of it. It's really uncomfortable, but it was worse than usual last night. When my temperature came down again, my sweat was sort of pooled up on the plastic so I was lying on a hard ridge with two long puddles of cold water on either side. I did ask the nurse if I could move or something but she just told me to go back to sleep. I'd like to see her trying to sleep on pools of icy water.

I felt dreadful all day. Dr Dove came round and I told him how rotten the beds are. He gave me a nasty look through those thick, glinty glasses of his, and later when he was feeling my tummy, he prodded it so hard with his horrid stubby fingers that it's still hurting.

Monday

I felt better this morning and got out of bed for a bit. Ward B6 is on the third floor so we have bars across the windows which must be to stop us from jumping out. I could see across a big area of waste land to our next door neighbours, Wormwood Scrubs. They have bars on their windows too. I think I saw a prisoner looking out. I suppose his lot is worse than mine but it's a toss up.

Friday

Ward rounds this afternoon. More weird hospital rules. We
have to be in bed, with the sheets pulled up tidily. No bedpans
allowed during ward rounds, even if you're desperate. No
books allowed in case they make the bed look untidy. We just
have to lie like rows of dummies while the consultant and his
gang of students walk round and make pronouncements
about us.

The consultant stopped at my bed and as per usual he didn't
even say 'hello' to me, he just asked a nurse to take one of my
dressings off so he could have a good gander at an interesting
case. Dr Dove was with him, prattling on about my treatment
and generally showing off. I wish I dared to say something to
the consultant but I just lay there and let him prod me about
as if I were a tailor's dummy. 'Very interesting case, Dove,' he
said when he'd finished, 'keep on with the steroids and the
sulfasalazine. Not sure we'll win, though. I think it'll be surgery
for this young lady.'

He walked off then with Dr Dove trotting along behind him,
but not before he'd given me his nasty smile. To be fair, Dr
Dove might have been trying to be nice, he knows how frightened of operations I am.

Tuesday

My birthday! One of the nurses came round with an enema and
I told her. 'Sweet sixteen?' she said. 'You're going to be a heartbreaker.' I don't think she's right. I've got nice hair but my eyes
are grass green. 'Heartbreaker' is kind, but something of an
exaggeration.

Wednesday

Last night was the worst ever. One of the (few) nice
Hammersmith nurses caught rabies. B6 has a little side ward
and they put Nurse Haydock in there. She screamed all night,
really screamed, like in a horror film, long, curdling screams
and incredibly loud. I could see dawn through the window bars
when they finally stopped but I don't know if any of us got
back to sleep. Later, they said she had died. I heard Nurse Luff
telling Mrs Delaney that it was a horrible death.

Saturday

Am I going mad or does Dr Dove fancy me? He keeps coming
and hanging round my bed for no reason, and he's taken to
examining me all the time. Sometimes he doesn't even call a
nurse in, I've heard the nurses giggling about it. He just draws
the curtains and makes me pull up my nightie. On the other
hand, he's being even nastier than usual.

    Yesterday when he was poking me about I told him I didn't
think being in hospital was doing me any good and he said,
'OK, I'll stop all your medication if that's how you feel.' He
looked so smug and ugly that I lost my temper and called
him rude names. He just stood there and stared at me. I hate
his scary, bulgy eyes behind those pebble glasses but I
shouldn't have called him Four-Eyes. Eventually I had to say I
was sorry. He gave that nasty little smirk of his and walked
off and left me with my nightie all pulled up and the
curtains still drawn. I lay there for ages because I was afraid
he'd come back and be cross if I'd opened the curtains. I
didn't cry, though.

Thursday

We've just been told ward B6 is going to be redecorated. It could certainly do with a change. Everyone's going to be moved to other wards. I wonder if I'm going to have a different Registrar or if Dr Dove looks after C6 too. I don't want to ask him, I'm getting rather frightened of the way he looks at me. I don't think he likes me.

Sunday

I haven't written anything for a long time. I'm starting to hurt less. One night, long after lights out, Dr Dove came on to the ward. He marched down to my bed and pulled the curtains. Then he pulled up my nightie and did something to me which really, really hurt. He didn't say anything until he'd finished and then he sort of hissed at me, 'Don't you ever dare tell a soul. They wouldn't believe you anyway.' I was crying so I just nodded at him and then he left. The next day, I was moved to C6 which has a different Registrar. I haven't seen Dr Dove since.

The notebook fell from Urban's lap. He leapt off the sofa, sending the cats flying, and crossed the room to where Spider still sat, curled in her chair. Bending forwards, he took both of her hands in his and pulled her gently until she was standing in front of him. Face pale, eyes huge, she stared up into his face. Then, as her head drooped forwards, he folded her into his arms. At first she held her body rigid, but then, as if giving up a long fight, she crumpled against his shoulder and began to cry.

For a long time Urban just held her and murmured calming words. 'It's over now. It's all right. You've been so brave.' As her sobbing continued, he began to stroke her back soothingly and was surprised to find that it wasn't ribby as he'd expected, but soft and well-covered. Her crying went on for a long time, and his shoulder felt quite damp when Spider's tears finally subsided. She drew back out of his arms a little, and reluctantly he let her go. Leading her over to the sofa, he went off in search of her bathroom and a box of tissues; then, while she was blowing her nose, he poured out more wine for both of them.

'You know something, Spider,' he said, sitting down on the sofa close beside her so that their arms were just touching. 'The world isn't divided between rich and poor, or even between commies and capitalists. The greatest division is between children with a secure family and those without. The lucky ones are Children of Light. But you and me, we are Children of Darkness.'

Spider gave a great sigh. Feeling her quivering against his shoulder, he put his arm round her, thinking that she was crying again. But when he looked down at her, he saw that she was actually shaking with laughter. 'Children of Darkness, are we? Urban, you're a mad twat, you know that? And that's enough frigging emotion to last me a year.'

His arm tightened around her. She was grinning up at him, eyes still bright with tears, and suddenly, colleague or no colleague, he couldn't stop himself. He bent forwards and kissed her. There was a gasp, and she pulled her head back to look at him. For a long moment, she stared into his eyes, and then with a slight smile on her parted lips, she lowered her eyelids and leaned up to find his mouth with hers.

He felt her melting against him, smelt the sweetly floral scent she always wore, ran his hands down the soft lines of her body, and suddenly they were tugging at their clothes, rolling off the sofa, and then her naked body was stretched out teasingly below him on the floor. Urban paused to stare at her. Spider was quite astonishingly beautiful. Even the long pink scar running down her abdomen seemed lovely to him. She reached an arm up to pull his mouth down to hers, and soon the two cats were wailing their disgust at the pair of writhing human bodies entwined on the carpet.

It wasn't until Greymalkin took a leap on to his back and clung to his bare flesh with his claws that Urban paused in his love-making. 'Bloody hell, that hurt! Talk about cattus interruptus.' Stark naked, he took a struggling Siamese under each arm, walked through the flat until he found a bedroom and popped them both inside. 'There,' he said, shutting the door. 'This scene isn't meant for voyeurs like you.'

He hurried back to find that Spider had pulled a couple of cushions down off the sofa and was lying against them, waiting for him. He thought fleetingly that the smooth curves of her bust and hips looked as pure as marble against the dark blue satin of the cushions. 'Hurry up,' she was smiling, holding her arms up to him. 'It's getting lonely down here.'

He was woken up by Spider mumuring into his ear, 'Shit, Urban. I can't believe I opened my heart *and* my legs to you in a single evening.'

He looked blearily about him to find that he was still on the floor, and that Spider had tucked a rug round his naked body. She was bending over him and had clearly been awake for some time. Her hair was damp from the shower and her breath smelt of toothpaste. Urban reached up to kiss her. Uncertain about the freshness of his own breath after that sleep, he avoided her mouth, just brushing her cheek with his lips instead. He felt embarrassed to be lying there with nothing on, when she was fully dressed, and struggled to find the right words. Eventually he said lamely, 'OK if I take a shower?' Wordlessly, she sat back on her heels and nodded, so he hurried off to the bathroom, the rug wrapped tightly around him.

While the water ran down over him, he tried to decide what he should do. It had happened so fast, he couldn't think rationally. Spider was breathtakingly beautiful, their love-making had been astonishing, but was that enough? He hadn't had time to work out how he felt about her, and more importantly, he had no idea how she might feel about him. As he towelled himself dry and stepped back into his clothes, he worked out the best approach. He'd wait for Spider to make it clear whether or not she wanted him to stay the night. Then he'd take things from there.

When he emerged from the bathroom, he found her sitting curled in her armchair again and apparently deep in a book. 'Did you find the soap and everything?' She looked up at him, her face that emotionless blank he'd often seen in the office. So that was it then. She obviously didn't want him to stay.

'Look,' he said, trying to keep his voice neutral. 'I've got an early start tomorrow.'

'Sure,' was all Spider said. 'Can you let yourself out?' She turned back to her book, and within a very few minutes he found himself walking alone through the streets of Pimlico.

He hadn't even got as far as Lupus Street before he was kicking himself for his idiocy. She was so lovely, so funny, so clever. She'd trusted him, had told him her terrible secret. She needed his care and protection. Maybe she had wanted him to stay, but didn't want to make the first move. He turned to go back, then stopped. She wasn't his type. She was too feisty. She was a colleague. And supposing she really hadn't wanted him to stay?

The coincidence of an approaching taxi and the sudden thought that Spider might come out of her flat at any moment and find him hovering there decided him. He'd sleep on it. Urban held up his hand and the cab swerved to a halt.

THIRTY-ONE

Mary had got up early after a sleepless night. How *could* she have accused Spider like that with absolutely no proof? No wonder Urban had been furious.

She was hovering outside Urban's office when he arrived just before eight. Following him in, she rushed to speak before he had even sat down. 'When you stormed out yesterday I realized how awful I must have sounded. Honestly, I can't believe Spider leaked anything confidential, or that she traded Pneumatech shares. Aiden Elginbrode must just have got it wrong. I'm really sorry. I've hardly slept a wink.'

'I didn't get a lot of sleep either.' Urban sounded tense, and as she looked at him she saw that his brown eyes had deep circles under them. In fact, for someone so handsome, he looked absolutely dreadful. 'And you can stop apologizing. You were right. Spider did leak those stories to Amy Flower.'

There was a long pause, during which Mary realized she was staring at Urban with her mouth wide open in surprise. Closing it, she struggled for something more intelligent to say than 'Goodness!'

She was saved by Urban, who shook his head and gave her a tired attempt at a smile. 'It's a bit complicated. Why don't we go out and get some breakfast? I'll be able to explain it all better after a gallon or two of black coffee.'

'That's a great idea.' Mary glanced at her watch. 'Can we meet in a quarter of an hour? I ought to let Aiden know where the newspaper leaks came from. And don't worry,' she added, seeing him frown, 'he's discretion personified.'

'Of course he is.' Urban got up to hold his office door open for her. 'I'll see you at Mamma's in fifteen minutes.'

Urban watched Mary as she bustled off down the corridor. Coming in to apologize like that. She really was one of the most principled people he knew. For a moment he felt almost happy. But when he turned and went into his office, the mood vanished. He stood leaning over his desk, keeping his back to the door so that no one passing by could read his face. What had he done? What should he do? How did she feel?

'Hi.' She was there, behind him. He could hear her breathing, smell her scent, but he couldn't bring himself to look round. 'Listen, Urban, last night, I've been thinking.' She sounded as nervous as he was. 'It's going to be embarrassing working together. I should go. I'll transfer to another office, New York maybe. Or San Francisco. That's even further away from you.'

He heard the catch in her voice and swung round. Spider was wearing a dress in some soft, fawn material. It hung straight down to her knees, making her look oddly childlike and vulnerable. She was pale, there were violet smudges under her eyes, he'd never seen her looking more beautiful. He gazed at her standing there, nervously biting her lips, and then he knew exactly how he felt. Knew with a sudden and absolute certainty. In two strides he had shut his office door. Then, wrapping his arms round Spider, he bent his head and was kissing her nose, her eyes, her chin, her throat, and then her mouth. Her lips parted and she pressed her wonderful body against him.

Phones began to ring, he heard voices outside, someone tapped on the door, but he ignored them all. As he held her against his chest and ran his hands slowly up and down her back, words he had never said before spilled out. 'I'm floored by love,' he murmured into her sweet-smelling hair. 'I adore you, I want to be with you.' He took a deep breath. 'I love you.' Urban looked down into her face. 'I love you, Spider,' he repeated.

She stared back at him, her eyes serious. Then her face broke into a grin. 'You asshole! Why the fuck didn't you tell me last night? I hardly slept at all.'

Ah well. It was as loving as he should have expected. 'Shut up, you stroppy cow.' He kissed her once again, hard. 'I didn't get any sleep either, thanks to you.' He couldn't bear to let go of her. He wanted to stand there the whole day, just hugging her and finding out all the things he didn't know about her. 'It's ridiculous,' the question suddenly occurred to him, 'but I don't even know your real name.'

'It's Minna. But I've never thought it suited me.'

'Minna.' He tried the name out, then kissed her again. 'You're right. Spider's better.'

A few minutes later, she said, 'Know something?' She reached up a hand and he felt her gently brushing his hair back off his forehead. 'You look ghastly. I hope you haven't got any client meetings today.'

'Meetings.' Urban let go of her. 'Oh, shit! Mary. I'm supposed to be having breakfast with her.'

Mary had been waiting in the Mamma Mia Trattoria for a good twenty minutes by the time Urban arrived. He sat down opposite her, out of breath. 'I'm so sorry, I got held up.'

'By something nice, obviously. You're grinning like the Cheshire Cat.'

'I'm not sure I ought to be telling you this, but Spider and I, we . . . er, you know.'

'No! You've got together? Heavens, Urban, that's absolutely wonderful news. Terrific. When did it happen?'

'I went to see Spider last night to ask her if she'd been leaking those stories, like you suggested. After she'd explained everything, well, then we . . . you know.' How sweet, he'd gone red.

A pot of coffee arrived and Mary thought it would be tactful to move the conversation on. 'Can you tell me why she did it? Talked to Amy Flower, I mean.'

'It was revenge, pure and simple. Spider came across Dove when she was a teenager. He did something so appalling that he deserves to be eviscerated and have his bowels burned in front of his nose.' A flash of deep anger crossed his face. 'Because of him, she's nervous as a cat about being touched. As a matter of fact she told me a few minutes ago that she's been keen on me for ages, but whenever she thought I was getting close her fear was triggered and she'd leap away.'

'Well, it sounds as if she's got over it now.'

Urban smiled. 'Oh yes, she's got over it.'

Mary decided that just at that moment she was more interested in hearing about the press leaks than Urban's love life. 'So Spider saw Alan Dove again, and then?' she prompted.

She watched while Urban stirred an enormous amount of sugar into a mug of black coffee. Eventually he went on, 'After we started working for Pneumatech, revenge just fell into her lap. After all, she had the facts. Spider says she arranged to meet Amy Flower last Wednesday, the day after Dove's AGM. She told her that the technical backing for the genomics research was dodgy. Amy Flower's first story appeared on Thursday.'

'And made Churngold Capital pull out of buying Dove's Lung Division.'

'Exactly.' Urban paused for some more coffee. 'Then when Dove rang me to ask if Lock Chase would do another valuation to help him find a replacement buyer, Spider obviously found out about it when we debated whether we should help Dove or not. She rang Amy Flower to tell her that Churngold Capital had pulled out, hence Friday's story.'

Two plates of bacon, eggs and fried bread were plonked in front of them. Mary kept away from the fried bread and forced herself not to have more than one egg. 'So you don't have to be sorry for anything,' Urban said kindly. 'You were right about Spider and you were right about Dove.'

There was still one thing he hadn't told her. She'd have to ask. 'And the share dealing?'

Urban smiled at her ruefully. 'To be quite honest, I didn't dare ask Spider about that. Not on top of everything else. I can't prove she didn't do any insider dealing, but she didn't. I just *know* she didn't.'

'I'm sure she didn't too. I completely believe she's straight.' Mary tugged thoughtfully at a loose strand of hair. 'And d'you know what? I'm going to prove it. Find out who *did* do the share deals. My chance to go after those scummy hedge funds may be blocked for the moment, but this sounds like straightforward insider trading. I can tackle that instead. I'll see if the Treasury will help me.'

'Did you manage to talk to Elginbrode just now?'

'No I didn't, unfortunately, I only got his assistant. He's away on annual leave. Odd man, he didn't tell me he was going when I saw him yesterday.'

'Perhaps it was a last-minute thing. Is he away for long?'

'Not back till late November. I asked if I could get hold of him while he's away but apparently it's virtually impossible. Guess where he's gone.' She raised an eyebrow, but Urban shook his head. 'He seems such an unimaginative old stick, but apparently he's a passionate troglodyte.'

'He's living in a cave?'

'Well, pot-holing actually. Exploring semi-inaccessible lime-stone formations in some remote part of China.'

At the table next to theirs a man was reading the *Daily Business*, his face hidden. As he shook the pages out, his arm nudged Mary's, making her jump with a sudden fear. Ivan Straw! She looked again. No, of course it wasn't Straw. That was blond hair peeping over the top of the newspaper. As the headline caught her eye she felt a slow smile spreading over her face.

'Quick, Urban! Go and grab a paper.'

Daily Business   *Tuesday 25 October 2005*

Pneumatech sacks Alan Dove
By Amy Flower, Senior Correspondent

Dr Alan Dove, founder and Chief Executive of Pneumatech Biosciences plc, has been sacked, a sad example of overweening ambition ruining a successful career.

So recently the darling of the stock market, Dove made a fatal error of judgement when he tried to complete two audacious deals simultaneously. Like the curate's egg, the outcome was good in parts. Buying Skinshine makes perfect strategic sense and could transform a good company into a great one. The rotten part was that he omitted to secure the funds to pay for it. Dr Dove compounded this error last Friday by implying in a statement that the sale of his Lung Division remained on track. As exclusively reported by this newspaper, that was not the case. There are no buyers.

The board of Pneumatech are left with the grisly task of trying to find alternative ways of funding the Skinshine purchase, while at the same time dealing with a company whose share price has gone into freefall. But Chairman Gregory Loach and his fellow Directors don't deserve a great deal of sympathy for the position they now find themselves in. The failure of the Pneumatech board to halt Dove's catastrophic risk-taking was nothing short of disgraceful.

Let's hope this hitherto ineffectual board finds the willpower to face up to any demands for a pay-off from their outgoing Chief Executive. Shareholders will be right behind them. They are understood to be bracing themselves for a fight over Dove's severance deal, which, if previous pay-outs to failed company bosses are anything to go by, is likely to be substantial.

On a personal note, I will be following this cautionary tale from a distance. I'm leaving shortly on a prolonged sabbatical and wish all my readers success and prosperity while I'm away.

THIRTY-TWO

More than a fortnight had passed since he had lost his job, but Alan Dove still found himself lifting the receiver to check that the phone wasn't out of order. His fall had been so sudden, so public and so cataclysmic that it was impossible for any of his acquaintance to have missed it, and yet on the day he had been sacked from Pneumatech, his normally frenetic telephone had fallen silent. His erstwhile friends, business companions and general hangers-on had dropped him like a piece of rubbish.

For days after his ejection from Pneumatech, he and Juliana crept about their London house like silent mourners, while on the street outside a gathering of journalists and photographers set up camp, hoping to get the Grief Pictures that are always so popular when someone successful has fallen. He himself had stayed firmly indoors, but Juliana had to make forays out to buy food. Every time she put her head out of the door during those first terrible days, he'd been startled afresh by the chattering of automatic shutters as cameras were pushed into her face.

As other news stories caught the headlines, the encampment outside their front door melted away and eventually he felt strong enough to make phone calls. Dove's first thought was Lock Chase. He'd paid them a great deal of money, so they owed him. They had a lot of clients and he was a bloody good Chief Executive. He was sure they could find him something to do if they kept their ears to the ground.

'Alan Dove here. Can I speak to Urban Palewski? It's urgent.'

'I'm sorry, Dr Dove, he's not available to take your call. Can I leave him a message?'

'Get him to call me as soon as possible.'

When a day had passed and the expected call from Urban hadn't come, Dove tried again. 'Dove here. Urban Palewski was going to call me back.'

'Mr Palewski's away from his office. May I leave him a message?'

'Well, how long's he going to be away from his office?'

'I'm afraid I don't know that. All I can do is to take a message for him.'

'Get him to ring me. It's urgent.'

After another day with no call from Lock Chase and another fruitless conversation with Urban's secretary, he went to find his wife. 'You wouldn't believe it. Those bastards at Lock Chase got a fortune out of me when I was running Pneumatech and now I can't even get my phone calls returned. Greedy sods. Offer you their umbrella then whip it away at the first sign of rain.'

'Perhaps they're disapproving at the moment.' Her sensible voice was calming.

'You may be right, though there's no reason I know of for Urban Palewski to disapprove of me. But since he won't talk, I'll try one of his sidekicks.'

'What about Mary Kersey. The dinner at Trister, you remember? Surely she'll want to help you.'

He went back to his study to make the call.

'Mary Kersey's office, Bella speaking. Oh good morning, Dr

Dove.' Was it his imagination or had the voice suddenly gone cold? 'I'm afraid Mary can't talk to you. No, I'm sorry but she can't.' The line went dead.

He would bloody well make someone there take his call. His clenched fists ground against his bowed head as he tried to remember the name of that other partner, the tall, black-haired woman. He'd hardly seen her. Some silly made-up name she had. Lovely face.

Minna. His eyes widened in shock as her name came back to him. Minna Wood. Spine-chilling as the night terrors, he saw her as she had looked fifteen years ago, staring up at him from a hospital pillow. 'Four-Eyes,' she had dared to call him, taunting as a Hawley-Wilson girl. He remembered his tormenting lust, the obsessive urgency of his need to crush that mesmerizing, defiant teenager. He'd never admitted to anyone the real reason why he'd abandoned his medical career. And he'd kept himself under iron control ever since.

But now he remembered. That face on the pillow. The Lock Chase partner. Those green eyes. That black hair. The ravishing mouth. Had she recognized him? Of course she had. That was why she'd kept out of his way. Perhaps she was going to come after him? Expose what he had done to her after all these years? He couldn't face that on top of what he was going through now. He might even be locked up. He'd read about what went on in those prisons.

Ivan recognized the voice on the phone straight away. 'For fuck's sake stop following me!' Dyengi's black-clad minder, watching him till he'd got the job done. 'Every time I turn round I see you there. It's like being stalked by the shadow of bloody death.'

'But for now I don't follow you.' The voice at the other end of the line sounded surprised. 'I am in Sveetzerland with Mr Dyengi. He want to speak to you.'

'Ivaan! You is bastard slow. Is two week since I tell you to kill her.'

'I'm on the case, I promise. I've got it planned.'

'Bloody shuts up. You deal with woman now or I come find you.'

'Yes, Platon.'

'And Ivaan. You keep secret or you ends up dead too. I hear everything. Police, judges, politicians. High-ups in many places tell things to me.'

Ivan was shaking when he put the phone down. God, he needed a drink.

Even in the sanctuary of her parish church, Mary couldn't help looking round nervously, as if Ivan Straw might suddenly pop up from behind a pew. Of course he wasn't there. She was being ridiculous. All the same, she glanced back over her shoulder before scurrying into the confessional box and drawing the curtain behind her.

'Bless me, Father, for I have sinned.'

'May you make your confession to the Lord with a humble and contrite heart.'

'It's Mary. I need to talk to you about Guy.'

'Oh dear, not problems again? I thought you were getting on so well. Don't worry about kneeling up straight. Sit back and tell me all about it.' Mary loved the way Peter lost any hint of crispness when he was hearing confessions. He always had all the time in the world. She settled herself as comfortably as she could on a needlepoint hassock.

'We'd be fine if he didn't keep worrying about my safety. Ever since Grace was hurt, Guy's been getting more and more irrational about it. And he's started nagging me about being in the office so much too. He says I'm not Superwoman and that Lock Chase is taking up too much of my time. This morning he even said I should give up work completely, which was incredibly annoying. He doesn't seem to understand that we couldn't possibly afford it.'

'To be honest, Mary dear, I'm not sure I understand it either. I'm quite sure you could live on a great deal less, it's just that you don't want to. You like having money to spend.'

Was he joking? From her darkened side of the confessional box, Mary peered through the grille at her parish priest, sitting in profile, brightly lit. No, he looked quite serious. He was completely wrong, though, and utterly impractical. It wasn't that she liked money, it was for Guy, for Grace, for Trister. They needed it.

Peter broke a long silence. 'And have the two of you talked about this? Calmly, I mean.'

It was uncanny. How had Peter guessed? Of course she hadn't had a calm conversation with Guy about his absurdly unrealistic ideas. But she would. 'I'm seeing him in Cambridge tonight, I'll talk to him then.'

'Well done, Mary. Now what else is bothering you?'

She knew what was bothering her. She couldn't stop thinking about him. The tall, thin figure. That narrow face watching her. 'This is going to sound hypocritical after what I said about Guy worrying, or maybe his anxiety's infectious. Anyway, I know it's silly but I keep thinking I'm being followed.' Peter looked so serene, staring out at his church from the other side of the grille. She should never have mentioned something so petty. 'I'm sorry. Even if I am being stalked, it's got nothing to do with confessing my sins.'

'What nonsense you do talk sometimes, it doesn't matter

what you say when you're in here. Now bow your head for a blessing.'

Mary closed her eyes and bent over her tightly clasped hands.

'May the Good Lord protect you and keep you from all harm and may the hand of anger never be lifted against you. In the name of the Father and of the Son and of the Holy Ghost.'

'Amen.'

The red light was flashing on Mary's BlackBerry. *'Working late, darling. Meet me in the Museum of Classical Archaeology.'*

'I'm not going to Pentecost College after all,' she said to the taxi driver who had picked her up at Cambridge station. 'Could you take me to the Classics Faculty instead, please?' Mary read Guy's message again, ridiculously pleased by the endearment. 'Darling.' She couldn't remember when he'd last called her that.

As the taxi swung left towards Sidgwick Avenue, she glanced out of the rear window. No one was following. Really, she must stop worrying in this idiotic way.

The faculty had just closed when Mary got there but the Porter opened the door for her. 'Evening, Mrs Kersey. Up from London, are you?'

'Yes I am, and I must say it's rather nice to get away. I'm meeting my husband in the museum. Do you mind if I go on up there?'

Mary wasn't at all surprised by Guy's choice of meeting place – it was somewhere they often arranged to see each other. Both of them liked to wander round the museum at dusk, after it was closed to visitors. The plaster casts of the ancients seemed more real when they loomed out of the fading light that filtered down through the long skylight.

A partition divided the room lengthways, and she and Guy

would always progress up the right-hand side, moving through time from the Archaic Style to the High Classical at the far end of the museum. There they would pause to admire Guy's favourites before returning down the further side of the partition, passing from the Late Classical through the Hellenists, to the Romans and back to the entrance again.

'Guy! Are you there?' Mary called as she pushed through the door. There was no answer. The museum's heavy silence was broken only by the occasional creaking of the glass in the skylight, contracting as it released the thin warmth of the November day.

She strolled down to the far end of the museum, expecting to find her husband absorbed by the High Classical. As she reached the Nike of Paionios, a flicker of movement from the next bay caught her eye. 'Guy?'

Turning her head sharply, she peered across at the pale draperies of a flying Nereid. Nothing. Of course there was nothing. She remembered another silent evening like this one, when she had thought she saw the headless seabird at this same Nereid's feet waddle suddenly forwards. Idiotic how the imagination was over-stimulated by solitude and twilight. But all the same, it was getting too dark to see the statues properly. And wherever was Guy? It wasn't like him to be late. That message. That 'darling'. Not quite right. Mary's breath came faster. Time to leave.

This time she heard rather than saw it. There *was* someone in Bay E. 'Who's there?' Mary called sharply. No answer but a laugh, brief but chilling.

Absurd to be worried, but she found herself walking fast towards the exit. At the sudden rush of feet she didn't stop to look, she ran. Much too far to the door. Heavy footsteps were catching up with her. Panicking, she darted into Bay C, searching wildly for somewhere to hide. The Ludovisi Throne? No. Far too low for cover. She raced to a gap in the central partition and slipped through it. In front of her, the Barberini Faun slumbered on his large plinth. Mary squeezed behind it. Only just in time.

Trying to stifle the noise of her frightened breathing, she heard her pursuer. The man hadn't spotted her yet, but peeping from behind the faun, Mary could just see him. Tall and thin. Impossible to make out his features in the fading light. As he hunted round the Aphrodite of Melos, he turned towards the skylight. Ivan Straw.

She almost called out to him. It was ridiculous hiding like this. He was only a banker. But she didn't call out. There was something in his look, something in that laugh. Instead, she peered around carefully. If she could just get as far as the Nike of Samothrace, she'd be able to dodge through to the busts of the Emperors. Plenty of places to hide there. Then another quick sprint and she'd be at the door. Her breath was coming in little gasps. She couldn't quite believe this was happening.

The floor creaked. His footsteps crept closer. She shrank back against the wall. A silence that seemed to go on for ever. Had he seen her? No. Thank God. He was moving away, back towards the far end of the museum. She took her chance. Heart pounding, she slipped out from behind the Faun and ran into Roman Portraiture. There was a wild shout. She fled past Domitian, Nero, Vespasian, their heads white ghosts in the twilight. He was catching up, he was close behind her. No time to hide. Mary pounded down through the final bay and almost reached the door and safety.

The Kore of Nikandre was her downfall. It was hard to see in the semi-darkness and she bumped against the narrow slab as she ran. Feeling it rock, she instinctively put out a steadying hand. It delayed her by a fraction of a second, all he needed. She managed one high scream before her voice was choked off by hands round her throat. She scrabbled at them, trying hopelessly to pull his long, thin fingers away from her windpipe. The hands were too strong for her. They were like bony cords, squeezing.

Mary did the only thing she could think of. She let her knees buckle and dropped towards the floor, forcing her attacker to bear the whole weight of her body. She heard him curse. His grasping hands weakened and slipped. She managed to scream again. Scrambling to her feet, she turned to face him.

He was coming at her again. His eyeballs were bloodshot, he looked quite mad. As he stretched out those long hands, she caught the stink of alcohol on his breath. Dear God! Protect me! He was gripping her arm, twisting it round behind her. 'Murder! Help!' she shrieked as his free hand reached for her throat.

She heard the door fly open. There was a shout. 'Mary!' The lights came on, and there was her husband darting towards her. The choking hands relaxed their grip as she felt him hauling Straw off. Gasping with relief, she clutched her bruised neck and turned round just in time to see Guy raising his fists. A moment later Straw was lying flat on the floor.

'Guy,' her voice came out in a croaky whisper, 'how did you know?'

'You didn't turn up at Pentecost so I came looking for you.' There was a movement on the floor. 'Stay still unless you want another thumping,' Guy said savagely. 'I told the Porter to call the police. Don't you dare move till they arrive.'

It was then that the shock hit her. With absolutely no regard for the fragility of the statue or the strict rules of the museum, Mary sat down heavily on the plaster feet of the Farnese Herakles.

*

This was how it had been last time. Excitement, exhilaration, euphoria. He'd made a brilliant shot at the pony, left the note in the girl's pocket, felt invincible, omnipotent. Then he'd lost it. Wretchedness, despair. He'd collapsed behind a tree and had almost been found by some half-witted cowman. The room seemed to swim around him. Grey walls, an iron table, a bolted door. Slumping across the table, he buried his head in his arms and wept.

As if from far away, he heard the sound of a key turning in a lock and then the sergeant's voice speaking quietly, close to his ear. 'Sorry to keep you, sir, I was just having a word with the doctor. You're in a poor state, he says.' Ivan heard the rattle of pills in a plastic bottle. 'We found these in your pocket. This is what you've been been taking, isn't it, Mr Straw? For manic depression. Bipolar disease as they call it nowadays.' The bottle was pushed under his nose so he could read the red-lettered warning on the label. 'See here, sir, you should never've taken these pills with alcohol.'

'Sorry, so sorry.' He knew that his words were slurred, but his lips wouldn't seem to coordinate with his brain.

'Our doctor's managed to speak to your own GP, sir. He says you live a completely normal life. Seems it was the drink pushed you over the edge.'

Over the edge, over the hedge, jump over the hedge, jump over the hedgie. Words spun round in his ears, making him feel sick. He rested his head on the cold iron of the table.

'I'll leave you to recover for a bit longer, sir.'

He was feeling more in control the next time the key turned in the lock, and managed to sit upright when the sergeant came in.

'Feeling better, are we, sir? Because I need to have a little chat with you.' There was a painful scraping of metal on concrete as he pulled up another chair. 'The lady you assaulted is here at the station. I've explained the situation to Mrs Kersey, concerning whether she wishes to press charges.'

The name knocked him backwards. Mrs Bloody Kersey. Sodding Oxbridge toff, la-di-da accent. He hated her, *hated* her. It was a while before he could concentrate again.

'So, between ourselves, she's been very understanding of your predicament, Mr Straw. "So he's really ill, is he? Then the poor man needs a psychiatrist, not a punishment." Those were her very words. Mr Kersey's tried to persuade her otherwise, but she's evidently a strong-willed lady and she's decided not to press charges against you.'

He could hardly believe it. 'So I can go?'

'In a while, sir, yes. When we know you're fully yourself again. And meanwhile, if you're agreeable, Mrs Kersey would like to see you. Her husband is with her, too.'

Husband. Bastard. Hit his fucking jaw. Flattened 'im. Flatten 'em. Platinum. I shoot the hippopotamus. Should have taken a bullet to her.

Floating in a confused limbo between rational thought and chaotic semi-consciousness, Ivan had a moment of clarity. If he saw Mary Kersey, apologized, blamed his illness and the drugs, she'd never even start to ask any dangerous questions. A bit of pretended self-abasement was a lot better than risking her unearthing the real reason why he'd tried to kill her.

As the sergeant opened the door again a few moments later, Ivan heard him say, 'Perhaps I should warn you both that Mr Straw is still rather disturbed.'

Disturbed, am I? Fucking half-wit copper. But as he tried to lift a mug to his lips, his hand shook so much that the hot tea slopped all over his clothes. 'I'm sorry,' he mumbled, looking down at his damp shirt. 'I'm a fool. The drink.' From miles away he heard his voice tailing off into something between a hiccup and a sob.

'But why?' That was Mrs Snooty Kersey trying to get an answer out of him. 'Why've you been following me? And why did you attack me?'

The fog cleared. He was in command again. 'For fifty million quid a year and the best job in the world. That's what your damned interfering cost me.' Perhaps he wasn't in total control yet. He couldn't stop his voice from rising to a shout.

'Steady now, sir. No need for that.'

'You leaked the Churngold Capital pull-out to the papers.'

'But that wasn't *me*.' She was interrupting him now. 'You've got that quite wrong.'

Ivan ignored her. Leaky cow. She was lying. 'That story cost one of my clients a fortune.' He'd been staring intently at her but now he could feel his eyes slipping away. The rambling words seemed to be coming from another mouth. 'Russian got me into this. Wanted me to kill her. Mrs Bloody Kersey. Didn't want to. He made me.'

Mary leaned forward, forcing him to look at her. 'This Russian. Presumably he's still out there? Still wants revenge?'

Revenge. Ivan's brain snapped back into the real world. How the hell had he come to mention the Russian? Thank God he hadn't said his name. 'Revenge? Oh, I'm sure not.' Good. He could talk quite smoothly. 'Russians are very volatile. He'll have forgotten all about it by now. Look, I'm sorry. Those pills.'

But the ghastly woman wouldn't let go. 'This Russian. Was it that short man you were with at Alan Dove's party? The one with the diamond studs? I've completely forgotten his name.' She turned her head. 'You remember, Guy, don't you? You tripped over him.'

Silly fucking cow, clinging on to her husband's arm like that.

Francesca clung on to him. Francesca. Off in France with sodding Daddy.

'I certainly do remember him. He had a philosopher's name. Aristotle? Socrates? Plato? Plato, that was it.'

'Of course! Well done, Guy. It wasn't Plato though, it was Platon. Platon Dyengi.'

'Platon Dyengi,' echoed her husband.

'*I hears everything. Police, judges, politicians.*' The words rattled round inside Ivan's head. He'd spared the woman's life and now she might as well have signed his death warrant.

'Could you sign this form for me, madam?' The sounds seemed to be drifting away from him. 'Just confirming you don't want to press charges.'

'Are you sure he's all right? He looks completely wiped out.'

'Don't worry, madam, we'll look after him. The doctor gave him a heavy tranquillizer, I expect that'll be it working now.' Their voices were receding as he struggled to stay conscious. 'And by the way, I took a note of that Russian who Mr Straw says was behind the attack. We'll pass the name up the line to Scotland Yard.'

THIRTY-THREE

Lawyers, financial advisers, headhunters, he was fed up with the whole boiling lot of them. He was fed up with sitting in his study all day too. Alan Dove stared blindly out at the empty Westminster side street. In truth, he just couldn't get down to fighting for a pay-off from Pneumatech and finding a new job. Whenever he tried to concentrate, the woman's face came flickering in front of his eyes.

The guilt was bad enough, he'd carried that for fifteen years, but the fear was worse. Would she expose him? Come after him? Take some terrible revenge? Feeling his heart thumping fast and erratically, he propped his head in his hands and tried to think rationally. A newspaper cutting on the desk in front of him caught his eye. He'd been taking legal advice about it earlier.

Daily Business   *Friday 21 October 2005*

Pneumatech Lung Division sale collapses
By Amy Flower, Senior Correspondent

'That journalist was remarkably well informed,' the solicitor acting for him had said. 'If we could prove that someone inside Pneumatech passed on a malicious leak, it might help your case for compensation from the company.'

Dove stared down at his desk. With one finger, he traced a

dark line zig-zagging through the green leather of his blotter. Well informed. Malicious leaks. Good God! Why hadn't he seen it? She'd known everything. Those leaks weren't from inside Pneumatech, they were from Lock Chase. And they weren't just malicious either. They were vengeance. She'd ruined him. She'd lost him his company, his reputation, his fortune, everything.

The realization came as a strange relief. Minna Wood had taken her revenge. He could go on with his life. Another thought struck him. His business world might be in tatters but his marriage was intact. He still had Juliana. Pushing his chair roughly back from his desk, Alan Dove felt quite light-hearted as he abandoned his study in search of solace and a cup of coffee.

His gloomy mood returned as he went downstairs into the huge basement kitchen. What a ridiculous extravagance. Just doing up this one room had cost a hundred grand, and yet it was utterly impractical, as he and Juliana were discovering now they no longer had staff to cook and clean for them. Styled in apple-green and silver, showing every speck of grease, it boasted a six-oven cooker, a built-in tandoor, marble surfaces banded with serpentine, a high-fashion rubber-tiled floor, yet not a single comfortable chair to sit in while you drank coffee with your wife.

Juliana was peeling potatoes while wobbling precariously on one of a pair of brushed-steel stools. 'Oh, there you are. I'll put on the cafetière.' As she wiped her hands and moved across the kitchen to get the coffee beans out, Dove wondered for the hundredth time how he could ever have coped without her. She had stayed so calm through all this ghastly business. Just looking at her bustling about made him feel more optimistic.

'How did you get on?' she asked.

'Not a bad morning all in all. It seems I may have a case for hanging on to my Pneumatech shares, and I've got a couple more meetings fixed up with headhunters. It's funny how some search firms will put themselves out to be helpful but others won't even give me the time of day. I tried a woman called Beth Scott just now. She was beating my door down when I was running a business, but today she wouldn't even take my call.'

'My dear, at times you can be a little abrupt. Perhaps you were short with this Beth Scott when she wanted to sell work to you?'

It was the kind of remark that might have irritated him in the old days, but not now, not with the one person who had stayed unquestioningly by his side. He smiled across at her. 'Perhaps I was.'

'Alan,' her voice tailed off. Her big brown eyes were peering at him anxiously.

'What is it?'

'Well, I . . .' The words came out in a rush. 'You know I don't like to pry into your working life, but I don't see quite why you're fighting so hard for this money from Pneumatech? Wouldn't it be best to walk away and start afresh?'

'You don't understand, Juliana.' Perching uncomfortably on his hard stool, he felt his worries flooding back. 'We live expensive lives, and I can't expect to be earning again immediately. It may take me a while to get another job. That's why I have to fight for proper compensation. How can I support you without money?'

As she fingered her chin in that tentative way of hers, he was surprised to see that she wasn't wearing nail varnish. 'I'm not sure I like the by-products of wealth any more,' she said slowly. 'Hairdressers, couture, make-up, it gets rather tiresome. And as for the newsmen on the doorstep, I didn't like that at all. I think they even sifted through our rubbish. To be honest, I'd like a simpler life.' She met his eye briefly, then looked away again. 'And I'd like to spend more time with you.'

He was struck by her words, the way she looked at him. It was as if she really cared for him. Tears pricked at the corners of his eyes. Embarrassed, he fumbled in his pocket for the antiseptic cloth that he always used to wipe his glasses. Feeling his wife pressing her own handkerchief into his hand, he grasped at her fingers. 'You can't want to be with me. I've failed.'

'Failed?' He could hear the astonishment in her voice. 'You? A man who's reached the top in two professions already? I'm just hoping I'll have you to myself before you start on your third career.'

He couldn't believe it. She wanted him. Him! He stared at her in amazement. Ten years they'd been married and he felt as if he hardly knew her. As Juliana extracted her fingers from his hand, he realized how hard he'd been gripping them. 'Sorry,' he mumbled, surprised by an unexpected pang. He wished she'd taken hold of his hand properly instead of pulling away like that.

Peering up at the silver and jade kitchen clock, another ridiculous extravagance, he saw that it was past midday. 'Come on, let's go out to lunch.'

'But Alan, if we're saving money, why don't we stay in? I've got plenty of food here. Come and see what you'd like.'

They went across to the fridge together and he stood close behind her as they peered inside. As she bent to look at one of the lower shelves, her bottom brushed hard against him. She straightened up, and as she did so, he realized that he didn't need the holding back, the iron self-control any more. Minna Wood had taken her revenge and now he was free. Reaching his arms around his wife, he could feel her heavy breasts through the wool of her jumper. He bent his head to kiss the nape of her neck and suddenly, instead of standing woodenly in his arms, he felt her pressing against him.

'Let's go upstairs,' he whispered into her ear.

'But what about your coffee?'

'Damn the coffee!'

Taking her hand, he pulled her away from the fridge and across the kitchen. At the bottom of the stairs, he stopped to kiss her before guiding her upwards, one hand on each side of her broad hips. He paused at each turn of the stairs in the tall, narrow house to kiss her again. Once they reached their bedroom, he expected her to retire to the bathroom to undress modestly and to emerge wrapped in a dressing-gown, as she always did. But this time she didn't leave him. Without even bothering to draw the curtains, she took all her clothes off, right there in front of him.

The sight of her naked white body was extraordinarily exciting. He tore at his trousers. As he tugged his pullover roughly over his head, his glasses flew off. He heard them fall on the floor but he didn't care. Juliana was in his arms, and then they were tumbling on to the bed together. His last sensible thought was that he would never have dreamed that his wife could be so uninhibited.

Afterwards, he lay quietly while Juliana dozed, her body curved heavy and relaxed beside him. He stroked her naked thigh and heard her sigh softly as she turned towards him. 'Alan?' Her voice was languid. 'Let's go to bed together every afternoon.'

He bent to kiss her shoulder, still not quite able to believe what had happened. He felt elated. He was in love, and with his own wife, of all people. A rush of optimism swept over him. They'd make a new life together, share each other's dreams, comfort each other. As he lay there, flooded with happiness, a sudden thought came to him. There must be no secrets between them. His beloved wife would help him to put his guilt behind him for ever. He had to share it with her straight away.

'Juliana,' he breathed into her ear, 'there's something I must tell you.' He kissed her earlobe as she wriggled into his arms.

'What is it?'

He couldn't bring himself to look at her while he talked. He lay on his back, hugging her to him, staring blindly upwards as the words came out. He didn't even try to make any excuses for what he'd done to Minna Wood.

She was silent when he had finished, so he propped himself up on one elbow to peer down at his wife. His glasses were lost somewhere on the bedroom floor, and without them he had to bend close to see her expression. As her face came into focus, he realized his mistake. Eyes wide, she was staring up at him in horror.

'Juliana?' Without a word, she rolled out of his arms and got up, her body becoming a blur as she moved away from him. 'Where are you going?' She moved further from his weak field of vision until she was a vague shape by the bedroom door. 'Come back!'

Out of the mist of his myopia her voice came to him, cold and flat. 'Have you forgotten what my father did to me? I couldn't stay an hour longer with someone who has done what you have done.'

Her father. Oh God, how *could* he have forgotten? 'But Juliana! My darling wife. Can't you forgive me?'

'For that, there is no forgiveness.' The door closed behind her.

THIRTY-FOUR

'Oh Mummy, look, they're so sweet! They're all wagging their tails at us!'

'Not wagging their tails, Gracie,' Sir John interrupted. 'They're waving their sterns.'

The only reason Mary had agreed to come to the hunt kennels again after that glacially slow afternoon with Minim was because of Guy's unease about Sir John's plan to take Grace along to the Boxing Day meet. Guy had tried very hard to persuade him out of the idea when he had raised it.

'I'm bound to say I think you're being rash, Father. You haven't ridden for years.'

'It's still four weeks till Christmas, plenty of time to get used to the saddle again.'

'But surely you can protest just as well from the ground as from the back of some lethal animal that's going to pitch and toss you all over Suffolk? Who's going to look after the farm when your tibia's been mashed into your ulna?'

'And what about Gracie?' Mary had added, wanting to support Guy's concern for his father. 'She's not going to be happy seeing you excavated from some muddy field and carried home on a trestle, is she?'

Sir John had smiled fondly at them both. 'Sorry, but I've got to do it. It's the devil, this banning business. Government attacking minorities just because they don't care for them. I've never broken a law in my life but I'm going to hunt again so I can break this bloody law.'

'But you haven't got a horse, Father.' Guy had sounded suddenly hopeful.

'All fixed. The Blythe Vale Hunt are lending me something to ride. Matter of fact I said I'd go down there this weekend to have a look.'

Grace had insisted on going with her grandfather to the hunt kennels, and Guy had asked Mary to go along too. 'Try and have a quiet word with Charley. Persuade him to lend Father a gentle old plod. And don't worry about lunch,' he added. 'I'll roast a chicken while you're out.'

At the kennels, they found Charley walking around among the hounds in the run, checking their pads and ears. 'Good morning Sir John, Mrs Kersey.' He briefly tipped his cap in Mary's direction. 'The Master's asked me to show you Sea Salt. He's a sound old fellow and he'll carry you as well as any.'

Shivering along after them as they walked over to the stables, Mary was relieved to learn that Sea Salt was both sound and old. 'And how are you getting on with that pony of yours, Grace?' she heard Charley calling over his shoulder. 'She's seen a hunt or two in her time. Nice little thing she is.'

'She's brilliant! Of course I'll always love Dimple the best,' Grace added hastily. Mary smiled at this, knowing that her daughter was fearful of offending the shade of her dead pony, 'But Minim does suit me. She never does anything frightening.'

'She just looks frightening,' put in Sir John cheerfully. 'Like a blonde orange. Never seen anything like it.'

'Now then,' Charley's calm voice interrupted Grace's shriek of laughter. 'You'll be getting my hounds all worked up with your noise.' He stopped beside the half-door of a loosebox over which a big grey head was peering inquiringly. 'Here he is, Sir John. What do you think?'

'I'm sure he'll be grand.' Patting the horse's neck, Sir John chatted to Charley while Sea Salt was tacked up. He lowered his voice, but Mary could hear him quite clearly in the still winter air. 'Dreadful business, my poor daughter-in-law being attacked by a maniac. My son saved her, you know. Punched the fellow's jaw.'

Roasting chickens, knocking grown men to the ground ... Mary was both disconcerted and delighted by Guy's unexpected talents. She sat down on a hay bale and thought about her husband. Everything would be fine if only he'd stop nagging her about her career. Either he was telling her it was dangerous: 'First there was Grace and Dimple, and now you and Ivan Straw. Supposing I'm not around next time it happens?' or he was complaining that she worked too hard: 'You're back doing those ridiculous eleven-hour days at Lock Chase and we never have a moment to ourselves. I'm starting to feel I'm married to a mirage.'

He was right. They weren't spending any time together. Fingering the stubbly ends of the hay with a gloved hand, she realized guiltily that they still hadn't had the talk she'd promised during her last confession to Peter. She really had intended to have a proper conversation with Guy that day she went to Cambridge, but Ivan Straw's mad attack had put it out of her mind, and since then she just hadn't had a moment. The run-up to the year end was a frantically busy time for her Lock Chase clients and there were all the presents to buy and the cards to write as well. Mary decided she'd just have to be realistic. Chatting to her husband must wait. After Christmas, she vowed to herself, that's when she'd make time to be with Guy.

There was a clatter of hooves on concrete as Sea Salt was led out of his stable. Sir John was still telling Charley about the attack. 'They let him go, can you believe it? Refused to press charges. I'd have locked him up and thrown away the key.'

Mary shivered as a thin wind whipped round the yard. Where was Ivan Straw? Had she done the right thing?

Ivan blinked hard, but he could see nothing in the pitch darkness. The heat strafed the back of his throat like burning phosphorus when he opened his mouth. He had no idea where he was, or how long he'd been there, but some things he could remember.

It had been a freezing night. He'd been wearing his thickest cashmere coat, but he'd still been cold. A biting wind had blown his trousers against his ankles as he hurried back to Wolkenbank. Occasionally he'd glanced back over his shoulder, hoping to see an empty taxi, but the streets of the City were silent and deserted. He'd walked faster, wishing he was at home in a hot bath instead of walking alone in the dark along an icy pavement. Suddenly, somewhere behind him, a car door had slammed. He'd heard an engine starting, turned and saw a pair of headlights creeping slowly towards him. He'd had to control a sudden urge to run. It was just some other City executive who'd been working late. He'd almost reached Wolkenbank when the car purred past and pulled up just ahead of him. A long, black limousine. Why was it stopping? One of the doors opened and he'd begun running, but far too late. He'd come to with a blinding headache, lying on the hard floor of this hot room in complete darkness.

He tried to stand up, though his legs felt weak. Staggering across the room, he stubbed his toes on an iron bedstead, burned his hand on the metal when he bent to touch it. He'd better move more carefully. He felt across the floor with his hands until he eventually found the door. Metal. Locked. No handle.

He beat his hands against it, oblivious to pain. Nothing. He shouted, pounded against the door with fists and heels, shouted again. Silence. Nothing but heat, darkness and the hammering of his heart.

The thirst crept up on him slowly. At first, it was just a dryness on the tongue, then a scratch at the back of the throat. He tried to ignore it, but once he realized he was thirsty, he couldn't think about anything else. The headache got worse, he felt sick, and all the time the thirst was growing. Panic began to take hold of him. He flung himself at where he thought the door was, stumbled, fell on the floor, feeling it with shaking hands. It was getting hotter. A nightmare thought occurred to him. He was inside an oven. He'd be slowly baked to death.

He leapt up, but his legs buckled under him. His head was pounding and he felt a sharp pain, a dagger sticking through his left eye and into his brain. He wanted to lie down but the floor was too hot. Fumbling around, his hand touched something. He'd missed it before. A glass. A glass full of something he couldn't see. Water, it must be water. He breathed a deep sigh of relief. Whoever had shut him in this room meant to frighten him, not to kill him.

He couldn't afford to lose a drop. Trying to stop his hand from trembling, he brought the glass to his parched lips and drank. His thirst was so great that he could taste nothing. He emptied the glass gratefully. It was only when he had finished that he realized what it was. Vodka. Worse than vodka. Vodka with salt.

Time passed, an hour, a day, a year, he had no idea. He burned himself when he sat down, felt dizziness and nausea when he stood up. Francesca burst in carrying jugs of iced water. 'Thank God, I knew you'd find me, doll.' He reached out a hand and she vanished. Alan Dove came to see him, his gargoyle face grinning. 'Hello, Ivan, let's go for a swim. The water's perfect.' He ran after Dove and dived head first into a boiling sea.

When he came to, he heard a noise. Scratching. A key in the door. He opened his mouth but his tongue was so swollen no sound would come out. 'Water,' his cracked lips mouthed into the darkness. The footsteps were retreating. Though invisible in the pitch darkness, he felt the walls spinning around him as he begged, 'Come back. Oh please come back.'

'I'm so glad you're back, Aiden, did you have a good holiday?' Mary asked. 'China, wasn't it?'

'Yes, indeed. I was exploring a series of limestone caves.' He looked across sharply, as if he were asking himself some question about her. 'I looked at some of the new surveillance technologies while I was there. Mind you,' he added, 'we're pretty hot on interception ourselves.' There was that sharp look again. 'On which subject, there's something I'd like to discuss with you.'

'Of course.' Surveillance? Interception? This man was no middle-ranking civil servant. He must have a much wider brief and a far higher rank than she'd been led to believe. Mary scrutinized his face. Anonymous, bland even. Forgettable. And yet today, for the first time, he'd let his blank mask slip. She wondered why.

Elginbrode brought her back to the present. 'But first, there was something specific you wanted to tell me. Pneumatech, was it?'

'Sorry, my mind wandered off for a moment. I need to let you know about those newspaper stories around the time of the AGM. But there's something else.' Mary paused. The whole thing still seemed quite extraordinary. 'I . . . well, you're going to find this very peculiar, but Ivan Straw, you remember?'

'Yes, indeed. Alan Dove's banker. From Wolkenbank.'

'He tried to strangle me. In Cambridge. In the Museum of Classical Archaeology, of all places.'

Elginbrode's eyebrows expressed his astonishment. 'He attacked you? Are you all right?'

'It was terrifying at the time.' She felt a little shiver as she remembered. 'But fortunately my husband had come looking for me. He knocked Ivan Straw right down,' she added, still proud of Guy's unexpected left hook.

'Incredible! Do you have any idea why Straw should do such a thing?'

'Well, it turns out he's bipolar and he wasn't very coherent when we talked to him. His gripe seemed to be over Pneumatech. He said a client had lost a lot of money when the Lung Division sale collapsed. He thought I'd talked to the *Daily Business*.'

'Strangling you over a newspaper leak seems a little extreme.'

'It does, doesn't it? But I think Mr Straw's client gets *very* upset when he loses money. He's one of those Russian oligarchs. Platon Dyengi.'

Elginbrode looked alarmed. 'You should take care, Mary.'

'Don't say it! I get quite enough warnings from my husband.' She smiled wryly at him. 'By the way, you were quite right about where the leaks originated. They did come from Lock Chase. It was one of my fellow Partners, Spider Wood.'

'And did she make money from them?'

'Good God, no. Talking to the *Daily Business* was an act of revenge for something Alan Dove had done. She never bought or sold a single share in Pneumatech, or in any other Lock Chase client for that matter.'

'Then I think we can put Miss Wood's involvement down to a happy chance. Happy, that is, for our share traders.' He leant back in his chair. 'The information they received allowed them to sell their holdings in Pneumatech before they lost any of the profit they'd made. For let's not forget . . .' Once again, Mary saw the intelligence behind Elginbrode's façade. 'Large purchases of Pneumatech shares were made immediately before Dr Dove announced his twin deals.'

'After which the share price shot up.'

'Precisely, Mary. If the people who bought shares then are also those who sold just before Miss Flower's articles caused the share price to collapse, then they have been prescient.'

'Insider trading, more like.'

'Exactly the subject I wanted to raise with you.'

There was such a long silence that Mary eventually felt she was expected to say something. 'So,' she ventured, 'what was it you wanted to ask?'

Elginbrode leant forward across his desk. 'Now that Alan Dove has met his nemesis,' he began, 'do you feel that the whole venture is completed, so to speak? Or would you be prepared to give me a little further assistance? You could be of considerable help in getting to the bottom of this nasty little piece of insider trading.'

The question took her by surprise. She'd love to help, but it would be yet another call on her time. What was it Guy had said? I'm married to a mirage. Elginbrode was looking at her expectantly, as if he had no doubt about her answer. And of course he was right. 'It's my duty to help you,' she said firmly. 'Inside traders are no better than thieves, and if I can prevent them stealing, then that's what I must do.'

'I was hoping you might feel that way.' A quick smile flashed across his face. 'Now there's someone I'd like to introduce you to.'

He must have pressed some invisible button, because almost

immediately his door flew open and a young woman sprang into the room.

Mary's first irreverent thought was that this was how Lot's wife might have looked when transformed into a pillar of salt. Over six foot tall, she was thin, with no discernable shape from nape to knee. She was also extraordinarily pale. Her wispy hair was nearer white than blonde and her face anaemic apart from a spattering of freckles across her nose. In sharp contrast to Mary's and Elginbrode's tidy suits, she wore a tight top with 'Looking For A Cowboy' written across her flat chest, while a pair of tatty jeans hung low on curveless hips, looking as if the slightest tug would bring them down round her ankles.

Expecting this skinny wisp to have a weedy voice to match, Mary was taken aback when her hand was grabbed and a voice roared, 'I'm Darleen and am I glad to meet you! Aiden's been talking y'all up big time. Seems we're sleuthing!'

'I'm glad you've introduced yourself, Darleen,' Elginbrode put in quietly, though Mary thought she caught the corners of his mouth quivering. 'Let me just explain who you are.' Before Darleen could interrupt, he said, 'You see Mary, Darleen here's an expert. A *serious* expert in the arcane world of information gathering. Telephones, computers, bank accounts, you name it, she can hack it.'

'Aw, come on, Aiden!'

'Her department in Texas has lent her to us on a year's secondment. Ostensibly she's learning from us but in reality it is we who are learning from her. A technological wizard, aren't you, Darleen?'

Darleen's reply was muffled by a toffee. 'Excuse me guys, have to eat.' She patted her concave stomach affectionately. 'There's nothing'll fill this sucker up. Ma reckons I got a worm.'

'Quite,' interrupted Elginbrode hastily. 'Now Mary, some background. Darleen's arrival happened to coincide with you asking me to keep an eye on Pneumatech. Since then, we've been monitoring telephone conversations in Dr Dove's areas of operation. Darleen and I set out some key words, rather obvious ones like "Pneumatech" and "F-ACE" and then she sat back and listened.'

'And picked up some traffic. Short and snappy. Suffolk,' put in Darleen.

'Presumably that would have been Dove himself talking, wouldn't it? He's in Suffolk at the weekends. So's Urban for that matter, and me.'

'No, Mary. I checked that out.' Darleen's voice seemed to be booming even louder. 'Y'all are too far east. Those key words were coming out to the west of you, Mary. Inner Suffolk you might say.'

Elginbrode's voice also seemed to be rising with something approaching excitement. 'So then we added a few other key words. Companies where we've had suspicions of insider trading in the recent past.'

'We sure picked up some smackers there, holy shit we did! Doverwhite, Seachest.'

'I believe we heard Dix Associates too.'

'No doubt about it, Aiden, I heard it!'

'So you see, Mary, this might mean nothing at all or it could mean something very interesting.' He looked quellingly at Darleen as if daring her to interrupt again. 'Somewhere to the west of you is someone with a normally untraceable telephone line. This someone is talking about some very specific companies where there's been shady share dealing. It's a long shot, but then you've lived at Trister for many years. I presume you'll either know or at least know of all the likely people in your area.'

'And we're talking a real small patch,' Darleen broke in. 'A handful of miles. Lucky as hell we're not talking big country. Like Texas.'

'Thank you, Darleen. As I was saying, is there anyone you can think of who might fit the bill? Rich, secretive. Quite possibly with no obvious source for their wealth.'

After a moment's thought Mary said doubtfully, 'I suppose there's Meg Dewey. Her house *is* to the west of ours and she *does* live in the absolute lap of luxury. Hot and cold running maids, gardeners by the shovelful, pictures you'd normally only see in a gallery. They're ridiculously generous with entertaining, too. Yet I can't see how they've got more than a handful of beans coming in. She doesn't work at all and her husband's a louche wine trader.'

'Meg Dewey you say?' Elginbrode scribbled the name down.

'But I can't believe Meg'd do anything involving work. She's *voluptuously* idle.' A vague memory came to her. Meg at Trister, talking to Alan Dove in the Great Hall. About shares. No. It was inconceivable that Meg was a closet inside trader. 'And I can't believe she'd do anything criminal.'

'Ostentatious expenditure, invisible means.' Elginbrode nodded thoughtfully. 'That rings an alarm bell. Anyone else we should be keeping an eye on?'

'What about Amy Flower? She seems rather central. And being a financial journalist she'd be well positioned to pick up inside information and sell it on.'

'You seen Amy round Suffolk? Reckon she's connected?' Darleen asked.

'Well, it may not be as big as Texas but Suffolk's not a *small* county. I haven't seen her myself though, no.'

'One must admit that Amy Fower's footprint is pervasive, but there's a problem.' Elginbrode was leaning back in his chair again. 'Were she to be selling information, she'd have made a deal of money.'

'But there's none to be found,' Darleen leapt in. 'I've been down that trail. Pay check comes in from the *Daily Business*, cash goes out on utilities, shopping and the like. Nothing suspicious in her bank account whatsoever.'

'Maybe she was paid in cash,' Mary suggested.

'Five-figure sums? Even in fifty-pound notes, that would be impractical.'

'Well, supposing she's working with someone she trusts?' Mary tried again. 'Maybe she hands over the information and they pay her later, when it's safe.'

'I sure as hell wouldn't trust anyone *that* much. Amy takes the risk, they take the cash and skedaddle?'

'You're right, Darleen,' Mary concluded. 'It's too ridiculous. Perhaps we're barking up completely the wrong tree with Amy Flower.'

'Maybe,' Elginbrode had that thoughtful frown on again, 'though instinct draws me to her. I'd like to see Miss Flower but she seems to have slipped off somewhere for a break.'

'Isn't she dating some politico?' Darleen scratched a thin arm vigorously. 'Tim Cusack, that's the sucker's name. Maybe we should check him out?'

'I agree. Someone should talk to him and I think it should be you, Mary. He'd be sure to see you with your background. Whereas Darleen, well, you're perhaps a little *noticeable* for his taste.'

Darleen had bounced out of the room and Mary was about to follow when Elginbrode called her back.

'Will you please take care? Your husband's quite right to be concerned. Ivan Straw's behaviour was extreme, to say the least.'

'Oh, but you should have seen him, it was really desperately sad. He's just ill. I'm sure he won't trouble me again.'

*

'Is done, Mr Dyengi. He dead now.'

'No trace?'

'No trace. Vodka and salty drink dehydrate him. Very hot room. No nice death. Take a long time. Head ache big, thirst very big, but leave no trace. Body show he eat salty food and drink too much, very bad with prescription. Police think silly boy. Or maybe suicide.'

'Dehydrate, good. He *yuzyk*, it swell horrible?'

'*Da*. The tongue stick far out when he die.'

'No one grass me to police and stay alive.' Platon Dyengi put down the phone.

THIRTY-FIVE

Having been taught from an early age that to lie was to sin, Mary sent Tim Cusack a message containing the simple truth that she'd like to talk to him about Amy Flower. Slightly to her surprise she got an almost immediate reply that he'd meet her in the House of Commons as soon as possible, and a date was fixed for early December.

'You've been here before?' Tim asked politely as he led Mary across the acreage of marble-floored, gothic stonework in the Central Lobby of the Houses of Parliament.

'More down the other end.' She jerked her head in the direction of the House of Lords. 'My uncle's the Earl of Ivybridge.'

'Ivybridge?' He stopped below the statue of some long-dead statesman and turned to face her. 'That's in Somerset, isn't it? Your family aren't constituents of mine, are they?'

'Not unless you represent Devon as well. My family home is Brink Castle. It's on the coast just to the west of Dartmouth.'

'Oh, I see. I hope you don't mind me asking, I'm in a key marginal and I need every vote I can get.' He led her to a green leather bench. 'So. You wanted to talk about Amy?'

'Please. It's in connection with some research Lock Chase have been doing for the Treasury. I need to talk to senior financial journalists like Amy Flower but I understand she's on a sabbatical. I thought you might know where she is so I can get in touch with her.'

She noticed his expression slipping dejectedly. 'I really wish I could help you, by God I do. Amy said she needed a break and then she just vanished. She's not answering her mobile, she's not at her house, I don't know where in the world she's got to. And I *had* hoped we could have spent Christmas together . . .' His voice trailed off.

'Maybe she'll be back in time for Christmas. Surely she'll want to see her family?'

'Actually she never talked about family. I'm not even sure she has a relation to her name.'

'No relations?' she prompted him.

Tim shook his head. 'The only family she seems to have are her cars.'

'Cars?' An alarm bell began to ring faintly. Cars weren't cheap.

'Vintage. Amy loves them like children. She keeps them down at a place on the river in Twickenham. I can give you the address if you like.'

Mary had a sudden thought. 'Did Amy ever mention Suffolk? Or someone called Meg Dewey?' Tim's blank face gave her the answer.

'Meg Dewey? Sorry, but no.' He got up to go. 'Do *please* tell Amy to ring me if you track her down.'

A sleety rain was falling as Mary plodded along the streets of Twickenham the following afternoon. After fifteen minutes of walking, she came to a particularly depressing cul-de-sac of 1950s brick-built houses. Her phone started to ring and she had to stop under a dripping tree to dig it out of her briefcase. It was Guy.

'I was just going into the British Museum and I thought I'd check on you before I have to turn my mobile off. D'you need a pugilist?'

'No, but I'd be glad of an umbrella.' She pressed herself against the trunk of the tree, where the rain didn't seem to be penetrating. 'As a matter of fact, I wouldn't mind some of your brain-power as well.'

'I'd have thought you had more than enough of your own, but I'm bound to say I'm flattered. Go on.'

'I told you this inside trading seems to be connected with Suffolk, didn't I? And Aiden Elginbrode says that people with ostentatious expenditure and no obvious income are often criminals. There's an idea I can't get out of my head. Meg's so rich. You don't think she could be a crook, do you?'

'Felonious Meg, it's an interesting thought. Any other clues?'

Mary flinched as a drop of icy water ran down her neck. 'Only one. A journalist called Amy Flower seems to have passed information to the inside traders but there's no sign she's been paid for it. It looks as if she trusts whoever she's working with implicitly, but I can't understand who *anyone* would trust that much.'

'My dear Mary.' Guy sounded quite offended. 'What about her husband?'

'She hasn't got one. But anyway, we're talking about a link between Amy Flower and Meg Dewey, not a married couple.' Another huge drop landed on her head. 'I'd better go, I'm getting soaked.'

'Wherever are you?' She could hear that note of anxiety creeping into his voice as she started walking again. 'Mary?'

'Near Richmond Bridge. I'm visiting a boatyard in a place

called Duck's Walk where Amy Flower's supposed to keep some cars. Oh, I think I've arrived.'

'Do be careful,' Guy started, but Mary snapped her phone shut before he could say any more.

Directly facing her was a grey concrete boathouse, beyond which the Thames rolled sluggishly down towards central London. Tarmac had been laid around the boathouse in balmier days, but now rank quills of grass pushed up through cracks in the surface and struggled for space against a tideline of plastic bags and discarded paper.

Her heart sank. The place looked completely shut up and deserted. There was not a sound from either the street behind her or the boathouse ahead. All she could hear was the steady patter of rain and the gurgle of the Thames flowing fast and high along its banks.

'You looking for me, hen?'

A head wearing a red woollen hat had popped out of a side door in the boathouse. Mary moved gratefully towards it calling, 'Hello! I'm looking for Amy Flower.'

'Well, ye'll no' find her here.' The man came out, brandishing a lethal-looking piece of steel and wood. Mary was backing away nervously when he said, 'Never mind this. There's a few bastards round here fancying a joyride. If they try to get in I break their wee heads with a starting handle, see? Come away in, hen, you're freezing. I'm Gordon,' he added, thrusting out an oily palm. 'Miss Amy's mechanic.'

Mary stepped cautiously into the boathouse and Gordon shut the outer door firmly behind her, creating an airlock before he opened a second door into the garage itself. Astonishingly, the clammy river-chill gave way to a blissfully warm, dry heat. Mary's first thought was how outrageous the heating bill must be. And then she thought, but who was paying for it?

'So Miss Flower,' she started tentatively, 'she must be a very rich woman to afford all this?'

'Miss Amy sent you here, did she?'

'Not exactly.' Mary couldn't bring herself to lie. 'It was Tim Cusack who suggested it.'

'Aye, I see.' She caught a hint of suspicion in his voice. 'He'll be wanting me to give you a wee tour of the cars, no doubt.' In the dim light of the boathouse Mary could see fifteen or twenty shapes huddled under protective dustsheets. Gordon swept the cover off the nearest one, revealing a long silver car of extraordinary elegance. 'Now here's a real beauty. A Bristol Beaufighter. Built in the 1970s she was. Bristol, now there's a great firm.'

Half an hour later they'd got to the fifth car, an Alvis Grey Lady from the early 1950s, and Mary had seen more than enough. There was a fortune here. The vintage cars, the luxurious warmth, the full-time mechanic – Amy Flower could never have afforded all this on a journalist's salary. But while Gordon explained much about the relative merits of the Maserati Quattroporte and the Lagonda Rapide, she couldn't persuade him to tell her anything about Amy. All he would say was that she'd be back. 'Miss Amy would never leave her cars for long. Loves them, she does.'

Gordon clearly loved the cars too, and seemed perfectly happy to talk about them for hours. It was only by using the excuse of having to get back to London that Mary finally escaped. 'If it's Richmond station you're after, you'll be quicker going down river, hen,' Gordon advised her as she left. 'You'll not get lost.'

Twenty minutes later, she was very lost indeed and was hurrying through heavy rain and in near-darkness along a deserted towpath. There should be a bridge. Take the second bridge, he'd said. Had she missed it? How could you possibly miss a whole bridge? She could hear the river rushing along just beside her. It was making unpleasant sucking noises, or was that her feet? Her shoes were completely soaked. Feet. Footsteps. Slopping along the towpath towards her. Oh God, no! Could it be Ivan Straw, coming to finish her off?

A sudden panic gripped her. She spun round and started to run back the way she'd come, splashing through puddles, her heavy briefcase banging against her leg. The trees made a tunnel overhead so that she couldn't see a thing. She skidded on wet leaves and fell hard on to her right knee. Forcing herself up again, she stumbled on. Was there anyone following her? She peered anxiously back over her shoulder. Too dark to see. The trees opened out and she caught a movement on the towpath ahead. Someone was coming.

Mary couldn't decide whether to go on or to run back again. The figure drew closer. It was a man, tall and familiar. 'Oh, Guy! It's you!' She threw herself into his arms. 'I was terrified. I seem to scare very easily at the moment,' she murmured into his shoulder.

'I'm not surprised.' Guy spoke to the top of her head.

'I don't believe this.' Mary peered up at him, trying to make out his face in the semi-darkness. 'Whatever are you doing on a towpath in Twickenham?'

'I've had a Eureka moment and I wanted to tell you about it. Well, the truth is, I was worried. I decided to chuck the British Museum and come here instead. I went to your boathouse in Duck's Walk and a ferocious Scot said he'd sent you this way. Since your sense of direction's appalling, I knew you'd get lost.' With an arm firmly around her shoulder, he added, 'Let's get back to civilization.'

With Guy by her side the towpath lost its terrors, and in a surprisingly short time they were sitting in a pub near Richmond Green drinking beer and warming their wet feet.

'So what was this Eureka moment of yours then?'

Feeling in one of his pockets, he pulled out a paperback and put it on the table between them. '*Little Women*.' Mary read the title upside down, then shook her head blankly. 'I'm completely in the dark.'

'I'm researching a paper on ancient and modern warfare and I found this on Grace's bookshelves. Does that give you a clue?'

'None at all.'

'The American Civil War?'

'I do vaguely remember that's when *Little Women* was set, though I haven't read it since I was a girl.'

'Just listen to this.' Guy opened the book at a page he'd marked and began to read. '"*Would you tell him?*" *asked Meg of her sisters.* "*He'll laugh,*" *said Amy warningly.* "*Who cares?*" *said Jo.* "*I guess he'll like it,*" *added Beth.*' Putting the book down, he grinned across at her. 'D'you see now? You asked me who you'd trust and the names gave me the idea.'

'You're a genius.' Mary was smiling too. 'Who *would* you trust? Your sister!'

'Amy and Meg.' Guy was looking thoughtful again. 'Why not another sister, or even two? A Beth and a Jo? I don't know anyone called Jo, but what about that headhunter I said you should see? Beth Scott.'

'D'you know, you might be right. I rather think her eyes were the same blue as Meg's. Criminal sisters. Surely that's unbelievable?'

'Not at all, it's *quite* believable. You don't read the classics enough. The Erinyes, the Sirens, the Harpies, it's astonishing how often sisters work together for unscrupulous ends. The Greeks drew from life, you know.'

'What d'you think I should do?'

'Sleep on it. If the idea still seems sane tomorrow you should tell your Mr Elginbrode.' Leaning forward, he took her hand and began to stroke it. 'You hair's gone all curly from the rain. You look like one of Rossetti's angels. Tell you what.' He stood up suddenly. 'Come to Cambridge with me. We'll pick up a bottle of champagne on the way and we can eat fish and chips in my bed. Come on!'

She got up too and leaned against his shoulder. It was a lovely idea, but out of the question. 'I can't, I'm afraid. I've got a client meeting first thing tomorrow morning.'

'Cancel the bloody client.' She was taken aback, Guy never swore. Now he was rubbing his thumbs along her shoulders. 'Come on,' he said again, 'we'll catch the nine-fifteen if we hurry. Bed before eleven.'

'It's impossible. My client's the Chief Executive of one of our biggest banks. I can't just cancel him. But why don't you sleep in the flat tonight?'

'You know I can't, I give seminars all morning. Please come back with me, Mary.' The hands on her shoulders were still. 'Champagne and chips in bed. Listening to the Cambridge bells. It'll be fun. We'll be silly and irresponsible, like we used to be.'

Mary thought of all the work her case team had put into tomorrow's meeting, the impossibility of not turning up to see one of her most important clients. 'I'm sorry.'

'I see.' Guy's hands fell from her shoulders.

'I simply can't let everyone down.'

'OK. I understand.'

In silence, they left the pub. Guy didn't kiss her as he put her into a taxi. 'Battersea, please,' he said to the driver before turning away. She looked out of the rear window but he didn't wave. She watched him walk straight into Richmond station to start his long trek back to Cambridge.

THIRTY-SIX

It took Mary a much longer time than usual to get to sleep. She kept seeing Guy's face as he turned into the station. He'd looked hurt, offended and profoundly sad. She really must find a way to spend time with him. She'd do it once Christmas was over. Life was always quieter between Boxing Day and New Year.

She was awake until long after midnight and was in a heavy sleep at seven the next morning when the telephone rang. Fighting the temptation to ignore it, she rolled over. 'Hello?' she mumbled.

'Hey there, Mary! Rise and shine!' Darleen's Texan twang boomed into her ear. Struggling to wake up, Mary's first thought was the impossibility of reconciling this thunderclap of a voice with Darleen's appearance, thin and quivery as a Lombardy poplar. 'Have I got a story for you!'

Reluctantly deciding that she was indeed awake, Mary sat up in bed and listened. 'Remember mentioning Mrs Meg Dewey of Suffolk? You'll never guess what I've found out. Got her mother's maiden name prior to blagging my way into her bank account. Now her mother's maiden name's Studley-Erskine. Posh-sounding but not interesting. But Mrs Dewey's own maiden name, that's *real* interesting. You'll never guess.'

'Flower?' Mary sat bolt upright, her hand trembling with excitement as she crushed the receiver against her ear.

'Right on, sucker! And there's more. Mrs Dewey sure has a

lot of accounts in faraway places with favourable tax regimes. And each one of them held nothing less than five million pounds sterling. Or equivaylent.' Darleen's voice dropped a decibel or two to denote bad news. 'Sad thing is most of them seem to have been emptied recently. Something's put the wind under the tail of your Mrs-Dewey-née-Flower. Aiden's told me to keep right on digging.'

'Darleen, while you're digging, I've had a little hunch. It may be mad but I think there might be another Flower sister. Could you see if you can find a Beth? Beth Scott she's called now.'

'Beth Scott? Sure will.'

An excited phone call from Darleen later that morning confirmed Mary's guess. Fortunately, her client had left and she was just winding things up with her case team when Bella popped her head round the meeting-room door to say there was an urgent call for her from the Treasury. With a brief, 'D'you mind hanging on for a minute?' Mary slipped out to take it.

'You Brits have a fine Record Office.' Darleen's forceful voice came down the line. 'Tracking that bunch of Flowers was a breeze, and here's the scoop. To Marcus and Madeleine Flower, three lovely daughters named Meg, Amy and Beth. Meg got hitched to Dominic Dewey, Beth hooked up with Jonathan Scott and split after a year. Amy's got no man as yet. Great news, hey? And Aiden wants to see us. Can you get your ass round to his office right away?'

'I suppose I could.' Mary had to join a long conference call that afternoon, but Bella would mind her back if she slipped out now for a couple of hours. 'I need to wrap up a meeting, then I'll come straight over.'

The case team was waiting for her as she'd asked. She smiled round at them. 'I'm so proud of you all, you've done a great job. I have the depressing feeling that our client still believes the good times are here for ever. But if he does go ahead with his barmy growth plans, when his bank crashes down around his arrogant ears we'll at least have the comfort of having warned him.'

Aiden Elginbrode was positively chuckling as Mary told him Guy's thoughts on sisters and crime. 'Furies, Sirens, Harpies, your husband is a wit of the first order, a *rara avis*.' As he said this, Mary realized with a pang that it was a long time since she'd heard Guy come out with one of his maddening Latin quotations.

'Is this Classical crap some kind of code?'

'Indeed it is, Darleen. Information of that type is frequently concealed from the wider world.' Elginbrode was looking quite skittish. 'Inside books.'

'I get you.' Darleen was dismissive. 'School stuff. But hey, Aiden, what d'you think? Three sisters doing inside trades big time. D'you reckon it makes sense?'

'I most certainly do. It makes the greatest sense.' The bland mask was firmly back in place. 'Sisters, yes. It wouldn't occur to most that there might be more than one female sibling blessed with a brain. And then the relationship is so easy to conceal through a marital change of surname. The family resemblance can be disguised too, with hair dye and the like.'

'And then there's the trust, isn't there?' put in Mary. 'Sisters are going to have total faith in each other.'

'You sure wouldn't say that if you met my sister, Sharran-Jayne. Wouldn't trust her further'n I could lob a ball of spit.'

'But the Flower sisters *do* seem to have trusted each other, don't they?' Mary pushed on with her argument. 'There's Meg at home doing the trades and managing the money. There's

Amy writing for a financial newspaper and picking up all sorts of interesting facts.'

'And Beth,' added Elginbrode. 'The headhunter. Ideally positioned. Endlessly made an insider by her clients who want to hire and fire in secret.'

'You reckon they been doing this for a while then?'

'I do, Darleen, I'm afraid I do. Judging by the amount of money you traced through Meg's accounts, they've been up to their tricks for years and they've made millions.'

'So what next? How do we nail these three slags?'

'There are the proper authorities, surely,' Mary said. 'Presumably we pass all this information on to them now?' She looked questioningly at Aiden Elginbrode, who seemed to be giving close examination to his fingertips.

'Oh, I don't think we'll do that,' he answered quietly, 'not unless we want to be interred in a tomb of bureaucracy and tied up with a big bow of red tape. No. I've evolved my own way of doing things. I and a few of my Treasury colleagues, that is. We let insider traders know that we know. We threaten them with dire penalties if they don't desist. It lacks the charm of trial and retribution but on the other hand it's effective. It does tend to stop them.'

Darleen looked disappointed at this, while Mary was simply confused. 'We let them know we know? How do we do that? Who does it?'

'Well, in this specific case, the answer seems astonishingly simple. You know them, Mary, you tell them.' There was a pause during which Darleen crunched angrily on a boiled sweet. 'I suggest you pay a call on Meg Dewey immediately. Ask her about her sisters. Tell her that life will be very much easier if she comes clean.'

'That's it, Mary! Get the hell out of here right now!'

Mary wasn't sure how she'd manage the embarrassment of confronting a friend and accusing her of insider trading, but reluctantly agreed that she would try. 'I simply can't get away from the office this afternoon, but I'll ring Meg this evening and ask if I can pop down to see her tomorrow.' She brightened as a thought struck her. 'It'll give me an excuse to go on to Trister. I love seeing Grace mid-week. Maybe I'll be able to see Guy as well.'

'Actually, Mary, I'd strongly recommend that once you've spoken to Meg you come straight back to London and pay a call on Beth Scott. And I wouldn't ring Mrs Scott in advance. They may be nervous of pursuit. After all, Amy has already vanished and Meg appears to have emptied the bank accounts.' Much to Mary's surprise, Elginbrode leaned across and patted her hand. 'You're a brave woman. Don't be afraid of being quite rough when you talk to Meg and Beth.'

'Yeah! Hit it, sister! Get the frighteners out. Scare the living shit out of them!' The door slammed shut behind Darleen, cutting off her final words of advice.

'Mary, just one thing before you go. I've been making inquiries concerning Messrs Dyengi and Straw. It seems that neither of them will be troubling you, for the moment at least. Platon Dyengi has upped sticks and gone to Geneva, while Ivan Straw has vanished completely. Suicide's a possibility, given the nature of his condition.'

'Oh, I do hope not. Does he have a family?'

'A young wife. One of my contacts in the police force visited their house. Apparently there's a shooting gallery in Mr Straw's basement.' Elginbrode looked sharply across at her. 'Your daughter's pony broke a foreleg, isn't that right?' Mary nodded, unclear where the conversation was going. 'And didn't you say she heard a shot before the pony tumbled over?' Mary nodded again. 'It occurs to me that a shot fired in such a way as to break the leg of a moving pony would require considerable skill.'

Perhaps it was because she hadn't slept properly, but the room seemed to sway. 'No. You don't . . . you can't mean it was Ivan Straw who shot at Dimple?' She shook her head in disbelief. 'But what about that note I found? Keep Away From Hedgies.'

'Mr Straw had a strong interest in frustrating our efforts to regulate the hedge fund industry. He worked closely with Mr Dyengi, who happens to be the prime investor in one of the hedge funds we were looking at. Dix Associates.'

Guy had always said that Dimple's death had nothing to do with Alan Dove. Could she have hated the wrong person all along? Mary's head drooped. She suddenly felt very tired.

'May I speak to Mrs Scott, please?'

'Who's calling?'

'Her brother-in-law.'

'Dommy? Where are you?'

'In a phone box on the Beccles road being asphyxiated by stale urine.'

'Heavens above, why?'

'Because I've had a peculiar phone call from Mary Kersey. That's Mary Kersey of Trister *and* Lock Chase *and* working for the Treasury. She wants to pay Meg a visit tomorrow and I'm suspicious. I didn't let on that Meg's vanished, because if Mary's here it'll give you time to get out.'

'Blast! I wasn't planning to leave Mumford Scott till next week. How long do you think I've got?'

'Well, I'll do my best to get her to stay for lunch. That is, if I don't perish in this disgusting telephone box. You might thank me for dashing out to warn you, Beth, you crabby old bitch.'

'You're an angel. Though why you're in a call box when there's a perfectly good untraceable line in Meg's study I can't begin to think.'

'I can never remember which one's which. Quartz, mica, feldspar, *too* confusing. I really can't manage without Meg.'

'Poor Dominic, but you'll be with her again soon. We all will.'

Mary had meant to leave London much earlier, but she'd had to go into Lock Chase first thing, and had spent longer there than she'd expected. By the time she'd got a taxi to Liverpool Street station, missed one train and had to wait an age for the next one, it was well after eleven before she arrived at West Hall.

'My dear Mary, you must be frozen.' Dominic sprang forward as she was shown into the Deweys' overheated drawing-room. 'Come and sit down. We'll have a lovely mug of mulled claret to drive out the cold. No, I insist,' he added as she began to shake her head. 'You must keep me company. I have a fear of becoming a sad old solitary toper now that Meg's done this vanishing act.'

'Meg's done a vanishing act?' As Mary's heart sank, she guessed that disappointment must be written clearly on her face. Dominic's expression seemed to mirror how she felt. He leaned across and clutched both her hands.

'Oh yes, Meg's gone. She's often teased me about running off with the postman and now it seems she has.' The doleful look passing, he added, 'But while the cat's away, this mouse intends to enjoy the cheese and here it comes.'

Heavy silver mugs of mulled claret were placed on a side table, enveloping Mary in a spicy mist of hot wine, brandy and cinnamon. With the wine had come little squares of toast, fried in butter and topped with cheese still bubbling from the grill.

Dominic held the plate out temptingly, but Mary managed not to take one. She'd lost well over a stone since the summer and she was determined not to pile it back on again.

While chattering and flitting around the room, Mary caught Dominic watching her covertly. He must be wondering what she was doing there. 'I'm so sorry about Meg. The thing is there were some questions I wanted to ask her. Can I ask you instead?'

'Only if you stay to lunch.'

'Oh, I'd love to but I really can't. I must be back in London this afternoon.'

'*Please*, Mary. To be honest I'm a tad lonely. We can eat almost straight away.'

He looked so sad, she couldn't say no. 'Well, if it's really quick.'

'Perfect. I'll go and tell Cook. Would you like a peek around my cellars to get your appetite up?'

Mary had a sudden fear that she might be letting herself in for an endurance test like Gordon's tour of Amy Flower's cars, but she needn't have worried. Dominic turned out to be a knowledgeable and entertaining host. He fluttered round the scarlet-painted cellars like a charming pipistrelle bat, alighting here and there to whip out a wine of particular interest.

'Oh look! A lovely Lebanese red with that rather special sanguinary flavour. Grown from soil soaked with the blood of young soldier boys.'

Over in a corner of the cellar, Mary noticed a pile of boxes. She looked again. Yes, they were definitely cases for packing wine in. Interrupting Dominic's running commentary, she said abruptly, 'Those are packing cases, aren't they? You're not going away, are you?'

There was a moment's pause. Did she catch an uncomfortable look in his eye? No, he was grinning at her. 'Packing cases? Oh no, those are *un*-packing cases. I thought I'd splash out on some decent claret to cheer myself up. But let me show you something unusual.' He grabbed her elbow, guiding her to the far end of his cellars. 'This 1943 Château Canon was made *during* the Second World War. A little piece of history, don't you think?'

It wasn't until they were sitting together in the mirrored dining-room that Mary managed to get a word in about Meg. 'Have you any idea where she might be?' Mary waited keenly for Dominic to reply.

Popping a mouthful of pressed terrine of goose liver topped with a little spoonful of black beer sorbet into his mouth, he chewed thoughtfully before saying, 'I've absolutely no idea where Meg's gone off to. But there's one thing I must tell you.' Mary leaned forward eagerly to hear what was coming. 'She'd *never* have let the cook over-sugar the sorbet like this. Too sweet and it simply ruins the combination of unctuous fat and bitter beer, don't you think?'

Several times during lunch, Mary tried to bring the conversation round to Meg, but Dominic just ran on about wine, the neighbourhood and his love of foreign travel. When the pudding arrived, she made another attempt. 'Could you tell me about Meg's sisters? Amy and Beth.'

Dominic's head was bent over his plate and Mary could see no change in his demeanour as she asked the question. Without replying, he tapped sharply on the dense sheet of chocolate, straight from the freezer, that lay across the top of his pudding. The icy chocolate snapped in half, revealing hot *crème caramel* beneath. 'Aah!' Dominic sniffed carefully. 'You're mad not to try this. Now what did you just say?'

Mary repeated the question and this time he met her eye. 'We never talked families, Meg and I. Never.'

She gave up. Whether Dominic knew everything or nothing,

she was going to make no progress at West Hall. Glancing at her watch, she was horrified to see that it was nearly two o'clock. She was forced to wait for what felt like hours as Dominic went off to look up the train timetable and then, having insisted on taking her to the station himself, took even more time to find coat, gloves and car keys. It was only because the train had been delayed up the line at Beccles that Mary caught it. She could have sworn that Dominic was driving slowly on purpose.

As the train pursued its leisurely way southwards across the Suffolk flatlands, Mary's phone rang. 'Mary?' Darleen's voice was unmistakable. 'You there? Can you hear me?'

Struggling to make herself heard over Darleen's vocal barrage, Mary shouted, 'Yes, I *can* hear you. Quite clearly.'

'Did you get your Mrs Dewey?'

'Done a bunk, I'm afraid. What news your end?'

'I've tracked down another barnload of cash. Three more accounts, all five million sterling, all recently emptied. Looks like they've been planning their escape for a while now. Reckon you better get over to Beth Scott before she high-tails out of there too.'

Mary looked anxiously at her watch. She couldn't bear it if the third sister got away. She simply *had* to get to Mumford Scott before they shut up shop for the night. Liverpool Street station was a morass of commuters. She fought her way out to the taxi queue and had to wait fifteen agonizing minutes before she was finally in a cab bound for Beth Scott's office.

'Curzon Street?' the driver said. 'It'll take a while to get you there. What with Christmas shoppers and all the roadworks we could be half an hour at least.' The taxi driver opened the glass partition fully so that he could give Mary the benefit of his views on London's traffic. Leaning back tiredly, she let the sound wash over her.

Having finally arrived at Mumford Scott, Mary was kept waiting a good ten minutes before Beth's secretary came tripping down the stairs. 'I'm dreadfully sorry to have kept you waiting, Mrs Kersey. I'm afraid you've missed Mrs Scott. She's taking a sabbatical and we're not sure when she's going to be back.'

Unable to speak, Mary nodded her thanks. The receptionist seemed happy to leave her in peace and she sat alone, thinking. So the last of the three sisters had escaped. She had so many questions and now there would be no answers. How did they cope with never seeing each other? Always pretending. And why did they do it? Was it just for the money? Was it for fun? What other reason could there be?

Mary pulled out her mobile. She suddenly had a terrible need to talk to Guy. They hadn't spoken since they'd parted at Richmond station. Two whole days without a phone call. Ever since they'd married, they'd never had even a single day without talking. She was tempted to ring him straight away, but first she'd better let Aiden Elginbrode know what had happened.

THIRTY-SEVEN

How beautiful on the mountains
Are the feet of one who brings good news.

A shaft of wintry sunlight burnished Peter's yellow hair into a bright halo. Mary thought how serene he looked, standing at the flower-covered altar in his white and gold vestments.

Listen! Your watchmen raise their voices
They shout with joy together.

Joyful faces packed the little church, children, parents, grand-parents, all celebrating Christmas morning together. Grace looked happy too, if in a bit of a daze. Her presents that morning had all been pony-related, and Mary knew she was seething with excitement about the next day when she'd be going out with the hunt for the first time.

She looked down at her hands. Guy had always given her a ring for Christmas. It had been a joke between them ever since they were undergraduates together at Cambridge all those years ago. Gothic skulls, plastic flowers, fake gemstones, she had a whole collection of them. This year he'd given her a fountain pen. Far more practical than a silly ring, more expensive too, but all the same, she'd much rather have had the ring.

What with the usual pre-Christmas panics at Lock Chase, and

Guy burying himself in his paper on warfare, she'd scarcely managed to see him. And when they did meet, he seemed distant. At first Mary had been piqued, then she'd been concerned, now she was miserable. She finally realized what she'd done by putting her career ahead of her marriage. She'd made her husband feel irrelevant. She longed to have things back the way they were, with his gentle intelligence, his daft rings and his endless Latin quotes.

Mary didn't listen to a word of the Gospel, or to any of Peter's Christmas sermon. For the rest of Mass, she kept her head bowed and prayed that she'd find a way to get her marriage back to normal.

Surely there wasn't usually such a big turnout for the Boxing Day meet? The little town of Stockbridge Oak was heaving with people, and Guy had to use his height to forge a way through the crowds. It was the law of unintended consequences, Mary concluded. The ban had drawn out people who didn't give a fig about hunting but would fight any law that stank of government bullying.

Guy found them a vantage point at the top of the High Street just as the Master appeared like a scarlet-coated centaur. As he rode his black Dutch Warmblood slowly down the road with the rest of the hunt processing behind him, the crowds made way for them like idolaters. Mary spotted her father-in-law, looking like one of his own ancestors in an old-fashioned hunting jacket and mounted on Sea Salt. She breathed a small sigh of relief as she saw that Grace was tucked close in behind him. At least she was safe so far.

As the hunt passed by, the crowd surged after them and Mary lost her footing. Instantly she felt Guy's hand on her elbow, ʼng her up. 'Thanks,' she smiled up into his face. He didn't answer, but he kept hold of her elbow while they followed the hunt along to the market square. At least that was something.

'A brace of Kerseys, how nice!' Mary swung round and saw Peter Cromwell pushing his way through to them.

'What are you doing here?' she asked. 'I didn't think you approved of hunting.'

'Indeed I don't. At least, I don't mind hunting for food, but I find it hard to believe that the good Lord meant his creation to be harried for pleasure. Ah, look . . .' He broke off to point through the throng of people. 'Here's a sad husband.' Mary followed Peter's finger to where Dominic Dewey was coming through the crowds clutching a polystyrene cup of mulled wine.

'Funny not to see Meg here, isn't it?' Dominic said as he came up to them. 'D'you remember how she always turned up swathed in furs? "I never wear fox to a meet," she used to say. "So tactless." She thought it smacked of *morituri te salutant*. It was always sable or mink on Boxing Day.'

'I'm sure you'll be seeing her again soon.' Mary hoped her words didn't sound uncharitably pointed. She'd never worked out whether Dominic knew exactly what Meg had been up to, or if he'd been an innocent bystander. 'No one can simply vanish from house and home for long.'

'Of course not, Mary.' Was that cunning she could see in Dominic's brown eyes? 'Quite impossible, I'd have thought.'

She was tempted to press him, but an admiring note in Guy's voice made them all turn round. 'Just look at that! Makes you proud to be English.'

The Master was weaving his way slowly towards them, pausing briefly in front of Stockbridge's eponymous oak tree. His black horse stood like a stone as he doffed his cap politely to the crowd. Mary thought fleetingly that he looked like some young Alexander rallying his troops for battle.

'I know you don't approve of all this, Mary,' Guy said, 'but you must admit, while our Master's a mouse on the ground, he's a giant on a horse.'

A horn sang out, and the hunt followed it away from the market square and off towards the fields that lapped the edges of the little town. Mary watched anxiously as Grace and Sir John trotted past the old oak tree and out of sight. 'Dear Lord,' she muttered under her breath, 'please help me to sort things out with Guy *and* bring Gracie home safely.'

She felt a moment's peace as they crossed the moat and saw Trister's mellow Tudor bricks glowing red in the thin sunshine, but it didn't last long. Guy vanished upstairs to work, and Mary couldn't settle down to doing anything constructive at all. At twilight, she heard the rattle of the trailer coming up the drive and threw down the knife she'd been using to cut ham for sandwiches. Pausing to shout up the stairs, 'Guy! They're back!' she rushed out into the chilly dusk to find Grace grinning hugely, splashed in mud and leading her tired pony down the ramp of the trailer.

As Mary paused on the doorstep to breathe a silent prayer of thanks, she heard her husband's step behind her. His hand caressed her shoulder briefly. 'Everything's all right now,' he said. Mary wanted to ask what he meant, but it was impossible with Grace shouting at them.

'It was fantastic! Minim went like smoke! You should have seen her, she jumped everything! Can we have some tea? I'm starving! Can you hang on a bit though? I have to look after Minim first.'

What with brushing down and feeding, then baths and changing, it was over an hour before Mary and her family were sitting in front of the kitchen fire and a huge tea. Grace talked non-stop.

'There was one fantastic bit, wasn't there, Grandpa?' Ignoring his muttered, 'Bloodthirsty little monster,' she rattled on with her story. 'Some man was showing off and he tried to jump a really high hedge from almost a standstill. Of course he couldn't do it. He fell off and bust his leg and you'll never guess what, they had to have the air ambulance in!'

'No! How absolutely terrifying,' said Mary, feeling her eyes widening in fear.

'Well, it *was* scary because this huge yellow helicopter came down really close to us. We were lucky to see it. They don't get the air ambulance out very often, do they, Grandpa?'

Sir John had no time to answer before Grace was off again, describing the gallops they'd had, the jumps she'd done, the jumps she'd decided not to do, interspersing everything with praise for her pony's general perfection. Even Mary was beginning to feel a little glazed, when Grace suddenly leapt up saying, 'I *must* go and check Minim's legs,' and was out of the door before anyone had a chance to answer.

'I'm bound to say,' said Guy into the sudden silence, 'I've always been led to believe that the only thing worse than hunting was having to listen to somebody else describing a hunt, and now I know it's true. Quick. Let's move through to the drawing-room before Grace comes back like some fearful old Jorrocks and starts telling us about it all over again.'

Sir John collapsed into a long armchair and stretched his feet towards the fire, his face hidden behind a newspaper. Glancing across at him, Mary thought he must be completely exhausted after the long day's hunting. She turned to Guy, longing to ask him if he'd meant anything particular with that 'Everything's all right now'. But of course she couldn't, not with his father there. She'd try something neutral instead.

'I was wondering about the book club. D'you think it'll manage to stagger on without Meg or Urban?'

'Urban's not going anywhere, is he?' Guy didn't sound very interested but she ploughed on.

'No, I didn't mean that. It's just that now he and Spider are an item, I expect they'll spend more time in London.'

'You may be right.'

A silence fell between them, broken only by the sound of Sir John's regular breathing. He must have fallen asleep. Mary leant back in her chair, staring up at the patterns that the firelight was making across the Jacobean plasterwork ceiling. This was her moment. She looked across at Guy and felt a rush of tenderness at the sight of that familiar, beaky profile and the lock of hair flopping down over his forehead. She'd neglected him. She *must* make things right between them. 'I don't think I've ever thanked you properly for working out that Meg had sisters. If it wasn't for you, no one would ever have guessed.'

'Sheer luck.'

His words might be dismissive, but Mary thought Guy sounded pleased. 'No, honestly, who'd have thought Meg Dewey, Beth Scott and Amy Flower were sisters, all making a fortune out of insider trading? It was entirely your idea.'

'Beth, Amy and Meg,' Guy mused. 'Three Flower girls out of a story book. I wonder who they were?'

'I must say, I still can't get to grips with Meg as a criminal. And I'd love to know *why* she did it.'

In the brief silence that followed, Sir John put down his newspaper, having not dozed off at all. 'Meg Dewey. Well, I'm blessed. Who'd have guessed she was little Meggy Flower? I might have recognized her if she hadn't gone blonde. Increased in scale a bit since I knew her, too. Mind you, she was still very young when I last saw the three girls.'

'Good heavens!' Mary interrupted. 'You didn't *know* them?'

'I'm godfather to one of them, I forget which. I was at prep school with Marcus Flower and we saw a lot of each other in the holidays. His family had a place called Cadle Hall, over towards Eye. He was sent off to some Scottish public school but I caught up with him again at university. We had a lot of fun there.' Sir John gazed into the fire until Mary prompted him to go on with his story.

'Oh yes, Marcus. He had far too much money, went off the rails, never did a stroke of work. Then of course he met Middy. Madeleine Studley-Erskine. Beautiful girl. Soft brown hair. Blue eyes. Wonderful figure. Marcus never looked at another woman. His parents let him abandon his degree to marry her.'

'And were they happy?'

'Blissfully, for a while. Mind you, there's a touch of dottiness in the Studley-Erskines and Middy had it. Fluttery girl she was, always reading children's books.' There was a thoughtful pause. 'Well I never, Amy, Beth and Meggy. Jane and I saw quite a bit of them when they were small. Cadle Hall's no distance away.'

Sir John paused again, and Mary guessed he was remembering his much loved wife. After a few minutes he picked up the thread of the past. 'We rather lost touch when Marcus had to sell up. He spent money like water, got into speculating and lost the lot in Kenyan coffee. Inevitable, I suppose, but idiotic, eh? Should have invested his fortune in British agriculture.'

The drawing-room door flew open suddenly, sucking a billow of smoke from the fireplace out into the room. 'Oh, sorry!' said Grace, bouncing into the room waving a sheet of green paper. 'Am I interrupting?'

'Slightly, darling,' Mary answered for him. 'Grandpa was just telling us a story about Mrs Dewey. He knew her when she was little. Did you want something particular?'

'I need you to sign this form before I go back to school. We're having a dance against Cobban Down next term and I've never been to a real one before. We have to be awfully proper. Mrs Tomkins called us all together at the end of last term to give us a few little hints on how to behave. Shall I tell you, it was really funny?'

Taking Mary's smile as a 'yes', Grace went on. 'There's to be No Touching and absolutely No Going Outside. If a boy turns off the lights as a joke we're to say in a Quiet But Clear voice, "Please turn the lights on! I am a Catholic."'

'Well, that should certainly do the trick,' said Guy drily. Mary burst out laughing and Grace joined in noisily.

When she'd stopped giggling, Mary said, 'You can stay if you like, but Grandpa was in the middle of a sad story, so you'll have to be quiet.'

'I'll sit like a mouse.' Grace squeaked a couple of times to make her point.

Mary turned to her father-in-law. 'Sorry about that. You were saying about Meg's father losing all his money. Is that why she and her sisters turned to crime, d'you think?'

'In the end I suppose it was.' Sir John scratched his head. 'Marcus started drinking heavily and Middy couldn't cope. He'd always protected her, now he needed protecting and she couldn't do that. She began shouting at him. Quarrels, tears, all that sort of thing, always about cash. Then they separated. Stupid, but there it was.'

Grace uncurled herself to ask, 'Did they do adultery?'

'Don't interrupt,' said Guy. 'Just let Grandpa get on with his story.'

'Sorree,' muttered Grace.

'It's all right, Gracie, adultery's not the only reason people get divorced. My friends' marriage fell apart over money. That's what changed those girls. They came to think you could only be happy if you were rich.' Sir John shook his head slowly. 'I never saw them again after the decree nisi. Sent to live with an aunt or some such. Marcus kept in touch for a while but Middy went batty. Smoking, drinking, pills. She died just a year after the divorce. Marcus vanished after that. Far East or South Seas was the rumour.' He paused. 'And all this time little Meggy's been living just down the road. Extraordinary. I wonder if she recognized me?'

'I'll bet she did,' said Mary. 'And she must have taken a big gamble that you wouldn't recognize *her*.'

A worried voice came from the floor. 'That's a horrid story. You won't get divorced and start taking pills, Mummy, will you?'

'Grace! Of course not.' Mary shifted in her chair so that she was looking straight at her husband. 'I love Daddy. I admire him more than anyone in the world. He's my best friend and I want to spend my whole life with him.'

Guy was looking back at her but his expression was unreadable. Mary held her breath.

'*Vivamus atque amemus.*'

Her breath came out in a huge sigh.

'What does that mean, Daddy?'

'A poet called Catullus wrote it,' Mary answered for him. 'It means, Let us live and let us love.'

'And I love Mummy.' Guy was smiling now, holding out his hand to her. 'In fact I might go so far as to say that my predilection for your mother is insurmountable.'

'Pompous ass!'

Later that evening, both Grace and Sir John having gone to bed exhausted, Mary went outside with Guy. It was a bitterly cold night. There was no moon, but the stars shone so brightly that they could clearly make out the moat and the dark line of trees beyond it. The silence was unbroken even by the usual sounds of wind in rushes or the low noises of the cows down in the barns. She shivered.

'You're cold, Mary. Do you want to go in?'

'Let's stay out for a few more minutes, it's so peaceful. And besides, there's something I want to tell you.'

'I'm listening.'

She took a big breath. What she had to say felt very important. 'You've been right, Guy, right all along. I got my priorities wrong. All that Superwoman stuff with my great career, making lots of money, I lost sight of what really matters. I've realized now though. I can't work eleven-hour days *and* bring work home at the weekends *and* be a decent wife and mother. I've been a nit to think anyone could do all that.'

Guy slipped an arm round her shoulders and hugged her but he didn't interrupt as she went on, 'I think we should take a proper holiday together.' She leaned her head back so that she could look up at his face. 'We never had a honeymoon, did we? How about Athens?'

'Or Jerusalem.' Guy smiled down at her. 'Let's toss for it.'

'As long as I can throw the coin this time,' she said teasingly. 'And when we get back, things are going to be different.' She wondered if he could hear the excitement in her voice. 'Aiden Elginbrode's asked me if I want to work for him, doing more investigations for the Treasury. He wouldn't be able to pay much but he did say he could recommend me for a non-executive directorship or two.'

'Heavens! Isn't being a company director risky these days?'

'Don't worry, I'd be very careful. I know I'm supposed to be an expert but I certainly wouldn't go on a bank board, for example.' Mary frowned at the silent moat. 'They're far too opaque, I'd never be sure I knew what was going on.' Sensing that Guy was about to say something, she hurried on. 'If I worked for Aiden, I'd have to leave Lock Chase and I wouldn't earn anything like as much as I do now. Would you mind that?'

There was a pause, then Guy said firmly, 'No, I wouldn't. Thanks to you we aren't broke like Meg's poor parents. In fact we even appear to have some savings in the bank. And you'd be at home more, wouldn't you? Gracie would love that and so would I.'

'Oh, that's *wonderful*.' Mary could hear her voice rising enthusiastically. 'I think being a tracker of scumbags and a righter of wrongs is the ideal job for a pious prig like me.'

'Pious perhaps, but not a prig.' He started rubbing her shoulders. 'Let's find a bottle of champagne and take it upstairs.'

'Lovely idea,' she said happily.

Withdrawn

**Indianapolis
Marion County
Public Library**

**Renew by Phone
269-5222**

**Renew on the Web
www.imcpl.org**

For General Library Information
please call 269-1700

DEMCO